Dark Champion

Also by Jo Beverley
in Large Print:

The Devil's Heiress
Devilish
The Dragon's Bride
Lord Wraybourne's Betrothed
The Stanforth Secrets
The Stolen Bride
An Unwilling Bride
Hazard
St. Raven

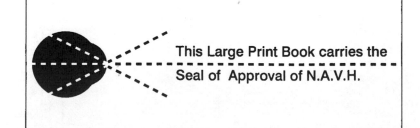

This Large Print Book carries the
Seal of Approval of N.A.V.H.

Dark Champion

Jo Beverley

Thorndike Press • Waterville, Maine

Published in 2003 by arrangement with NAL Signet, a member of Penguin Putnam, Inc.

Thorndike Press® Large Print Core Series.

The tree indicium is a trademark of Thorndike Press.

The text of this Large Print edition is unabridged.
Other aspects of the book may vary from the original edition.

Set in 16 pt. Plantin by Ramona A. Watson.

Printed in the United States on permanent paper.

Library of Congress Cataloging-in-Publication Data

Beverley, Jo.
    Dark champion / Jo Beverley.
        p. cm.
    ISBN 0-7862-5397-5 (lg. print : hc : alk. paper)
    1. Great Britain — History — Henry I, 1100–1135 — Fiction.   2. Knights and knighthood — Fiction.   3. Large type books.   I. Title.
PR9199.3.B424D37 2003
    813'.54—dc21   2003044485

The original 1993 edition of *Dark Champion* was dedicated to the GEnie Romex online group, now a victim of technological change. I am still grateful for that wonderful community, and especially for the help I received there from Suzanne Parnell who, as I said, "let me plunder her expert knowledge of the early Middle Ages."

These days I am very grateful for the wonders of the World Wide Web, where original documents and generous experts are bountiful, and where lovers of historical romance can gather so easily. I have a Web site at www.jobev.com.

Chapter One

England, 1101

Imogen of Carrisford stood in the dark cold, shivering at the muted sounds of horror. Even here in her castle's secret ways, she could not escape the distant clash of arms, the howls of battle rage, the frantic bellowed orders and screams of terror.

Screams of death.

The clamor told of horrors beyond her imagining, but her small spy hole revealed only the beautiful great hall of Carrisford Castle, empty, untouched, and gilded by torchlight and candlelight. The only violence there was in the precious wall hangings, where silken warriors fought with gilded swords.

The trestles had been broken down after the evening meal, but the mighty oaken high table sat in its place with the two solid great chairs behind it. Her father's chair and her own.

Her father was dead.

A flagon of wine and some goblets told of the meeting so rudely disturbed. She and her father's officers had been making sad but orderly plans for the future. One silver goblet lay on its side, red wine soaking into the wood and dripping slowly down onto the rush mats.

The only sign of disarray.

The peaceful, familiar chamber tempted her to leave her dank hiding place, but she stayed. Sir Gilbert de Valens, her father's marshal, had thrust her into the secret space between the walls and bade her remain there at all costs. The invaders — whoever they were — had surely come for one thing only. The Treasure of Carrisford.

Herself. The heiress to all her father's vast wealth and properties.

The secret way was narrow, only wide enough for most men to pass sideways. Though Imogen was not as large as most men, her body sometimes brushed the outer wall, and the dampness which seeped through the massive stones crept chillingly into her gown.

Or perhaps the chill came from terror.

Or perhaps it came just from the agony of waiting.

Imogen would much rather have been out among the noise than cowering here. As mistress of Carrisford, surely she should be with her people.

They were invaded, but *how?*

Carrisford was a mighty, impregnable fortress. Her father said it could hold against the whole of England.

She stifled a whimper. Her father was dead.

The bereavement, the raw and recent loss, swelled up to drown out even the sounds of horror. How could Bernard of Carrisford, mighty lord of west England, die so quickly of a minor hunting wound?

Father Wulfgan said it was the hand of God. Her chaplain had instructed her to mark well how such a fate could strike down the mighty as easily as the low. He was right, she supposed. The simple gash had festered, and before they knew it her father had the wound fever and neither hot iron nor poultice, woundwort nor holy water, had stopped the spread.

In his death agony Bernard had dictated a plea to the king for protection; then he had commanded that the castle be sealed tight, that no one other than the king's envoy be admitted, high or low. All to safeguard his only child, now vulnerable at sixteen to the first greedy man to hear the news. Now trembling in this cold dark hole.

It was impossible, but it had happened. Before the earth was smooth on Lord Bernard's grave, a greedy man had heard, and come, and entered. It could only be treachery, but that was for later. For now it was Imogen's duty to escape this brutal wooing.

The clamor grew louder and Imogen

flinched back from the hole. But then she pressed her eye close again, seeking any evidence of what was happening. A piercing scream told of violence just out of sight. Was that her Aunt Constance? Surely not. Who would hurt such a sweet, gentle lady?

Imogen gave thanks that there were few innocents to suffer here. Her own two girlhood companions had recently left to marry, and her father's squire and pages had set off for their family homes yesterday after the funeral.

Which left only Aunt Constance.

If only Imogen's aunt had been in the hall when the alarm was given. But the dear lady had taken no interest in political matters, and had been in her beloved garden. Heaven only knew what was happening to her now.

Sweet Jesu, what was happening?

One of the great hall doors swung open and Sir Gilbert de Valens staggered into view, swaying from exhaustion and the weakness of wounds. There had been no time for him to arm; his bare head was matted with blood, his tunic torn and stained. His sword hung wearily from his right hand and blood dripped from his useless left with mesmerizing regularity.

Imogen found herself watching those droplets of scarlet blood. *Drip. Drip. Drip.*

Now that the true face of violence was before her, she felt numb rather than afraid. She supposed she was as safe as possible.

Only the family and a few senior servants knew of the secret passages. The chink she was looking through was disguised by a shield hung on the wall. . . .

Her father had taught her all these things.

Her father was dead.

Drip. Drip. Drip. That wound needed binding. She must go to aid Sir Gilbert. Soon his very life would drip away into the rushes and it was her duty as Lady of Carrisford to aid the sick and wounded. Even as she formed the thought, the half-open doors were slammed back to bounce against the walls. A monstrous figure appeared in the entrance, backed by a horde of villainous, howling followers.

Arnulf of Warbrick!

He was a giant of a man — tall and massive. Under his chain mail his belly swelled like a monstrous pregnancy, and as he swaggered into the room his tree trunk legs were far apart, unable to meet.

Warbrick. Vile Warbrick, brutal brother of the infamous Robert de Belleme. . . .

When Warbrick had come courting Imogen in satin and velvet, she had been hard-pressed not to laugh at such a barrel of a man. There was nothing amusing about the demon before her now. Every word of his reputation for bestial cruelty and superhuman strength was surely true.

And he came to wed her.

11

"Ha! Sir Gilbert!" he bellowed. "Where's the pretty morsel?"

"Lady Imogen has already left to go to the king," Sir Gilbert said faintly. "Leave us in peace, Lord Warbrick."

Warbrick advanced on the knight. Gilbert raised his sword, but it wavered. Warbrick took the man's wrist in his beefy paw and controlled him with ease. "You lie. I have had the roads watched for days. The only one to leave here for the east was the messenger you sent to the king, seeking his protection for the girl."

Gilbert fell to his knees. Imogen felt her own legs weaken with fear. If Warbrick knew of the message, he had stopped it. No aid was on the way.

Warbrick took the older man's throat in his fist. "Where is she?"

"Gone," Sir Gilbert choked out.

"Where!" Warbrick's gross face flushed purple with rage and he shook Sir Gilbert like a dog with a rat.

There was only a rattling noise. With a snarl Warbrick threw the man aside. Imogen stared in blank horror at her father's friend and faithful vassal. His throat had been crushed.

She began to tremble. Nothing could stop it. She was sure the men in the room could hear her teeth as they clashed together hard enough to break.

She couldn't move.

She couldn't think.

A woman ran into the room, fleeing some terror but finding worse. It was Janine, Imogen's middle-aged handmaid. She stopped and tried to back out again, but two of the soldiers seized her.

At a word from Warbrick they threw her down on the table and yanked her skirts up over her head. Her shrieks and futile prayers were muffled. The men grasped her kicking legs and held them apart. Warbrick opened his clothing to let free a monstrous phallus. He thrust into Janine and pumped at her. The woman shrieked at the first assault, then her cries took on the rhythm of Warbrick's thrusts in a mesmerizing way.

Janine gave short, high-pitched despairing screams. Warbrick grunted. His gross body thumped, thumped, thumped.

Imogen found she was moaning in horror in time with the rape, and thrust her fist into her mouth to stifle the noise. That was her fate if she were caught.

She supposed Warbrick would marry her before he threw her down and thrust into her, but there the difference would end. She had no doubt that if she fought him he would have his ruffian soldiers hold her down for his pleasure.

She wanted to look away but was transfixed. To look away would be to abandon Janine, to abandon Sir Gilbert's already cooling corpse.

Imogen watched as Warbrick readjusted his clothes and nodded to one of Janine's captors. The man grinned and repeated his master's crime. The maid's shrieks changed into an altogether more dreadful moan of despair.

Imogen couldn't stand this anymore. Sir Gilbert had instructed her to stay in the secret passage no matter what happened, but Sir Gilbert was dead. Imogen was what Warbrick wanted, and if she surrendered the horrors would cease. Janine would be left alone. She began to sidle along the narrow space toward the entrance slit.

The thought of giving herself up to Warbrick brought bile to her throat, but to be doing something was an immense relief. After all, she might be able to escape before marriage formalities could be arranged. If not, she thought sickly, she could always kill herself.

Away from the spy hole there was little light, but Imogen knew she had only to follow the passage to find the exit beneath the west stairs. She worked her way by feel alone, grateful for the blackness around her. Nothing to see, little to hear, but at long last something to do.

A faint gleam of light told her she was near the exit. She moved more quickly.

Abruptly, the light was obscured. Imogen gasped and shrank back.

"My lady?" someone whispered.

"Siward?" She sagged with relief. "Oh, Siward. We can't allow this to go on. I must give myself up to Warbrick."

"I was affeared you'd be thinking that," her seneschal said, and his fist connected with her jaw. That was the last Imogen knew.

Imogen came to her senses in the woods. There was a moon, so it was not pitch-dark, but under the heavy canopy of summer foliage it was close enough. Imogen was first aware of a very painful jaw and rubbed it, muttering unflattering comments about the perpetrator.

Then she remembered.

Sir Gilbert.

Janine.

Warbrick.

Siward must have forced some potion into her to keep her unconscious for so long, and perhaps that was why she felt so numb. It was a relief to be so. Her memory could repeat scenes of horror for her again and again — she thought it would do so for the rest of her life — but it was like a mummer's play. It did not touch her.

Or not too much. Her teeth began to chatter again, and she clenched her jaws to stop them.

Then winced at the pain.

She buried her swimming head in her

hands. What was happening now back in the castle, her beautiful, tranquil home?

Immediately, her mind shied away.

She looked up and made out Siward sitting nearby. A few dark shapes showed that other people had escaped.

"Siward," whispered Imogen, "you have done a terrible thing. What will happen to my people with Warbrick tearing Carrisford apart looking for me?"

He was hunched over, and she realized he was an old man, and that he too was accustomed to an orderly life. At her words, however, he straightened and spoke firmly. "What will happen to your people if Warbrick forces you to wed him and thus becomes Lord of Carrisford, lady? Sir Gilbert deputed me to keep you safe, and so I will. You must stay out of that devil's hands."

Imogen pressed her hands to her face. He was right, she supposed. For her sins, she was the Lady of Carrisford and the heir to the castle. She was the key to possession of great wealth and power and must act for the good of all her people. A leader had to be willing to sacrifice a few for the good of the many.

But it was hard. She could not forget her maid crying for pity and for help. . . .

"Janine," she moaned. "Did you see . . . ? Oh, Siward, did you see?"

Wordlessly, he gathered her into his arms

16

and she shuddered there, far beyond tears.

Imogen had never experienced violence, and today she had near drowned in it. She had never seen the act between man and woman before, but now the picture was imprinted on her mind and the sounds rang in her head.

And she would have to come to that some day with some man. . . .

She thrust that thought away before it truly drove her mad. Not Warbrick. At least, not Warbrick. If she could keep out of his hands, perhaps she could bear it. Not all men could be so vile.

Siward's voice broke into her panicked thoughts. "We can't stay here, lady. It's not safe. Where shall we take you?"

Imogen looked up in shock. She'd thought her people had the matter all in hand, but here they were looking to her to lead them.

She had no idea what to do.

Until two days past she had been the pampered daughter of Bernard of Carrisford, great lord of Gloucestershire. Her days had been an orderly succession of music, needlework, hawking, and reading the treasured manuscripts in her father's possession.

Until the past spring her future had been securely planned to continue in this pattern. She had been betrothed at ten to Lord Gerald of Huntwich, a pleasant and able man fifteen years her senior who would surely have secured her peace forever.

17

He had always treated her with the same kindly indulgence offered by her father, and had been content to wait for her woman's courses to come upon her before taking her into his home. That had happened, however, in April, and the wedding date had been settled for October 20, Imogen's seventeenth birthday.

But in June Gerald had eaten tainted fish and died of the gripe.

Imogen's father had brought her the news, awkward because he feared that she would be upset, and irritated at this disruption of his plans. Upset, too, at the loss of a friend.

"You'd think the man would have more sense," he grumbled. "Now there'll be a stirring, and with times so unsettled I've no mind to choose you a new husband just yet."

Imogen was silently testing the fact that she felt only mild regret at the death. How strange. "God keep his soul," she said, grateful for the needlework which occupied her hands and eyes. "What will happen now?"

Lord Bernard suddenly chuckled and dropped into a chair. "Every eligible man in England will be sniffing around you, dearling." He flicked the parchment in his hand. "Some are hot off the mark. Here's a polite note of condolence from Lancaster, with the news he'll be passing by next week."

Imogen looked up sharply. "Lancaster! His son is too young, surely."

"Aye, but his wife died just past Christmas, if you remember. He's hunting for himself." He must have seen the shadow of doubt cross her face. "He's only a year or two older than Huntwich, Imogen, and a powerful man. He'd keep you safe."

Imogen was fond enough of the Earl of Lancaster as an acquaintance of her father's — another big, powerful man stepping gingerly through England's tangled politics. As a husband, however, she found she did not care for him. He dressed too richly, his hands were too soft, and she thought he was sly rather than clever. Imogen had been sheltered by her father, but she still appreciated an honest fighting man. Her father was an honest opponent and could still hold his own in combat.

She was not nervous about the matter, however, for she knew her father would not force her into a match she disliked.

"Do I have any other suitors yet?" she asked, beginning to like the thought of being courted. At ten she had been little interested in the matter; now it might be fun.

Lord Bernard ran off a shrewd list of the men who would doubtless make moves to gain one of England's greatest heiresses for themselves or their sons. "But I'll make no decisions yet, dearling. I'm not sure of Henry

Beauclerk's ability to hold his throne. I've sworn my oath so I'll hold true to him, but I don't know about others. If Henry's still king come Michaelmas, we'll see who the men of power are then."

It was less than a year since the ascent of the new king — Henry I, called Beauclerk — and the king's older brother Robert, Duke of Normandy, was still contesting the succession. Robert was even now gathering a fleet to invade England as his father, William the Conqueror, had done.

Imogen shuddered. "Will you have to fight, Father?"

He shrugged wearily. "We all do what we have to do, daughter. Never forget that. Protect you as I may, doubtless the time will come when you will have to bite into gall to maintain our honor, or even to survive." He pushed up out of the chair and chucked her under the chin. "For now, dearling, enjoy yourself. I doubt not you'll have the might of England prancing through here in silks and tissue, and so long as you choose a man of honor, you can have your pick of 'em."

It had been as her father had predicted. For a while Imogen had enjoyed a pleasant summer entertaining the eligible men of England in their silk and tissue.

Then in July the Duke of Normandy had invaded, and Lord Bernard had marched out to support his king. Courtship games had halted. In early August, however, the duke had quailed before King Henry and his supporters, and slunk back across the Channel.

Lord Bernard and his men had returned without a scratch, and Imogen had been surrounded by eager suitors again. It had been far too much fun to cut short and her father had not pressed her.

Which, with hindsight, had been a mistake.

If Gerald had lived, or if Imogen had been legally betrothed to another, Warbrick would have been unlikely to have tried such a crude wooing. Now there was little to prevent a man from forcing a match.

She had escaped the trap, but only for the moment. Imogen shuddered at the thought of her fate at Warbrick's hands. His brutality was only exceeded by that of his brother, Belleme. Belleme's first wife had died by violence, and his second, Agnes of Ponthieu, had fled him a broken woman.

Imogen knew she had truly been mad to want to give herself into Warbrick's power. Why had she thought he would wait for a marriage ceremony to claim her? If she fell into the hands of any ruthless, godless man, it would be rape and imprisonment until the formalities were completed. And could even the king undo such an alliance?

She clung to Siward. She wanted to burrow into the leaves on the forest floor and hide like the hunted creature she was, but as he said, there was no safety here. As soon as Warbrick was sure she was not in the castle, he would tear Gloucestershire apart in the search for her.

She needed someone of equal power to protect her.

Siward stroked her head. "We could try to get you east to the king, lady." He sounded dubious, and with reason. Warbrick's land lay to the east and his men watched the road.

Imogen reminded herself that she was her father's heir, heir to his responsibilities as well as his wealth. She removed herself from the steward's arms and forced herself to think, to lead.

"No. That's the road Warbrick will watch most closely. And who's to say where the king is, or if he's able to come to my aid? He's likely still watching the coast in case his brother changes his mind again. It would take at least a week of walking just to reach London, and if Warbrick didn't stop us, I fear some other hazard would." She looked around. "Did any of my father's men-at-arms escape?"

"None that I know of, lady."

Totally undefended. Imogen had never in her life stepped out of her castle unguarded, and now she felt naked before the world, but she forced her voice to steadiness as she said, "We must seek aid closer by, then."

Siward shook his head. "But where, lady?

To the north and east are Warbrick and Belleme. To the south is Sir Kyle. To the west is Cleeve."

Imogen shivered. Put like that it was a withering choice. "Sir Kyle would do me no harm," she said, thinking of the elderly knight who held Breedon Castle for the Earl of Lancaster.

"And little good, I fear, lady. You know well enough that he's an old man and of a nervous disposition. He's been secure, for no one had reason to risk Lancaster's wrath, but you would be enough to tempt Warbrick to take the risk. If Warbrick and his jackals arrived at Breedon's gates, old Kyle would hand you over."

"Surely not," protested Imogen, but she knew it was true. She was fighting the obvious source of help. "You think I should go to Cleeve?" she whispered. "But it's in the hands of the one they call Bastard FitzRoger!"

"Cleeve's your only chance against Warbrick unless you want to hide in the woods until the king comes."

An owl hooted and there was a scurrying in the undergrowth. Imogen felt like that small animal, frantically hiding from predators.

She turned away that puling image. She was Imogen of Carrisford. She was a wolf at bay, not a rabbit. What she needed was an ally.

"Is FitzRoger as hard a man as they say?" she asked.

Siward rubbed his long nose. "He's not been hereabouts long enough to tell, lady, only since January. And not about the place that much, what with helping the king establish himself and driving off the duke. All we know of him is rumors and gossip. You know he was maybe son to old Roger of Cleeve but raised in France. Came over with the new king and looked up his family, so to speak. That weakling brother of his was still lord then, but when Lord Hugh died without heir, the king gave FitzRoger the place."

Imogen did know this, and more. Rumor said the bastard had killed his brother. Lord Bernard had said little on the subject, however, and Imogen had been too busy teasing suitors to care. Old Roger of Cleeve and his son had been such an unpleasant pair that Carrisford had had nothing to do with them.

"The local people must have some opinion of him," she said.

Siward shrugged. "He's a young man, they say, but well proved in war and tourney, and close to the king."

A man able to stand against Warbrick and Belleme, perhaps, but at what cost to herself? "I have heard he is a harsh man," she whispered.

"Aye," said Siward. "He's taken Castle Cleeve in a firm grip, sure enough."

A vision of Warbrick's fist around Gilbert's throat flashed through Imogen's mind, and bile choked her. She forced herself to ignore it. "You almost sound as if you approve of him, Siward."

"It's not for me to approve or disapprove, lady."

"What I mean," asked Imogen impatiently, "is do you think FitzRoger is a lesser risk than Warbrick? You know my father sheltered me. I don't *know* enough."

"There's no risk with Warbrick," said Siward flatly. "There's just certainty of evil. From what they say, FitzRoger's a hard man and a good soldier. That's what you need right now, lady. He'll likely help you, for Cleeve and Warbrick have long been at odds. Besides, he's the king's man, and Belleme and his family are a thorn in King Henry's side. I judge FitzRoger rich and strong and brave enough to stand against Warbrick, do he choose to, maybe even take vengeance for what was done this day."

Vengeance.

As soon as the word was spoken Imogen knew she wanted it, hungered for it. Her home had been despoiled in the most vile manner. Her people had been abused and slaughtered. She wanted her castle back, but more than that, she wanted Warbrick dead in the dirt for what he had done.

To achieve that, she'd pay any price.

She sat up straight. "Then I had best go to FitzRoger and enlist his aid," she said. "Now let us think how I can make my way there safely."

Chapter Two

The next day, as the sun began to set, an elderly couple hobbled along the edge of the dusty road leading to Castle Cleeve. The edge of the road was the wise place to walk, for the wide track was busy and each horse and cart sent up clouds of dust. The traffic coming and going to the Stern castle on the crag was largely military.

The man was gray-haired, dirty, and stooped beneath an enormous pack. The woman's hair color could not be told, for she had a grubby white headrail over it, but she looked as if it should be gray too. For all that, she couldn't be as old as her man, for she was clearly well-advanced in pregnancy. Despite this she too stooped beneath a load nearly as large as his and hobbled like a crone.

Imogen looked up as the castle came into view and felt nothing but relief. It no longer mattered to her if the devil himself waited at the end of the journey; she could hardly go another step. If it wasn't for the sturdy staff Siward had cut for her, she would have given up hours ago. Her feet were merely balls of agony on the ends of numb-weary legs, and her back screamed with the desire to be straight again.

Their disguise had been wise, however, for they had encountered Warbrick's men along the way, checking among all travelers for Imogen of Carrisford. When they had faced such scrutiny Imogen had been grateful Siward had insisted that every detail be exact. For the rest of the journey she had simply been miserable.

Her hair beneath the filthy cloth was caked with grease and dirt, just in case anyone decided to look for the famous honey-and-gold hair of the Treasure of Carrisford. Her fine leather shoes had been discarded in favor of peasant sandals tied on with coarse linen strips. Her feet had started out looking like bandaged sores: now they felt like them. Her clothes from the skin up were of the poorest sort and unclean. Her own smell revolted her, the pack straps galled her, and she was itching from bites.

Worst of all was the paunch Siward had constructed and which she had bound to her body with the wide winding cloths commonly used by pregnant women. The effect was of a woman well gone with child, and the deceit would not be detected unless the cloths were removed.

The pregnancy had been her own idea. It would further mislead the hunters, she had thought, and surely give some protection from rape and cruelty. More important, if she could maintain the deceit it could prove even more useful. Should FitzRoger turn out to be more predator than paladin, he would hesitate to wed a woman who carried another man's brat. That would be to risk having to acknowledge it as his own.

If there seemed any danger of a forced wedding, she would claim the child to be fathered by Gerald of Huntwich. As she had been legally betrothed to him, that should muddy the inheritance situation enough to make any man hesitate. She'd considered herself very clever to have thought up such a plan, but now she cursed it.

The bag filled with bracken and sand had not felt heavy at first, but now it dragged on her bent body. She was convinced even a real babe would not be so hard to carry.

There was one good thing to all this: she no longer needed to act to appear to be a downtrodden peasant rather than a rich young lady. She looked toward the castle as refuge indeed. There she could shed her rags and become once more Lady Imogen, the Treasure of Carrisford, the Power of the West.

Though it hurt her neck to look up, Imogen studied Bastard FitzRoger's keep. Castle Cleeve was harsher than Carrisford, and less graceful in its lines, but it inspired confidence. It was set on a rocky elevation and the keep was protected by a deep, steep-sided ditch which ran straight up to its tall, defensive walls. Before the gate the ditch was broken by a causeway just wide enough to allow a single cart to cross. As she and Siward hobbled their way toward it, Imogen admitted she would not like to be an enemy faced with crossing it under fire.

They paused for a brief rest at the end of the causeway. The sun was beginning to set and many people were passing in and out of the castle to find their places for the evening meal and sleep. Still, there seemed more activity than she would have expected.

"What do you think is going on?" she asked Siward.

"Who's to say?" he grunted wearily. "Perhaps FitzRoger's just arrived, or is just leaving."

"Leaving," Imogen echoed in alarm. "He can't leave now!"

"He won't go anywhere," Siward assured her, "once he hears your news. You can drop the pack now, my lady. We're safe."

But Imogen looked at the causeway and the well-guarded gate at the end of it and held on to caution. "They seem to let people in and out quite readily," she murmured. "Perhaps it would be wiser to keep our disguises until we find out what's going on. Till we discover more of FitzRoger. It should be easy enough to sense what his people think of him."

"If you don't ask the Bastard's help," Siward asked with a touch of impatience, "what will you do?"

Thought of a further journey was beyond Imogen, but she still felt wary. She remembered her father saying, "Go with your instincts, child. You have a gift for it." So be it. She could carry her burdens a little longer.

They began to make their slow way across the causeway behind a young man and a woman who looked like entertainers of some sort. Imogen bitterly envied their light step.

She looked down and saw a bloodstain on the cloths binding her right foot.

She gave a little cry and staggered. Siward grasped her and she found she was at the very edge of the steep drop. In her exhaustion she had been weaving as she walked. She looked down dizzily at the sharp stones far below and staggered away from the edge. Then she looked again at her feet. They had felt so sore, but she had never imagined them actually bleeding.

"Come on!" said Siward roughly. "Move on, woman!"

Imogen looked up to see that the entertainers had stopped and were staring at them. She wasn't sure she could go on, but neither could she stay here —

"Move on! Move on!" bellowed a voice and she looked up to see two armed horsemen at the castle end of the narrow path, holding back their prancing horses and beckoning. "Get a move on!" one shouted again. "Get out of the way, curse you!"

The fear that they'd ride them all off the cliff gave Imogen strength and she staggered forward as quickly as she could. The horsemen waited, however, then as soon as the people were across they charged off down the narrow strip of land as if it were acres wide.

Seeing their urgency, Imogen took heart. Surely Castle Cleeve could not be such a bad place if soldiers on urgent business hesitated to ride peasants to their death. And a castle would take its character from its lord.

They approached the guards. The two men surveyed them without great interest. "Business?"

Siward looked to Imogen. She had expected to just walk in, announce her identity, and enlist the aid of Lord FitzRoger. Now that she wanted to maintain anonymity, what reason could they give for coming here?

"We come to seek justice, sir," she muttered in a thick accent. "Justice of Lord FitzRoger."

One guard rubbed his broken nose. "Well, you've come at a had time, woman. The master's a mite busy."

"Aye," said the other with a grin. "But he is dishing out justice, Harry!"

Both of them laughed coarsely at this, and

Imogen's feelings about the place changed. She had the urge to flee, but the guards were waving them through. "Go on in. He might find time to heed your plea. Wait to the right of the gate-house."

"Wait" translated in Imogen's numb mind to "rest." She forced her painful feet down the long dark passage toward the busy castle bailey — an arch-framed picture gilded by the evening sun.

They walked out into pandemonium. A small army of people seemed to be milling around, along with horses, dogs, hawks, and assorted livestock. Lord FitzRoger was undoubtedly busy. Imogen didn't much care anymore. She found an empty bit of wall, dropped her pack, and sat on it with a bump. She looked at her feet and wondered if it would be better or worse to take off the cloths and sandals.

"What do you want to do now?" muttered Siward as he took his bent stance next to her.

Never move again, thought Imogen. But she was Imogen of Carrisford and her people depended upon her. She must act. But, please God, not for a minute or two.

"Get a feel for the place," she murmured back. Her instinct was still sending a warning, though she could see no reason for it. "Do you think we could make it to London like this?" she asked.

Siward flashed her a look. "It'd be terrible risky, lady. Unprotected strangers are always in danger, and these are chancy times. Could you walk that far?"

"I might be able to," she complained, "with decent shoes."

"Starving peasants don't have decent shoes," he replied.

Imogen fell silent and worked at making sense of the scene around her.

Packhorses were being loaded; weapons were being carried here and there. It definitely spoke of a journey and looked like preparation for war. Was it possible Duke Robert had invaded again? Since Belleme and Warbrick had thrown their forces behind Duke Robert, the attack on her castle might have been part of a wider plan.

To add to the evidence of war, she could hear the clamor of an active smithy off to one side, doubtless fixing up swords and mail.

On the other hand, it was said that the king was moving against those who had proved traitor. FitzRoger was the king's man: perhaps he was planning a punitive mission.

Against Warbrick and Belleme?

The noise of people and animals all around was deafening, but another sound began to stand out. Regular repetitive screams. Memories of Janine sprang into Imogen's mind and she used her staff to push herself to her feet. Was she to witness another rape?

No, never.

The crowd shifted.

Imogen saw the cause of the noise.

A man was tied to a post and another was wielding a long whip. It was a flogging. A number of soldiers stood rigidly watching, though most people were paying little attention.

Was this such a regular occurrence here?

Each time the lash bit, the victim let out a hoarse, guttural scream. Imogen was amazed he was still conscious — his back was such a bloody mess that the strokes no longer made any visible difference.

The man wielding the whip was also stripped to the waist and she could see hard, contoured muscles rippling across wide shoulders with each swing.

He stopped.

He simply stood there, like a lord watching a show, as his victim was untied and carried away and another man was dragged trembling to the post. The sun moved past a tower, and the scene, which had been in shade, was suddenly grotesquely gilded. The body of the man with the whip seemed to be made of gold and the sun struck red in his black hair.

Then the smooth swing of the bloody whip started again. For a few strokes the prisoner merely jerked as the lash bit, but then the cries of pain began again, more loudly. Each stroke cut a clear new welt.

Imogen turned away blindly, fighting the urge to vomit. This was hell on earth, not a place to seek help.

"We're leaving," she said to Siward.

"What? Why?"

"This place is as bad as Warbrick Castle."

Siward grabbed her arm. "What? Because of a whipping? Your father had many a man whipped. You just didn't see it."

"Not like that," Imogen protested.

"Sometimes like that, aye. He protected you too well, lady. Find out first what those men did before you judge." He called out to a passing servant carrying trays of ale around. "Ho, my friend. Someone's getting a fine stinging there. What's the cause?"

"Drunkenness. But there's only one cause 'round here, granddad," replied the cocky youth with a grin. "Not following the master's orders." He hurried on.

"Drunkenness!" Imogen hissed. "He's having a man half killed for *drunkenness?*"

Siward shrugged. "I said FitzRoger was a firm lord, and so it proves. Drink can cause a lot of trouble. You'd be mad to scurry away from here just because of a bit of tough justice. He's hardly likely to have *you* whipped." When she did not agree, he shook his head and said, "At least wait till the morrow, lady, and until you've seen the man himself. It would be madness to go without sleep and venture out in the dark."

Imogen collapsed back down on her pack, knowing she was too weary to go anywhere now.

Had her father truly ordered such punishments? She supposed he had but not where she would witness it. Her world had been a peaceful, civilized place — a place where the guards never had to use their weapons, where a guest was always welcomed with smiles and courtesy, and where justice was mild and understanding.

Her father had created such a world for her, but she saw now it had largely been an illusion. Men had marched from Carrisford to war, but it had always been accomplished much more as a parade than a military expedition. The wounded, she now recollected, had always been cared for at the infirmary maintained by her father at the local monastery. The worst she had actually seen was the healed results of war — the occasional missing limb or patched eye.

Imogen had been raised to do her duty as a noble lady, and to care for the sick and injured, but her care had been confined to minor wounds and those diseases unlikely to do her any harm.

Her life at Carrisford Castle had been idyllic, but an illusion. This was reality — Castle Cleeve and Warbrick.

Her delightful childhood had been poor preparation for all this. Siward was right. The least she could do was wait, and listen, and find out what kind of man this Bastard FitzRoger was.

The cocky young man with the ale pots was pushing his way back toward the brewhouse. He stopped. "Here," he said, and pushed a half-empty flagon at them, then carried on.

Siward called out a blessing and passed the pot to Imogen. She took a deep draft to ease her dusty throat, too thirsty to care that one or more had already drunk from it. It was good ale. Another point in Castle Cleeve's favor. She passed the rest to Siward and he drained it with a grunt of satisfaction, wiping his mouth on his dirty sleeve afterward.

Imogen supposed that was the sort of thing she should do and copied him tentatively. She hardly touched the cloth to her lips. She couldn't identify the smells that assailed her from it, and didn't want to. Then she cursed herself for a pampered nothing. What did a little dirt and discomfort matter when the future of her people was at stake?

She struggled to her feet, moaning slightly when they took her body's weight again. Quickly, she grasped her staff. The rest seemed to have made the pain worse, not better. It felt as if sharp hot coals were pressing all over her feet and every part of her body screamed.

"It's as well I'm supposed to hobble," she muttered as she eased into an almost vertical position. "Let's see what there is to learn."

Siward looked down at her feet and muttered a horrified curse. "Lady, you must not —"

"We are here to save Carrisford," she said grimly. "My feet are not so bad, and the sooner I am easy in my mind about approaching FitzRoger for aid, the sooner I will be able to put aside this disguise."

They started to circle the crowded courtyard, keeping close to the wall where they were less likely to be trampled by a destrier or knocked flying by a hurrying servant. Even so, they had to stop and start to allow for the constant coming and going from the storage rooms in the wall.

Imogen began to take heart. She noted the overall good humor of the busy throng. There were curses and shouts to get out of the way, but generally people made way and jokes were as common as insults. A slight change in the cacophony alerted her and she looked over to the whipping post. It was empty, no sign of the punished or the punisher. Thank God for that.

A smell caught her attention and cramped her belly. Baking bread. Her stomach growled with the reminder that there had been nothing except water and that swig of ale for over twenty-four hours. No wonder her spirit was so weak.

"Can we ask for some?" she whispered, scarce able to believe how desperately she wanted even a crust.

"No harm in asking." Siward made his way to the bake-house door. Imogen peeped in after him and saw the baker and his men, stripped down to loincloths in the intense heat as they shoveled loaves in and out of the stone ovens.

"Any scraps for poor folks?" Siward whined. The baker looked up and nodded curtly. A young boy picked up a loaf which had fallen into the dirt and tossed it to them. Siward caught it and called a blessing as they escaped into the cool of the bailey. As they pushed their way toward a quiet corner, Imogen felt something wrong. She yelped and grabbed the base of her slipping paunch. The bandages were loosening.

A middle-aged woman was beside her in an instant. "A pain?" she asked. "Are you due yet?"

Imogen shook her head desperately. "No. Not for weeks."

"Thought not. Probably just kicked you funny. Where're you from, dear?"

Imogen was having to keep hold of her weighted paunch to stop it sagging and she looked frantically at Siward to answer.

He acted the selfish man and took a large

40

bite out of the fresh loaf, making Imogen's mouth water. Then he mumbled, "Tatridge." It was a village on the border of Carrisford, Warbrick and Cleeve land.

"No wonder you're on the road then, things being as they are —" The woman broke off and cocked her head. Doubtless one of the many shouts had been directed at her. "Have to go. Just find a place to sit, dear." She bustled off.

Siward immediately passed the loaf to Imogen and she took a huge bite. It was delicious; still warm from the oven. The slight grittiness of earth didn't bother her at all. "The winding cloths are coming loose," she mumbled with a full mouth.

"Why not let it go?" he asked. "It's served its purpose."

Imogen shook her head as she swallowed. She hadn't told Siward her full plan for her guise of pregnancy. He'd have a fit at the thought of the Lady of Carrisford appearing to be with child while without husband. "Enough people have seen me like this," she said. "If we want to leave without speaking to FitzRoger, we'd best not attract attention." With great willpower she passed the rest of the loaf back, but he shook his head.

"You have it. I've had enough."

He was doubtless lying, but Imogen found she couldn't continue the protest and settled to enjoying the last of the loaf.

"I must say that grabbing at yourself looked very real," said Siward. "I half expected you to drop a babe at any moment. But you'd best not go around clutching yourself or we'll have the midwife hovering. Move back in this corner and I'll see what I can do."

Imogen squeezed into a shadowy corner half behind some bales of hay, and Siward groped under the back of her skirts to try to tuck the loose end of the winding cloths back in. Imogen stared at the sky, trying not to look as embarrassed as she felt at the whole thing.

"Hey, you old goat," called a big soldier who was carrying a bundle of pikes as if they were sticks. "You're a spicy one, aren't you? Everyone can see you've done your work on your woman. Can't you wait till nightfall to plow her?" He burst out laughing and all the nearby people looked over and sniggered.

Siward cursed, and Imogen covered her red face with her hands.

"Haven't got that many years left for it," Siward called back amiably. "Got to take every chance I get!"

There was a huge gust of laughter from the crowd. "Well, I'm glad you brought your own with you, then. There's few enough women around here as it is and you'd doubtless exhaust the lot of 'em in one night!" The soldier rolled on his way, still laughing. Everyone else lost interest and got on with their work.

Imogen turned to rest her head for a moment against the cool stone wall. This was getting worse by the minute. "Can we just find a quiet corner and hope no one knows we're there?" she asked faintly.

"Come on," Siward said, and though he tried to sound comforting, she heard the amusement in his voice. Everyone thought they'd been . . . And nobody thought it was wrong, merely funny.

Imogen began to wonder whether she might not be best suited to life in the cloister, as Father Wulfgan said. These last few days since her father's death the Carrisford chaplain had been urging the advantages of the religious life on Imogen. His arguments about a life of penance and prayer being a sure path to eternal bliss had not carried much weight, but now Imogen could see one great advantage. If she entered a cloister, she wouldn't have to marry. There'd be no man fumbling at her body.

She'd never end up like . . . like Janine.

She hobbled after Siward. She couldn't help thinking, too, that in the cloister she'd have good shoes and clean clothes. There'd be regular food and some of the elegancies of life — music and books. She'd be taken care of and she wouldn't have to take risks because people depended on her.

You sniveling little coward, she berated herself, and made herself walk a little faster despite the pain. You took delight in being Imogen of Carrisford when all it required of you was pleasure. Now it demands work and sacrifice, and you shrink back. All of Carrisford depends on you, and you think only of your comfort. It is time to prove yourself worthy of your father. Though he was a gentle, civilized man, Bernard of Carrisford held his own and cared for his own. His people were safe within his governance. As his daughter, you can do no less.

Imogen stiffened her resolve.

First she must regain her castle and wreak vengeance on Warbrick for his acts.

Then she must find and marry a man as good and strong as her father so that the like would never happen again.

Then, she resolved grimly, she must endure the disgusting things men do to women so as to bear sons. She would raise them to be good, strong men like her father so that her people would be cared for from generation to generation.

She was dragged out of these lofty resolutions when she realized her "baby" was lopsided. She couldn't bear to ask Siward to fiddle around with the supports again, and so she put her right hand under the sagging side, pushed up and held it there. She only hoped she'd got it even.

They'd just found what seemed to be a quiet corner, with boxes convenient for sitting, when a voice shouted, "Hey you! Granddad!" They turned.

It was the burly guard from the gate. "What're you doing, wandering all over? Didn't I tell you to wait nearby? Lord FitzRoger'll see you now."

Imogen flashed panic at Siward. They hadn't had a chance to question people, to find out what FitzRoger was really like.

Siward put an arm around her and said, "My wife's not feeling well . . ."

"Master wants to see you," the man stated. "She can be sick later." When they hesitated, he seized them by the arms and began to haul them along. He moved at such speed, that every part of Imogen's body complained and she let out a scream.

"None of that, woman," the guard growled. "I'm beginning to think there's something fishy about you two. You wanted justice from the Lord of Cleeve, and by the Rood you'll get it."

Chapter Three

Imogen stumbled along as best she could, clutching her paunch and biting her lip to stop further moans.

"Harry, what are you doing?"

The guard stopped as if he'd run into a wall. There was bluster in his voice as he said, "Bringing these peasants to you, me lord. The ones I told you of."

Imogen looked up and her heart chilled.

It was the man with the whip.

She couldn't mistake him, though his bare torso was now covered by a dark shirt. His clothing was plain and he wore only a studded leather belt with pouch and knife, but there was no mistaking his authority. It had to be Bastard FitzRoger.

He whipped his own malefactors? Imogen thought in horror, and her instinct took her a step backward.

On the surface there was nothing to fear. He was clean, personable, and civilized. His features were fine and lean, his eyes a clear green; on a woman they would have been called beautiful. His dark hair rippled down onto his shoulders in the latest fashion her father had so deplored. He was tall and had broad shoulders and strong legs, yet a fine-ness in his build denied the looming brutality of some fighting men. He was nothing at all like Warbrick.

So why was Imogen's heart racing? Why had her throat constricted beyond hope of speech? Why was her instinct screaming that she should flee?

Perhaps because of the coldness of those arresting green eyes. As they flicked over her, they seemed to see to her soul and not like what they found there. He glanced at the guard and Imogen was sure she felt the man's hand tremble before he let her go. A simple nod and Harry made himself scarce.

Bastard FitzRoger sat on a convenient keg, one knee raised to support his arm. "You came to seek justice? State your case. I don't have much time." The voice was crisp and impersonal, and she could only be glad of it. The last thing any human being would want would be to attract the interest of this man.

Imogen's voice was frozen. What could they say that would get them out of Castle Cleeve immediately?

Siward nervously filled the gap. "We were thrown off our property, lord. By Lord Warbrick."

Imogen saw a spark of interest at the name. She remembered they'd come here be-cause Cleeve and Warbrick were old foes, come here seeking vengeance. That had not changed. Why was she quailing because Bastard FitzRoger had proved to be a hard man? She was looking for a champion, not a troubadour. FitzRoger seemed just the sort of person to be able to help her regain her castle, and the fact that he made her shiver was nothing to do with the matter.

"Where was this property?" FitzRoger asked.

Siward glanced for guidance at Imogen, but her mind had gone blank. "Tatridge," he said at last.

"Carrisford land?"

"Aye, lord."

"Do you know the castle?"

Siward hesitated, then said, "Aye, lord."

"Tell me about it."

"Lord, we're only simple folk come to get justice —"

"Tell me about it." The voice was not raised, but the command was imperative.

Even Siward stuttered slightly as he replied, "L-lord, I don't know what you want to know. Ask me questions and I'll do my best to answer them."

Imogen watched in fascination as Bastard FitzRoger turned a heavy gold ring on his right hand. He had well-shaped hands which promised both strength and deftness, but the movement transfixed her with its silent menace.

"How many entrances?" he asked at last.

"Just the main gate and the postern," Siward said.

And that wasn't true, thought Imogen, for there was an entrance which connected with the secret passageways. She supposed Siward had used it in getting her out of the castle.

"How is the main gate protected?"

"There's a drawbridge and portcullis, lord. The passage beyond is narrow, well-guarded, and has murder holes. Like this one."

"Do you know how many men garrison the place?"

"No, lord, but enough."

"What about the postern?"

"Two guards, I believe, and it leads to a narrow passage with a farther door before the castle proper."

Imogen saw the sharpness in FitzRoger's eyes, and stiffened. He suspected something. "You are surprisingly well informed for a peasant."

Visions of the whipping post flashed before Imogen's eyes. She heard a moan and realized with shame it came from herself. The green eyes turned to impale her.

"Sit down, woman," he said sharply. "There's a box behind you. And if you're going to drop the babe, go find the goodwives." Imogen complied before her trembling legs gave way. He had already turned back to Siward. "Well?" It was like the crack of his whip.

49

"My brother's a guard there, lord." Imogen could have kissed Siward for his calm, convincing answer.

FitzRoger's eyes traveled them both, and such was the power of his gaze that Imogen was astonished he didn't realize her identity immediately. He was clearly alert to the fact that they were not what they seemed.

Suddenly his questions and the bustle around them clicked together to make a whole picture and her heart gave a little leap. "You are going to attack Carrisford," she said.

He stood smoothly and came to her, an unpleasant smile sparking on his lean face. The farce was over, it said, and now we'll see sport. "And you are very gently spoken for one brought so low."

Imogen was still frightened of him, but the implications overwhelmed fear with hope. FitzRoger had heard her plight, and was already preparing to ride to her rescue. She rose and abandoned deception. "Are you going to attack Carrisford, Lord FitzRoger?"

He hooked a thumb in his belt and studied her. "That is my intention, woman."

She smiled up mistily. "Thank you."

He did look slightly bemused by that. "In what way will my actions serve you?"

Imogen stood as straight as she could. "I am Imogen of Carrisford," she said with dignity. "As you see, I do not need rescue, but I have come to you for aid, as a knight and vassal of our liege the king, in regaining my home from Lord Warbrick and wreaking vengeance for foul deeds."

The green eyes widened. Imogen rather thought she'd rendered him speechless. When he took a breath, she realized he had not in fact been breathing normally for a few seconds.

"Lady Imogen," he said, and something gleamed in his eyes. It reminded her of a cat sighting a mouse far from its hole. She took a hasty step back, but she had forgotten to hold her paunch and it slipped. Her grab to support it drew his eyes and the blade-sharp coldness snapped back.

"I think I will need proof of your identity, lady."

"Proof? How can I prove who I am?"

"Your condition argues against you being the Flower of the West . . ." His eyes wandered over her, stripping her of her dirt and disguise. "Or at least suggests a very strange tale. Come with me." He turned and strode toward the keep, confident that they would follow.

They did so, but slowly. Imogen simply could not force her swollen feet to move more quickly.

He turned back, sharp displeasure on his face, but then he looked at her feet. He moved quickly to swing her into his arms. She gasped in surprise but could not but be grateful for the relief from agony.

51

"You stink," he commented.

"I'm sorry," she replied with as much dignity as her position allowed. "There are also fleas." With a degree of malice, she added, "Which are doubtless even now moving with relish from my dirt to your cleaner flesh."

As he began to mount the wooden steps up to the entrance to the keep he looked her over with a frown. "Take off your headcloth."

Silently thanking Siward, Imogen obeyed and saw his grimace at the greasy mess revealed. He would not be able to tell whether it was her famous hair or not. Her instinct was working furiously and telling her not to lower her guard with Bastard FitzRoger. The more she kept him uncertain, the better. Her pregnancy was definitely a good idea and she would maintain it until she was sure of his honesty, or — more likely — until she was safe in the protection of the king.

Imogen couldn't help but notice, however, that her porter was very strong. He was climbing the steep stairs quickly without any change of breathing, and she was not a particularly dainty lady. She was of average height and well-rounded. Her father had always told her she had excellent hips for childbearing.

Since she had sought out this man she should be pleased at his strength, but instead it made her nervous. Imogen was, for the first time, having to consider a protector's strength being used against her. The plain truth was that Bastard FitzRoger could do with her as he wished, and all she had to oppose him was her wits.

On the other hand his very strength was having a peculiar effect upon her. Protected as she had been, she had rarely even touched a man other than her father. Now, under her hand she could feel a rock-hard shoulder — but warm, living, moving rock. His arms, his torso, all had the same vital firmness.

Her father had been a big man and very strong, but he hadn't been so *hard*. It was as if all Lord Bernard's massive strength had been condensed down into this man's slighter form — rocklike and singing with power. It frightened her, but it also excited her in the strangest way. . . .

She told herself to stop such thoughts. She was in danger of losing her wits altogether. It had been a horrendous few days, but she could not afford to give way. Not yet.

The simple question was, how far could she trust this man?

She doubted she could trust any man.

In desperation she clung to one clear thought. Whether he was a kind man or not, Lord FitzRoger had heard of her plight and already been on his way to champion the damsel in distress.

FitzRoger carried her through the arched

doorway into the castle hall. It was a large chamber hung with cloths and banners, but it had a harsh, crude feel to it quite unlike her own elegant home. The walls were unpainted stone, the hangings were crude and dirty, and the rushes on the wooden floor were stale. It was also deserted. She supposed everyone was busy outside preparing for the relief of Carrisford. That cheered her.

FitzRoger walked straight across the room and into a narrow tower staircase. This proved more difficult to negotiate with her in his arms, but he managed it, and without banging her head or her feet. She had to admire his competence.

The upper floor of the keep was divided into a number of plain rooms. He stopped in the first and lowered her to sit on the floor. There was a bed there and she looked at it meaningfully.

"The fleas," he said coolly, brushing his hands as if he had just carried a noisome load. Which she supposed he had. "I will send some women and a bathtub. I am willing to assume you are Imogen of Carrisford until it is proved otherwise, and treat you accordingly. But do not attempt to leave this room without my permission."

He didn't need to make threats. It was clear from his tone and expression that what the young man had said was true. There was only one crime in Castle Cleeve: not following the

54

master's orders. And justice would be swift and ruthless.

He turned toward the stairs and Imogen called out, "Stop! Please, what has happened to my man?"

He turned back sharply, his gaze traveling her swollen body. "What is he to you?"

"My seneschal," she said quickly. "He is an old man. Be kind to him."

"He will be given the same care as you for now." He again moved to leave.

"Lord FitzRoger," she called, and he turned with a touch of impatience.

"Will you help me regain Carrisford?"

Then he did smile. "Yes, of course, Lady Imogen. I am already preparing and tomorrow we ride. You, of course, will want to accompany us."

It was spoken as an edged challenge, but Imogen matched his smile. "I will insist upon it, my lord."

With a nod, he left.

Brave words did not make brave hearts, however. Alone for a blessed moment, Imogen sagged back on the floor. It was tempting to give way to tears. Her father was dead. Her home was despoiled and in the hands of a cruel enemy. Her maid had been viciously treated, perhaps killed. She didn't know what had happened to her beloved aunt. She was alone in the hands of a cold, unpredictable stranger.

She forced back the tears and the weakness that inspired them. She was Bernard of Carrisford's daughter and she would prove herself worthy.

She turned her mind to Bastard FitzRoger. She had little experience of such men; under her father's eye, no man had ever dared be other than courteous to her.

How was she to judge such a dark power?

How could she be sure, for example, that once he had regained her castle he would turn over control to her? The king, of course, would see to her affairs as soon as he became aware of the situation, but FitzRoger could drain the place of supplies and cause serious damage before then. If, she thought bleakly, Warbrick left anything of value after doing the same thing.

There was also the concern that FitzRoger was reputed to be high in the king's favor. If he did steal from her, would the king enforce the law and grant her reparation? Henry Beauclerk would not have crossed Bernard of Carrisford, but would he pay much attention to his daughter?

Of course, an additional problem was that the king would now have the choosing of her husband. Sweet Virgin, was ever an untried maid so beset with problems?

Imogen had to wonder when the idea of wooing her would occur to FitzRoger. She had not heard that he was already wed or betrothed, so he would have to see her as a ripe plum for the picking. She had no intention of marrying such a man, so her pregnancy could turn out to be very useful indeed.

Three women came in with a tub and lined the inside with thick linen cloths. Imogen was soothed by this evidence of gentle living in such a rough hall. They went away and returned with pails of hot and cold water and filled the tub, adding herbs. One laid out clean clothes for Imogen to wear.

The women eyed her disgusting state curiously but were otherwise as respectful as she could wish. They would have bathed her, but Imogen could not allow that. She sent them away and they obeyed quite readily. Imogen had to admit that she wouldn't touch herself either if she didn't have to.

As soon as she was alone she ripped off the foul rags, the paunch, and the sandals. She scratched some of the worst bites, and sank with a blissful sigh into the water. Her feet stung, but it would do them good to be cleaned.

It felt so very, very good.

It would have been easy to fall asleep in the steamy comfort of the bath, but the women would soon return, and so Imogen took up the cloth and the pot of soap and began to wash. When she saw how foul she was, she scrubbed viciously at every inch of her body.

When she started to wash her feet, however, she hissed with agony and stopped. More careful cleaning showed they were in a terrible state. They were puffed up almost beyond recognition. There were swollen blisters all over the soles, and weeping, bleeding sores on the sides where the thongs had rubbed. How had she walked on them? How was she to walk now?

Dabbing at them gingerly, she tried to tell herself that they'd be better in a little while with the soaking.

She resumed the attack on the rest of her body, then turned her attention to her hair. She soaked it, did what she could with the soap, then rinsed it with clean water. She really did need a maidservant to help with this task, for her hair was thick and wavy and fell to below her hips.

Would she ever have dear Janine back to brush and braid her hair? That raised unbearable thoughts, however, and she pushed them away.

When she was as clean as possible Imogen stood, but a moment on her feet had her back sitting, tears in her eyes from the pain. Sweet Savior, what was she to do?

Eventually, she climbed out of her bath by hoisting herself on her hands and falling out onto her bottom. She discovered there was a spot on each heel which could take some weight without protest, and so she managed to dry herself. Then she shuffled over to her paunch and bound it on, and pulled the clean cotton shift on top.

At last she was, just possibly, safe.

Safe? she scoffed. How safe was she when she couldn't even walk? She was as helpless as a babe.

She eyed the low bed. If she was lying on it when the maids returned, perhaps no one need know just how vulnerable she was. She worked her way awkwardly over to the bed and hoisted herself onto it. Surely by morning she would be able to walk.

Why was she so afraid, when she was in the keep of an ally? Apart from his coldness, the Lord of Cleeve was being a perfect knight. He had been willing to hear and aid two destitute peasants, as a good lord should. He had given her a room, clean clothes, and a bath. He was preparing to recover her castle.

She suddenly wondered why the Lord of Cleeve had not been among her suitors.

He had been busy since coming to Cleeve, of course, occupied with taking control of his property and helping the king repel invasion, but other men as busy had found time to at least express interest. With Carrisford and Cleeve lands adjoining there would have been arguments in favor of the match.

Of course, he could well have realized that someone of such dubious origins would not have been a strong contender. Lord Roger of Cleeve had denied both paternity and the legality of the marriage to the Bastard's mother. This man's taking of the name FitzRoger had been a calculated taunt at the man he claimed as father. It was only since the coronation of his friend and patron, Henry Beauclerk, that Lord FitzRoger had obtained validation of his legitimacy. He had not yet managed to shed the nickname Bastard, and perhaps never would.

Imogen doubted that anyone actually used it to his face.

Imogen nodded, satisfied that she understood the situation. He'd either never thought he'd have a chance of wedding Imogen of Carrisford or he'd approached her father and been dismissed. Now he could well be thinking that doing her this service would bring him into favor. He still was not the sort of husband she wanted, but she would try to be kind when the time came to dismiss him. His irregular origins were not his fault.

The women peeped in. Imogen smiled and allowed them to come and clear away the bath. One produced a comb and began to work it through Imogen's wet hair. "It's so long, lady. And I swear it looks like gold where it's drying. Such beauty . . ."

Then one of the maids gave a squeal of horror and pointed at a bloody patch on the sheet. "Oh, lady! Your poor feet!"

Before Imogen could prevent it the woman ran off to get help. Soon a monk appeared along with the master of the castle.

"This is Brother Patrick, Lady Imogen," said FitzRoger. "He's more accustomed to sword cuts and saddle sores, but he should be able to tend your wounds."

Imogen thought of protesting but guessed that if she did, the master would simply upend her and present her feet to the monk. Anyway, her feet did hurt and she wanted the use of them tomorrow.

FitzRoger leaned against a wall, arms folded, and watched as Brother Patrick inspected the damage. The monk shook his head in a worrying way, then set to work, cleaning the weeping flesh then smearing salve and applying bandages. It hurt.

Throughout the painful ordeal Imogen's awareness of FitzRoger's impassive observation firmed her courage. She'd pledge her soul to the devil before she'd whine with those cold green eyes on her.

"How bad are they, Brother Patrick?" FitzRoger asked as the monk began to bind her feet.

"Not as bad as they look, my lord. As long as no infection sets in, they will heal."

Imogen caught her breath at the very notion that they might not heal. She remembered her father dying in agony from a festering wound and a chill swept through her.

She looked up and her eyes were caught by FitzRoger's. "They will heal unless you are foolish," he said. "I've seen enough wounds." Despite the brusque tone, it was almost as if he realized her fears and was offering comfort.

He strolled closer to the bed. "You improve with washing," he said casually, "no matter who you are. You do fit the description of the Carrisford heiress."

"That is hardly surprising."

A light flickered in his eyes. "Robust," he said, "with gingerish hair."

Imogen gaped. "It is not *ginger!*"

He picked up a strand, letting it fall before she could slap his hand away. "If it's not, then perhaps you are not the Carrisford heiress. I wonder what the penalty should be for impersonating a highborn lady?"

Despite the fact that she could never be found guilty of such a crime, Imogen felt a tremor of fear. "You have no right to punish me."

"You have placed yourself under my governance."

She glared up at him. "I have not. I have come to you, equal to equal, for aid against my enemies. My father was always an ally of Cleeve."

The monk finished his work. "Please do not walk on those feet for at least two days, Lady Imogen," he said, "and send for me if there should be any increase of pain or swelling of the legs."

At least her confrontation with FitzRoger had distracted her from Brother Patrick's final ministrations.

But two days? "I can't stay off my feet for two days," she protested.

"You must if you want them to heal," said the monk. "And don't try to wear shoes."

Brother Patrick left and Imogen looked down with disgust at the bandaged lumps at the ends of her legs. How could her body betray her at this crucial time?

Then she realized the women had also left.

She was alone at the uncertain mercy of Bastard FitzRoger, and forbidden to make any attempt to escape on pain of death from festering feet.

She could feel the pounding of her heart but kept her chin up and her expression stern.

At least FitzRoger moved away from her, going to sit on a bench beneath the narrow window. The sun was low now and fiery. It touched his dark hair and tunic with red, so that Imogen was reminded of the devil.

He raised a thoughtful finger to his lips as he studied her. "There are stories," he said at last, "of secret ways into Carrisford. Do you know those ways?"

Imogen's heart skipped a beat. This was not what she had expected. Even the existence of those secret ways was a family secret, a sacred trust. How had he heard of them? She remained silent.

His expression hardened. "If Warbrick holds the castle, you want him out of there, do you not?"

"Yes."

"Then you must tell me all you know about the place."

It made sense, but it had always been strongly impressed on Imogen that a secret escape is also a secret entrance, and a known secret is no use to anyone. "You said you were taking me with you to Carrisford," she said at last.

"Hardly practical anymore."

Imogen wanted nothing more than to stay in this bed and be taken care of, but she could see her duty. "I can ride," she said.

She expected an immediate protest. No one ever allowed the Flower of the West to put herself in danger or discomfort. If had often chafed her.

Instead he nodded. "It will not be easy, but if you insist it can be done. We should be in no great need of speed."

"Then," said Imogen, "I will tell you what you need to know when you need to know it."

"What I need to know?" he echoed. He turned that heavy ring again, then rose smoothly and moved toward the bed. "Did you not say we are allies, Lady Imogen?"

She pressed back into the pillows and nodded, dry mouthed.

"Allies are honor-bound to help one another." He raised one foot and rested it on the bed frame, leaning forward on his knee, looming over her. "In all ways."

Imogen remembered thinking that he did not loom. Foolish error.

"Can you read and write at all?" he asked.

She was startled back into her voice. "Yes."

"Then I will have some parchment sent up with pens and ink. Draw a plan of the castle and put on it all the information you know. Everything." It was as if she had never spoken. "Tomorrow we're going to Carrisford, Ginger. If you withhold any useful information, I'll take it out of your skin. If you deceive me, I'll strangle you myself."

She believed him. She would have disappeared under the bed if she'd been able, but she kept her chin up and her eyes on him. "Then you do believe I am who I claim to be?" It came out a little thin, but she was proud of having got it out at all.

"I said I'd treat you as such until proved wrong, didn't I?"

He leaned forward and picked up a strand of her long hair, twisting it around his finger. "If you are playing a part, sweet Ginger," he said softly, "I recommend that tomorrow you take any opportunity that presents to run — swelling feet or no."

Imogen was frozen.

Then he released her hair and straightened. "I'll have a supper sent up along with the writing materials. Good night."

He was gone and she could breathe again, try to calm her hammering heart. Her instincts had been right all along. She had snared a dragon, not a hunting hound, and was as likely to be its dinner as its mistress.

She closed her eyes on tears. She wanted her father back to guide her, Aunt Constance to fuss, Janine to comb her hair and lay out her beautiful clothes and jewels. She wanted her home. She didn't want to be in a strange place, alone, and having to be brave.

She had no choice. She remembered her father's words and knew that the taste of gall was on her lips.

After she had eaten the plain but adequate supper, Imogen drew a careful plan of Carrisford for Bastard FitzRoger. She told herself she did it because he was her champion and was going to win back her home for her. She knew she also drew it to pacify him.

She even included the section of the passageways which ran behind the walls of the great hall, for they would be easy to find by anyone who suspected their presence, and the link between them and the lower ones was hidden.

Despite her fear, however, she did not include the lower passages or the entrance they provided to the castle.

After all, it was possible that Warbrick had abandoned Carrisford when he found her missing. It would be utter foolishness to give away the family secrets unless absolutely necessary.

All the same, she chewed the quill nervously, wondering what FitzRoger would do when he realized most of the secret passageways weren't shown.

Of course he wouldn't whip her.

But neither was he a man to make idle threats. . . .

Fear and confusion about the nature of her paladin — not to mention the bulk of the unaccustomed paunch and her sore feet — should have kept Imogen from sleep, but exhaustion was stronger. She slept deep and dreamless and was only reluctantly roused at dawn by a serving woman.

Imogen discovered she was in a worse state than the day before. She ached all over and the sores on her feet protested at the lightest touch. She briefly thought of changing her mind and staying there in comfort until her home was secure again, but she could not. She was Imogen of Carrisford and her duty called her there. Lord knows what FitzRoger would get up to if she was not with him to protect the interests of herself and her people.

It was awkward to dress, even with two women to help her, but she managed it. Then she ate a breakfast of bread, cold pork, and ale while her hair was worked into two fat plaits. By the time this was done her spirits had improved. With movement some of her stiffness had eased, and she was cheered by the thought that soon her home would be secure once more, and she safe in it.

The clothes provided were simple garments of linen and wool, but clean and colorful, as opposed to the rags she had worn for her flight. The women brought some large shoes which would fit over her bandages, but they hurt, and after one tentative attempt at standing Imogen found Brother Patrick had been wise to suggest she stay off her feet entirely. The slightest weight on them was excruciating. If she wasn't going to stand, never mind walk, she had no need of shoes.

One of the women was bold enough to venture a protest. "You shouldn't go anywhere today, lady. You bide here with us, and let the master handle matters."

Imogen gritted her teeth. "I will be able to ride."

When she was ready to travel, one of the maids went to find someone to carry her. Imogen braced herself for another encounter with FitzRoger.

However, it was a stranger who entered her

room. He was a handsome young man of high rank, already dressed in mail but with brown curls uncovered. "Lady Imogen," he said, and bowed. "I am Renald de Lisle who has the honor of carrying you to your horse." His expressive dark eyes suggested he had fought the hordes of darkness for the right to be her porter.

He was clearly French, not Norman. It showed in the way he spoke the language, and in his mannerisms. Imogen could not help but smile in the face of his unconcealed delight at his task. Why could not all men be as appealing?

Though not quite as tall as FitzRoger, he was of more massive build, with heavy shoulders and a broad chest. He picked her up without effort. Imogen leaned at ease against his mailed chest. She noticed that though he had the same strength as FitzRoger, Sir Renald didn't cause her to turn giddy.

It all went to show it had just been exhaustion and hunger.

Sir Renald smelled slightly of herbs, perhaps from his clothing. She tried to remember what FitzRoger had smelled like. But then her stink would have blotted out any odor more subtle than vinegar. What a way to be first seen by a man, she thought with despair. He would probably never forget her standing there in grimy rags, eight months gone, and half crippled.

Sir Renald broke into her thoughts. "Such a pleasant duty," he said cheerfully. "I thanked my brother-in-arms most warmly for appointing me his deputy."

"You refer to Lord FitzRoger?"

"Indeed. We are brothers of the heart, demoiselle. We were poor together as we sold our swords. We vowed that if we became rich we would be rich together. And here we are."

The warmth in his voice was startling. How extraordinary to think of cold FitzRoger having any friend, especially such a friend. Sir Renald carried her out of the keep and Imogen savored fresh morning sunshine and a light breeze that caught at the edge of her skirts. A good day for victory.

"And what do you do for the Lord of Cleeve, Sir Renald?" she asked as they began the descent to the crowded, noisy bailey.

"At the present I am his master-at-arms as he shapes up these lazy rogues he has inherited from his brother. One day, as his riches increase, he will give me land of my own. Me, I do not care. I have food, a roof over my head, fine clothing, and enough fighting to dispel boredom. I am in Paradise."

Just then he carried her past the blood-darkened whipping post. The previous day's scene returned to her mind, and she saw again Bastard FitzRoger wielding that whip. She heard the men screaming. And their only crime had been a bit too much to drink.

Imogen shuddered. Paradise? Only the coarsest type of man would find Castle Cleeve a paradise. Just let these warriors wrest her castle back — it was all they were good for — and she would seek out a sensitive, civilized husband, another man like Gerald of Huntwich.

Instead of being put on a horse of her own, Imogen was settled to ride pillion behind a solid, middle-aged soldier. He told her gruffly his name was Bert, and it was clear he wasn't too pleased with his role in this day's events. Imogen wasn't too pleased with the arrangement herself, but within moments she had to admit that she would have found it hard to manage a horse. Stirrups would have been out of the question. Sitting sideways on the pillion seat, she found her feet gave her no pain. She hooked her hand over Bert's leather belt and resigned herself.

Sir Renald kissed her hand gallantly before he left to mount his gray destrier. FitzRoger rode past bareheaded. His squire rode behind bearing his shield and helmet.

FitzRoger's eyes traveled over his force, taking in every detail. Without hesitation or hurry they passed over Imogen. She could imagine his mind ticking off: ". . . one heiress, mounted . . ." Then they were off at a steady pace which should bring them to Carrisford, she reckoned, by late afternoon.

It was a pleasant day for riding and

without even the work of guiding a horse, Imogen settled to enjoy it. The Castle Cleeve lands appeared to have given good crops and fat kine were in the meadows. There was much unused land, though. She had heard that FitzRoger's brother, Hugh, had not been a good lord, so perhaps these lacks could be laid at his door.

The people were busy with the last of the harvest. They looked up and watched their lord as he passed. There were no friendly cheers such as had regularly greeted Lord Bernard, but nor was there sullen resentment. It was as if they took their tone from him and were cool.

FitzRoger occasionally rode away from the line of troops to speak to a group or inspect something. Always checking, she thought sourly. Nothing was allowed to escape his perceptive green eyes.

Her father had been a good lord and had been deeply loved. She didn't think that was the case with Bastard FitzRoger, which was hardly surprising. Who would love such a harsh man? But she saw that he was respected. She thought how significant it was that they all called him "the master." Discipline among his men was as tight as the shine on every visible piece of metal, and yet the soldiers sang as they rode and any grumbles were humorous ones.

Imogen decided with irritation to put aside

this obsession with her paladin — her champion. He was nothing more to her than a tool.

She'd help him to take Carrisford, even show him the secret entrance if necessary, then she would settle to restoring her home and holding it safe. She would, of course, give him a suitable reward for his help and that would be that. She'd make sure the next message to the king got through. Henry would crush Warbrick as he deserved, and then Imogen would carefully select a husband.

She began to run her previous suitors through her mind. To her surprise, she found them an unsatisfactory lot. From safe within her father's protection they had seemed well enough, but now it was clear that one had been too stupid, another too cruel, another too clumsy, another too vain, another too old . . .

FitzRoger was making one of his periodic rides along the line and he pulled up his chestnut beside her. "You frown, lady. Are you in pain?"

"No, my lord."

"Tired? If so, I'm sorry for it but we cannot stop."

"I have no problem except tedium, Lord FitzRoger."

"Some people pray daily for a tedious life, Lady Imogen. I'm afraid you must wait for excitement until the fighting starts."

Annoyingly, he was gone before she could think of a fitting response. She twisted to follow his progress down the column. He stopped here and there for a word or a joke. Or a rebuke. Imogen saw one man turn pasty white after a few quiet words.

Despite FitzRoger's saying they could not stop, they did stop three times — to rest and water the horses. The comfort of the horses, after all, was much more important than that of a mere heiress. At each halt Sir Renald carried her to a shady spot and settled her on a blanket there.

He never lingered, however, but was off with FitzRoger making another round of men and mounts, checking, encouraging, admonishing. Imogen had never had anything to do with warfare before, and she began to suspect it was as much a matter of organization and planning as violent action.

At the third halt food was served — bread, cheese, and ale. Sir Renald brought Imogen her portion, but then went off with his friend on the usual inspection. After a while, however, the two men came and threw themselves down beside her, sharing a skin of ale and a loaf.

It was past noon and the day had turned hot. Sir Renald pushed back his mailed hood to reveal damp hair. "I hate summer fighting," he grumbled.

"Lose some fat," said his friend unsympathetically.

"I am not fat," Sir Renald rebutted. "Only an inhuman monster such as yourself would not feel the heat with thick felt, heavy iron, and a surcoat on."

"I feel the heat," said FitzRoger. "But I enjoy a campaign whatever the weather." He turned to Imogen. "I hope you are not overheated, lady." His tone implied that the sentence could be completed ". . . for I'm not going to do a plague-ridden thing about it."

"Since I have on only two thin garments, my lord, it would be churlish of me to complain."

He deliberately eyed her swollen body. "Women in your condition tend to feel the heat."

Imogen knew her cheeks were flaming as if she roasted. She needed to get the conversation on a different track. "Can you tell me what has become of my seneschal, my lord?"

"Strange," he mused, "how any mention of your impending motherhood seems to bring him to your mind. I wouldn't have thought such an elderly man to your taste, but women are strange creatures . . ."

Imogen was about to protest this fiercely when she detected a glint of humor in his eyes. The wretch was daring to tease her! The only response to such impudence was to ignore it. "He is my trusted servant," she said coldly.

"Then your trusted servant is back at

75

Cleeve in safe but considerate captivity."

Imogen stared at him. He was holding Siward hostage. "It would be dishonorable to mistreat an old and faithful retainer."

"If you behave yourself he will not be mistreated," he countered blandly. At his signal the camp began to prepare to leave — gathering up scraps and tightening girths. As FitzRoger uncoiled to his feet, he asked, "Who, then, is the father of this most inconvenient child?"

Imogen looked down. "I cannot tell you that," she answered with perfect honesty.

He grasped her chin and raised it so she had to face him. "You are not secretly married?"

"If I had a husband I would have no need of *your* protection, would I?"

"That would depend on the husband." He let her go and strode away to supervise the reassembly of the fighting force. Imogen wanted to hurl a lethal projectile at his arrogant back.

Renald de Lisle bent and lifted her into his arms.

"Sir Renald," said Imogen tartly, "though you doubtless feel your friend has all the virtues, I find him uncivil and unkind."

She felt his rumble of laughter as a wave through her body. "Of course I don't think he's a paragon of virtue. He's a rogue like me. But he's a man of his word. What promises he makes he will keep, and that's more than can be said for most men." He deposited her once more in the pillion saddle.

Imogen shivered. When she thought of some of the promises Bastard FitzRoger had made to her, de Lisle's words offered no comfort at all.

Chapter Four

They drew close to Carrisford Castle in the late afternoon. FitzRoger held most of his force back in the cover of the woodland, then he, de Lisle, and a few others went forward to survey the situation. Imogen had no intention of being excluded, and persuaded Bert to ride forward to join them. The men were still within the shelter of the trees, but on a rise which gave an excellent view of Carrisford Castle.

Imogen's throat tightened at the sight of her home, whole and unblemished on its rise of land near the river. Wisps of destructive smoke rose from the nearby village, though, which looked deserted though not entirely wrecked.

She turned her gaze back to the castle, seeking signs of damage. The tall, square keep and two mighty walls forming an inner and an outer bailey were unbroken, and still fused smoothly with the scrubby rock of the hill upon which they sat. The main entrance, approached by a long, sloping path up to the lowered drawbridge, was watched over by two gate towers. The portcullis was invitingly raised.

She had prepared herself for a gutted ruin, but it was as beautiful as ever.

"He's gone," she murmured.

FitzRoger turned to look at her. "Or he's set a trap for you or anyone else who seeks to claim the place."

Imogen bit her lip. If she had returned here alone, she would have ridden up to the castle, rejoicing in recovering it. How naive she was.

"What do we do, then?" she asked.

"Observe and scout."

They all moved slightly back, and the whole force dismounted and looked to their horses. When Sir Renald lifted her down, she persuaded him to make her a place to sit up on the rise where she could see her home. He ensconced her behind some undergrowth, but she was still able to see quite well. She would still swear the place was empty.

A short while later a few men rode off, doubtless to seek news throughout the neighborhood. A few more slipped away on foot, venturing closer to the castle. FitzRoger came forward, and without a word to Imogen sat quietly against a tree and watched the castle like a hawk.

Imogen found herself spending more time watching her paladin than the silent castle. There was little to choose between them, she thought sourly. He was as still and as cold as a stone fortress. What an ability he had to be immobile. Even in the shade it was still hot and she was sure armor was not the most comfortable dress, and yet he sat as still as a statue.

His profile had a carved quality, she thought. Very clean, severe lines —

A disturbance behind them, down near the encampment, interrupted her study. In a second he was gone, heading toward the voices.

Imogen wriggled around and saw that one of the soldiers had returned with a peasant who instantly fell to his knees before the Lord of Castle Cleeve. Imogen instinctively moved to join them, then hissed with pain and sat again, cursing her feet. She *hated* being tied to a spot like this.

As if he'd heard, FitzRoger returned to her, picked her up, and carried her back down the slope. He came to stand before the peasant, who was now on his feet but shaking with fear. Imogen thought he might be the local hurdle maker but wasn't sure.

"Who is this?" FitzRoger demanded of the man.

"That be Lady Imogen," the man gabbled. "Lord Bernard's daughter. The Treasure of Carrisford. O, my lady, right glad I am to see you safe. Such a time —"

"Enough," FitzRoger said, and the man fell silent. "The lady will be returned to her rights in Carrisford, and order will be restored. You have nothing to fear, but you must stay here until all is settled."

The man was led off, bowing and scraping — rather more to FitzRoger than to her, Imogen thought.

FitzRoger carried her back and set her down again on her blanket. He looked her over all afresh. "So, Lady Imogen. You undoubtedly have a tale to tell. When is the babe due?"

Imogen swallowed. "Late September," she said, thinking another month seemed about right.

"Hmm," he said with a raised brow. "You must have had a merry Yuletide."

Before she could think of an appropriately scathing retort he walked away and settled back to his watching post.

Imogen kept an eye on him as she tried to think of a tale to tell which would account for her supposed state. It was impossible to imagine that her father would not have noticed such a bulging waistline and arranged her marriage. In fact, she realized with concern, just about anyone in the locality would be able to tell FitzRoger she'd been properly indented in the middle only two days since. Her deception could not last long, but she needed to be out of FitzRoger's power before he learned the truth.

She looked over and wondered just what his reaction would be to having been fooled. The thought sent shivers down her spine.

He tensed and she turned to see what he had seen. Nothing.

"What is it?" she whispered.

He ignored her. She had an urge to crawl over to him and demand his attention, but she hated to think of the sight she'd be at the end of it. She turned instead to stare at the castle with as much intensity as he. Finally she saw it. A slight movement as someone, emboldened by dusk, peered over a battlement. It could be a nervous servant, but it could be a concealed guard.

"If Warbrick and his men had left," she said, half to herself, "and there were servants still in the castle, there'd be no reason for them to conceal themselves."

"Exactly." He slid sinuously from his watching post and came to loom over her, thumbs tucked into his sword belt. "Time for you to tell me all your secrets, Imogen of Carrisford." A slight hand signal brought Sir Renald and two other men. "Well?" he said.

She hated being tied to the ground at his feet like this. He was deliberately using her incapacity to terrify and control her, and she loathed him for it. "It is a family secret," she said firmly, meeting his eyes, even though it hurt her neck to do so.

"Then consider me family," he said with a cold smile.

"Hardly."

He dropped to one knee so that at least

their eyes were level. "You claim to want Warbrick out of Carrisford, demoiselle."

"I do."

"Then prove it."

Imogen found having those cold green eyes on a level with hers, and barely a foot away, was even worse than having him towering over her. Like an icy wind, his intent gaze numbed her senses, stole her voice.

"Ty," said Sir Renald humorously, "stop glaring at the girl. You'll scare what wits she's got out of her entirely."

Imogen expected FitzRoger to gut the man for his impudence, but instead he collapsed back to sit on the ground, arms around his knees. His expression was still unfriendly toward her, but it did not have that numbing power. "You think she's a half-wit?" he asked his friend dryly. "It would explain a great deal."

"I have all my wits!" Imogen burst out. "Though if I'd been using them, you are the last person I would have gone to for aid."

"Where then?" he asked sweetly. He was even smiling. Imogen decided his glare was horrible, but his smile was worse. She was sure he smiled at his enemies before he ran his sword through them.

"To the king," she said boldly.

He raised one brow. "If you'd thought there was any chance of reaching Henry, you'd have gone east yesterday."

She frowned at a sudden thought. "Since Warbrick was at Carrisford, I should have gone east, through his land!"

The men all looked at her with disbelief. "I think half-wit is generous, Renald," said FitzRoger, and Imogen had to admit that had been a stupid thing to say.

"Still," FitzRoger continued, "she presumably has the knowledge of the secret passages in her muddled head somewhere. The question is how to get at it."

"There's a key to every person," said Sir Renald.

"Mess up her feet a bit more," said a massive blond-haired man casually, making Imogen instinctively scuttle backward. She saw the man's eyes widen. A nervous turn of her head showed a chilling expression on FitzRoger's face as he gazed at him.

Again, Sir Renald was the peacemaker. "Use *your* wits, Will. This is the sweet demoiselle we are rescuing from the vile monster. Save your nasty streak for him. I'm sure when Lady Imogen has considered the matter she'll see sense."

Imogen rather thought there was a warning in those last words, but she couldn't seem to think straight. Though Bastard FitzRoger had willingly come to her aid, her instincts screamed that she shouldn't trust him entirely. After she was in control of her property, she didn't want him knowing its secrets.

She swallowed and licked dry lips. "It's clear there are few people left in the castle, even if they are soldiers. If there were many, they wouldn't be able to stay invisible. It should be no great matter to take the place."

"Of course not," said FitzRoger amiably. "Why don't you lead the way up to the gate?"

She stared at him. As soon as she became aware it was open, she closed her mouth with a snap. "I am not a soldier."

"Whoever leads the way is going to get killed, soldier or not," he remarked pleasantly. "Don't you think the honor should be yours, since it's your castle?"

He twisted everything she said. The world didn't make any sense anymore. "But I'm the whole point of this," she heard herself say. "If I'm dead, Carrisford will revert to the Crown." It sounded terribly selfish. *Was* it her duty to lead the force? She supposed if she were a man it would be. . . .

"How true," FitzRoger said with a sigh. "What a shame. In that case, Lady Imogen, perhaps you should nominate a deputy. Who would you like to see killed in your place? Myself? Renald? The nasty man who wants to mangle your feet?"

She had been right to distrust his smile. When it focused on her, she felt her face flame. "I don't know," she mumbled sullenly.

"The decisions are all yours," he said implacably. "Perhaps you would prefer that we turn around and return peacefully to Castle Cleeve. That way nobody need so much as prick his finger."

Imogen buried her head in her arms, fighting an urge to weep, an urge to scream. If she had a weapon she would have tried to silence that mocking voice in any way she could.

The worst thing was that he was right. He didn't have to bludgeon her over the head with it. A direct attack would be successful but would cost lives. A sneak attack through the secret entrance could well be bloodless, at least on their side.

She raised her head and gave him a stare she hoped would blister his soul. "Get me some ink and parchment."

It was there so quickly she knew it had been waiting to hand. Stony-faced she began to sketch in the failing light, explaining as she went.

"The entrance in the cliff is very hard to find. Even when you're close you won't be able to see it. It's above an arrowhead rock, however, and if you just follow the way the arrow points, you will come to it. It's the merest slit and the very largest men will not fit through." She looked at him and said with relish, "Even you will probably not be able to go through in armor."

He was silent and impassive.

"The passage is dark and very narrow," she continued. "But any man who can squeeze through the entrance can make it through the passage. It would be best to use no light as it is awkward enough to sidle along without extra things to hold, and there's nothing to see. The floor is smooth, and there are no outcroppings or other hazards. You just have to have faith that all is well ahead of you." She shuddered slightly at the memory of the few times she had gone through the deepest passages. Total dark. The feeling that one was in an ever-narrowing space without end.

She looked up and saw something strange. His eyes were not so green. No, that was not it. His pupils were unusually large. "Go on," he said a little sharply.

"The darkness does end," she said. "When the entrance joins the castle passageways, there is light through narrow slits in the walls. Or at least," she added doubtfully, "there is during the day. Light or not, you'll know you're there because the passage widens slightly and the walls are dressed stone, not rock. There is a door at that point into the castle proper. It opens into the storage cellars."

She looked around. She had their close attention.

"If you continue in the passage there are steps up. Over the top step there is another door, a trapdoor into the floor of the garde-robe off the solar. It should push open but has been little used . . ."

She carried on drawing and explaining until all the secret ways were laid out for them. Then she handed the parchment over to FitzRoger. "After this is all over, the entrance will have to be sealed," she stated.

"Undoubtedly," he said, but her words seemed to amuse him, which worried her.

"I think I should lead the party to take this route," said Sir Renald, and reached for the parchment.

"No."

There was a cold, hard edge to the word which sounded strange to Imogen, but she was past trying to make sense of all this. She just wanted her home and security back.

The men left her alone as they waited for darkness to fall. Cold meat and ale were passed around and she was given some, but otherwise she was ignored. Clearly she was now of no further use. She fretted about her decision to reveal the secret passages. But what else could she have done?

She cast bitter looks at FitzRoger, Renald, and the other knights, who sat together making plans. Or perhaps just gossiping. There was occasional soft laughter.

Imogen lay down, for sitting was becoming hard on her backside. She tentatively tried putting weight on her feet and decided it was still a bad idea. She probably could crawl around the camp on hands and knees, but that was hardly attractive.

Eventually it became clear she was going to have to do something. She had determinedly ignored her body's needs all day and been moderate in drink, but her bladder could not be contained indefinitely.

She cast a wary eye at the men, and then quietly rolled over onto her hands and knees and began to work her way behind some bushes. Her skirt practically strangled her until she gathered it up under her paunch. Her feet hurt every time she jarred them, and soon her knees were complaining violently.

"Trying to escape? Or are you going to take the castle single-handed after all?"

Caught on all fours like an animal, her skirt bunched up so he could see most of her legs, Imogen hated him then more than she'd ever hated anyone, even Warbrick. No, not more than Warbrick. "I need to piss," she mumbled.

There was a sharp sound that she recognized as laughter. Trust him to find such a thing funny. "I suppose you do. How easily we forget these simple things." He sounded sympathetic, almost friendly. Her ears must be playing tricks. She began her laborious crawl again.

"Stop that!" he said sharply. "Turn around

and I'll carry you into some privacy. Beyond that I have no suggestions. I doubt it will be simple, after all."

From pride Imogen would have refused his aid, but she feared he would just haul her up anyway, which would likely show him how unstable her "baby" was. She rolled over to sit and glared up at him. "This isn't funny."

He did look well-disposed. "No. I hurt my feet once and I remember how awkward it made simple things. And men have certain advantages." He scooped her up and she struggled to get her skirts around her legs. "Stop wriggling or I'll drop you," he said.

She stopped, but she colored when she saw how appreciatively he eyed her bared legs.

Once they were behind some bushy yew, he lowered her gently enough to the ground and left. She watched suspiciously, but he stopped a few paces away and leaned against a tree to wait. This courteous behavior confused her more than his callousness.

She managed her business kneeling and then made sure her clothes were all in order before calling him. When she was in his arms again, she asked, "What kind of man are you?"

"What kind of question is that? I'm just a man."

She shook her head. "Should I trust you?"

"You shouldn't be let out without a keeper," he replied caustically. "If I say yes, will you believe me?"

He put her back down on her blanket. The light was already fading to that misty nothing when everything seems magic. His colors were all muted and the lines of his body appeared finer and more fragile.

"Yes," she replied, surprising them both. He rose abruptly and left her.

In a few moments he returned with a heavy woolen cloak and dropped it by her. "You may want to sleep. It will be a long night."

When he began to leave she said, "So, Lord FitzRoger, can I trust you?"

His voice floated back on the misty air. "Yes and no, Lady Imogen. Yes and no."

And that, she thought, probably proved his words true, and offered little assurance at all.

The last of the scouts slipped back into the camp and reported. She could hear none of their words, but the preparations went smoothly forward so she assumed everything was as they had thought.

She saw FitzRoger start to peel off his armor and de Lisle go over to speak to him. She would swear the two men were arguing. About her?

Then de Lisle started to undress and FitzRoger replaced his hauberk. A change of plan?

To confirm her suspicions, de Lisle came over to her. He was wearing a dark leather jerkin over dark hose and had smeared dirt over his face.

"Any final advice, little flower?" he asked.

"I thought Lord FitzRoger was to lead the way into the castle."

"I persuaded him that staying behind was one of the prices of leadership," he replied with a flash of teeth. "If you sent him on a route of destruction, little one, you will destroy only me."

"Why would I want to destroy my rescuer?" she asked uneasily.

He laughed softly and touched her cheek with a callused finger. "Your senses tell you to flee, yes? Your senses are wise. But it is too late, little flower, and in the end you will not mind so much being plucked." Before she could question him further, he leaned forward and kissed her lips, hard and firm. "For luck, my pretty blossom."

With that he was gone, leaving her trembling and with a tangled warning in her mind. Who or what was going to pluck the blossom? He must have meant FitzRoger. She was doubly, trebly glad of her supposed pregnancy.

When FitzRoger came over and sat by her side, she challenged him. "Do you mean to act honestly by me, my lord?"

He was chewing on a stalk of grass. "I'm going to take your castle back for you, am I not?"

"And then what?"

He turned to face her. "Do you want me to ride straight home again?"

"If I said yes, would you?"

She heard the clink of his mail as he shrugged. "Of course not. What would be the point? Warbrick would be right back. You'd be running again. I'd be here again with it all to do over. Though my men could use the exercise, your feet would never take the strain."

Imogen had a violent urge to throw something particularly noxious at him. "What, then, will you do?"

"It is your castle, Lady Imogen. I am merely your strong right arm."

Which sounded all very well except that she could hear the amusement in his voice. And she couldn't think of anything to suggest other than the obvious. "Then I suppose I must ask you to man the castle until I can reorganize Carrisford's defenses."

"I am completely at your service, my lady." He stood, bowed, and went to take up his watching post again.

Imogen glared after him. She had just invited him to rule her castle. She felt like the half-wit he'd called her; and yet, stretch her mind as she could, she could see no alternative until the king sent her aid.

And when the king sent aid, he would almost certainly send it in the form of a husband. Her life was twisting out of her control, and no matter how she tried she wasn't able to stop the process.

She lay down on her back with a sigh and pulled the heavy cloak over her. It smelled of wool, horse, and sweat, but also of lavender and sandlewood. It was a strangely comforting blend of aromas, mingling as it did hard work and elegance.

The only trace of power she had left was to choose a husband before the king made his wishes known. But who should be the man of her choice?

She began another depressing review of her suitors. They hadn't improved. The two most favored by her father had been Lord Richard of Yelston, and the Earl of Lancaster.

The Lord of Yelston was a gruff, no-nonsense man of forty who had already buried two wives. One had died of some wasting disease, and the other of fever, so the deaths could hardly be laid at his door, but it was not a reassuring history. Lord Richard had been favored by her father for his courage and unflinching honor, but even Lord Bernard had been forced to admit that the man's attitude to women was not kindly. As far as Lord Richard was concerned, women were to be seen and not heard, and their main purpose in life was to breed sons, even though he already had three, one of whom was older than Imogen.

The Earl of Lancaster was a little younger and a great deal more sophisticated. He was a man of wealth and power, and under the previous king he had been a valued royal adviser. As a suitor he had proved to be a much more congenial companion than Sir Richard. Imogen still had those doubts, however, about his personal courage and competence. She was convinced that he was not, at heart, a strong man.

She ran through her other suitors without finding better.

The leaves above her were black against the gray of the cloudy sky. Though it wasn't cold, there was a dampness in the night air and Imogen pulled the cloak closer, wishing for another, better choice, wishing for her father's guidance. Perhaps she should let the king choose her husband after all.

But she did not know Henry Beauclerk, and the thought of being handed over, body and soul, to a stranger terrified her.

She pulled her mind away from that distant problem to the more immediate. How long would it take de Lisle and the dozen men who'd accompanied him to reach the castle and make their way in? They'd go cautiously, for those in the castle would maintain close watch, and there was a three-quarter moon to light the scene. Mostly the moon was muted by the clouds, but every now and then it would sail out, and clear white light would flood the castle and the open slopes leading up to it.

She guessed it would take them hours.

Hours for her to wait with only the occasional soft voices from the soldiers, the scurry of night creatures, and the screech of a hunting owl. Hours during which her recent experience of violence grew larger in her mind until she would almost give up her land and abandon her people not to have more blood shed in her name.

Then her scurrying mind threw up a fact. She sat up with a jerk. "Oh, Sweet Jesu!"

FitzRoger heard and came over. "You are sick?"

"No!" She grabbed the cold metal which covered his arm. "I forgot. How could I have forgotten?"

He twisted out of her hands and took his own ungentle grip on her shoulders. "Make sense! What did you forget?"

"The trap!" she gasped, thinking of smiling de Lisle, who would surely be in the lead. "The trap. My father had a trap installed two years ago after he felt knowledge of our secrets had escaped."

"What trap?" he asked in a voice like a blade on her heart.

"A swinging stone. If not stepped on right it tips the person down into an oubliette." She felt him stiffen. "But that is not all! It triggers an alarm." At the look in his eyes she cringed. He let go of her. In fact, he threw her away.

"How could you forget such a thing?"

"It's so new," she gasped, tears welling. "I have never traveled the secret ways since it was put there. I was remembering what I had known . . . Surely if someone were to follow quickly they could warn them!"

He was already stripping off his chain hauberk and the padded haqueton he wore beneath. "Tell me exactly what is involved. And this time don't forget anything."

"But shouldn't you stay here —"

"I've already studied the ways. Get on with it." He was in dark braies, chausses, and linen tunic. Now he rubbed dirt into his face.

Imogen collected her wits. "Where the rock ends and the stone begins," she explained quickly, "there are three lines gouged in the right-hand wall at shoulder height. If the leader stretches out from there he will find three more at his fingertips. He must step forward so his foot comes down at that fingertip distance. Then he must step forward as far again. It is supposed to be a normal long stride for an average man. Nothing extraordinary except that in the passageways one tends to shuffle." Imogen had never felt so ashamed and heartsick in her life. "I'm sorry," she whispered. "I truly am. I like Sir Renald."

"But you'd sleep easy if I was in the lead?" he asked unpleasantly. "Your instincts are finely honed, are they not? Pray, Imogen of Carrisford, that I reach them in time."

With that he had a quick word with his

lieutenants and ran off toward the castle.

Imogen sat up to watch, harboring the irrational notion that by keeping her eyes fixed on him she could in some way help. Because she knew he was there she could follow his progress — a moving shadow in the dark. And because he took little care in his haste to reach his men. He ran fleetly down the slope from the trees and then started up the scrubland leading to the castle walls. She lost him then and could only guess where he was.

Then the moon sailed out from behind the clouds. Every detail of the landscape seemed as bright as day.

FitzRoger fell to the ground and lay perfectly still, but to Imogen he looked as visible as if he lay black on pristine snow. She waited with thumping heart for a cry of warning from the castle, for the whine of an arrow speeding to its mark.

Then the clouds brought darkness, and in that instant he was moving and she could breathe again. Dear Lord, how did a leader send armies into battle knowing some of the men went to meet death? She found it impossible to contemplate even one man losing his life in her enterprise.

Even if he reached de Lisle and the plan went forward, was it possible that she could win back Carrisford without loss of life? She looked down at the shadowy shapes of FitzRoger's force, sitting quietly, some perhaps dozing, as they awaited the call to action.

Would some of them die tonight?

Which?

Another man came over to take up FitzRoger's watching post. It was the burly fair-haired knight de Lisle had called Will, the one who had wanted to torture her. Was Bastard FitzRoger squeamish about torture? It seemed unlikely. He'd doubtless known he could win her compliance without going to such trouble.

FitzRoger was out of sight now, presumably beginning to scale the rough cliff.

The silence began to grate on her, and the waiting, and so she murmured to the shadowy figure nearby, "Is there to be a signal when they are through?"

"A fire if possible, but any sign of life will be a signal." His tone was very curt.

"But what if it is the alarm?"

"What alarm?"

Imogen realized FitzRoger had not explained the problem to his men, but it seemed to her they should know. She told Sir William, not needing to look to see his disgust.

"You're a dim-witted little trollop, aren't you?" he said in disgust. "What a . . ." He swung closer. "He's gone to stop them?"

She shrank from the sharpness in his voice. "Or to tell them the way to get past the trap."

"But they'll likely already be in the passage when he catches them?"

"Yes, but he should be able to get to them before the trap. It's at the far end, close to the first exit."

The man snarled into her face. "After all the work we had to persuade him not to go! Do you know what you've done, my lady Imogen? You've sent him off to the one thing he can't do."

Imogen flinched back against the tree. "What do you mean?"

"His father threw him in an oubliette once. Left him there for weeks. The one thing Bastard FitzRoger can't endure is closed, dark spaces."

"His father!" Imogen echoed in horror. "But then why did he go? He said it was because he'd already studied the route . . ."

"True enough." The menace lessened as Sir William ran his hands through his hair. "And from what you said, I'm too broad. But he hates to admit there's anything he can't do." He turned hard again and flashed her a nasty look. "Heiress or no, you're a great deal more trouble than you're worth." With that he stalked away.

Chapter Five

Imogen lay back and fought tears. She wished she were dead. A week ago her world had been one of beauty, joy, and safety and nothing had prepared her for change.

She could never take her father's place. She lacked the appropriate knowledge. She lacked the fortitude. She lacked the harshness. Who was she to drive men to suffering and death, to send them to face their private demons?

She knew what it was to have an irrational fear; she was terrified of rats. True, rats could bite, which darkness couldn't, but still she imagined how it would feel to be in a room full of rats, to go into a room full of rats of her own accord. Could she do that to save a friend? She honestly didn't know. She was in a fine sweat just thinking about it.

And what kind of father, she wondered, threw his son into an oubliette?

She reviewed the gossip about Roger of Cleeve and the FitzRoger bastard. Old Sir Roger had married and sired a number of children, all sickly, most dying young, until he found himself with one sickly heir and no chance of better as long as his wife lived. On a visit to Normandy he'd got a girl with child — a daughter of a poor knight, it was said, and of birth enough for marriage if he'd been free.

And then he was free. The story went that he'd received news that his wife was dead and promptly married his concubine two months before the babe was due.

Then he'd returned to England and found the king was offering him a rich heiress as a reward for his service. Bitter at having to miss such an opportunity, he'd returned to Normandy to try to buy his way out of his hasty marriage. When he found his wife had delivered an eight-month babe, he'd promptly had the marriage annulled on the grounds that he had not consummated it, which was technically true, and that the child was not his, which was generally held to be doubtful.

Much good it had done him, thought Imogen, who had never liked the brutal man. His rich second wife had proved even more unfruitful than his first and never even conceived.

If the tale was true, it would seem that Bastard FitzRoger was not really a bastard. He surely must have proved his birth to have inherited from his half-brother.

As for the rest, she could imagine old Roger of Cleeve throwing an unwanted child in an oubliette, but she had not thought he and his supposed son had ever met. The Bastard had been raised by his mother's family in Normandy. Perhaps that family had been the one who had caused his fear. Such a family disgrace would not have been treated kindly.

Again she knew how fortunate she had been in her birth and upbringing, and she was touched with pity for that unwanted child, denied and mistreated by both sides of his family. . . .

Activity jerked her upright, and she looked at the castle. The first dim wisps of dawn lit the sky, but a brighter light came from a fire blazing in the outer bailey of Carrisford Castle.

"They're in," she said with relief. The alarm had not been triggered. FitzRoger must have overcome his fears.

Her excited hope returned. "We've won!"

"We hope." Sir William grunted and called for his horse. "You stay here," he barked at Imogen as he pulled up his mailed coif and jammed his helmet on top. He swung into the saddle and gathered his men with the cry, "FitzRoger!"

The mounted force swept over the rise and down toward the castle crying their leader's name, desperate to get involved before the fighting was over.

Imogen watched, kneeling up straight, her heart pounding with excitement and fear. The soldiers hurtled down the incline, then began the longer and more dangerous ride up to the open gate. This was the time when arrows or pitch could rain down. She bit her lip and prayed. . . .

Nothing.

The men charged into the castle without opposition.

"It's safe!" Imogen cried, and looked around for Bert. "I have to be there. Please. It's all clear. Can't we go?"

The stolid man didn't move. "Sir William said to wait for word."

"But what did Lord FitzRoger say?" Imogen asked with cunning.

The man scratched his thinning hair. "Don't know as he did, lady," he admitted. Imogen could see how much he, too, wanted to be in the action.

"Then I think we should go down. After all, it's clear the castle is taken." He was weakening. She looked around at the six men and extra horses. "We're more at risk here now. If Lord Warbrick is prowling around, he could take us easily."

The men eyed one another and conferred briefly, but the issue was never in doubt. One of them lifted Imogen onto the pillion, and they set off jauntily to the castle.

Imogen was practically bouncing with excitement. At any moment she would be back in her home, and she hadn't had to wait for Bastard FitzRoger to come and get her.

Even though she knew her side must be victorious, Imogen's nerves prickled as they rode up to the gaping maw of Carrisford's entrance. She had never before viewed her home's defenses with the eyes of an attacker, and it was all too easy to imagine a hail of arrows from the two mighty gate towers, or an ambush waiting in the long, dark, narrow tunnel.

And at the end of the tunnel was a scene from hell. Armed men were lit by the blood red of dancing flames. Riderless horses milled about, plunging. There were shouts, crashes and the occasional scream of agony.

It was as bad as Warbrick's raid.

Euphoria fled and memory made her teeth chatter — why had she thought this would be bloodless? She tugged on Bert's belt and croaked a demand that he turn back, but the battle fever had caught him. He was already spurring in, yelling, "FitzRoger!"

Imogen closed her eyes and held on for dear life.

Then they were in the middle of hell. Clash of arms. Yelled instructions. Roaring flames. Smashing wood. She opened her eyes to see a frenzied, riderless horse pulverize a corpse with its steel-shod hooves.

She shut them again. "Not ours," she prayed. "Please God, not ours."

"Nay, they're not ours," Bert reassured her.

He didn't sound too bothered by the state of affairs, but he said, "For all that the fun's over, I'm not rightly sure you should be here, lady."

Tumult lessened. Imogen dared another look and found matters much improved. Bert had steered his fretful horse back close by the wall, away from the mayhem. He was stretching to look around and she knew he was looking for his master.

He still didn't seem anxious, however, and his calm eased her fears. "I'm safer here than up in the woods," she said firmly, as much to herself as to him. She set to taking in what was happening.

As her senses organized the chaos, she saw that most of the frenzied action was directed to putting out the fire and catching the loose horses. They were milling about because the stable sheds were on fire. The fighting was mostly over.

Where was FitzRoger?

That brought an alarmed thought.

Was he already taking possession of the keep? Her keep. She looked up and saw it standing square and strong on the motte, apparently untouched and uninhabited. *She* should be the first one there.

"Perhaps we should go to the inner bailey," she suggested.

"Nay," said Bert flatly. "We'll stay here."

And that was that, Imogen supposed. What

it was to be deprived of the use of one's feet. Here she was, perched like a queen on her throne and unable to do anything useful at all, while FitzRoger could be ransacking her home.

Someone ran by and Bert called out. "Is it all clear, Nathan?"

"Pretty well!" was the cheerful reply. "Fine bit of action, that. Go see if you can drive those horses there into the inner bailey, Bert, away from the flames. They're going to bash someone's head in, elsewise."

"Where's the master?"

"Dunno. Him nor Sir Renald. It's every man for himself, but it'll still be hell to pay if we don't act smart."

Bert muttered to himself but began to work his mount toward a bunch of wild-eyed horses.

"Hold tight, lady. I'm just going to encourage 'em that way a bit."

Every man for himself. Looking around, Imogen saw the chaos this implied. Most of the men had laid down their weapons and were trying to put out the fire which roared and sent flaming banners up into the sky. It had spread to a number of storage sheds, but she didn't think it could do much harm unless it grew so hot it burst the walls.

A few men were still dashing in and out of wall chambers and nooks, looking for lurking enemies. A few others were gathering up the loose horses. The men were doing useful things, but there was no apparent command. She was surprised. It was not what she'd expected from FitzRoger's force after the control and planning she'd witnessed so far. So this was what it came to once the fighting began.

Bert began to herd four horses toward the wide gate leading to the inner bailey. He started to whistle. Jokes were shouted back and forth. Everyone seemed pretty happy with the state of affairs, despite a number of gruesome corpses.

Imogen assumed none of them were theirs.

Imogen, however, was increasingly dismayed. She was just beginning to take in the shambles of what had once been her beautiful home. The walls might still be standing, but within, it was a wreck. Among the corpses of men and horses, she saw the domestic animals — sheep, pigs, milch cows, poultry. All wantonly slaughtered.

She reminded herself that Warbrick had been the invader, and he and his men were doubtless responsible for the killing, as well as for the broken doors and smashed barrels. When she saw one of FitzRoger's men rip the remains of a door off its hinges, however, she swore silently at all men, her rescuers included.

As Bert's large horse walked placidly on, herding the agitated horses toward the inner bailey, Imogen shut out the scene around her and began planning the recovery of Carrisford. Soon she would have it peaceful and happy again, just as it had been in her father's day.

Where *were* her people?

She prayed none of the corpses were of castle people. Surely they would have fled to safety? If not, Warbrick would not have killed them *all*.

Would he?

She was not at all sure there were limits to that brute's evil.

Had he ransacked the place? She looked up again at the keep. After two battles had been fought over it, how much would be left of the elegant home created by her father?

She would build it again, she told herself firmly. There was ample treasure hidden in a secret strongroom. Stock and provisions would have to be purchased, and —

A black shape flew out of a wall chamber and lunged at them. Imogen screamed. Bert was carried off the horse. Imogen had relaxed her hold on his belt and so she stayed on, sprawled facedown over the saddle. She clutched the pommel for dear life as the horse sidled and plunged around the two men struggling beneath its hooves. Imogen groped for the dangling reins.

She couldn't reach them.

The attacker plunged a dagger into Bert. His cry of agony clashed with her own scream: *"No! Help!"*

Her fingers touched leather at last, and she grabbed the reins. She fought to get astride the plunging horse, cursing the awkward saddle and her skirts, screaming for help, hearing her voice swallowed by the racket all around.

Another hand on the reins. Someone else was trying to mount, fighting her for the horse. A frantic, grimacing face was thrust at hers, then a hand grabbed her ankle. "The heiress, eh? You're coming with me."

Imogen smashed a fist into his nose. She almost fell off, but her attacker howled and lost his grip. She grabbed the saddle with one hand and held on to the reins for dear life with the other.

She hit out with her elbow and screamed, *"Help! Help! Carrisford! FitzRoger!"*

"Hell-born bitch!" The attacker raised his dagger and stabbed viciously at her hand on the reins. She snatched it back just in time and the blade went into the horse. It screamed and reared. Imogen was flung stunned to the ground.

She came to her wits when hooves reared above her in the demonic red firelight. She rolled away, covering her head with her arms. When she rolled to sit, the horse had plunged away, but the man was coming at her again, drawing his sword. "Hell-born bitch!"

She scuttled back on her behind and yelled

thought of poor Bert. Would he live to face his master's displeasure?

"It was my fault," she confessed. "I told Bert we'd be in danger up there. It could have been true." Noises were lessening and she judged they had passed through into the inner bailey. She opened her eyes a crack.

Yes, they were out of hell. This looked more like the home she knew. There was no firelight, but the misty dawn light was picking out details from shadow. Horses, resting now they were away from the fire. Men doing quiet, purposeful things.

Then she saw more bodies. Some women.

"Who are they?" she asked in a whisper. "The dead."

"Some yours, mostly Warbrick's," he answered. "I haven't had time to check. I had scouted the area, Lady Imogen. Wherever Warbrick is, he isn't around here. You were perfectly safe where I left you. We would all be better off if you would learn to do as you are told."

He was probably right. He would have sent for her when the fire was out, order had been restored, and all the bodies were neatly stored, if not buried. Just like her father, he would have shielded her from this unpleasantness.

Imogen found she resented it.

"My father protected me too well," she said. "I was never allowed to see violence or cruelty. But this is all for me, isn't it? I

and yelled, hoarser and hoarser. It was no good. She prayed instead. "Angels and saints above, aid me —"

She bumped up against something soft and glanced down. Shrieked when she saw she was sitting on a corpse. Looked up to see her attacker looming over her with his sword high. "If I'm going to rot, I'll take you with me!" howled the man.

She grabbed the shield lying by the corpse's hand and dragged it over herself.

The sword smashed down on the shield so her ears rang. The force of the blow seemed to bruise her whole body, and it drove her down onto the corpse beneath her. The dead man gave an eerie whistle as air was forced out of his lungs.

The breath was knocked out of her own. She wanted nothing more than to huddle beneath the long, solid piece of wood and metal like a snail in its shell, but that would be to die for sure. She forced herself to look up to anticipate the next blow.

There was no other blow. Even as her attacker grinned and prepared to kill her, Bastard FitzRoger launched himself at him.

The man whirled to meet the new threat.

Imogen cried out a useless warning. FitzRoger wore no armor and carried only a light sword, while the other man wore mail and wielded a great sword. It was suicide.

The great sword whistled down. It would

slice the lighter man in two. Her paladin blocked it. The mighty clang made Imogen's ears ring and her arms ache in sympathy. Had she truly blocked a blow such as that? No wonder she felt as if she had been trampled.

How many more such blows could her defender take? A touch on any part of his unarmored body would mean death.

Why was she just lying here?

She heaved off the shield and pulled herself up to her knees, shrieking, *"To FitzRoger! FitzRoger!"*

At last, men heard. They turned and ran toward them, but it was too late. FitzRoger ducked a swing and his sword bit deep into his opponent's unguarded leg. As the man howled and went down, FitzRoger stamped on his sword hand and kicked him in the head. The man reeled onto his back. FitzRoger thrust his blade into the man's throat. The scream turned to a gurgle, and then to silence.

FitzRoger wrenched his sword free.

Imogen rolled over and was violently sick. She retched on and on even after her stomach was raw and empty. When the heaving stopped, she looked down. She had spewed up all over the corpse. She screamed as she scuffled backward.

She bumped against something and swiveled, her arms raised in futile protection.

FitzRoger hunkered down beside her. "It's all right," he said quite gently. He laid a hand on her shoulder. "Are you badly hurt?"

She jerked away. "You killed him!"

"That's my job, Lady Imogen," he replied levelly. "Where are you hurt?"

"You kicked him." Knights weren't supposed to kick one another in the head. She began to tell him so. "You're not supposed to do that. I'm sure you're not . . ."

She shook her head and couldn't seem to stop. While she was shaking her head she couldn't think, and she didn't want to think —

A sharp slap on her cheek jerked her back into her wits and she stared at him.

"I'm going to lift you," he said. "If it hurts too much, let me know."

He swung her up. After a pause in case she wished to tell him of a hurt, he began to pick his way across the bailey with Imogen in his arms.

"You shouldn't have kicked him," she repeated earnestly.

"You're probably correct. I'll do a penance."

With that settled, Imogen shut her eyes and blocked them against the leather of his jerkin. Then she flinched away. He stank of blood. "Just get me away from here," she begged.

"Of course. You had no business being here."

She heard the chill in his voice and

should be part of it. I don't want to be shielded anymore."

"A worthy notion but don't overstrain yourself. Reality can be too much for some people and you get in the way. Where is your room?"

She wanted to fight him, to object to the way he was dismissing her as a useless burden. But she was so tired, so heartsick . . .

"In the southeast corner of the keep," she said.

Was it possible that her room was still there, undisturbed, with its silken hangings, its precious glass window, her lyre and books? She prayed it might be so.

"There's a stairway up the side of the keep," she said, "but it might be easier to use the wider stairs in the great hall."

Despite her words he headed for the narrow door which led to the stairs built into the wall, and she remembered the scene she had witnessed in the hall. Was it really only two days ago? Was the room still running blood? No, of course, it would at least have dried by now.

She closed her eyes again. If there were horrors, she didn't want to see.

Only when she felt the familiar contours of her bed did she open her eyes. It was her room, but it didn't look right. The walls were bare. The place was littered with debris. The light was wrong.

The rising sun should have been glinting through red, yellow, and blue, but instead it washed in without interruption. She gave a little cry as she saw only scraps of her precious window clinging to the frame.

Miserably, she took in the rest of the destruction. The wall hangings had been torn down and shredded, her chests spilled out and the gowns ripped apart. Wanton destruction. She could imagine the enraged Warbrick rending her garments with his bare hands.

FitzRoger nudged one pile with his foot. "You really did upset him, didn't you?" he said, and smiled at her.

And Imogen found herself echoing the smile, even if weakly. Suddenly the destruction seemed a prize of victory, not a defeat. She scrubbed away the tears which had trickled down her cheeks. "Clearly I did."

He went to the window and she guessed he was checking the state of affairs in the castle. Always checking, always alert for trouble. "I haven't seen many castle people," he said. "Most of the dead are Warbrick's. We lost two as far as I know."

"Is my aunt here?"

"I've seen no sign of a lady."

Imogen wanted to ask about Bert, but didn't dare. If he was dead, it was all her fault.

"Once your pennant flies again," FitzRoger said, "your people should return." He turned back. "Until then, we're all going to eat sparingly, and you are going to have very rough handmaids. Are you injured?"

"No," she said with surprise. "I ache even more after taking that blow on the shield, but I don't think I'm hurt at all."

"You did very well. You didn't try to hold the shield away from you or you'd have broken your arms, and the corpse cushioned the blow."

Imogen wanted to deny that she'd planned to use a dead body for such a purpose, but it seemed too much effort.

He leaned out of the window and called something, then turned back. "Is there anything you need?" he asked, adding, "Urgently."

Imogen decided that a cool drink and clean clothes weren't what he had in mind and shook her head. She wondered again where he had been earlier while his men coped alone.

Her heart missed a beat. Plundering her secret treasure chamber?

"The men lacked leadership out there," she probed. "Shouldn't you have been organizing matters?"

He flashed her a guarded look. "They did well enough. What's the matter? Afraid this laborer isn't worthy of his hire? But then, Lady Imogen, we haven't discussed payment yet."

Her instinct shrieked that she'd just hit a

nerve, but before she could pursue it, he said, "I'll leave a guard on the door. This time stay where you're put. I'll come for you when we have the place in some kind of order." With that he was gone before she could object or ask further questions.

She found she had little desire to do so. She was home and Bastard FitzRoger, despite his many shortcomings, would take care of things. She was exhausted, not just from a night with little sleep, but from all the terror and stress of the last two days.

She surrendered her world for a time into stronger hands. As she drifted into sleep she took surprising comfort from that crisp voice saying, "You did very well."

Yes, she had done very well. She had, after all, got her castle back. Perhaps her father would have been proud of her.

Imogen awoke parched, weak, and with a headache, surprised to find it was still early morning. The sun was just beginning to fully light the room. A noise made her sit up quickly and a woman came to her bedside.

"Martha?" queried Imogen, recognizing one of the castle women. She was a particularly skillful weaver. Had it perhaps all been a terrible dream? But then she looked around and saw that though her room had been tidied, there was still an open space where her window had been, and bare walls which had so recently been hung with silk.

That meant Janine had been real, and the corpse, and FitzRoger plunging his sword in that man's throat. . . .

"There, there, Lady Imogen," said the middle-aged woman soothingly, stroking back Imogen's hair. "It's all right now, lovey. Likely you'll want a bit of something. You've slept a whole day. The master said to have soup for you when you woke so we've kept it warm on the fire here." She bustled over to the brazier and scooped liquid from a pot into a wooden bowl.

"Everything got broken," the woman said with a shake of the head. "All the pottery smashed. All the glass. The fine silver goblets crushed flat —" She broke off. "But then, you don't want to worry your head about such things now, lovey. We still have the woodenware." She placed the bowl in Imogen's hands and gave her a wooden spoon. "There you are, my lady. You eat that and you'll feel better. Master'll take care of everything."

Master. Master. Master. It hammered in Imogen's aching head. She looked up at the woman. "FitzRoger is *not* master of Carris-ford."

"Well no," the woman said. "Not exactly. But he's taking care of things right well, lady, now he's over his sickness."

"Sickness?" Imogen asked in alarm, with

vague notions of plague striking to add to her miseries.

"Threw up like he'd eaten bad meat, he did," confided Martha. "Some of us were hiding in the back end of the stores when Lord FitzRoger and his men came out of a wall. Gave us a right turn, I can tell you, but we soon saw it weren't more of Warbrick's louts. He were white and shaking, though, and the others were virtually carrying him. Then he threw up something terrible. We didn't know who he was, so we didn't let on we were there. He seems well enough now."

Imogen began to eat the soup and digest this information. Bad meat? Or just being in closed, dark spaces? She knew she'd throw up if obliged to make her way through a room full of rats. She felt some sympathy, and increased admiration for the courage that had sent him after his men.

However, she also saw a weapon, and she might need one in the coming days. She didn't delude herself that Bastard FitzRoger would prove easy to handle.

She worked on eating all the soup, determined to have her faculties working as soon as possible. How could she have slept away such a crucial day and left him in control?

She wondered how much food was left in the castle, and what damage Warbrick's men had done to the land nearby which would supply more.

More important, had FitzRoger discovered her father's treasure store? From his talk of payment, it would appear not, and yet only a fool would assume the obvious with that man. She took comfort from Martha's story. If he had been so badly affected by the passageways, he wouldn't be inclined to explore further, and she didn't think he would entrust such a mission to another.

Once she had access to her gold, she could pay him off, no matter what price he put on his services. She was very, very rich. Her grandfather had married a great heiress, and neither her father nor her grandfather had disdained trading ventures. Though not the most powerful, Carrisford was probably the wealthiest holding in the land.

Which was as well, given the state everything was in. Once FitzRoger was dealt with, Imogen would make good any damage and buy new supplies. She couldn't do any of this, however, until she could get to the treasure chamber by herself. She, too, wouldn't entrust such a mission to another.

Since FitzRoger seemed to want to be in charge, she thought sourly, let him use his own resources to put things right for now.

The next most important thing was her marriage . . .

That was when Imogen realized she was no longer pregnant. Her shape was flat and smooth under her shift. "Where did it go?"

she demanded, her hands on her abdomen.

The woman looked at her and understood. "That thing you were wearing, my lady? We took it off to make you comfortable. Whatever it was for, there's no need for such anymore and it isn't right, you pretending such a thing. What your poor father would say!"

Her defense against hasty marriage was gone!

"Does Lord FitzRoger know?" Perhaps she could resume it and persuade the women to keep silent.

"He came to look in on you a couple of times. He didn't say anything." The woman chuckled. "Did you let him think you was with child, my lady? Well, I never. Naughty girl."

Imogen moaned slightly at this new twist in the tangled skein of her life. Now how was she to prevent a forced marriage if he decided on it?

Martha hurried over. "Poor hinny," she crooned. "There, there. Don't you worry. Everything's going to be all right, you'll see. The Lord of Cleeve will look after you right well."

Imogen opened her mouth to object, and then shut it again with a snap. The woman's indulgent tone was infuriating, but it wouldn't be fair to blister her for it. It was the way everyone had always treated her — with proud, kindly indulgence. Imogen of

Carrisford, the Flower of the West, her father's greatest treasure.

And like most treasures, protected, ornamental, and largely useless.

Siward, in knocking her out and taking her away from the castle against her will, had been acting as usual. Then she'd just done as everyone suggested and gone to FitzRoger, who'd carried her to the capture of her own castle like an unwanted bundle. No wonder he was doing exactly as he wished now with no notion of seeking her approval.

Not true, her conscience argued. She had petitioned him to take back her castle and to man it until she could make other arrangements. She'd even asked him to take her away from the fire and the blood and the death.

Such times were over, however. She put aside the empty bowl and sat up straighter. It was time to assert herself as Lady of Carrisford. The first thing was to see if she could walk.

"Martha," she said, "let's see if we can get these bandages off."

"Oh, my lady. Do you think that's wise? Master said —"

"Lord FitzRoger," Imogen corrected sharply, "if you must quote him at all."

The woman's eyes opened wide, but she said, "*Lord FitzRoger* told us they were hurt right badly and the monk who tended them said to keep off them."

"He said no such thing," Imogen declared. "I want to see how they're healing." She reached forward and began to untie the bandages herself. Muttering, Martha came to help.

When they came to the end they were stuck. "There, see?" said the woman triumphantly. "They need longer."

Imogen, on the other hand, was touching her wounds and deciding they weren't too bad after all. The worst blisters, still red and raw, were on the sides of her feet where the knotted thongs had rubbed. Those on the soles were healing fast.

"Soak them off," she said. When the woman opened her mouth to argue, Imogen gave her such a glare that she hastily did as she was bid.

With a bowl of warm water and patience, Imogen was soon free of bandages. She tentatively put her weight on her feet, then smiled. They were virtually painless. She walked across the room, delighting in mobility, once taken for granted. She had bruises and aches in other places, but none that she couldn't ignore.

"You still can't put shoes on," said Martha rather smugly.

"Do I have any shoes left?" Imogen asked.

It appeared she had a few. The silk slippers were gone, but the leather shoes had proved too difficult to destroy. It was soon clear, however, that Martha was right and Imogen could not bear them. They immediately rubbed on raw, weeping flesh.

"I'll go barefoot," Imogen declared.

"My lady!"

"Not a word!" Imogen commanded. "I refuse to skulk here in my own castle waiting for someone to come and carry me around like a babe. Now," she went on, "let's see if there are any clothes still wearable." Imogen was determined to appear before the people of the castle as mistress.

First, Imogen had Martha wash her hair properly, then, as the light brightened into daylight, she and Martha sifted through the remains of her beautiful garments. Imogen felt like weeping at the sight of her favorite gowns ripped to pieces, some even soiled with urine and feces, but she wouldn't allow herself that kind of weakness. Some could be patched and mended.

Martha and Imogen set to work and soon they had made some garments decent, if not restored to their former elegance.

Imogen was happy enough to discard her borrowed coarse clothing and put on a fine shift and a tawny linen kirtle, embroidered at neck and hem with gold thread. Over it she put a light tunic of rust red silk, with bands of white and red at hem, cuff, and neck. Her jeweled girdles were all gone and so she cut a sash from a ruined gown of brown samite and bound it around her waist, puffing the shimmering silk into elegant draping above it.

"There," she said triumphantly. "Do I not look like the lady of the castle?"

"Indeed you do," said a mocking voice.

Imogen spun around to see Bastard Fitz-Roger studying her.

Chapter Six

If she looked the lady, he surely looked the lord. Where had he obtained such fine clothes? Was he deliberately trying to beat her at her own game?

He was leaning against the doorjamb, arms folded. His tunic was of heavy dark green silk, finely worked in gold and black. The sleeves ended at his elbows, but he wore rich golden bracelets on each wrist. A leather belt was buckled with gold, and his knife hung in an engraved gold sheath. Of course he wore his heavy golden ring. For the first time he looked like a powerful lord. Imogen resented her own lack of bullion, and looked closely to check that none that he wore was familiar.

No, it all appeared to be his own.

An impressive collection of adornment, carelessly worn.

There was its equal and better in Carrisford's treasure chests, though, and Imogen itched to get to it and put this man in his place. "As soon as I can reach the king," she said firmly, "I am going to complain of Warbrick and get my jewelry back."

A lazy smile creased his eyes. "I'll give you some if you want."

"No thank you. I prefer my own."

"Warbrick will deny having any of it."

"How can he do that? Half the country will recognize it as soon as it appears."

He pushed off from the jamb and entered the room.

"He'll have it melted down. If necessary he'll throw it in the ocean. He'll do anything rather than give it back to you after you thwarted him."

That was dismaying, but again Imogen felt warm pride at the notion that she had thwarted Warbrick. It had been a hard path, set with difficult choices, but she had traveled it. Now, all she had to do was rid herself of her escort — yes, that's how she would think of him, her escort — and rebuild her life.

Her "escort" turned to Martha, and at a gesture the woman curtsied her way out. Imogen's pretty bubble popped and the truth was laid clear. This man was more than escort; he'd risked his life and that of his men for her, and was now an unpredictable force in her home.

"You must have other jewels," he said.

That snapped her wits back to the main point. He was sniffing on the trail of the treasure. No wonder he was being so pleasant. Well, she might be a half-wit at times, but she wasn't as foolish as that. "No, I don't," she lied.

He walked toward her. Imogen stopped herself from retreating. "The jewels given Imogen of Carrisford by her father are famous. You kept them all in your chamber?"

"Yes."

Cool fingers gripped her chin. "Even if you were so foolish, your father was not."

"Unhand me, sirrah!"

He did, but only to grip her shoulders. His emerald eyes blazed down at her. "Are you determined not to trust me? If your jewels are hidden in the secret passageways, there are a dozen men who know those ways now. I wouldn't trust most of them with a shilling, never mind a small fortune."

"They're your men," she retorted. "Doubtless they take their standards from their *master*."

His eyes narrowed. "Are you challenging me?" he asked softly.

It took effort, but Imogen kept her chin up and said, "Yes."

And meant it.

Something flashed in his eyes that sent a shiver straight through her. "You are a foolish child."

"So it would appear. I went to you for help. I'm learning fast, though."

He forced her slightly closer. Thin linen and silk did nothing to protect her body from his hard warmth, and her breathing fractured. . . .

"What are you learning?" he asked softly.

Imogen was no longer having to fight to meet his gaze. Rather, she could not look away. His eyes, she discovered, were not particularly unkind; they were almost warm. . . .

Fool, she berated herself, and tore her eyes away. "Not to trust men," she snapped.

He let her go and stepped away as if she were nothing. He turned to face her. "Am I supposed to have been your teacher?"

Imogen refused to answer.

"In what way have I proved untrustworthy, Lady Imogen?"

Her wanton body wanted that moment of warmth, of closeness, back. Imogen hated the wanting. Moreover she couldn't think of an accusation to make in answer to his challenge. She suspected him of many things, but his behavior thus far had been exemplary.

She was forced to resort to history. "You went to Castle Cleeve to help your brother. Then, oh so conveniently, he died."

His face hardened. "Don't make accusations, Ginger, unless you're willing to back them with your life. That's merely gossip."

"But it's true."

He studied her, hands on hips. "You think I intend to take Carrisford from you?"

Imogen didn't know for sure, but only decisive statements got through to this man. "Yes," she said.

He raised a brow. "Then you *were* foolish to come to me, weren't you?"

"I didn't know you then."

"And now you do?"

"Yes. You're hard, ruthless, and take whatever you want."

He smiled coldly and stepped closer again. "Then aren't you a little foolish to be throwing down the gauntlet? Perhaps I want you."

Imogen's nerve broke. She retreated a few steps, desperately wanting her paunch back. "You don't."

His smile widened but didn't warm. "Perhaps I find angry little cats desirable." A few more smooth steps and she was pressed against the wall with him barring any escape.

"I'll scream," she warned.

He merely raised one sardonic brow. The castle was full to bursting with his men.

"You won't rape me," she said desperately. "I'd tell the king and you'd pay the price."

"I don't rape," he said quite gently, and there was that touch of warmth in his face again. "Many men want you, Ginger, and for more than your castle. You're very beautiful, you know, and your hair . . ."

She and Martha had not yet formed Imogen's hair into plaits, and his eyes traveled its silky thickness down her body. Imogen felt

131

her knees weaken, and it wasn't with fear.

He leaned his arms on the wall on either side of her. Imogen found she felt strangely encompassed rather than trapped. Her heart was racing and dizziness was fogging her wits. She knew she shouldn't let him do this, and yet, and yet . . .

"Stop it," she whispered.

"Stop what?" he whispered back.

She stared at him and he lowered his lips gently to hers. They were soft and warm. Why had she thought they would be cold and hard?

He angled his head slightly and kissed her more firmly. Imogen raised her hands to push him away, but instinct took over and her hands slid up to rest on his shoulders — rock-hard shoulders, but flesh-warm beneath the silk.

His lips moved gently, caressing hers. She had never been kissed like this before. She liked it more than she had thought she would.

His tongue came out and ran along her lips like spice and fire. She gasped. His tongue moved in to run along the inside of her lips.

Imogen jerked back. "You mustn't! This is a dread sin!"

"Is it?" he queried. There was genuine warm humor in him now. His right hand moved to gather a handful of her hair and cradle her head. His thumb stroked down her cheek like fire. "It's not so evil to kiss, Imogen."

"Father Wulfgan says it is. . . ." Imogen knew she had to stop this before something terrible happened. The chaplain had warned her that such kisses led to lewd touching; lewd touching led to lust.

And lust led straight to the fires of hell.

Surely it was a brush with the fires of hell that had her so burning hot. . . .

She ducked from between his arms and put the width of the room between them.

FitzRoger made no attempt to stop her but merely turned to lean against the wall, arms crossed. "Is he a scrawny priest with crippled hands? The one trying to impose penances on us for taking lives?"

She nodded and put a hand over her mouth. "Oh, but he'll give me terrible penances. I'll be on my knees for a week. All this killing over me. Letting you kiss me. And pretending to be . . ." She trailed off and eyed him nervously.

"I knew it was false, Ginger."

That hurt her pride. "I don't believe you."

"I don't lie. Or only when it's absolutely necessary."

"How did you know, then?"

"After your adventure yesterday, it was knocked out of place. I'd wondered before. It seemed very unlikely."

"Why didn't you say something?"

He shrugged. "I was interested to see how long you could keep up the pretense. It was a cunning disguise, well carried out. When I first saw you I really thought you were going to give birth any minute. Another idea of your seneschal's, I suppose."

"No," Imogen said proudly. "It was mine. He just helped."

FitzRoger's brows raised and he gave a nod which was an accolade.

"How is Siward?" she challenged.

"I've sent for him." He pushed off from the wall and walked toward her. "You've done very well, you know, whoever's was the guiding hand. You escaped from Warbrick and suffered that disgusting disguise. At least," he said with a twitch of his lips, "it disgusted me. You walked till your feet were in shreds and still had spirit to stand up to me — figuratively, if not literally. Yes, for an untried girl, you've done very well."

Imogen felt a new warmth start in her toes and spread up her body until it was a rosy flush in her cheeks. Pure, delicious pride. "I was terrified," she admitted shyly. "I hated all that dirt. I hated being so alone and without protection. I hated having to make decisions. I just wanted to throw myself on your mercy and let you take care of everything."

"We all get terrified, and once we learn to be clean we hate dirt. Some decisions never become easy. You did very well."

He really wasn't such a bad man, after all. "Were you terrified in the passageways?" she asked gently.

All warmth fled and his eyes widened. "What?"

"You fear close spaces. Sir William told me."

His eyes turned cold. "Did he? He exaggerated. Do you wish to come down to the hall for breakfast? Shall I carry you?"

Imogen shivered and knew better than to mention what Martha had said about him being sick. "I wish to attend mass," she said quickly. She certainly needed all the holy guidance available. "I want to go to the chapel and pray for the dead as I wait for Father Wulfgan."

"It'll be a long wait. I've thrown your chaplain out."

"You've *what?*"

"I'll not have such a guilt-mongerer about my men. I'll find you a more suitable replacement."

Heat roared into Imogen. The heat of rage. "Get him back!" she snapped. "This is *my* castle, FitzRoger, and he is *my* priest!"

He didn't even blink. "I am your defender, and I must do what's best for *my* men."

Imogen leaned forward. "You doubtless want a priest who'll pander to your evil ways," she snarled, "and blink at all your wicked mischief. But I'll have Father Wulfgan back and make sure he calls fire and brimstone down on your black heart!"

He stood there unmoved, and even amused.

He was ignoring her.

Imogen swung back and hit him with all the force she could command.

The sound of her hand on his face seemed to echo and the mark flared there. His face went utterly still, his eyes wide and emerald cold.

He, the agile warrior, had made no move to evade the blow.

Imogen couldn't breathe. He'd kill her. . . .

Then he relaxed. It was nothing distinct, just an easing throughout his whole body. "You must be allowed some powers, I suppose," he said. "But I give you fair warning, do anything like that in public and you'll rue it bitterly."

With that he turned and left. Imogen collapsed, legs atremble, relieved to still be alive. She'd never hit a man before in her life. Of course, she'd never encountered a man like Bastard FitzRoger, and her father would have murdered any man who so much as looked boldly at Imogen of Carrisford.

This one had kissed her. Her breathing wavered at the remembered magic of his lips on hers. It had been uncommonly sweet. He had seemed quite different then — warmer, gentler.

Then it had all evaporated when she'd spoken of his fear in the passageways. She supposed a man would not like it known he was afraid of such a thing. She understood that.

Then he'd told her he'd thrown out her priest.

Her mind began to clear. She moved beyond dalliance and pique to consider his parting words about "powers," and "authority."

What had he meant, "*allowed* some powers"? And what authority should not be challenged? Who was in control of Carrisford?

Did he think a kiss and a few kind words could buy her and her castle? She laughed out loud. He doubtless thought just that, but he wouldn't make much progress when his benign mask slipped at every little thing to reveal the cold, hard tyrant underneath.

With a start, she realized he had not said anything about getting Father Wulfgan back. When next they met she would insist on it.

That would show who commanded in Carrisford.

FitzRoger went through the linked rooms that led to the majestic wide staircase which ran straight down the side of the great hall. Carrisford Castle was a magnificent building, far more sophisticated than any other he had seen in England. He wouldn't mind incorporating some of the elegancies here into Cleeve one day when he had time and funds for it.

Funds made him think of the heiress and smile slightly.

A spirited creature, and one with brains when she remembered to use them. But pampered to death. Still, he'd been honest when he said she had done well, especially for one so protected all her life.

He entered the hall, which had an unusual vaulted ceiling, brightly painted walls, and a lot of narrow windows. With the shutters back in this fine weather, they allowed in the sunlight to make the room warm and bright.

The soldier in him said they were unnecessary and hazardous, but he liked the way they brightened the room. The hall at Cleeve was always gloomy.

The room had been cleared of the more obvious signs of carnage and looked very fine to him, but he knew from the comments of the servants that it fell far short of its former glory. There had been embroidered hangings, and displays of arms, and gold and silver on the sideboard shelves. The tablecloths had all been of woven patterns or embroidered.

He'd seen the weaving sheds in the bailey where the looms and frames stood idle for lack of the women to work them. There weren't that many dead, so they must be around somewhere. Presumably they could re-create the simpler hangings, though he suspected the finer ones had been imported from Italy and the East.

He would like to restore Imogen of Carrisford's home for her. He began to plan the restoration work. Food, supplies, tableware, hangings, table linen . . .

The trestles were still set up for breakfast — bare of cloths — but the meal, such as it was, was over and the hall was deserted. FitzRoger hefted a jug, found it still had some ale in it, and filled a wooden beaker. He added ale and wine to his list of requirements. Carrisford had some ale, and the brew house had already started operation again, but Warbrick had opened the cocks on all the casks of wine. Heaven knows when the stink would leave the cellars.

Even with supplies, living would be sparse here for a while. . . .

His thoughts were interrupted by Renald de Lisle's jovial voice. "Unless that's a maidenly blush, my friend, the lady slapped your face. I thought you said she'd be easy to persuade."

"I haven't tried to persuade her of anything yet." He poured ale for Renald.

"Then why did she hit you?"

FitzRoger's lips twitched. "She wouldn't like to admit it, but I think it was because I stopped kissing her." His friend choked on the ale. "Her excuse was something else. That priest, Renald, the one who was screaming about us doing penance for each life taken."

De Lisle nodded.

"Get him back."

Renald looked over in surprise. "Why? He doubtless believes in hair shirts and flagellation."

"The Flower of the West commands."

"Ah," murmured Renald. "You think to buy her favors with sweets? Buy her favors with her own sweets? When are you going to tell the luscious little blossom that she hasn't been rescued so much as plucked?"

"You make her sound less like a rosebud and more like a scrawny hen. If I'm going to marry her, I might as well make it as easy on her as I can. Perhaps she'll just think of it as being transplanted into new earth."

"At least with her carrying a child, you have plenty of time to confuse and persuade her. And kill the man who made her that way."

"It was her seneschal," said FitzRoger, taking another draft of ale.

"That old man!" de Lisle exclaimed, his hand flying to his sword. "I'll gut him."

FitzRoger put a hand over Renald's. "I think you have a taste for flowers too," he said, quite pleasantly. "Lose it, my friend. She's mine." He removed his hand and refilled Renald's mug. "The seneschal is being brought here to take over the running of the castle."

"You'll overlook such behavior?" exclaimed Renald, his fine eyes flashing. "I most certainly will not."

"Lady Imogen assures me it was done with her consent," said FitzRoger blandly. "Was, in fact, her own idea. She's very proud of the achievement, and if she isn't unhappy, who am I to take offense?"

De Lisle was staring at him as if he'd grown an extra head. FitzRoger glanced up and drew his friend's attention to the stairs. Imogen was gingerly descending them, startlingly beautiful in bright silks, and remarkably shapely for one so far gone with child. And obviously not the victim of a sudden miscarriage.

"It was all a hoax?" Renald asked blankly. "I'm surprised you didn't beat her for it."

"I don't crush such a lovely blossom, not even for perfume. I'd guessed," he said softly, "and it really didn't make any difference except that it gave her a false sense of security." He walked forward and offered his arm to Imogen of Carrisford.

Imogen eyed him warily, but he seemed calm. She was pleased to see that her handprint on his lean cheek had faded, though she couldn't help wishing that the full strength of her arm could make a more lasting impression.

"How are your feet?" he asked kindly. "I will see if there's a cobbler available to fashion some kind of footwear for you."

"I can walk for short distances."

Imogen had been concentrating on the stairs and FitzRoger as she descended, but now she looked around the hall and could have wept. There was little sign of mayhem except for some raw gashes on woodwork, but the place was stripped naked. The beautiful hangings were gone, the floor was bare, the sideboards held no goblets and dishes, and there were so few people. Only the three of them in here at the moment, and no sound of bustle nearby.

Where was everyone?

Afraid. They would return.

The sight of four hounds curled near the table was reassuring, until she realized they weren't her father's familiar hounds, or her own pair, but strange dogs belonging to strangers.

This place scarcely seemed like her home at all.

She would restore Carrisford, she promised herself, restore it as it had been such a short time ago. For that she would need a little help from FitzRoger, but she must make it clear that he was her instrument in this, and that was all.

She addressed him in a brisk, authoritative tone. "There is obviously a great deal of work to be done, my lord. After breakfast I will inspect the castle and interview what people are still here. I must see what can be repaired and what needs to be ordered. If there are military needs, Lord FitzRoger, you must tell me of them and I will see if they can be met."

Though she kept her voice firm, Imogen's heart was pounding as she threw this challenge down. She was as good as relegating him to captain of the guard.

"Of course," he said as he escorted her to one of the two large chairs. "Your main requirement is men-at-arms, Lady Imogen. I'm afraid none of your father's garrison survived."

It was like a blow. "All? All dead?"

He nodded and poured her ale. "Warbrick was thorough."

"As were you!" she replied angrily. "I saw you kill that man after you had him at your mercy."

"As am I," he agreed, and continued. "You will, of course, make some provision for the families of the dead men."

"Of course," she said, though it hadn't immediately come to mind. So many things to be borne in mind.

"I have rather more men than I need at present," he said. "I would be willing to hire twenty to you for a period. Twenty men is an adequate garrison for Carrisford, and should be able to hold it against everything but a long siege."

Imogen flicked him a wary glance. He was politely impassive and impossible to read. With his men garrisoning the castle, she'd be as good as a prisoner in her own home, but what alternative did she have? Until the king came, or sent his agent, she was at FitzRoger's mercy. Her only hope was the dubious one of his good intentions, and the rather better one that he — unlike Warbrick — would not want to cross the king.

"Thank you, Lord FitzRoger. I will take the garrison until other arrangements can be made."

He nodded. "This place should be impregnable. Warbrick must have been given access to the castle."

"I know," said Imogen with a frown. "I don't know who would do such a thing."

"Possibly one of the garrison. If so, Warbrick has taken care of the problem for you."

"Impossible," Imogen protested. "They had all been my father's men for years. I cannot believe one would suddenly turn traitor."

He sat in the other chair and sliced a half loaf and some cheese, passing it to her. "Lady Imogen, the survivors' stories suggest that most of the garrison was drugged before the invasion."

"So it *must* have been someone in the castle. I can scarce believe it. . . ."

"Were there any strangers here?"

"No," she said as she nibbled the cheese. "There were no travelers those last days. Only some monks from Glastonbury Abbey.

And once my father was known to be dying, the castle was sealed."

She saw FitzRoger and de Lisle share a glance and then the darker man slipped away. "Monks!" she exclaimed. "That cannot be."

"You have a remarkable reverence for religion, Lady Imogen. A habit is easy enough to put on."

"But they were here from before my father's injury, even. And they had tonsures, I am sure of it."

"And were the tonsures as brown as their faces?"

"I don't know," she confessed. There had never been any need in Carrisford to inspect strangers closely, or doubt people's goodwill. At least not that she had been aware of. She looked up at him. "Am I never to trust anyone again?"

He tore off part of the crust, but turned it in his fingers rather than eating it. "At least learn to give your trust sparingly, Lady Imogen. You've made a good beginning," he added with a dry smile. "You don't trust me." He at last took a crisp bite of the bread and chewed it. "What you need is to marry, demoiselle, then your husband will take care of all these things for you."

Here it comes, thought Imogen, and stiffened her spine. "I don't want to be taken care of anymore, Lord FitzRoger."

"You want to fight your own battles?" he

asked skeptically. "Drill your own soldiers? Command your own executions? Squeeze information out of your own traitors?"

How did he always make her seem a fool? Imogen glared at him. "I will petition the king for a husband, then."

He laughed out loud. "He will be enchanted. He has any number of debtors to pay."

Imogen had already realized that, but what was the alternative? None of her suitors appealed.

"My father left me to King Henry's care," Imogen said, trying to sound more assured than she felt. "It is my duty to wait on his will."

"Very likely," said FitzRoger, "but it is one thing to leave the choice to the king, and another to go to him and ask his consent to your wedding a particular man. As long as your choice is reasonable he has no right to object and can only demand a fee for his blessing."

Imogen eyed him uncertainly. His words made sense, but he had already admitted that she was wise not to trust him.

"I know Henry and his current situation," he added. "To gain the approval of the English of his claim to the Crown, he has had to promise much relief from taxes. If you leave the choice to him, Lady Imogen, he will sell you to the highest bidder. Even Warbrick is possible."

Imogen paled. "He couldn't. Not after everything."

"It's not very likely, I admit, because that whole family is out of favor. They chose to back Normandy in the recent conflict. But it all depends on what Warbrick is willing to pay, or promise. Warbrick might think it worth a lot to have the Treasure of Carrisford in his grasp, and Henry could well see it as desirable to suborn Belleme's brother."

Imogen considered this scenario. Robert de Belleme was using the unrest, the conflict between the Conqueror's sons over England, to try to carve out a fief for himself here on the borders. King Henry would definitely consider any means to weaken the man, but she doubted he'd be fool enough to trust Warbrick with the power represented by Carrisford.

She called FitzRoger's bluff. "You're deliberately trying to frighten me," she said, and saw that she had scored a hit. "What do you want, Lord FitzRoger? State it clearly."

Again there was that gleam of admiration in his eyes, and he nodded. "Your welfare."

She would not be wit-softened again. "I find that hard to believe."

He showed no disappointment at her tone. "As you will. Whom then do you wish to marry, demoiselle?"

She was relieved that he accepted the situation so calmly, and he had been correct in advising that she face the king with the choice already made. After all, there doubtless were other men *like* Warbrick seeking a rich bride. Imogen reviewed her discouraging list of suitors.

Finally she said, "It will have to be Sir Richard of Yelston or the Earl of Lancaster."

"Really?" he said.

He hadn't given up. He wanted her to choose him. She couldn't bear this cat-and-mouse game. "I will not marry you," she said firmly.

Not even a twitch. "Negative decisions are not very productive, Lady Imogen. Whom then will you marry?"

She had to put an end to this. "The Earl of Lancaster," she declared. "He has power enough to see to my security, and has stood friend to our family for many years. He even sent his personal physician — a man of great skill — to tend my father . . ." To no avail, she thought sadly.

"Then you had best send him a message to tell him of his good fortune, demoiselle."

Imogen had expected more protests. Thrown off balance, she began to retreat. Perhaps with time a better prospect would occur to her. "I need to have Carrisford restored to its glory," she said, "before I can hold a wedding." She rose to her feet.

"As you will, Lady Imogen," he said amiably. "Just tell me when you need a messenger."

"I can find my own messenger," she declared. He raised a brow and she realized she couldn't.

She was tempted to hit him again. How did he bring out the very worst in her? She realized in time that there were servants in the hall now.

"Very wise," he murmured.

"Let me make it clear," Imogen said with icy precision. "You, My Lord of Cleeve, are the last man in England I would ever consider marrying." With that, she stalked back up the stairs, even though it hurt her feet.

De Lisle returned in time to catch the end of this. He looked amused. "The monks were here when Warbrick got in, but they were among the dead."

"Warbrick wouldn't balk at killing his own tools."

Renald watched Imogen disappear around the bend at the top of the stairs. "You do have a way with women, don't you?"

FitzRoger cut more cheese. "What of the priest?"

"I've sent some men to trace him. He can't have traveled far. Apparently he's crippled in the feet as well as the hands. Made a pilgrimage to Jerusalem, was captured and crucified by some infidels. The people 'round here regard him as a regular saint. They don't *like* him, but they revere him. By the way, he would have nothing to do with the monks. Said they were vicious and ungodly."

"Vices, not habits," mused FitzRoger. "When you find the priest, bring him back slowly."

"What's going on? First you throw him out, then you want him back. Now you want him back, but not soon."

FitzRoger turned his great golden ring thoughtfully. "I think I'm going to have to seduce my future wife. The last thing I need is a resident thorny conscience."

Renald hooted with laughter. "I think you've got a long way to go, Ty, before you get Imogen of Carrisford soft and rosy beneath you. You heard her. You're the last man in England she would consider marrying, and she said it like she meant it."

FitzRoger just smiled. "She did, didn't she?"

Chapter Seven

To Imogen's disgust, her short foray into the hall had brought up some of the blisters on the soft soles of her feet. She fumed against her body's weakness but set her mind to action. Even if she had to stay in her bed, she did not need to be powerless.

She sent Martha to find youngsters who would not be needed for other work and set them to being her eyes and ears.

Soon she had reports of who was dead or injured, and who just missing. As FitzRoger had said, all the garrison were dead, along with five servants, the monks, and Janine.

"Is there news of my aunt?" Imogen asked the boy who was reporting.

"Laid to rest in the chapel vault yesterday," said the lad cheerily.

"Dead?" It hit her like a blow. She had just assumed that Aunt Constance had been spirited away too, and would soon return. Why would anyone kill such a kind lady? "Buried?" she asked. "Without a word to me?" Anger rose to drown grief. "How *dare* he?"

The boy took a step back. "You were sick, lady."

"He could have waited."

The boy kept wisely silent. She waved him away and grief returned. She was truly, truly alone.

She pressed her hands to her face. She would not cry. She had promised herself she would not cry. Constance had gone to her heavenly reward, as had her father, Janine, all the soldiers. They were much happier now than before, or so the Church would say. She called up Father Wulfgan's teaching. This life was just a brief moment of pain and sorrow. It was the afterlife that we should long for.

It didn't, she discovered, ease the grief of those left behind alone.

The sense of loss almost overwhelmed her, but she knew that if she once gave in she could drown in it. She remembered a village woman who had lost all her children to a fever. The poor soul had wandered mindlessly about the area, and then one day had been found in the millpond. Imogen could not afford that road; too many people depended upon her. She pushed all thoughts of her losses away and set her mind to restoring her home.

She reminded herself to ask if Brother Patrick was around. She probably needed more salve for her feet. That reminded her of Lancaster's physician. What had become of him? He had trained in Spain, and was much more skilled than a soldier's monk.

Enquiries merely discovered that he had disappeared during the sack, but that no body had been found. It was assumed that he and his servants had escaped.

So Imogen asked for Brother Patrick's help. The monk applied a salve to her sores and again recommended that she keep off her feet as much as possible. "I understand your impatience, Lady Imogen," the man said, "but each adventure delays the healing. And if you were to venture into the bailey I fear infection."

Imogen had to accept that lying in bed for a few more days was her fate. She continued her administration from there.

She discovered that a handful of Carrisford servants had weathered the siege by hiding, and that they were being helped with essential tasks by FitzRoger's men. Imogen sent lads out to the nearest villages to spread the news that she was in control of Carrisford once more, and that everything should return to normal. Her people should return to their places, and the village headmen should send supplies.

Carrisford had always been good to its people and she knew they would rally to her support now.

Her little messengers told her that the wine in the cellars had been drained, and that Lord FitzRoger — or the master, as her people would keep calling him — had already brought in some supplies from Cleeve and sent for more.

Frowning, she made notes on waxed tablets, keeping tally of what she owed him. Once she was mobile again, she would find a way to slip down to the secret treasure vault and bring up enough coin to pay him off.

It would be very dangerous to be in that man's debt.

She would also bring up some of her jewels. He must be brought to realize that Imogen of Carrisford was not a poverty-stricken suppliant but a great lady.

The grains had fortunately only been spilled out of the bins and much had been recovered, so bread was in production, but what joints had been available had gone. There was meat, however, for the slaughtered stock had been butchered for use.

Then she was told FitzRoger had gone off hunting. That hardly seemed necessary with so many carcasses around. She curled her lip at the thought that he was off amusing himself when there was so much work to be done.

All the same, Imogen was surprised at how the knowledge that he was out of the castle affected her. She was keyed up for another assault on her. Now, with him gone, she felt freer, but also nervously vulnerable. What if Warbrick returned?

She stopped in her record keeping and

sucked on the end of her stylus. Freedom or security. It was a choice.

I choose freedom, she thought firmly, but wondered if the secret entry had been sealed. That was a task FitzRoger could delegate; he would not need to enter the passages himself. She made a note to check on it. It made her very nervous to think of the secret ways lying open now they were known.

Her precious supply of spices was apparently missing, along with the fine carved chest that held them. Her chests of cloth — the silks and sendals, samites and tissues — had been spilled out into the bailey and stamped into the dirt. Curse Warbrick. One day she'd see him dead for what he had done. As soon as there were enough servants, she would have some women do the best they could in cleaning the lengths of cloth. She would surely need new clothes from somewhere and she wasn't sure she should spend coin on adornment just yet.

Though most of the stock would soon have been slaughtered before winter, some would have to be replaced. She would prefer to offer coin directly but had none. She sent for laying hens and milch cows anyway. Surely Imogen of Carrisford's word was good.

Every time she looked up she was aware of her missing window and her bare walls, and was reminded of the destruction wreaked throughout the castle. She put it behind her.

Time enough for elegance later. For the moment it was the necessities of life which concerned her.

Feeling as if she trespassed, she sent a boy to report on the state of the soldiers and armory, and on the progress of repairs. He brought back reassurance of security. The men all knew their business and were well armed. Those not on guard duty spent their time in repairing weapons.

She should have known FitzRoger would not have left the castle vulnerable. She remembered that time after the castle had been taken, when the men — unsupervised — had acted efficiently. He kept a well-trained force.

And they had been unsupervised because their leader was spewing up his terror of closed dark spaces in the arms of his lieutenant.

Imogen pushed that image away. It softened her to think of FitzRoger's point of vulnerability, and that was dangerous. He would give no quarter in this fight, and anyway, look how he had reacted when she had mentioned it.

She frowned over the problem her supposed champion represented. He had his fingers into everything in Carrisford, and his men were her guards. He had all the people thinking of him as the master, and he'd even buried her aunt without Imogen's authority or presence.

She had better winkle the man out of Carrisford before he put down roots!

The only way to do that, however, was through the king, and that would lead to her speedy marriage to a man of King Henry's choosing.

She found she had chewed the end of her wooden stylus almost to a pulp. She threw it down in disgust.

Henry Beauclerk had only been on the throne of England for a year and Imogen had no idea what to expect from him. FitzRoger claimed he would sell her to the highest bidder, and FitzRoger was said to be close enough to the king to know. King Henry's right to the throne was being challenged, and he was also plagued by Belleme and a number of other restless barons. He doubtless did have wavering supporters to buy.

But surely he would never sink so low as to try to buy Belleme or his brothers with her?

Then she remembered her father discussing the rumors that Henry Beauclerk had been behind the death of his brother, King William Rufus, who had so conveniently died of an arrow while hunting. Lord Bernard had been warily watching the new king, withholding judgment. If a man would kill his brother, would he balk at anything?

Imogen felt as if her mind were whirling in circles. If she didn't want to submit to the king's whim, she had only two alternatives. She could offer herself to one of her established suitors — probably Lancaster — or accept the unspoken proposal of Bastard FitzRoger.

She collapsed back against her pillows and tried to think straightly about her choices. The king was a gamble and Imogen was not a gambler.

Lancaster then.

Lancaster was many years her senior, but that was not unusual, and not a matter to take into consideration. She knew her duty as Lady of Carrisford. She should not look for someone pleasing, but for a strong and just lord for her people.

It was as well, she thought dryly, that she could put aside her own tastes if the choice lay between Lancaster and FitzRoger. Neither appealed to her. One older, and seeking always the easy way, not the right. One younger, hard, and frightening.

But, whispered a tiny part of her mind, he would not seek the easy way.

Then she sat up straight.

As wife to Lancaster she would have to live at his principal castle in the north of the country. She would rarely return to Gloucestershire. After all, Lancaster owned Breedon, which lay in this part of the country, and had scarcely ever visited there even when he had come to Carrisford to court her.

Marriage to Lancaster would mean leaving Carrisford.

How could she care for Carrisford from so far away? How could she know if all was well, if justice was fair, if succor was given in times of hardship?

These questions had never arisen when her father was alive to care for his land. He had not been an old man, and it had been assumed that Lord Bernard would live to see a son of hers hold Carrisford after him. Now, however, everything was different. Having just taken Carrisford in her grasp, having suffered to save it, was Imogen now to abandon it?

She saw a hateful decision rearing up to face her.

After all, every mighty lord in England — king's choice or her own — had the same disadvantage. They would expect her to live on their estates far away from Carrisford.

Every lord except Warbrick and FitzRoger, whose principal estates bordered hers.

Warbrick was out of the question.

The Castle Cleeve land adjoined hers. Moving between the two would be easy.

Though she disliked him, FitzRoger had impressed her with his competence. If handled properly, he would keep both estates safe, and she was certain he would not shirk his duties through indolence.

Imogen wiped damp palms on her skirt as her mind skittered around the point.

Martha came in with a pile of laundry.

"What do the people think of Lord Fitz-Roger?" Imogen asked the woman.

Martha laid her load down and considered it. "He's got a hard edge on him, that's for sure, lady. People 'round here have had it soft, and many a one's tried to shirk or whine, but they soon found it better to work." She began to sort the wash. "He's a fair man, though," she said, "and keeps his men in line. I've not had so much as a pinched bottom." She sounded a little regretful.

Imogen licked her lips. "And . . . and has he whipped anyone?"

"Whipped?" asked the woman in surprise. "Not that I've heard of, my lady. Not but what that Sir Renald don't carry a lash and sting a body here or there if they try to malinger. Some people 'round here are bone idle."

Imogen felt dizzy. "Sir Renald?" She'd thought him so gentle. But that wasn't the biggest surprise. "Are you saying my father was lax in the running of Carrisford?"

Martha looked up in alarm. "Lord, no, lady! Sir Bernard were a fine man and a great lord. But times have changed. Under your father everything had gone along smoothly for, well, for nigh on twenty years. There were people aplenty and everything always kept in first order. Now everything's in disarray and half the people are missing."

She shook out a sheet that still had boot prints on it. "Look at this. See what I mean? Lazy work." She threw it on the floor to go back to the laundry. "All have to work twice as hard and many don't like it much, lady. It wouldn't surprise me if some of those that fled just aren't hearing that all's well, hoping most of the work'll be done by the time they return to claim their place."

Imogen knew her people and that had the ring of truth. Life had been soft and easy at Carrisford — for her and for everyone.

Suddenly she knew what FitzRoger was out hunting. He'd never waste his time chasing deer when they had too much meat. He was chasing her missing servants. She remembered that terrible whipping post.

"By the Grail," she muttered, "if he bullies my people . . ."

She commanded that her bed be moved over to the window so that she could observe the goings-on in both baileys. She'd see exactly what FitzRoger was up to when he returned.

She put aside her momentous decision, waiting to see what would be revealed next.

FitzRoger returned alone. She noted that he had ridden out bareheaded in only a leather jerkin sewn with metal rings. She supposed with disgust that it would stop an arrow if he were lucky.

Then she wondered why she was worried about his safety.

Because he was her temporary bulwark against the world?

No, because she'd decided to marry him.

All unconsciously, the decision was made.

She studied the man with new eyes. He was hers. He was her strong right arm. He should protect himself better for he would be no use to her wounded.

It was all very practical.

Why, then, was her mouth dry, her heart pounding? Was it fear? It didn't feel like fear.

He tossed his reins to a man and walked briskly toward the main tower with a smooth, easy grace which denied hours in the saddle. By the Virgin, she'd *like* to see him weakened, at least limping!

She bit her lip when she realized that directly contradicted her previous thought. He was going to drive her mad.

He passed out of sight but not out of mind. He would be a good lord to Carrisford, she admitted, but would he be a good husband?

Would he be kind? She thought he would if she didn't cross him. Would he beat her? The answer was yes if she did something to deserve it. She shivered, but was surprised not to feel great fear. She realized she believed him just.

She hoped to heaven she was right. He could kill her with one blow.

Would he allow her some hand in the running of Carrisford?

Yes, he would, she decided, because that would be her condition for the marriage. She must remember her worth and set her price high.

And what, she thought hesitantly, of the marriage bed?

She remembered Janine and pressed a hand over her eyes, fighting nausea. It would not, could not, be as bad as that for her.

There would be a bed, not a table. She would not fight and so no one would have to hold her down. FitzRoger was surely not so . . . so gross as Warbrick, she told herself, remembering that huge, engorged phallus.

It was a normal thing, after all, and necessary for children. She could endure it as other women had since Eve. She had broken her arm once and had it set without one cry. It was simply a matter of closing the eyes and thinking of something else.

It would merely be another taste of the gall.

Now, the sooner she told him, the sooner it would all be done, and she could settle to restoring Carrisford. She listened for his brisk footsteps.

After a little while Imogen realized he wasn't coming hotfoot to report to her. That annoyed her, but she controlled her irritation. Letting FitzRoger catch her constantly on the raw was to play into his arms.

She tapped her finger and considered strategy. She could send for him and acquaint him with her decision. It was tempting to get it over with, but Imogen knew it would be wiser to wait and make him try some more of his dainty maneuvers. Then she would be able to settle on better terms.

It was just like bargaining with an itinerant merchant, and Imogen had always been good at that. The first rule was not to show how interested one was in the goods.

She became aware of noises and looked out to see FitzRoger's men on horseback driving some of the castle people into the outer bailey like a herd of sheep. At least the people didn't look to be beaten or frightened. She set herself to watch.

FitzRoger came out again and waited as the group progressed to the inner bailey. They were filed toward him. He spoke to each and consulted a listing in his hand.

She caught her breath. That was the record of the castle staff. He had no right to be using it without a word to her!

Each one was given something and sent off to their job. When the sun shot a gleam from one of the items being handed over, Imogen realized he was giving them a silver farthing each. It could be seen as a rehiring fee. It was a crafty move designed to soothe any grievances, but she felt herself seething. It meant that as far as they were concerned they had been hired by *him!*

More people who saw him as the master.

She felt her teeth ache from the pressure she was exerting on them and muttered a few unpleasant curses in his direction. She imagined she had a bow and was sighting on his back. No, not his back — that was still protected by that leather jerkin. His neck. Could she hit his neck at this distance? She was a good shot with her small bow and thought she could.

She imagined an arrow hissing through the air to strike —

He suddenly turned and looked up at her. She almost cowered back as if she really had sent that arrow. Then he raised a hand in salute and turned back to the servants.

They, however, had followed his look and now set up a cheer. "Hail to Lady Imogen! Hail to Carrisford!"

She grinned and waved back.

That for you, Bastard FitzRoger. They know their true liege.

Their genuine pleasure at her safety heartened her, but it still galled her that he was down there acting as her deputy, perhaps even seen already as her lord, while she was trapped here by her cursed blistered feet.

She lay back and shut her eyes. *Oh, Father,* she prayed silently to her earthly father, not her heavenly one, *am I doing the right thing? Why did you not prepare me better? I always expected to choose a husband under your guidance, and then live for many years with the knowledge of your protection.*

What would you think of Bastard FitzRoger? He frightens me, Father; but I think you'd like him. He's good at what he does and you always liked people who are good at what they do.

I wish I didn't have to marry him, Father; but I have to marry someone. You always made it clear that was my duty, and now I find he seems the obvious choice, the only choice. It's very strange. It's as if I'm impelled toward him. Is this the instinct you always spoke of or is it madness?

Watch over me, Father. Guide me. . . .

She heard the door open and her eyes flicked open to see Bastard FitzRoger in the doorway.

"Were you sleeping?" he asked. "I'm sorry if I woke you." He'd taken off his jerkin and was dressed only in braies and a fine linen shirt, belted at the waist. The unlaced neck revealed his finely muscled chest glossed by sweat.

Imogen hastily sat up and grabbed for her wits. "I was thinking of my father."

He perched on the end of her bed. It seemed shockingly intimate and she almost protested, but there were enough important things to fight over without descending to the petty.

"You have scarce had time to grieve, have you?" he said. "From the stories of how Lord Bernard doted on you, you must miss him."

"Of course I miss him. But he didn't *dote*.

He . . . he loved me." Her voice almost broke and she took a deep breath, praying that she wouldn't let the tears escape.

"It is acceptable to cry, you know, when someone so close dies."

Imogen won the battle. "I'll *never* cry before you, FitzRoger. That I vow."

That stillness came over his face that she knew was anger, tightly controlled. "I hope at least that you never cry because of me," he said quietly, "though I suspect you will." He rose. "If you're in the mood for grieving, I should leave you in peace."

He was halfway to the door before she cried, "Stop!"

He turned, mildly surprised, but not as surprised as she. Imogen had no idea why it seemed so important to keep him here. This wasn't the time to tell him she'd marry him.

"Surely we have things to discuss," Imogen said.

"Do we?"

She remembered her grievances. "You buried my aunt without me."

"It was necessary."

"You could have waited a day. I wanted to say farewell. She was very dear to me."

Imogen couldn't read his expression, but it wasn't inimical. "I'm sorry," he said. "It seemed better to get it over with."

She could hardly demand that poor Aunt Constance be disinterred. "What about the people you have just rounded up and herded back here like sheep?"

He relaxed and humor glinted in his eyes. "They seemed to have forgotten the way home. I merely guided them."

"I won't have them punished," she told him.

"Not at all? No matter what they do?"

He was laughing at her again. "I mean, I won't have any flogging at Carrisford. I don't forget what I saw at Cleeve."

"Ah," he said, sobering. "You feel compassion for those two wretches, do you? That *is* Christian charity."

Imogen was being made to feel in the wrong, when she knew she wasn't. "Being drunk is not praiseworthy, but hardly calls for such brutal punishment."

He was no longer laughing, but very serious. "Imogen, I am at times harsh, but never brutal. I permit no man of mine to drink more than weak ale on duty, and they all know it. Those men were not only drunk, but guilty of rape while wine-mad. One of their victims was a mere child, who died of it. I would have been in my rights to hang them, but I wanted the lesson to the other men of like mind to be more memorable."

Imogen didn't know what to say. Rape. A child. How young a child?

He shrugged, misinterpreting her silence. "Unless you see the victim, I suppose such punishment does seem cruel. I assure you, I have no intention of punishing those people I just brought in. That would be to dissuade the others."

"They will come as soon as they hear," she protested. "Doubtless the news of events here is slow to travel."

"News of events here is traveling faster than wildfire, Lady Imogen. I hardly feel you need to send a message to the king. He'll already have heard. Doubtless your more optimistic suitors will be pounding on the door any day, too, including the worthy Lancaster. Am I to admit them?"

That was dragging the conversation to the point with a vengeance.

"What alternative is there?" she asked dry mouthed, hoping to make him take the first step.

She saw recognition flash in his eyes like green fire and her nerve almost faltered. "Me," he said softly. "Better the devil you know . . ."

He was still very controlled and yet she could tell from his eyes, from a minor change in his breathing, that he wanted her — or more precisely, wanted Carrisford — very badly indeed.

That put her in a position of power.

She took a deep breath. "I want Carrisford," she said, striving with all her will to match his control.

He came closer, three steps, to stand at the

end of her bed. "What do you mean?"

"I rule in Carrisford after we are wed."

He considered it and her intently. "Will you raise your own force?" It was not a taunt. It was a straightforward negotiating question. At last he was taking her seriously.

"No," she said crisply. "As my husband you will do that for me, and command it. But it will be paid separately out of Carrisford income. Land grants will be Carrisford land. Everything will be kept separate, and here I will administrate."

He nodded slightly as he considered. "Are we to live together?"

She heard "sleep together" and knew she had colored. "Of course. It is no great distance between our castles. I expect we will move between them. It will be easy to go from one to the other in time of need."

Imogen's heart was pounding, but it was with excitement, not fear. He was listening, really listening. He was not angry that she was setting terms. The power was like wine to her senses.

"And I want vengeance," she said. "Vengeance against Warbrick."

"His head on a platter?" he queried, then shrugged. "I'll kill him for you, Imogen, never fear."

"Kill him?" Imogen echoed, taken aback.

"You don't want him dead?" he asked. "You do have a forgiving nature, don't you?"

"It's not that," Imogen said, unsure how to put her concern into words.

She could swear a smile hovered on his face before being controlled. "You're worried about my safety," he declared. "That's quite endearing. I can't think who last has been concerned about me in that way."

"You're not much use to me dead," Imogen said defensively, though in truth she had been appalled at the thought of him facing mighty Warbrick, and was touched by the genuine pleasure he had almost shown at her concern.

No one had cared . . . ?

"How true," he said, without apparent offense. "So those are your conditions. That you administrate Carrisford, and that I kill Warbrick for you."

It sounded so cut-and-dried. "Yes," said Imogen, "but I don't expect you to kill Warbrick immediately. I'll take your word on it."

"Good, because I can't find him at the moment."

"You're looking?"

"Would I ignore such an enemy? He hasn't returned to his castle, nor does he appear to be close by. It's possible that he's gone to Belleme at Arundel. There'll be fighting soon between the king and Belleme. I have to point out that it's possible that the matter of your vengeance will be taken out of my hands, or that Warbrick and Belleme will flee beyond my reach."

"You're being very honest," said Imogen, almost suspicious at this goodwill.

"I told you, I always am honest if I can be. I intend to deal honestly with you if you will allow it."

That was reassuringly convincing. "Then I won't hold you to your word about Warbrick if circumstances make it impossible." She was amazingly comforted by her decision now it was done. "Now," she said briskly, "if we're to wed, there are a number of matters to be seen to. We must discover how Carrisford was invaded and punish the traitors. Have you made any progress? And, of course, the entrance to the passages must be sealed —"

"Not so fast, Imogen. What exactly did you mean by 'administrate at Carrisford'?"

Imogen was knocked off balance. He wasn't going to refuse the plum that was falling into his hand, so why this quibbling? "Running the household," she said, "taking in rents, allocating labor, and dispensing funds as needed." That was the easy part. She threw in the extra like a challenge. "Justice."

Still no outrage. "And if a tenant refuses due rent, or is attacked by outlaws or another lord? If a malfeant needs to be apprehended?"

She met his eyes unflinchingly. "Then the men you provide will obey *my* instructions and go to enforce *my* will. Won't they, FitzRoger?"

He smiled. There was distinct admiration there and it warmed her like a fierce fire. "Assuredly they will," he promised. Then added, "Under my advice."

It was like a spray from the Irish Sea. *"What?"*

"You may administer Carrisford as your own, Imogen, but you will heed my advice. My men will obey you, but they will still be my men. If you say 'Go' and I say 'Stay,' they will stay."

She found herself kneeling up on the bed facing him, sore feet or no. "That's not fair!"

"That is reality." He grasped her shoulders before she could pull herself out of range. "It's not a bad deal you've negotiated. Are we to be wed?"

"No!"

He shook his head and waited. Imogen's mouth twitched with the desire to tell him to go to hell and take his men with him. Still and all, she would have Carrisford, which was more than Lancaster, or probably any other man in England, would give her.

"Yes," she said.

His eyes flashed victory and his hands tightened. Imogen pulled back, but he drew her closer anyway. She was held against his body, feeling his warmth through his soft shirt. She smelled herbs from the chests in which his clothes were stored, but he'd been out in the sun most of the day and there was a tang of horse, sweat, and fresh air that weakened her knees so that she suspected he was holding her up.

"What are you doing?" she protested, but faintly.

He smiled down at her. "I'm not going to throw you on the bed and ravish you, Ginger. Don't you think a kiss is in order?" His hands slid around her, one to curve around her nape, the other to rest like fire in the small of her back.

"No," she said, but rather unsteadily. "This is a practical, dynastic arrangement."

He tilted up her chin, laughter in his eyes. "Just practical?" he teased.

"I wouldn't have chosen you," she said firmly, "if you weren't a neighbor with a strong right arm."

He was unoffended. "Then we're well suited. I wouldn't have chosen you if you didn't own a large chunk of England."

Before she could spit out her offense at that, his lips were on hers. His hand cradled her head and there was really nothing she could do about it except submit.

Kissing was very strange, she decided. It was a silly business of lips to lips, and yet it made her feel soft and warm, like a hot herb-scented bath, or a potent wine. The feel of his body against hers, only thin silk and fine linen between them, somehow made it worse. Or better.

At least it wasn't a sin anymore. . . .

She found her arms had gone around him — for support, she told herself, so she didn't fall off the bed.

The hard, resilient muscles of his torso flexed against her hands. She could almost feel the leashed power humming in them, humming into her so that she tingled all over. A shudder rippled through her. . . .

He drew back and dropped a kiss on the end of her nose. He looked quite different. Younger. Warmer. His voice was softer when he murmured, "As I said, Imogen, we're well suited."

That brought her grievance back with a thump and she raised her chin. "Very well suited. You're strong and I'm rich."

He laughed and let her go, once more his old, hard-edged self. "I've proved my strength, Ginger. Why don't you prove your wealth?"

He was after the treasure again. She gathered her scattered wits. She'd not give him a sniff of it until he'd signed the marriage contracts giving her control of Carrisford.

He took in her silence and shook his head. "I wonder if you'll ever fight me about something that really matters. You'll lose, Ginger."

Imogen knelt up straight as a spear. "I will not. I am Imogen of Carrisford and you are *nobody!*"

At the look on his face she quailed inside, though she wouldn't let herself retreat.

"If we fight," he said quietly, "I will win, because you are Imogen of Carrisford and I, until recently, *was* nobody. I know how to fight in ways you've never dreamed of. You don't know what the world's like, Ginger, and if you're a good girl, I'll make sure you never find out."

He left before she could reply, his footsteps light down the spiral staircase.

"I hate you, Bastard FitzRoger!" she screamed.

The footsteps stopped.

Imogen froze, her heart pounding. She'd never used that name to him before.

After a heart-stopping moment the footsteps started again, going down. Imogen collapsed back onto the bed. He wasn't going to take retaliation.

A little part of her was disappointed.

A short time later Renald de Lisle came up with a sheet of parchment, ink and pens.

"What are they for?" Imogen asked suspiciously.

"Your marriage contract. Ty suggested that since you're the one with most leisure, you should write it out."

Imogen blinked. "FitzRoger's leaving me to write it as I wish?"

"Apparently," said de Lisle with a grin.

176

"Ah, I wish I had spun gold hair and deep blue eyes. I'd have a castle out of him in no time."

"Only if you married him," said Imogen tartly.

"True. And only if I had a mighty castle in the first place." He gestured to the blank parchment. "It is for you to state your terms as you wish, little flower."

When he had gone Imogen considered the space and what she could write. But in the end she wrote what they had agreed on — excepting the matter of Warbrick — even including his supervision of her rule of Carrisford. It was the way of the world, and he doubtless wouldn't sign it otherwise.

Chapter Eight

"Lady Imogen! Did you hear the king is coming?" Martha's round face was rosy with excitement.

"*What?*"

"The king's heard of the wickedness here and he's coming to your aid. An armed party of knights came with a messenger."

Imogen shut her gaping mouth with a snap. "And nobody told me? Get FitzRoger up here!"

Martha's eyes were like saucers at this tone, but she scuttled off.

Imogen fumed — at herself as much as anyone. It was nearly sunset and after writing out the contract she'd sat here for hours fretting about her marriage, when she knew she'd made the right decision.

Wasting time.

Imagining all the clever things she could have said to put FitzRoger in his place.

Wasting time.

Remembering that kiss. Wondering when he'd kiss her again.

Wasting time.

If she'd kept her attention on the bailey,

she would have seen the king's men arrive.

FitzRoger came in, a picture of knightly courtesy. "You want something, my lady? To come down to the hall for the meal, perhaps?"

"No . . . Yes . . . Maybe. What I want," said Imogen, getting a grip on herself, "is to speak to the king's messenger."

He wasn't abashed or ashamed. "Why?"

She hissed in a breath. "Because this is my castle, FitzRoger, and he is bringing a message to *me*."

"No, he wasn't. He was bringing a message to me, asking me to rescue the poor damsel in distress. It was only because the messenger heard I was already in Carrisford that he came here at all."

"Oh." Imogen felt like a pricked bubble. She rallied. It was, after all, still her castle. "I would still like to speak to him."

"I'm afraid he's already gone on with his escort to take a message to Warbrick, summoning him for judgment."

"A fat lot of good that will do," snapped Imogen.

"We all know that," he said patiently. "But the proper forms have to be followed."

Imogen glared at him, thwarted. She was being ignored and circumvented but didn't know what to do about it. Perhaps she would be better advised to marry the indolent Earl of Lancaster after all. She could run rings around him.

"So the king is to visit here," she said thoughtfully.

"Yes. He should be here tomorrow. He can witness our marriage."

"I'll not be wed in such haste," Imogen declared. She definitely wasn't ready to commit herself yet.

"What point is there in delay? It will only tempt another man to try to seize you."

Imogen smiled at him. "You don't seem to have much faith in your ability to protect me, do you, Lord FitzRoger?"

He moved close to the bed. Looming again. "I can hold you fast, never fear, Imogen. But once there's a chance you carry my child, you're a less attractive plum. You used that device for your own protection, if you remember?"

"Yes," said Imogen, and hated the fact that she blushed.

"So once we are married there will be less necessity for me to hover by your side. That will be a relief, won't it?"

"Yes," said Imogen again. What else could she say?

"And if we're wed before the king and the great lords of the land, a marauder would have no hope of contesting the validity of the match, would he?"

She looked away from his challenging eyes. "I suppose not."

"So we should be married tomorrow, shouldn't we?"

Imogen fought it, but in the end she sighed and said, "Yes." She felt a perfect fool again.

She looked up resentfully.

He smiled, almost kindly, and picked up a strand of her hair. She slapped at his hand, but this time he didn't let go and her hair was yanked.

"Ow! Let go. I am not yours yet to do with as you please!"

"You mean," he murmured, rubbing the strand of hair between his long fingers, "that by tomorrow night you will be sweetly acquiescent?"

Imogen had been trying very hard not to think about such things. . . . Tomorrow night! "If I marry you," she said thinly, "I will try to be a dutiful wife."

"If?" It was like the snap of a whip.

She forced herself to meet his cool eyes, but her throat was dry and her heart was like a wild horse in her breast.

"We have an agreement, Ginger," he said quietly.

"Then stop mauling me, FitzRoger, until I have to put up with it."

He let her hair drift free of his fingers and moved away. Imogen didn't know why she said these things. They were pointless and didn't bring her any satisfaction. Rather, they seemed to cause a sick knot of misery to

181

lodge in her chest, threatening to choke her.

He was looking at her soberly, but he suddenly smiled. "You'll feel a lot better when you can fight me on your feet, you know."

"But I'll still lose — according to you."

"Nothing is ever certain in war. You have some dangerous weapons, bride of mine. For now, however, I would rest if I were you, so you can walk to your wedding and make your curtsy to the king."

"By Mary's crown," she gasped, other problems fading. "We are in no state to receive the king!"

"Don't worry. I've sent for additional supplies and goods from Cleeve, and called in more from your people here."

Don't worry, don't worry. What was she? A babe in arms? "That was for me to do."

He sighed impatiently. "I hope you learn to pick your battles with more care, Imogen. I have no desire to run Carrisford, and if you want to take over the domestic organization of Cleeve, you're welcome to that too. But you're stuck in your bed. That does hinder things."

"You could at least consult me," she said, feeling in the wrong again.

"I have merely given everything into the hands of your seneschal. He seems competent."

"Siward's back?" asked Imogen in delight, and then found a new grievance. No one had told her that either, and Siward hadn't come to see her.

"He's been busy," explained FitzRoger. At her startled look he said, "Your every thought shows on your face, Ginger."

Imogen hurled a pillow at him.

He caught it. "Do I gather you don't want me to carry you down to dinner?"

"I certainly do not," she snapped, "and I am thinking of taking to wearing a mask."

"Very wise. I wear one all the time." He tossed the pillow back and left.

Imogen knew truth when she heard it.

What, she wondered, was guarded by the mask? Perhaps it was that softer, younger man she had glimpsed when they kissed. She hugged the pillow pensively. If she married the Earl of Lancaster, she would never find out. She knew she was definitely not going to marry the Earl of Lancaster.

She was going to marry Bastard FitzRoger, even if he did send shivers down her spine. Perhaps because he sent shivers down her spine.

How old was he? At first he had seemed ageless, but she thought he could not be ten years her senior.

Martha returned, somewhat tentatively, with a tray of food. "The master said you wished to eat here."

That hadn't been what she'd meant and she was sure he knew it, but Imogen was tired of fighting. "That's correct," she said. "I must be strong for tomorrow when the king arrives."

"And for your wedding," Martha said as she laid the tray on Imogen's lap. The woman chuckled. "And I always thought you'd end up married to one of those old fogies your father favored. You've certainly got an eye for a lusty male, I'll grant you that."

Imogen felt the heat rush into her face. "Martha, you are impudent!"

The woman pulled a face, but she shut up. She was, Imogen reminded herself, just a weaver promoted to maid. It was time to think of gathering some proper attendants. She needed to train someone to take Janine's place.

As for Aunt Constance's position, Imogen had no other available female relatives in England. . . .

Lusty? As she chewed mutton stewed in rosemary, Martha's word echoed in Imogen's head.

The shivery excitement, half fear, half pleasure, was that lust? All her life Father Wulfgan had warned her against lust. When she remembered Janine, all his warnings took on new depth, except that they seemed to be about avoiding temptation. What was tempting about that kind of invasion?

Truly, as Father Wulfgan said, lust was the path to hell. It must be that men were

184

tempted and women suffered. But honesty compelled Imogen to acknowledge that in FitzRoger's arms she had not suffered.

Yet.

The devil could be very cunning, she reminded herself. He always made sin appear attractive. These thoughts reminded her that the fight over Father Wulfgan had never been resolved. "Martha," Imogen said, "has Father Wulfgan returned to Carrisford?"

"That old crow," muttered Martha but fell silent at the look in Imogen's eyes. "I don't think so, lady. The master . . . Lord FitzRoger threw him out."

"And I ordered him returned. Who prayed over the graves of my aunt and the others, then?"

"The master's monk, Brother Patrick did, lady."

Imogen saw a strong weapon and smiled. "Martha, go to Lord FitzRoger and tell him I will not be wed except by Father Wulfgan."

Martha was wide-eyed again. "Lady . . ."

"Go!" Imogen commanded.

Martha scuttled out. Her mutterings could be heard receding down the stairs.

Imogen half expected the appearance of FitzRoger, complete with acidic arguments, and could hardly eat the rest of her meal for nervous excitement. Instead, before the sun was down, gaunt Father Wulfgan stalked in.

"Daughter," he declared, "you are in the devil's maw!"

"I am safe from Warbrick," Imogen countered. She immediately felt reduced to a child by this man.

"From one devil to another. Cast out the evil one now, my child!"

"Lord FitzRoger?"

"He is the hand of death on the land," thundered the priest. "He repents not the spilling of blood. He is the devil's spawn and his seed will poison the ground on which it falls."

Imogen wondered why she'd been so desperate to have her chaplain back. Truly, Fitz-Roger had turned her wits.

Father Wulfgan was not an old man, but he had been at Carrisford as long as Imogen could remember. He was short and nothing but bone and sinew, which was not surprising in view of the severity of his self-imposed penances. In his sallow, sunken face, his brilliant blue eyes burned like fire.

Imogen swallowed. "You think it would be wrong for me to marry FitzRoger, Father?"

"Better by far to join the sisters at Hillsborough."

Again it was tempting. No hard choices. No marriage bed to endure.

"My father wished me to marry," Imogen said, half hoping, half fearing to be persuaded otherwise.

The priest scowled bitterly but conceded the point. "Your father wished you to marry Lord Gerald, daughter, or another such sober man. Not this impious warmonger."

"FitzRoger did not start this war," Imogen protested. "I went to him for help."

"He is a man of war," Wulfgan countered fiercely. "He has been a mercenary — an accursed soul. He has gathered wealth through the wickedness of tourneys. He has come into this part of the land for nothing but war. He and Warbrick. There is nothing to chose between them."

"Warbrick is foul!"

"They are all men who live by the sword!" declared Wulfgan. "The fratricidal king is another of the same breed. They kill in their own cause, and do not seek repentance for the blood they spill!"

Imogen realized she would get no sense out of Wulfgan on politics. His obsessions were bloodshed and lust, and it was the latter she wished to speak of, not the former.

"But I must marry a strong man, Father," she said. "You would not want me in the power of such as Warbrick or Belleme."

He clutched the crucifix he wore on a cord around his neck. "The Lord will be your protection, my child."

"He didn't protect me a few days ago!" snapped Imogen. She didn't remember Father Wulfgan sounding silly before.

Wulfgan's eyes flashed fire at her. "Undutiful child! You are safe, are you not? Doubt not the Lord's ways!"

Imogen pounced. "Then FitzRoger was the Lord's right arm!"

Wulfgan stepped back in horror. "Why do you shout his name so?" he hissed. "What is this man to you?"

Imogen was once more a nervous sinner making confession. She buried all thought of two heated kisses. "He . . . he is my champion, Father — a righteous paladin."

The priest leaned forward. "A paladin serves for the good of his soul, not for gain, daughter in Christ. Does that describe this man?"

Imogen had no good answer.

"No," said the priest. "He is a mercenary who kills for gold."

Imogen swayed back a little. "He has asked for no payment, Father."

His spittly mouth turned up in a sneer. "Except yourself."

"No," said Imogen. "That was my idea."

Father Wulfgan jerked back. *"What?"*

"He is strong," she explained quickly, "and his land marches with mine so that I can watch over Carrisford."

The priest eyed her suspiciously. "And there is no lust in your heart for him?"

Now they were at the point. "I don't know," Imogen whispered.

Down in the hall, Renald and FitzRoger were playing chess. The raised voice of the priest could be heard now and then.

"Are you going to let him harangue her all night?" Renald asked.

"She demanded him back," said FitzRoger, moving a bishop. "Perhaps she'll think better of the idea."

"Very clever. But he's doubtless exhorting her to give up the marriage and you've nothing signed and sealed."

"It's your move."

Renald pushed a pawn over a square and FitzRoger took it.

"I wouldn't leave her alone with that fanatic," Renald persisted.

"The priest won't turn her off the marriage," said FitzRoger, twirling the silver pawn in his fingers. "The Flower of the West is getting everything she wants. Including me."

Renald laughed. "You've melted her already? No wonder you promised her the earth. She'll be too befuddled to insist on it."

FitzRoger dropped the pawn into the box. "No, my friend. I haven't melted her, and if I'm any judge, she'll demand every letter of her rights. Are you not interested in the game?"

Renald recognized his friend's tone and dropped the subject. He looked at the board and grimaced as he realized how little chance he had of saving his king.

Up in Imogen's room, Father Wulfgan was sitting on the bed so that, pressed back against the wall though she was, Imogen's eyes were still only inches from his. He stank, but she should be used to that — he mortified his flesh through uncleanliness as well as starvation and flagellation.

"It is good that you do not recognize lust, my child."

That wasn't the problem. Imogen wished she could tell Father Wulfgan that she had witnessed lust at its most foul, and have the memory wiped away like the sins in confession. The words wouldn't come, though. To speak of it would make it more real.

"But . . . but how do I avoid it, Father," she whispered, "if I do not know what it is?"

He laid his twisted hand over hers. "The easiest way, daughter in Christ, is to be celibate."

"But I am to marry."

"Married couples have lived a pure life. Holy Edward, king of this land not fifty years since, took a wife and yet kept himself free of all vileness."

How fortunate his wife was, thought Imogen, imagining a comfortable world of hugs and kisses which never progressed to vileness.

But then she remembered her father's scathing comments about King Edward. It was that celibate marriage which had left England without a clear heir and ripe for plucking by Normandy.

Somehow, she couldn't imagine FitzRoger praying his wedding night away. "I . . . I think Lord FitzRoger will want children, Father."

"Then let him get them as he was got," snarled Wulfgan, "on women whose feet are already set on the path to hell."

Imogen felt a spurt of pure outrage at the idea and kept her lashes lowered, her face as still as possible. If FitzRoger could read her like a book, doubtless Father Wulfgan could too.

"I believe it will be my duty as a wife to bear my lord's children." And I want to, she thought, even at the price of pain. The image of presenting FitzRoger with his first child turned her innards warm with longing.

The priest sighed. "Few have the strength for a chaste marriage," he conceded.

Imogen looked up. "So how do I fulfill my duty to bear children, Father, but yet avoid lust?"

Wulfgan sat back, looking as if he had bitten into a green apple. "It is simple enough. You must avoid pleasure in the marriage bed, my child, and things that might lead to pleasure. Remember always that your vile flesh is the enemy of the spirit. Reject it. Mortify it. When your flesh takes pleasure, you know you are in sin."

"Pleasure?" Imogen asked blankly. The fires of lust were one thing, but where was the danger of pleasure in the marriage bed? He must mean the kisses. This was all very confusing.

Wulfgan patted her cheek with a gnarled hand. "Your very bewilderment shows you to be pure, my child. I have told you in the past of those acts you must avoid if you are to escape damnation — the tongue in the mouth, the hand on the breast . . ."

Imogen looked down, wishing her face would not flare with heat.

Wulfgan sighed. "I soil your innocence by talking of such things, and now I fear I must distress you further, dear child. I have wished to save you from all this, but you are right in saying it is your duty to wed. The path of duty is often set with the fiery pits of temptation. Let me tell you now of other fearful things the devil may put before you. . . ."

Imogen hardly slept that night for thinking of the extraordinary things Father Wulfgan had spoken of, things that went far beyond anything she had seen or imagined. Some practices revolted her, and she certainly couldn't imagine FitzRoger wishing to behave so ludicrously, but she had to acknowledge that the devil was cunning. Some of the acts described had created in her a tangled excitement which might be the dreaded lust.

And lust would not only condemn her to hell; it would mark her offspring and ruin all enterprises of the family. Men, according to Father Wulfgan, were weak in the face of lust. It was for women to avoid leading them into temptation.

Imogen wasn't clear how, except that she wasn't to flaunt her naked body before her husband or touch him in one of the wicked ways described.

As if she would.

Imogen greeted the rising sun with sick anxiety, and set herself willingly to the prescribed day of fasting and prayer. Martha protested this, saying Imogen needed her strength, but the ribald look in the woman's eyes just increased Imogen's resolve. She must be spiritually resolute, not physically.

Martha went away muttering.

Though Imogen tried hard to concentrate on purity and prayer, strange images kept intruding on her prayers.

FitzRoger's long-fingered hands, and the feel of their callused strength on her body.

The taste of his mouth joined with hers.

The sick ache inside when he held her.

That gentling warmth that had come into his austere face just once or twice in tender moments.

Surely that couldn't be a sign of damnation, could it?

She prayed harder.

In the afternoon, she heard the clamor of the king's arrival and greeted it with relief.

It marked the beginning of the end.

Chapter Nine

Martha rushed in, excited and glad to be doing something, and tidied Imogen's appearance. Soon the king arrived in her room, accompanied by FitzRoger and Henry's personal physician. The man examined her feet and pronounced them to be as well as possible, and fit for walking if she were careful. He applied his own healing salve, then left.

As this was going on, Imogen studied the king, wondering what would have happened if she had left her fate completely in his hands.

Henry Beauclerk was in his thirties and not a particularly handsome man, but he had the presence of a king. He was stocky and strong, with thick dark hair hanging in fashionable curls on his shoulders and over his brow, and vivid dark eyes. Crisp dark hair grew on his brawny arms, too, and down onto his strong, short-fingered hands.

Though he clearly enjoyed fine dressing, he was no more ostentatious than any other nobleman. If she could get at her treasure, Imogen decided, she could easily cast him in the shade. Then she remembered her father's warning that it was not wise to flaunt wealth before princes.

Perhaps that was why FitzRoger was dressed in a simple linen tunic of red woven with black, with only one bracelet and his ring by the way of ornament.

The king was in a good humor, and his eyes gleamed merrily as he teased her and FitzRoger about the coming wedding.

When he spoke of Warbrick, however, his expression turned cold and hard as a blade. Henry Beauclerk, born fourth in line and landless, had struggled to survive, and had fought to grasp and hold the throne of England. He was not a man to cross.

Then Imogen noted something else.

For all the difference in their ages, FitzRoger and the king were as close as brothers. Henry leaned on FitzRoger's shoulder, teasing and being — very judiciously — teased back. They addressed each other as Hal and Ty.

Then, like a bolt from heaven, she remembered that when the king had commanded a man to rescue her, it had been FitzRoger who had been called to serve.

It was as good as a declaration that FitzRoger was to be her husband.

She wondered bitterly why he had bothered to woo her. All the concessions she had so carefully written down were as words written on water, for the king would never take Imogen's side against his beloved "Ty." And what *was* her future husband's full name? It seemed absurd that she alone did not know it or dare to use it.

She was just the fool FitzRoger had once called her, pacified by illusory powers like a babe pacified by a sucker.

She eyed the two jovial men bitterly. Perhaps she would delight Wulfgan's ascetic heart after all and take her body and her treasure to the convent at Hillsborough. That was the one option the king could not oppose.

Perhaps FitzRoger read her like a book again, for when the king left, he stayed behind, a watchful expression in his eyes. A hint of cold humor there made Imogen grit her teeth.

She challenged him directly. "Why did you pretend I had a choice? The king would have trussed me like a Michaelmas goose and presented me to you on a platter."

He leaned against a wall, arms folded, and didn't deny the charge. "You might have chosen Lancaster. That would have been a mistake, but he's sufficiently influential to have made problems. Henry would not want to offend such a powerful baron while his hold on the Crown is still uneasy."

"I could still choose Lancaster. I've agreed to nothing publicly."

"No. He sent a message pressing his claim. I replied that you are now promised to me."

Imogen gasped. "Without a word to me?"

"There was no need to consult you. You had already given your word to marry me. You will marry me, Imogen. Resign yourself. You won't find it too arduous if you behave yourself."

Fury swept through her. He was dismissing her again, and he was too far away to hit. Imogen beat the bed with her fists. "Doesn't it bother you to be marrying someone who hates you so?"

He said nothing, but he did shield his eyes with his lids for a betraying moment.

Imogen scented blood. "What makes you safe from a knife in the night or poison in your cup, FitzRoger?"

"The fire on which they burn a woman who kills her husband?"

"I'm sure I could be cunning enough to avoid that."

"I'm sure you could, too. The truth is that I will be vulnerable to your malice as you will be vulnerable to mine."

Imogen shivered. "Is that a threat?"

"It is a fact. Tonight I will sleep by your side, Imogen. If you wish to use a blade on me, there will be little I can do about it." He slipped his knife out of its sheath and tossed it gleaming on the bed. "In case you don't have one sharp enough. Novices go for the chest, which is far too chancy and well protected. If you want to kill me, Ginger, slice open my belly or cut my throat. But cut deep the first chance. You won't get a second."

With that he was gone.

Imogen picked up the long knife with shaking fingers and carefully tested the blade. Despite her care, she still cut her thumb. The knife was wickedly sharp — a hunting knife, not a table knife. She imagined slashing it through skin and muscle. . . .

She sucked her own salty blood thoughtfully. What was she to do? What choices did she realistically have? None but the convent, and honesty told her that wasn't for her.

She wished this wasn't her wedding day. She wished her father were alive to look after her. She wished FitzRoger would at least *pretend* to be gentle.

Fine chance there was of that. But at least he didn't pretend to virtues he could never possess. He had, in his own way, been honest, and she had decided to marry him for good and logical reasons. Those reasons had not changed.

And his first gift to her had been a knife to kill him with.

Imogen placed the knife neatly on a chest by her bed. Perhaps if he were ever vile enough, she would find the courage to use it.

Imogen spent the rest of the day mending the dress she had chosen for her wedding and trying to think no further than that. She could not help but regret, however, that her finery was so limited. Only a mended gown to wear, and no jewelry at all.

Ridiculously, that trivial problem did bring a few tears to sting at her eyes. Perhaps she should weaken and tell FitzRoger where her jewels were hidden.

Just then Martha bustled in with a carved chest in her hands, her eyes glittering with excitement. "For you, lady!" the woman exclaimed as she put the box on the bed. "From the master!"

Imogen eyed the box suspiciously. She was wary of anything sent by FitzRoger, and reminded of the story of the ancients and the gift that had conquered Troy.

This gift, at least, could not conceal an army. It was a domed chest about two hands long, finely carved with woodland scenes and bound in silver. It had a lock, but the key was in it. She turned it and lifted the lid to expose leather pouches. She opened one to spill a golden girdle.

Another contained a bracelet, another rings. Soon the bed was covered with a flashing carpet of earrings, fillets, collars, brooches, and even ancient fibulas. There was every kind of metal and design — filigree, ribbon work, chains, stones.

Martha was gasping and oohing, but Imogen turned the ornaments thoughtfully. This haphazard collection was all of women's pieces, and as FitzRoger had not had time to purchase them, they must be loot. They were all good pieces, but it was a collection without pattern or meaning. Doubtless whatever had been up for grabs at the time.

A mercenary's loot.

Even so, she was touched by the lavishness of the gift, and that FitzRoger had thought of her problem. Perhaps the chest had contained an army of invasion after all, an army designed to invade her heart.

Imogen laughed at that. Probably such riches would turn the heads of most women, but when FitzRoger finally saw her true jewelry, he would realize these were mere trinkets.

All the same, she was touched, and could approach her wedding a little easier in her mind.

Imogen stood for the first time in over a day. Her feet did not hurt much and she discovered that FitzRoger had been right again. The world did look better when she was standing on her own.

Martha helped her into a cream silk kirtle and the darned red silk tunic. Imogen investigated the loot and clasped a girdle of gold filigree set with ivory flowers around her waist and a collar of gold and garnets around her neck. There were two narrow gold bracelets of ancient design and she slipped them onto her wrists. That was enough. There was no need for ostentation and she reminded herself that it was not wise to flaunt wealth before princes.

She replaced the rest of the jewelry, locked the chest, and then tucked the key under the girdle. She had nowhere else secure to keep it.

Martha combed out her long hair. "Oh, but it's so pretty," the woman said as it crackled along the comb. "And so long. It's a wonder for sure. I don't know what color it is, lady. Gold? Copper?"

"Lord FitzRoger says it's ginger."

"He never did!" The woman chuckled. "I'll be bound he says something else tonight, lady."

Imogen stiffened. "What do you mean?"

"Men say these things when they're wooing, lady. They like to tease. But when they're all hot and bothered, they say the truth."

Imogen turned to look at her. "Hot and bothered? In lust, do you mean?"

"If you like, lady. Turn 'round do, so I can finish this off."

Imogen turned. Martha was a married woman and might be able to advise her. "Er . . . is it hard in the marriage bed to . . . to be good, Martha?"

"Good, lady?"

Imogen licked her lips. She found she couldn't speak of the practices described by Father Wulfgan. "To do right. You know . . . Not to offend."

Imogen felt the woman's hand stroke her head briefly. "Don't you fret, lambkin. He won't expect you to be clever. It'll be all right."

Clever? Imogen's heart thumped. What had clever to do with it? She abandoned questions which only seemed to make matters worse. She knew she had been cossetted and protected, and Father Wulfgan had told her only what she *shouldn't* do. What if there were things she was supposed to know that she didn't know?

She would hate to give FitzRoger another reason to call her a silly child.

When it was time to go down, Imogen's nerves were on edge and her legs felt unsteady. She tried her softest shoes but found they immediately galled the sides of her feet. She would have to go down barefoot and this made her feel even worse, as if she were entering the great hall only half dressed.

There was no help for it. Imogen reminded herself that she was Imogen of Carrisford, great heiress of the west, and set out to her wedding.

Alone, for she had no female attendant of stature, Imogen walked through the rooms and began to descend the wide staircase into the great hall. Her head felt fogged. It could be because of her sore feet, or the fasting.

She thought it was fear.

She was amazed to find that the hall

looked ready for royalty and a wedding. There were hangings on the walls — not as fine as those destroyed by Warbrick, but better than nothing. The trestle tables set up for the meal were covered with snowy cloths. The rushes on the floor were clean and, she detected, strewn with rosemary and lavender to sweeten the air.

The large oak high table was not yet laid, for it was covered with the betrothal documents, but the nobles gathered around it were drinking wine from fine silver and gold vessels. The empty sideboards now held plates and even some precious glass.

It must all have come from Cleeve.

Something alerted the men. Silence fell as they turned to look at her.

Imogen's steps faltered under all those assessing eyes. Hard eyes, mercenary eyes. To them she was just wealth and power on legs.

She gave thanks at that moment for FitzRoger's trinkets, which allowed her at least the appearance of a great heiress. She regretted, however, that she had not agreed to be carried down to her betrothal; her dizziness was growing worse. She put a steadying hand against the wall.

Then she steeled herself. She was strong, and must prove it. By God, she would need to be strong as the wife of Bastard FitzRoger.

She saw him.

In the few brief days since they had met

she had seen FitzRoger half naked, in armor, in gory leather, and in silk, but she had never seen him in such finery as this. He clearly had plenty more loot of a masculine sort.

He was sleek and hard in the green and gold of his colors. His dark hair glittered in a beam of light, and heavy gold ornaments glowed so that he outshone even his prince. He dominated the room, the King of England included. So much for not flaunting wealth before princes. It was as well he and Henry were friends or such unconscious arrogance could cost him his head.

And she had called him a nobody. He clearly was anything but.

She had learned to read him a little. She knew that just now he was concerned that she would fail to complete the walk she had set herself.

The concern didn't hearten her. It was the same coolheaded concern he gave to his men's fighting fitness, his animals' good health, and his weapons' edge. Everything Bastard FitzRoger possessed was expected to fulfill its purpose perfectly. He made no move to help her.

She would marry him for his strength and hardness, and be grateful she knew it was war she entered, not love.

But one does not go into war alone. As she walked down the long staircase, Imogen wished she had someone familiar by her side.

Her father and aunt were dead. Janine had met her bloody end in this very hall but five days past.

Unwise thought.

The memory burst back on Imogen and she faltered. She immediately picked up her pace again, though her heart was pounding and bloodred shadows were threatening her vision. She would *not* faint in front of them.

Now, however, instead of a richly dressed wedding party she saw brutes in armor, blood dripping from sword points, and Janine . . .

She saw the woman held stretched across the table. She heard her guttural screams for mercy as her rapist thrust into her, grunting in rhythm. Grunt, grunt, grunt —

Dear God, it was the same table!

She came to the present frozen with horror, staring at the oak boards spread with documents. Was it her imagination that there were bloodstains?

A hand took hers, burning hot against the chill of her flesh. She looked up into the sympathetic dark eyes of FitzRoger's friend, Renald de Lisle.

"You should not have walked, Lady Imogen," he chided gently. "Now you must sit." He guided her to the great chair set by the table. She glanced at the king, but he waved a negligent hand.

"No, no, Lady Imogen. I insist. Ty has told us of your stubborn pride. I commend you, but it would be foolishness to take it too far."

Stubborn pride? Her eyes met FitzRoger's. Was that really what he saw? How strange. She felt feeble, so unable to take charge of her own destiny. After all, this wedding was an admission that without some man at her side she was like a rabbit flung among wolves. She was grateful to sit, however. It lessened the chance that she would faint.

Renald poured her wine, but before she could drink, a long brown hand removed her cup and replaced it with a goblet of water. "We are supposed to fast," said FitzRoger. "Remember? If we don't, all our works will turn to evil and you'll give birth to rabbits."

Imogen looked at him in shock. "What?"

His smile was cool. "That's what Father Wulfgan says. The priest you value so."

Imogen looked over at Wulfgan, huddling darkly over his psalter, clearly dissociating himself from this event. Was that why FitzRoger sounded angry?

She sipped the water to ease her dry mouth.

The king stepped forward into the silence. "As your father entrusted you to my care, Lady Imogen, I am honored to guide you in this matter of your marriage. Perhaps you would like me to explain all these documents."

"She knows them well, sire," said Fitz-Roger. "She was the scribe."

"Indeed." The king looked at her with more respect. "You have won a gifted bride, Ty, as well as a beautiful one. But does she understand what she has written?"

They spoke as if she wasn't there. "She does!" snapped Imogen, and then looked at the startled king in horror. "I beg your pardon, sire."

Again he waved a hand. "No matter. This has been a hard time for you, Lady Imogen, and we make allowances. It is our wish to see you safe in the protection of the Lord of Cleeve. Tell me, then, what is in the documents, so that we may all give testimony that you enter this betrothal with full understanding."

So that she couldn't seek annulment later on the grounds that she had been forced or deceived.

Imogen clasped her hands on the table and said, "I agree to marry Lord FitzRoger of Cleeve. I will retain overlordship of Carrisford for myself and it will pass to one or more of my children excepting only the eldest son, who will inherit Castle Cleeve and whatever other properties my . . . my husband may gain in his life." She looked up and found her eyes locked with FitzRoger's. In a painful way it was welcome. She had noticed this before. His cool gaze strengthened her where sympathy would make her crumble. She'd do anything rather than snivel before him.

"My husband," she said as if to him alone, "on my behalf will defend Carrisford and provide the knight's fee due to you, sire, for the estate." Meaningless possession, in other words.

"I, through my officers," she continued, "will be responsible for the civil administration of Carrisford and its holdings, and for all costs incurred there."

"Under your husband's guidance," prompted the king.

"I beg pardon, sire?"

"It does say" — he pushed forward a document and pointed to a section with a bejeweled finger — "you are responsible et cetera 'under the guidance of Lord FitzRoger, my husband.' That should say 'Tyron FitzRoger.' Where's my clerk?"

A monk came forward, scraped off the word *Lord*, and wrote in *Tyron*. So now she knew his full name.

"Do you agree to this, Lady Imogen?" the king continued. "It would hardly be acceptable for a girl of sixteen to rule her own estate, but we must be sure you understand all this. These words do sharply limit your authority."

Imogen looked up again at Bastard FitzRoger. "I know it."

"And accept it?" queried the king.

"And accept it."

"Is there a dower property?" asked one of

the other men. "It is irregular that there not be."

FitzRoger answered that. "Since the lady comes to this marriage more well endowed than I," he said dryly, "it seemed superfluous. The granting of her title to her lands constitutes her dower, since I have just won them back for her."

Crudely put, but accurate. "I accept it as such," Imogen said flatly.

"Good," said the king jovially. "Then I see no impediment and it remains only for all to witness this betrothal."

Imogen took the offered pen and signed her life away, adding the cross that made it a holy vow. She watched as FitzRoger put his signature and cross below hers, and then all the witnesses followed suit, with mark, seal, or letters. She was now committed, for a betrothal was binding and she had freely consented before witnesses. It was a relief of sorts to have no further choice. She felt light-headed and detached from the action and the cheerful voices around her.

She was snapped out of her thoughts when FitzRoger took her hand. "Now you must swear fealty for Carrisford to Henry."

Henry sat, and Imogen rose to kneel before him and place her hands in his, vassal to liege. It was a solemn moment, and one she found joy in, for she had won this honor for herself by courage as great as any knight in the field.

When that was complete, it was time for the oath taking. Her wedding.

FitzRoger eyed her with that same impersonal concern. "It would not be wise to walk across the bailey with open sores on your feet. There is a chair here which can be carried."

Imogen looked bemusedly at the chair he indicated. A simple seat with a back had been attached to two long poles. Two sturdy men stood ready to carry her on them. A sudden relief told her how much she had dreaded having to step out into the mud and dung.

"Thank you," she said. For all he'd done for her, it was the first time she had truly felt grateful.

"Renald arranged it," he said.

She should have known FitzRoger wouldn't have wasted time on her problem when she could always be carried in someone's arms, probably his. She'd had her fill of that. Imogen smiled at the other man and went to sit in the chair.

She clutched the sides as it was hoisted up, then they were on their way in a bizarre kind of procession. Father Wulfgan walked at the front bearing a crucifix and looking as if he wished he were anywhere else in the world but here.

Imogen could sympathize.

Her porters managed to carry her down

the steps from the doorway of the great hall to the castle bailey without tipping her out, and there the inhabitants of Carrisford were crowded to witness the nuptials of their lady and their liberator.

They let out a cheer as the procession appeared. Imogen heard her own name, the king's, and FitzRoger's, but she noticed how few of the crowd were Carrisford people. Many were doubtless busy preparing the feast, but a great number of her people had not yet returned to the castle. The bulk of the crowd around her now were FitzRoger's small army and the king's escort.

It made it clear how illusory any notion of choice had been.

Wulfgan disappeared into the chapel and her porters put the chair down by the church door where a cloth had been laid for her to stand on. More of Sir Renald's thoughtfulness? She saw with a sigh that it had once been a fine embroidered depiction of a hunt which had hung in her father's chamber. It covered the ground adequately enough, but was slashed almost to ribbons. How long would it take to bring her savaged home back to the richness it had once known?

The king came to stand beside her, and FitzRoger took his place on Henry's other side.

Wulfgan reappeared. He had merely put his stole over his patched black robe and looked more suited to a funeral than a wedding, especially in view of his expression. He proceeded to read out the betrothal documents in his deep and sonorous voice, making them sound like a list of crimes awaiting punishment.

"Tyron FitzRoger of Castle Cleeve," he intoned at last. "Do you agree to these dispositions and attest to this being your true and honest mark?"

"I do."

"Imogen of Carrisford. Do you agree to these dispositions and attest to this being your true and honest mark?" He made it sound like the most heinous accusation.

Imogen swallowed. "I do," she whispered.

"And are all here present willing to stand witness to this agreement having been freely made?"

There was a rumble of ayes.

"So be it," said Father Wulfgan in disgust, which wasn't part of the correct procedure. "If you must, get on with it."

Imogen looked around and saw that the king was fighting laughter at this performance. She bit her lip. She wasn't used to finding Father Wulfgan funny, and it felt like a sin. She glanced at her husband-to-be, but he was looking at the priest in that cool, assessing way that boded no good. Any inclination to laugh disappeared.

The king took Imogen's cold right hand,

gave it a little squeeze, then placed it in Fitz-Roger's right hand. Her husband's touch was warm and firm. She then placed her left hand on top of both, making three arms of a cross. The cross was complete when his free hand came over to slip a plain gold ring onto her ring finger.

"With this ring I thee wed," he said, "with this gold I thee honor, and with this dowry I thee endow."

And thank you for my castle back, Lord FitzRoger. Imogen would have liked dearly to avoid the next part, but stiffly she knelt and kissed his hand. "I submit myself to your authority, my lord husband."

Only then did she realize how hard it would be for her to rise again without hurting her feet. She looked up in instinctive appeal.

He put his hands to her waist and lifted her smoothly to her feet. She knew his strength, but again it startled her, for he was not a massive man. He did not release her, but held her there against him. She could feel their bodies move together as they breathed, hear the faint rustle of his gold braid brushing against her silk. She looked up, wondering what he intended.

He lowered his head and gave her the formal kiss, the lightest possible touching of his lips to hers.

"Do you think the old crow intends to

bless us?" he asked against her lips, and with the glint of cynical amusement in his eyes.

Trust Bastard FitzRoger to poke fun at a man of God. "That is no way to speak of a holy priest."

"It's a perfect way to speak of this one," he replied, and stepped away from her.

It appeared Father Wulfgan did intend to bless the union, for he stood ready, hand held high. The married couple turned to face the priest, who looked as if he had swallowed gall.

"It is better to marry than to burn," he intoned. "Marriage is ordained for those who fail to find true union with Christ through blessed chastity. It has some virtue, however, in that through your unclean union you may create those better able to serve God in purity. Pray for it."

Imogen heard some stifled guffaws from the nearby men and flashed an alarmed look around. The king was red in the face, but whether from anger or the desire to laugh she was unsure. She didn't dare look at FitzRoger.

"You are not necessarily consigned to the fires of hell," admitted the priest. "You may still live your lives in a manner pleasing to God. The most noble way is to herewith dedicate yourselves to holy chastity within marriage, perhaps more noble than the life of the cloister, for you must deal with the devil's urgings every day."

He left a hopeful silence, then sighed. "Alas, few are capable of that great trial. Take care, then, to use your body's lust only for procreation. Control it, lest it control you. Be abstinent on Fridays and Sundays, on all holy eves, in Lent and in Advent. Avoid one another whenever possible for fear of the devil's urging and come not together once a child begins to grow. Above all, avoid pleasure in your carnality, for that will surely lead to the birth of monsters."

He gave them a final glare, now more sorrowful than angry, made a sign of the cross, and sang out, "God of Abraham, Isaac and Jacob, bless these young people and sow in their hearts the seed of eternal life."

With that he stalked into his chapel and the door clanged shut behind him.

"By the Rood," said the king. "If the Archbishop of Canterbury had been of that stamp at my wedding, I fear for the future of the country. I'd have been terrified to get Matilda with child."

"They venerate Edward for that saintly penance," FitzRoger said dryly. "You missed your chance at sainthood, Hal."

"I pass it by happily every night I am with my dear Mald." The king gave Imogen a hearty kiss that left her dizzy, and FitzRoger a buffet that almost toppled him. "And that's how it's done, my friend. That kiss you gave her makes me think that sour-mouthed priest has weakened your brain, or at least the parts of you most needed tonight! Going to take up holy chastity after all?"

"Not at all," said FitzRoger, rubbing his arm. "But my carnal urges can wait while my empty stomach can't." He swept up Imogen into his arms and dumped her in her chair. "To the feast!" he declared.

The procession circled the bailey before re-entering the keep. The people cheered, waved hats and scarves, and threw corn for fertility. Children and animals ran around in all directions. Whistles and drums came out to make music.

A woman ran up with a chaplet of celandine and forget-me-not and crowned Imogen. "Bless you and your lord this happy day, lady!"

Imogen's heart began to dance and her doubts eased. No matter what difficulties were to come, she had done her duty by her people and they were truly happy. Her father's death had left these people as well as herself unprotected. Death and suffering had followed. Now, however, because of her marriage they had a new lord, a strong lord, one able to protect them.

Her people had seen FitzRoger at work in Carrisford for the past three days, first fighting, then clearing up the mess, and they were happy with her choice.

She even gave the new lord a tentative

smile and received a cool one in return.

At the base of the steps which led up to the great hall of the keep, FitzRoger's men were gathered. They unsheathed their swords and saluted. He took a pouch from his belt and poured a stream of silver pennies into her hand.

"Largesse," he said. "Since you won't use your own money."

Some of her happiness drained away. The treasure again. He probably thought this marriage entitled him to help himself from the strongboxes, but that was for Carrisford, not Cleeve. She looked down and saw the bracelets on her wrists. She would return these ornaments once she had her own. She should have thought, however, to make provision for this rite.

She threw the coins into the crowd and he did the same. The cheers and blessings intensified.

"Many children, and sturdy!" called a woman waving a gleaming coin.

"God bless you both!" cried another.

"A boy in a ninemonth!"

"Aye!" called a man. "Pound her well tonight, master! Fill her up quick!"

Other lewd suggestions followed.

The rude, raucous shouts swelled up, calling cheerfully of lust and violation. Imogen began to feel as if she were drowning in them. The jovial faces became screaming maws, attacking villains. Then they became Warbrick's men laughing at their lord's rape and awaiting their turn. . . .

She only became aware that her hands were white on the chair when FitzRoger began to prize them off. "Let go," he said as a quiet command. "I insist on carrying you up these stairs, wife, stubborn pride or not."

She was aware only of blind panic, of a desire to escape him and the marriage bed. "I can't . . ."

Then she was in his arms. "Yes, you can," he said. When she squirmed he added shortly, "Don't fight me here, Imogen, or I'll drop you on your sweet behind."

She surrendered. It wasn't his fault God had cursed womankind with such horrible duties, though she couldn't understand why everyone was so jovial about it. Funereal solemnity would seem more appropriate than cheers.

She would dearly like some sympathy.

She wearily rested her cheek against the soft velvet of his tunic, but a bit of gold braid scratched her. She jerked away. "That's typical," she snapped.

"What?"

"You do nothing but hurt me."

He looked down with a frown, and licked quickly at the sting on her cheek. "I made you bleed already? And I will do so again tonight. You're doubtless right in all your misgivings."

She shuddered at this heartless confirmation of her fears.

"Stop shivering, Imogen," he said with more than a touch of impatience. "It's a woman's fate to bleed on her wedding night. Others have survived it, and so will you. If you'll just stop squabbling with me, you'll find this marriage quite tolerable."

She glared up at him. "I am not a child, FitzRoger. Stop treating me as one."

"I will always treat you as you deserve," he said, and it silenced her. She very much feared she was behaving like a child, but she was so frightened. Frightened of everything, but especially of the marriage bed. She shivered again as they moved into the cool of the hall.

He settled her in a chair behind the high table. "You are quivering like an aspen," he remarked with real concern. "I thought you had more spirit than this."

Imogen looked down at the table, covered now by rich cloths. "I have unfortunate memories, my lord. Is that surprising? Doubtless in time they will pass." It was particularly bitter fate, however, that had her eat her bridal feast off the table upon which her maid had been so brutally violated.

She thought she felt the brush of his hand against her shoulder, but perhaps she was mistaken. When she looked up, he was moving toward the bench on her left hand as the king took the chair on her right.

Imogen looked around and had to admit that the feast appeared to have been well done. All the tables were piled with bread and a rich assortment of dishes. It was almost as fine as before Warbrick, but it bothered her that it was a strange finery, not truly that of her home.

Her home, her past, was gone.

Some traces of the familiar remained, however. Gray-haired Siward came forward to bow to the king and to her. Imogen smiled and reached out a hand to him. "You look well, Siward. How happy I am to see you."

"I'm well enough, lady." He grinned. "And better for seeing you in your place with a strong man by your side!"

"Thank you, my man," said the king with a wink.

The seneschal went red with confusion and retreated quickly.

Imogen glanced at FitzRoger, the strong man by her side. People seemed to think she was pleasing herself this day, that she should be happy. She wanted to stand and scream at them that she was making a *sacrifice* for them, one equally as bad as the walk to Cleeve, and this time for a lifetime.

Oh, stop it, she told herself. There's no longer any point in what-ifs and regrets. You've made your bed, Imogen, and will have to lie on it.

Thoughts of bed made her feel sick.

She grasped the ruby glass by her place and drained it.

"We were supposed to have shared the loving cup," FitzRoger said dryly, and summoned a server to refill the handsome goblet. He put his lips to the place where hers had been and drained it in turn. "If we can't share," he commented, "at least we can be equal."

"We are hardly that."

"Are we not? Then entertain the king, wife, while I make do with surly Sir William. Proof of our inequality, I grant you."

Imogen was astonished. He thought she was saying he was her *inferior?* She remembered calling him a nobody; had it drawn blood? She hoped so, even though it was a weapon without an edge. In terms of property brought to this marriage it was true, but it was power that counted, not wealth, and he had all the power.

"That reminds me," she said, and pulled out the key. "You had best keep this, my lord. I have nowhere secure to carry it."

He took the key and turned it in his fingers. "No thanks for my paltry offerings?"

Imogen felt her face flame. "Of . . . of course," she stammered. "It was good of you to think of it."

"But they are not really up to the Carrisford standards? You must make allowances. I wasn't expecting a bride quite so soon. I will commission something more worthy."

"There is no need," said Imogen. "I have plenty . . ."

"When you finally decide to open your treasure house," he completed. "But you must at least allow me to give you a morning gift . . ." — his eyes held hers — ". . . in the morning."

Imogen swallowed. The morning gift would be a symbol of his dowry gift to her, but it would also be testimony that he was satisfied with his wife in all ways. She did intend to be acquiescent, but she wasn't at all sure he would be satisfied.

She turned with relief to the king.

The king had brought his own musicians and was tapping a finger in time with the music. He, too, looked highly satisfied with events. Imogen pushed back a number of bitter comments she could make on the king's care of her, and reminded herself that she was Lady of Carrisford and must be courteous to guests.

As she washed her fingers in the bowl provided, she said, "I must thank you, sire, for coming to my aid."

The king too washed in the perfumed water, then allowed his attendant to dry his hands. "I came as soon as I heard of your plight, Lady Imogen. But it would have been too late, I fear, if you had not saved yourself and enlisted worthy help."

The first dishes were presented and the king selected a choice piece of fowl to place on her trencher. Imogen looked at it. Despite a day's fasting, she wasn't sure she could swallow solid food.

"You think highly of Lord FitzRoger, sire."

"He is a trustworthy friend," said Henry simply, chewing with relish, "and I have few enough of them. He will hold you safe. This is finely cooked."

Whether I want to be held or not. "He is very efficient," Imogen admitted, referring as much to this feast as to anything.

Henry laughed. "The very word! Efficient. He even kills efficiently."

Imogen's appetite diminished even more. She had seen FitzRoger kill, and knew what the king meant. No question of correct knightly behavior, or of quarter, just expeditious slaughter.

She shuddered. She had no doubt Fitz-Roger would slit her throat as dispassionately as he had dispatched that man in the bailey, did he have cause. How many men had he killed? Tens, hundreds? She threw off the macabre thought. A paladin had to be able to kill.

"I am surprised Lord FitzRoger was not already betrothed elsewhere, sire," she said, and attempted a nibble of the chicken.

"Are you? Until recently he was a landless man, and said to be a bastard. He was my friend, but I was a landless man, too. We have both found good fortune, Lady Imogen, and good wives." He toasted her and she felt obliged to smile.

It was strained. Her taunt that FitzRoger was nobody had more edge than she'd thought. A glance to the side showed her FitzRoger engaged in talk. She wished she knew more of his history.

Imogen spoke softly to the king. "For a landless man, he has done well."

"For a landless bastard, he has done remarkably well, and all by the use of his sword, lady. He won his knighthood by merit alone, and survived for years as a mercenary and tourney champion. You have gained one of the foremost soldiers of the age."

Imogen flicked another glance at her husband, but she was not really surprised by that description. She could believe that everything Tyron FitzRoger did, he would do well.

"That's why I want him strong in this part of the country," Henry continued. "He came here with orders to secure Cleeve and make alliance with your father. Matters have turned out even better."

Imogen wanted to protest that dismissal of her father's death and all that had followed, but she knew the king was looking at matters simply in the light of cold strategy. With his brother still likely to try to seize the Crown, Belleme engaged in insurrection, and the Welsh always restive, a loyal power base in the west was essential.

Had FitzRoger made approaches to her father in the last months? It was likely, and she would not necessarily have been informed.

It was strange to think that FitzRoger might consult more with her than her father had.

"If my husband were to fight Warbrick," Imogen asked the king, "would he win?"

"In single combat? Such matters are in the hands of God, Lady Imogen, but Ty hasn't been bested since he became a man."

"And how old is he?" She needed to know.

The king seemed amused by her questions, but indulgent. "Twenty-six. Perhaps I should have been more specific. He hasn't been bested since he was eighteen."

"And who defeated him then, sire?"

"I did," said the king. "It's how we met."

Imogen fiddled with her food, trying to come to terms with her husband.

Twenty-six and one of the foremost soldiers of the age.

Undefeated in single combat, efficient in military matters.

She had called him a nobody. She had challenged him.

She might have to again if he tried to violate their agreement.

She shivered slightly, and he turned, alert.

"You are not eating, Imogen. You should."

Fearing to be forced, Imogen took another bite of saffron chicken and made herself chew and swallow it, though her nervous stomach rebelled.

He frowned slightly and laid a warm hand on her cold one. It felt comforting, but she saw it as imprisonment, and pulled away. He filled the ruby cup again and pushed it toward her.

"Drink, at least."

Imogen obeyed. Her restless anxiety was gaining his attention, and she did not want that, so she tried to look calm and happy as she listened to the musicians and watched the tumblers. She recognized two of the entertainers as the couple that had crossed the causeway into Cleeve that day so long ago — four days ago.

They had been free then, and still were.

She was not free, and had not been free from the day of her birth.

The effort to smile soon made her cheeks ache. She wished this farce of a feast was over except for what must follow.

Two of the king's hounds lay at his feet. When Imogen was faced with a large chunk of beef on her trencher, she slid it down to be snapped up by them. The king noticed, but merely quirked a brow and stopped serving her food.

Imogen was grateful. The only thing that could make this day worse was if she threw up.

She seemed to be the only person present not in the highest spirits.

In the face of the best food and wine, all the men ate heartily and drank deeply. Perhaps FitzRoger would get drunk. She took to watching the goblet she shared with him, but it sat untouched through most of the meal.

Eventually the food was gone and there was only drinking left. There seemed to be an endless supply of good wine.

All from Cleeve.

The noise — drums, pipes, shouts, laughter — seemed to fill her head to bursting.

FitzRoger touched Imogen's hand to gain her attention. "I think it's time we completed this business," he said, as if he could think of a hundred more interesting things to do. "The king has graciously insisted that we use the principal chamber, the one that was your father's. Your woman awaits you there. Don't be afraid. Only the king and a few others need witness the bedding." He smiled slightly. "I don't suppose there's any point in asking Father Wulfgan to bless the nuptial bed, is there?"

"You should not laugh at him," she said angrily to hide the tight hand of panic squeezing her gut. "He is right. Lust is the work of the devil. He told me a newly married couple should abstain for three days to prove that they are in control of the flesh."

To her surprise he kissed her hand. "It won't be as bad as you think, Imogen. I promise you."

"You won't hurt me?" she whispered, hoping against hope for reassurance.

He placed a finger gently over her lips. "Hush. We'll talk later. Go up."

Chapter Ten

Imogen rose to her feet. They gave her little pain, she discovered, perhaps because her mind was so frantic over other problems. As she walked to the stairs, there were some whistles and shouted comments, suddenly hushed. She glanced back, but Tyron FitzRoger was impassive. She knew, however, that with a look he had silenced both his own men and the king's.

She found her father's room subtly altered. She had known FitzRoger had taken it for his own, but she hadn't been prepared. His chests and hangings had replaced those familiar to her. Even though her father's possessions had doubtless been stolen or destroyed by Warbrick, she resented this invasion.

Her father's great bed was the same, however, except that it was now strewn with rose petals. Martha was there, grinning as if this were a joyous event.

Imogen wondered if she was going to disgrace herself after all by fainting onto those rose-strewn sheets. She really did feel very strange. He'd been right again. She should have eaten. This weakness doubtless came of too much rich wine on an empty stomach.

"Come you in, my lady, and let's ready you," said Martha cheerfully. The woman had taken some of the plentiful wine, that much was clear. In no time at all, Imogen found herself stripped naked, her hair combed out again to lie like silk all around her. Despite the warmth of the day, she shivered.

"There now," said Martha. "You mustn't catch cold." She tenderly wrapped a blue wool cloak around Imogen. "You just sit down here and I'll go give the sign you're ready. What a shame you've no family to see you wed, my lady, but never you mind. You've found a good man to hold you fast."

Imogen shivered again.

All too soon the room was invaded by FitzRoger, the king, Renald, and a stranger — one of the king's men. "The Lord Jarrold," the king told her as FitzRoger stripped.

Soon he was naked before her. Imogen hadn't thought she would look, but her eyes took on a will of their own, wandering over his sun-darkened body.

She was surprised at how beautiful it appeared, for it really was not. There were plenty of scars, but they seemed to enhance rather than detract. He was broad in the shoulders and slender of flank, but contoured everywhere with hard muscle without a gentling layer of fat. She could see now how he could be so strong without great bulk.

She met his eyes and saw he was giving her time to look at him, to learn him.

She lowered her eyes and told herself that she had merely been admiring his attributes as a warrior in her service. That was, after all, why she had married him.

She heard laughter and glanced up. Under her horrified eyes, the unalarming softness between his legs began to swell and reach.

"By the sepulcher, your body knows its job," declared Henry jovially. "And no wonder, with such a morsel ready for it."

Martha whipped off Imogen's cloak. She instinctively covered herself with her hands.

"Perfect in every way," declared the king. "Into bed with you both and at it! Make me fine soldiers for England."

Despite the cover it offered, Imogen had to be pushed into the bed by Martha. FitzRoger slid into bed from the other side and, under the covers, held her down with an iron-hard arm.

With a few more jovial comments, the king, the lords, and Martha left.

As soon as they were alone, FitzRoger let Imogen go.

She didn't try to escape. There was no refuge available and her fears were irrational. Fighting them, and determined not to make an undignified scene, she lay still on her back, opened her legs wide, shut her eyes tight, and waited.

Nothing happened. When she could bear the waiting no longer, she opened her eyes a crack and saw him lying on his side, head supported on his hand, watching her.

"Am I doing it wrong?" she asked anxiously. "What should I do?"

"What exactly are you doing?" he queried.

She felt her face flame. "You know."

He leaned forward and kissed her lips gently. "If I know, sweeting, why not let me take charge?"

"Because you always take charge," she said in despair.

"Only when I know what I'm doing," he pointed out with a touch of humor.

"You always think you know what you're doing," she retorted. "Very well, since you know what you're doing, just do it. And I hope I get with child because then we won't have to do it again for a year or so."

"Oh," he said as he slipped an arm around her, "it will be at least a couple of months before we know whether my seed has taken root. We'll have to keep trying until we're sure."

Imogen found herself plastered up against his iron-hard body with that *thing* poking at her. Panic flooded her again, and she pushed away with all her might. "No! I won't! I can't!"

He released her and her own push almost flung her off the bed. "What are you afraid of?" he asked with a frown. "Or why are you so afraid? Everybody does this, and most people find some pleasure in it."

Pleasure! "No, I won't," she said again, wriggling right to the edge of the bed.

He sighed. "Can't you trust me a little, Imogen?"

"No," she said baldly.

His lips tightened. "If you are a flower, Imogen of Carrisford, the best I can imagine is a thistle. Can I at least expect you to do as you're told?"

"Oh, you have me all nicely terrified," she said nastily. "I wouldn't dare disobey the *master.*"

"Good," he said. He gripped her arm and dragged her into the middle of the bed, then moved so he was half on top of her. When she pushed at him, he said, "Stop that."

She did.

"Good again. Now lie still."

Trembling at the look in his eyes, she did so, and opened her legs. "Close your legs," he said quietly. "I don't like you lying there like a sacrificial offering. Try to relax."

"Relax!" she repeated incredulously, but got no response.

His callused hand moved onto her body near the hip and began to travel. It was a firm touch. A stroke. It moved over her belly and up her ribs to her shoulder. She couldn't imagine what the purpose of it was but had to admit that it was pleasant. She even liked the slight abrasion of his hand's roughness against her delicate skin.

"You're not a thistle," he said softly. "Your skin is like rose petals. . . ."

He moved away from her a little so that he could stroke parts of her as yet untouched, parts never before touched by a man. He ran his hand up her thigh, his thumb brushing the curls there before moving up to circle her belly.

She squirmed. "What are you doing?"

"Gentling you." The sun was almost down, but there was enough light left to show her his fine-drawn impassive features. He did not look lustful, but as if he concentrated on things other than the physical. This was not what she had expected at all.

"Gentling me?"

He glanced at her with a flash of humor. "Like a high-strung filly."

"I am not a horse," she muttered, but even so she could feel herself grow soft and warm as that hand roamed over her skin.

"That's good." His hand brushed over her right breast, then her left. "Father Wulfgan would definitely not approve."

She grabbed his hand with both of hers. "Stop that! He said that was one of the worst sins, to let a man touch me there!"

With a twist he captured both her hands in his and held them over her head. "Did he warn you about this?" His mouth came down to her nipple and covered it.

Imogen screamed at full pitch. He let go of her wrists and her breast and clapped a hand over her mouth. "For the Lord's sake!"

She looked up over his hand and saw amusement and exasperation. He was infuriating. When he relaxed his clasp she bit him.

He flung himself out of the bed. "I don't believe this," he said, shaking his sore hand. "I'm beginning to think we'll have to do it your way after all."

Imogen looked at him, fixated by the phallus sticking straight out in front. *Just* like Warbrick. "No," she said, and scuttled as far away as the bed would allow. "I want to go to a cloister."

He looked at her coldly. "Don't be such a coward."

"The marriage isn't consummated," she said desperately. "It can be annulled. You have no right to keep me from being a Bride of Christ. Father Wulfgan says —"

He pointed a finger at her. "Say one more word about that priest and he dies."

She gasped.

He came back to the bed and covered himself, put out a long arm, and pulled her against him again. She wriggled to try to escape, but she might as well have tried to escape iron bands. That *thing* pressed against her thigh like an oaken staff. She pushed back mightily and made no impression at all.

He blew softly against her ear and his voice was warm as he said, "Unless, of course, you want to list all the things he says will send us to hell so I can demonstrate? I suspect I've acquired the best informed virgin in England."

She could never break free and so she stopped trying. "You're a heretic," she protested weakly. "You make fun of a living saint . . ."

He turned her and pressed her flat on the bed on her stomach, hand hard in her lower back. When she didn't struggle, his hand started to wander again, this time over her back. It was magic. Father Wulfgan had not said anything about a hand on the back. Imogen allowed herself to relax and enjoy it.

"Your body is God's own creation," he said softly as his hand explored her spine. "And a fine piece of work it is."

"The flesh should be mortified," she breathed.

"I'll whip you if you insist on it."

She chuckled. "As if I would."

"Good. I wouldn't enjoy marking this satiny smoothness . . ." His hand was tracing the curve of her buttocks.

Imogen wriggled, her breath catching.

"What interests me," FitzRoger murmured against her ear, so his warm breath tickled it and made her squirm even more, "is where the good father learned just how evil carnality can be."

Imogen was aware of melting, of bones grown soft and muscles grown weak. "He always says he was once a wicked man," she breathed.

"His replacement will be pure from birth," he promised.

Imogen's bones and muscles regained their strength. She pushed up to look him in the eye. "He's my priest and he stays, FitzRoger. I rule Carrisford."

"Under my advice," he reminded her, pushing her down again. "I'm not having that man here."

She pushed up again, but before she could give him her opinion of that, he flipped her over and covered her lips with his own. His leg held her down and one hand wove in her hair so she couldn't escape.

She resolutely kept her teeth and lips tightly closed.

After a while he moved very slightly back. "Open them."

She shook her head.

"I think we're back to you doing as you're told, Imogen," he warned.

"You are —" His lips met hers, soft and gentle, and she found she didn't want to fight him over this. She enjoyed his kisses, and kisses couldn't be so very wicked. When his tongue ran quickly along her inner lip, she shivered with the remembered fire.

When he pushed farther to touch his tongue to hers, she jerked back, remembering more of Father Wulfgan's warnings. If a man put his tongue in a woman's mouth, it triggered a poison, and the woman died. . . .

FitzRoger would not let her escape, though. She fought him, but his tongue invaded her mouth. . . .

No poison burst forward to kill her.

Imogen surrendered to the magical sensation. Just perhaps Father Wulfgan was mistaken about a few things. After all, as FitzRoger said, how would a living saint know?

She felt him relax in response to her surrender. He turned her head this way and that, their tongues meeting in his mouth and hers. She tasted the moist warmth of him and was lost.

Imogen only slowly began to notice that he was rubbing their bodies together at the hip as if he wanted to get at her. It was coming, then, was it? Well, she knew it had to. This kissing was all very well, but it couldn't put off the other forever. He was trying to give her something sweet, like honey to help the medicine down. She remembered her words: "You do nothing but hurt me." He'd admitted it would be that way tonight.

She reminded herself it wasn't his fault. She'd never thought God had been very fair to Eve and her daughters, but God was God.

Was it time to open her legs yet?

The long kiss ended and Imogen braced for the onslaught, but his head moved down in one long lick to her breast.

Oh no. What a penance she'd have to do! She grabbed his hair.

"Let go."

No one could deny that tone of command. Her hands fell limp onto his shoulders. "It's not my fault, God," she muttered, and heard what sounded like a groan.

Then his tongue circled her nipple. It felt most strange. Next it flicked at her nipple and she shivered.

"That is a sin," she whispered.

"No it isn't," he said with such authority that she didn't dare protest again.

Shivery feelings were swirling around her body. His mouth moved to her other breast. It settled on it, warm and wet, and he began to suckle like a baby. The most extraordinary sensation shot through her and her whole body tensed. She gripped his hair again, but not to pull him away.

Imogen took in a great shuddering breath. An ache was growing within her, bringing a fever to her mind. Her hips moved of themselves and she clutched more desperately at him.

He kept sucking and nibbling as his hand wandered, dizzying her. Her hips heaved as if

possessed. Her whole body was hot, writhing, and twitching.

"I'm tormented by devils!" she cried.

He looked up, eyes dark and bright. "And you know how we have to drive them out, don't you, sweeting?" His hand slid between her thighs, which opened wide at his touch. Imogen instinctively closed them, but he was already within.

"Truly?" she gasped. She stared at him as her hope of salvation. "I can't bear this."

"They'll torment you forever unless we do. Now it's time to open your legs."

She obeyed and his fingers moved against her. She whimpered.

"Do you feel a pain here?" he asked.

"Yes," she said, but hesitantly, for she wasn't sure it was exactly a pain, but whatever it was was getting worse.

She stared at him. His eyes were darkened, his cheeks flushed with color. He looked warm and soft again, and the change she saw in him seemed to make the devils in her dance more wildly.

His fingers slid up within her a little, rotating. "And here?" he whispered.

Imogen closed her eyes and it was as if she could see inside herself to a swirling pit of demons, cavorting and jabbing at her with fiery brands. Something cramped beyond where his fingers moved. "Higher," she gasped.

"That's why I'm equipped to go higher, Imogen. To rid you of your devils."

Oh, now it all made sense. She thrust up urgently against his hand. He moved it against the throbbing ache, but the torment just intensified. Instinct, not duty, drove her to stretch herself wider to him. "Do it then," she gasped. "I'm going to die!"

"No you're not," he said huskily. "Your paladin is going to save you."

He was between her legs and she felt that hardness against her ache. "Yes," she said. "Oh yes."

"Yes," he said, as breathlessly as she. "You're a hard woman to save from the devils, Imogen of Carrisford."

The devils were spreading throughout her body. She clutched him. "Hurry!" she cried out. "Hurry!" She felt him begin to fill her, stretching her. The tightness was astonishing and came close to pain, but it was promising relief from the greater torment. "So good," she muttered. "So good."

"Yes," he groaned and kissed her. With his mouth hot and soft over hers he breathed, "My flower, my treasure, my ultimate pleasure. . . ."

That shocked her eyes open. *"Pleasure!"* It was as if Wulfgan himself loomed over the bed. "No!" she shrieked, and pushed against him with all her might. "Think of our children!"

His jaw clenched and his eyes shot green fire. "Wulfgan is dead," he promised grimly, and pushed into her.

Pain, excruciating pain, struck. God's judgment!

Imogen kicked and squirmed. "You're a devil yourself! Sweet Savior, help me!"

Now she knew why Janine had screamed.

She beat at him, crying. "Stop. Please stop." It was like trying to move a boulder. She went for his eyes. He seized her wrists and stilled her breathlessly.

"Imogen. Stop this."

His voice came from a distance. She saw only Warbrick thrusting into her screaming maid, felt only a monstrous imprisonment and invasion, and terrible, terrible pain. Powerless before his great strength, Imogen echoed Janine's plea, with the same tearful despair. "Sweet Mary, aid me!"

She was free.

Imogen rolled out of the bed and huddled on the floor, shaking so she feared she was rattling the castle walls. She couldn't bring herself to look to see if the monster was coming after her.

Then she heard the click of the latch. It was like a key turning, bringing back sanity, bleak sanity, to her tangled mind. Fearfully she uncurled from her defensive position enough to peer over the bed at the room.

It was empty.

He had gone. FitzRoger had gone.

Imogen broke into soul-shaking sobs that spoke of relief, and anguish, and a deep mysterious loss.

When Renald de Lisle finally found his small wall chamber — a somewhat difficult matter after the quantity of wine he'd drunk — he found the bridegroom lying on the narrow bed, hands behind his head, staring at the beams. In the small amount of dying sun slicing in the slit window, it was hard to see anything except Ty's shape.

Renald struggled for his wits but still couldn't think of anything safe or sensible to say.

It was Ty who spoke. "I said I didn't bruise flowers," he said. "I lied."

Renald looked at the flagon of wine he was carrying. There wasn't much left, but he sloshed it into a wooden cup and set it by the bed. "Went hard, did it?" he said, not really believing it. Ty had tricks enough and the girl had been practically eating out of his hand these last few days.

Ty was completely immobile, which was a very bad sign. Renald hoped it wasn't the little bride his friend wanted to kill, for he supposed he'd have to try to save her, which was to greet death himself.

"You were right about the priest," Ty said at last, quite calmly. "I was too clever by far there." After a long, heavy silence, he added, "Keep him out of my sight."

So that's who he wanted to kill. Renald hadn't the slightest idea what had happened in the marriage bed, but dealing with Father Wulfgan seemed a simple enough matter. "I'll sh-send him on his way tomorrow."

Silence.

"Now?" Renald queried, knowing himself incapable.

"He will stay as long as Imogen wishes him to stay."

Renald gave up and let his wine-sodden legs buckle so he was sitting on the floor, leaning against the bed. "There'sh wine by your head. Plenty more below . . . Get drunk. I am."

"That's obvious." Two strong arms hooked under Renald's and hauled him onto the narrow bed. Ty's steps moved away.

Renald couldn't keep his eyes open and it was too dim to be a useful effort anyway, but he struggled to use his brain. He knew he was needed here and wished to Jerusalem he hadn't drunk so deep.

He'd thought a full-blooded celebration was in order.

"Wha' happened?" he asked.

There was no audible emotion in his friend's voice when he replied. "Nothing extraordinary. Go to sleep, Renald. I may be lacking in many respects, but I'm still capable of handling a military emergency if one should arise."

Renald heard the curtain rustle as his friend left.

By the wounds, he wished he hadn't drunk so deep. But the drink took him anyway.

Imogen didn't know what had happened to her, except that time had passed. Had she slept? Fainted?

The room that had been bloodred with the setting sun was now silvered by the moon. It was her father's room, where she had always been safe; the place she'd played as a child, and come to as she grew to ask questions and discuss problems.

Now, however, it was no longer safe. It was tainted by an alien smell and troubling memories.

Violence. Death. Corpses. . . .

Memory clicked in.

Bastard FitzRoger. Her husband.

She shuddered as she remembered what had occurred. She remembered it all, the pleasure and the pain.

Pleasure? Yes, she remembered pleasure. She remembered, too, her husband's face when matters had been right between them. He'd let his mask fall for her, and she'd seen the man, and the soul within the man.

So briefly sweet.

Then she'd fought him, and screamed. She'd seen him as Warbrick, monstrous and vicious.

He'd left her.

She was sure the mask was back firmly in place.

She covered her face with shame.

What had she done?

She could try to blame FitzRoger for the disaster. She could say that he should have waited, given her longer to grow accustomed, but he'd been gentle with her. She remembered begging him to do what he was doing and do more of it.

Until the pain.

Had it been the pain she'd fought, or the pleasure? The pain had been far worse than she'd imagined, but the pleasure had frightened her too. Frightened her into her worst nightmares.

Father Wulfgan was right. Pleasure did lead straight to hell.

FitzRoger seemed to think that pleasure in the marriage act was not wrong, but he had not been to the Holy Land and been nailed to a cross for his faith. He did not fast most days of the year and whip himself with metal-tipped thongs.

And now FitzRoger was proved to be wrong, for the terror and pain that had come between them must be a punishment for their lust. If he'd simply entered her, it would surely have gone much better.

Imogen knew she had virtue, harsh virtue, on her side — but still, her instinct said that she had done very badly this night.

What must FitzRoger have felt, with her screaming and fighting beneath him as he did only as he thought best?

Could she do otherwise next time?

Imogen rested her head on the bed. She wished she had someone, anyone, to advise her, or even just to hold her. "Father, Father," she moaned. "Why did you have to die? It was so . . . so *careless* of you! I need to talk to you."

She gave a choke of laughter. She could almost hear her practical father pointing out that if he hadn't so carelessly died she would not be in this predicament. *And, Imogen, my darling, you must grow up, and quickly.*

Imogen sat up straight. It was almost as if she *could* hear her father, here in the room where they had shared their most precious private times.

You have been plunged into a torrent of the evils I tried so hard to spare you. But you have chosen your course — not a bad course — and you must see it through.

Was she going mad? Imogen didn't know, but this moment of communication was too precious to risk with skepticism. She closed her eyes tightly and framed a question. *Do you approve of him, Father?*

He is not what I would have chosen for you, my child. I confess I had a father's distaste for giving you to a lusty young stallion. But he will serve you well if you let him. And re-

member that you must serve him.

In the marriage bed?

Not only in that. Perhaps least of all in that, daughter. No man is so strong as to be able to stand alone. Look to your husband's needs.

Needs? Imogen tried to imagine how FitzRoger might need her other than as bed partner and mother to his children. He had perhaps hinted that she should manage the domestic arrangements at Cleeve, and as his wife that was now her duty.

That must be what her father meant, but this did not address her current problem. She must learn to tolerate the marriage bed.

What of Father Wulfgan? she asked. *Is he right about lust?*

She could swear she could hear the worldly humor that had marked Bernard of Carrisford. *Saints are sent to irritate our tenderest spots rather than ease us, Imogen, and Wulfgan is very good at irritating. That is why I brought him to Carrisford, for I was always a worldly man, but I had heed to my soul and knew I needed the goad of a stern conscience. But even saints do not always know the truth, daughter. Have you forgotten your lessons? Listen respectfully to all who have the authority to advise you, but take the decision from within your own heart. And then accept the consequences.*

Accept the consequences.

"Sweet heaven," she murmured. "Consequences."

What would be the consequences of this night's work?

She had to do something.

She leaped up and pulled on her clothes. She didn't know what she should do, except that she must find her husband.

Where was he?

She went to peep out of the door, hoping that he would be hovering there. He wasn't. She could hear raucous celebration still going on in the hall. There seemed a remarkable amount of feminine squealing, but she couldn't be distracted by that. She supposed the castle women were enjoying themselves, too.

Where would FitzRoger have gone? Surely he wouldn't have rejoined the carouse below on his wedding night. That would be to shame her terribly.

Perhaps she deserved that shame. She rubbed away tears and made herself think. There were other rooms and wall chambers, but on instinct she took the narrow circular staircase which led up to the battlements.

She found her husband there, standing by the battlements, looking out as if on guard at a landscape washed white by the large low moon.

FitzRoger was not on guard. On the far side of the square space the watchcorn was keeping watch, horn and bell at the ready to sound alarm.

FitzRoger was still and calm, but something about him stabbed a pain near Imogen's heart, a pain that was largely guilt.

She didn't want to deal with this. She wanted to creep away and let someone else sort everything out, but she was done with such weakness. She said a brief prayer to her father and walked over to her husband.

He sensed her at the last moment and spun around, a knife flashing in his hand, halted inches from her body.

He let out a hissing breath. "Don't ever creep up on me, Imogen."

"I'm sorry," she said shakily. "I didn't think . . ."

She could swear he was shaken too. "Start thinking," he said sharply.

Imogen bit her lip. She wanted to speak of things that had to be said, but not when he was angry, and not where the watchcorn would hear every word.

He must have caught her anxious glance at the studiously oblivious guard, for he moved away from the battlements, silently leading the way to the stairs, back down to their room.

Imogen grabbed his arm — she couldn't go back there yet — then jerked her hand away from his hard flesh as if burned.

He stopped and looked at her. In the chill moonlight he seemed to be carved of stone, cold stone. Then he moved. Almost hesitantly, he put a hand on her waist, and the

251

hand was warm. When she made no retreat, he drew her gently against him, his arms encircling her.

Imogen shuddered as she leaned her head against his shoulder. She hadn't known how much she needed to be held.

Tears swelled in her, and she knew it would do her good to weep here within the strong encompassment of his arms, but her tears would surely hurt him and she had hurt him enough. She won the aching battle with them.

It was comfort enough just to be held. She hoped it was comfort for him to hold her. . . .

It was only when he softly said, "There is a perfectly good bed below," that she realized she was drifting off to sleep. Perhaps had slept.

She stirred and saw from the position of the moon that quite some time had passed.

"You need sleep, too," she said, and realized it was an invitation of sorts. She hoped it was not an invitation to disaster.

She couldn't read him. He was more relaxed than before, but guarded. Without a word, he guided her toward the stairs with his hand on her back, then went down their blackness ahead of her.

The castle was quiet now. The carouse must finally be over.

The solar seemed strangely normal when

they reentered it, though eerie in the moon-light. She had expected it to be marked by what had occurred.

Still he didn't speak, so Imogen braced herself to break the silence. "I'm sorry," she said. "I didn't behave at all well."

He was standing calmly in the center of the room. "What has that to do with it? I'm sorry I couldn't make it easier for you."

His flat tone bruised her. She wished she could explain some of the devils he hadn't been able to exorcise, but the words would choke her. "I'm sure it will be better next time," she offered.

She saw rather than heard the sigh. "Go to bed." He turned toward the door.

"Where are you going?" she cried in alarm.

He turned back. "It's all right. You hardly ate at the feast, and I'd forgotten that you probably took that business of fasting seriously. You'll feel better with some food in you."

"You mean you didn't fast?" she asked in dismay.

"No," he said, and she could almost feel his effort at patience. "And if you give birth to rabbits, Imogen, I vow I'll make pil-grimage to Jerusalem on my knees."

"Oh, don't say that!"

"Imogen, women do not give birth to rab-bits."

"With God all things are possible." She won-dered if he were heretic enough to deny *that*.

"Doubtless. But I'm sure God has better things to do with his omnipotence."

Imogen bit her lip. That sounded both true and sacrilegious. "And the monsters?" she asked.

He moved back, a step closer to her. "Imogen, women do give birth to strange children — crippled, even lacking limbs. I once saw a babe like a Cyclops, with only one eye. You must have seen some unfortunates, even in Carrisford. But I don't believe God made them that way as punishment for adultery or unseemly pleasure. I've seen animals similarly deformed. Did they also enjoy themselves too much?"

Imogen couldn't think what to say to that. She *had* once seen a lamb with six legs.

He touched her cheek very gently, and she could swear there was a trace of a smile on his face. "My biggest crime, I think, is to forget how young and naive you are. Sometimes you are so brave and strong. Go to bed. I'll be back shortly."

Chapter Eleven

Young and naive. That hurt, though it was doubtless true. She was trying, though. Did that count for nothing? He had said that sometimes she was brave and strong, and that comforted her.

When he'd gone, Imogen made a light and lit a candle, then remade the bed. She distastefully brushed all the crushed rose petals onto the floor. A perfume rose from them but it didn't please her; she preferred the other smell, the musky one which she recognized as his.

She stood looking at the bed, hands clasped tight. He thought her problem was just religious scruples, but she knew in her heart it wasn't. It was that other, darker, fear that lay between them, only exacerbated by Wulfgan's preaching.

She didn't want the fear, but she didn't seem to be able to control it. Such a thing should surely be under her control. When she was clearheaded, like now, she knew FitzRoger was no Warbrick, that he was not trying to rape her, that she wanted to be joined with him.

At the time, however, it had been like rats. No amount of thought could stop her fleeing a rat. Nothing could make her willingly touch one. She was sure that it was that fear that had caused the pain. Was it possible that nothing could make her welcome his invasion of her body?

She covered her face with her hands. That would surely be hell.

It *had* to be within her control.

Imogen gathered her courage and slipped out of her clothes and between the cool sheets, clearing her mind so that she would behave properly this time.

She brought to mind some holy martyrs. If Saint Catherine could endure the wheel, and Saint Agatha having her breasts cut off . . . Too late, she remembered that these stories supported Wulfgan's preaching, for the martyrs had been punished — and sanctified — for refusing to sully themselves with men.

She thought instead of the walk to Cleeve, which had been horrible and frightening, but it had to be done and so she had done it. This too was something that had to be done.

FitzRoger came in with a piled trencher, a flagon, and two goblets. Thoughts both noble and philosophical were swamped by simple hunger. Imogen's stomach rumbled and she sat up in the bed eagerly. With a quizzical smile, he placed the food before her. She grabbed a piece of cold saffron chicken and bit into it with a sound in her throat that was almost a purr.

It was gone quickly and she began on an almond honey cake, ending by licking the crumbs from her fingers. Suddenly embarrassed by her greed, she looked up at him. He was watching her, catlike, but did not seem to be displeased. He offered her a goblet of wine.

She tried a smile as she reached for it. "Thank you, my lord."

He held on to the silver goblet when she would have taken it. "Tyron," he corrected. "Or Ty. Or even Bastard, if you wish."

She tentatively allowed herself to tease. "Bastard," she said.

His lips twitched and he gave up the goblet.

"Do you not mind?" she asked, watching him over the rim.

"I've been called that all my life behind my back, but I've killed men who used it to my face."

She considered him. He was being pleasant, but the mask was firmly in place. She wished he'd let it drop again. "What will you do to me, then, if I use it?"

"I've given you permission, haven't I? And if you need someone to mortify your flesh, I'm sure Wulfgan will oblige." She saw him catch himself on that spurt of irritation. He went on calmly, almost lightly. "However, if you call me Bastard in public, wife, you can

257

explain the ramifications of my mother's relationship with Roger of Cleeve."

Imogen felt as if she were tiptoeing through daggers, but that deliberate use of the word *wife* strengthened her. He was not rejecting her. "What are the ramifications, then?" she asked.

He moved to lie on the bed, his back to one of the foot-posts, facing her. His shoes almost touched her knees. "My mother married Roger of Cleeve and I have documents to prove it, though he sought to have them destroyed. When the marriage became inconvenient, he had it annulled on the grounds that I wasn't his child. I was born a month early and he could prove that nine months before he had been in England."

"Were you small?"

"Very. That didn't concern him, or count with the Church court he took the case to. The bishop found a generous donation to his coffers much more interesting."

"But now your birth is validated."

"Yes. Money and power now weigh the other side of the scale."

Imogen almost protested that sounded remarkably irreverent, but she held her tongue.

He carried on. "It was made easier, of course, by the fact that there is no contesting heir."

"Your half brother Hugh being conveniently dead." Then she wished she *had* held her tongue. It was said Hugh choked at the table, but there were rumors . . .

It was a particular look in his eyes that distracted Imogen. She realized she was sitting up naked in the bed for this meal and conversation. With a squeak she moved to slip under the covers, but — lightning fast — he snared the sheet.

She remembered her good intentions and froze. Her heart was pounding, and she knew she must be rose-red, but she didn't fight him.

"You're lovely," he said. "There's no reason to hide from me."

"Modesty," she countered, then bit her lip.

A momentary lowering of his lids was all the evidence of the impatience she knew he felt. "It isn't immodest for you to be naked before your husband," he said in that same calm, authoritative voice he had used before. Situation and memory combined to render Imogen miserably self-conscious.

He tossed the sheet over her and left the bed. Imogen knew she'd failed again. What on earth was she to do about all this? Despite good intentions, she feared that if he tried again to consummate the marriage, the same terrible thing would happen.

But without it, they were not truly wed.

He was standing by the narrow window looking out at the bailey, his arm raised against the wall. It was shadowy in that dark corner of the room, but the muted moonlight deepened the angles of his body and made him appear even harder than he was.

But she had seen tonight that he was not hard.

"I wish you would come to bed," she whispered into the gray half-light. "Please." She knew it might sound like an invitation to repeat his act and she didn't want that. But she knew it would be disastrous if he stayed by that window all night long.

She thought he would refuse, but then he stripped off his clothes and joined her. He lay on his side again, and played with a strand of her hair. "What would you do if I started all over again, I wonder?"

Imogen swallowed. "Submit," she said bravely.

"That's what I thought. Go to sleep, Ginger. We both need our sleep."

When Imogen awoke it was bright daylight outdoors and she was alone in the bed. She leaned up to scan the room, but he was not there. Dread leaped into her. An unconsummated wedding night. What was going to happen to her now?

She heard men and horses in the bailey and shot upright in the bed. He was leaving!

Before she could act, the door opened and FitzRoger came in. Imogen grabbed for the sheet, then stopped herself, trying not to mind her nakedness, absorbing the vast relief that he was still here.

Unless he had come to announce his departure.

He picked up her shift from the floor and tossed it to her. As soon as she was in it, he opened the door wide and two servants came in to lay a cloth on a table and spread meat, bread, and ale.

When they were gone, her husband said, "Good morning. You look well rested."

"Yes." Then she wondered if that was the wrong answer. Should she have lain awake worrying? Had he? The idea seemed ridiculous, and he looked his usual unruffled, austere self.

He gestured to the table and she climbed out of bed and joined him there. She picked up a bread roll, wishing she could think of something light and clever to say. The fresh, warm bread reminded her of the bread she had eaten at Cleeve. If she hadn't traveled there, what would have become of her?

Warbrick, perhaps. She'd be dead in that case, for she would have killed herself. On this sweet, sunny day with birds singing and the smell of the warm earth in the air she was glad to be alive.

She might have made it through to the king, though. Then she would have been delivered to FitzRoger without the chance to make terms.

Perhaps she could have insisted that there

had been an agreement that she wed Lancaster. She thought of Lancaster in the marriage bed. His hands were fleshy and clammy. He licked his lips a lot so they always appeared moist, and bad teeth made his breath foul. She knew with certainty that scream as she might, Lancaster would not have halted the consummation. . . .

"What's the matter?" FitzRoger asked her alertly.

"Nothing."

She could see he didn't believe her. All his formidable attentiveness was now focused on her; she was a problem to be solved. It unnerved her.

"Are people up yet?" she asked.

He poured her some ale and she downed it in a gulp.

"A few bleary servants and the unfortunate guards who pulled duty last night. I gather," he added dryly, "everybody except them had an excellent time."

Except us, thought Imogen, and concentrated on her bread. "I suppose I should go down and organize things . . ."

"Hardly. We are allowed some indulgence. Or at least, you are. Hal is already up and raring for a hunt." He took a piece of meat and bit into it.

Imogen looked up, feeling she was being pushed into her pampered corner again. "I like to hunt," she challenged.

"Not today you don't."

"Am I to be confined to my room, then?"

He made a sudden movement, abruptly controlled. "Imogen, Carrisford is yours. Go where you want. Do as you wish. Hunt if you wish. I'm sure my reputation can stand the implications, and you obviously don't care about yours."

Then she understood and blushed. If she rode all day, people would know the marriage had not been consummated, or would think that she had not been a virgin. "I won't hunt," she said.

"As you will."

She shook her head miserably. Those moments of warmth before the disaster had been brief but potent. She could not forget them, and she wanted them back. She wanted to discuss what had happened, now, in the safety of daylight. She wanted to tell him of her demons, and apologize for her silliness. She couldn't think of words that wouldn't choke her.

"What you need," he said briskly, "is some women. Do you have relatives who would come to live with you?"

She shook her head. Since he was looking away, she had to force words out. "No. There was just my . . . my aunt. My father has . . . had relatives in Flanders, but they are strangers. . . ."

"I will arrange something. For the immediate, I will ask for some nuns from Hillsborough. I'm sure you will be comfortable with such companions."

"Very well." Imogen was more concerned with ways to melt FitzRoger's icy shell than with companions.

She wanted the teasing, relaxed companion back. The longing was a physical pain in her chest, deepened by the fact that she had doubtless made it impossible. He would not seek such a disastrous scene again.

He would have to.

Unless he abandoned subtlety and raped her.

"Don't look at me like that," he said sharply. "I'm not going to attack you again." He rose from the table, flipped open a chest and grabbed a pair of hawking gloves and a whip, then headed for the door. "Rest."

Trying for humor, Imogen said, "Is that an order?"

He was already at the door. He looked back and shook his head. "Do as you wish. Carrisford is yours. You've earned it."

From her window Imogen watched the hunt leave. The king must have a hard head, for he and FitzRoger appeared to be the only ones really relishing a day in the saddle. The rest hauled themselves onto their horses as if their muscles were string and their heads fire. Imogen couldn't help but giggle, especially when one knight mounted only to topple off the other side.

As if sensing her, FitzRoger looked up. His face assumed an appropriately fond expression and he blew a kiss. Imogen didn't have to force a smile as she shyly waved.

The king said something. She guessed from his gesture that he was offering to allow her husband to stay behind. FitzRoger refused and made a remark that caused humor among those nearby. Imogen knew it would have been something lewd, but that was expected of a bridegroom.

The falconers came out with the hawks and some men took their own on their wrists. Her husband did. It was a fine peregrine, and the cruel head sought his voice, the neck curved under his gentle touch.

In what condition were her mews? And what of her own merlin? There were so many parts of Carrisford she still had not even considered. She feared the worst.

Leashed hounds strained, pulling their handlers toward the gate and the open country. There had been no sign of her father's fine dogs since the sack. They must have been stolen or killed.

The king gave the signal and the party streamed out.

And the horses. What of the horses? She sighed, having little hope that her snow-white palfrey, Ysolde, had escaped Warbrick.

Trapped by her feet, and by her tangled obsession with FitzRoger, she had not even begun to face her responsibilities. Now it was time. It was also time to go to her treasure store and put the administration of Carrisford on the right footing. It was not so much a distrust of FitzRoger anymore as a desire to prove herself responsible and worthy.

Worthy of him.

On the other hand, she had to admit that she didn't want to give him free access to the treasure.

Could she both trust and not trust a man at the same time?

Yes. She trusted him in personal matters, but she didn't trust him not to put his interests and those of the king before hers. Both FitzRoger and the king were new men and power-hungry. Her husband wanted to make Cleeve great, and the king wanted a power base in this part of the country. Imogen didn't oppose those aims, but her first priority was to restore Carrisford.

She scowled down at her feet, for she didn't want to go through the dusty passageways to the treasure chamber barefoot. Again she tried a pair of shoes but could feel the pressure on sensitive spots. She *could* wear them for a while, but the price would be to undo most of the healing. She muttered a few curses that would have gained her a scolding from her aunt and a severe penance from Father Wulfgan.

Where was Martha? She wasn't much of an attendant, but she was all Imogen had. The woman was doubtless still sleeping off the carouse.

Imogen decided she could do without Martha. Though she had never done such a thing before in her life, she dressed herself. It was no difficulty to get into a simple kirtle and tunic, though it was hard to arrange the garments pleasingly when she could not see herself.

She brushed out her hair, but trying to plait it proved beyond her; it was too long and thick. When she tried, the plaits did not look right at all. She would have to leave it loose.

As a married lady she was entitled to wear a veil on her head, but she didn't have such a thing or anything to hold it on. A check of FitzRoger's jewel chest proved that it contained no circlets. She could use a circle of cloth, as serf women did, but that seemed to be more lowering than going bareheaded.

She had plenty of circlets in the treasure chamber.

She clicked her tongue with frustrated impatience.

In the end she abandoned the effort to look matronly and went down the hall barefoot, with her hair uncovered and loose to her thighs. If anyone cared to make a scandal out of it, they could. She knew no one would even try to make a scandal out of anything Bastard FitzRoger's wife did. There was pride in that thought.

When she took in the scene in the hall, she bit her lip on laughter. There was such an air of fragility. Judging from the condition of the survivors, it certainly had been a magnificent debauch. Renald de Lisle was sprawled at the high table, his head in his hands.

Imogen walked up behind him. "Good morning, Sir Renald."

Even though she'd spoken quietly, he jerked as if she'd yelled, but then he gathered his manners and stood unsteadily to seat her.

"Good morning, little flower." He looked at her rather closely and said, "You appear none the worse for wear." Then he winced at his own words.

"I am none the worse, thank you," said Imogen, then colored at the admission that could be. Surely he wouldn't take it as such. She did not want to give anyone a hint that her wedding night had been incomplete. "In fact," she added quickly, "I would have said that I am in better shape than most of the castle today. You chose not to hunt?"

"I am left behind in command. I'm not sure if that was a kindness or not. My whole body rebels at the thought of riding, but those men will come back from a day in the open air in a better state than I will be."

A woman sauntered into the hall, hitching her loose gaudy gown up over lush breasts. She strolled over to a table and poured herself a goblet of ale, running a casual hand over the shoulder of a nearby guard. Just as casually the guard put an arm around her and pulled her close.

"Who is that?" Imogen demanded. "That woman isn't from Carrisford!"

Renald sat up sharply, then cursed and clutched his head. "Visitor," he said. "I'll send her on her way."

"But who . . . ?" Imogen realized there were a few other strange women about and none of them seemed to be doing any work. "The lazy sluts!" She was half on her feet when Renald tugged her down.

"Hush! Don't make a fuss." He looked slightly harassed. "They're whores from Hereford."

Imogen gaped. *"In my castle?* Is this FitzRoger's doing?"

"Keep your voice down!" he hissed, wincing in pain. "Yes, but you don't know Beauclerk. He's a lusty man, and those with him follow his style. If you didn't want every woman in Carrisford unable to walk today, we had to bring some in."

Imogen opened and shut her mouth a few times. "Very well," she said at last, "but I won't have them in my hall, king or not."

"Of course not. I'll see to it, but without a

fuss. Ty should have . . ." He slid her a look. "He's not quite himself this morning."

Imogen kept her face calm. So the efficiency had slipped a little. She was pleased to know it. She lowered her eyes demurely. "It doubtless takes some getting used to, being a married man."

"I'm sure it does. And how do you feel about being a married woman?"

She glanced at him, wondering at his tone. But even between her husband and Renald there must be some secrets. "What choice did I ever have?" she asked, standing and shaking out her skirts. "At the moment I am more concerned about being Lady of Carrisford. Remove those women from my hall, Sir Renald. And you will make it known that if the servants are not busily about their work within the hour, I will be after them with a whip."

A spark of admiration lit his bloodshot eyes. "Yes, my lady!"

Imogen stalked out of the hall to the steps that led down to the bailey, but was brought to a frustrated halt. She couldn't go down there barefoot.

Raging at her feet, she went through the wooden buttery and down steps to the storage rooms and cellars. These were cleaner, but not kind to her bare feet.

In the lowest floor of the keep she was met by the dismaying sight of empty shelves, little more solid," she said. "In case I have need to go into the bailey."

The man pursed his lips then picked up the one that was toe and heel. "This one, lady. See, I can add a little extra soft leather along the sides, which should give protection and not pain you. With a raised cork sole, you would be above any foulness."

"How long will that take?"

"The sandal you can have within minutes, lady, but the other will take until tomorrow."

Imogen sighed but agreed. "It is a shame you didn't come a few days earlier, Master Cedric, rather than working on these efforts at a distance."

The man looked up. "But I was told not to come until today, lady. Your feet were doubtless not ready for shoon."

Imogen's bubble of contentment burst. FitzRoger, as usual, had thought of everything. He wanted her mobile — doubtless so she could take up her duties in the castle — but had not intended that she have the freedom of her castle until she was securely bound to him.

It was completely in character. Kindness, but always judicious kindness.

Her calculating husband hadn't counted, of course, on the marriage still being unconsummated today.

For the first time, Imogen wondered why it wasn't.

She remembered thinking that Lancaster

broken containers, spilled goods, and the stink of leaked wine and ale. Though she had been told, she hadn't expected it to be quite this bad.

FitzRoger had brought in supplies for the wedding. Could he not have had the mess cleared up too?

She quickly brushed aside that peevish thought. He had been busy and shorthanded, and this was her work, not his.

But to put all right would be a tremendous amount of work. She needed people and money.

She had money aplenty but could not reach it. The passage to the treasure vault was deliberately unwelcoming — dank and muddy, and in some places inches deep in water. It was made to appear a part of the secret ways which had been abandoned. It would be insanity to attempt it in bare feet.

With a sigh, Imogen gave up all thought of reaching her treasure until she could wear good solid shoes. She climbed a narrow circular staircase to her tower chamber.

It was only when she entered the room and saw how little it contained that she realized it wasn't her chamber anymore. Unless, that was, FitzRoger chose not to share his quarters. She didn't know how she felt about that. She knew it would not be wise for them to advertise their problems by sleeping apart, and yet she feared that if they were together it would come to that terrible intimacy again.

She gripped her hands tightly. It had to be done. Without consummation, the marriage was incomplete. It was voidable.

She suddenly realized her virginity provided the means of escape. Of course, while she was totally in the power of FitzRoger and the king there was nothing she could do, but if the situation were to continue for a period of time, and if the balance of power should shift . . .

Imogen went over to the gaping space where her beautiful window had been and looked over her castle and her land.

Did she want to escape the marriage?

Her husband was a hard man, and not one she was sure she could entirely trust. His power was uncertain, for the issue of the crown was not settled between Henry Beauclerk and his brother. If Henry fell, FitzRoger would fall too, and perhaps take Carrisford with him.

A wise woman would flee Bastard FitzRoger, and yet the thought brought a shadow of pain. In some strange way he was already a part of her life; his leaving would cause a gaping hole.

Before Imogen could tussle with the problem further, Martha burst in. "There you are, my lady! What're you doing here? I've been that worried! There's a man here for you. I'll go get him."

She was gone before Imogen had time to question her.

Imogen didn't know who she expected to appear, but it certainly wasn't the slight, middle-aged tradesman who bowed in. "Lady Imogen of Carrisford?"

Imogen agreed this was so.

"Cedric of Ross, master shoemaker," he announced with pride. "Your husband ordered footwear for you." He opened his pack and spilled out a half dozen pairs of rather incomplete shoes. Mere sandals, really.

Bemused, Imogen picked up one which was all heel and toe with nothing in between. "How would it stay on, Master Cedric?"

"None of these are complete, lady. Lord FitzRoger sent a pair of your shoes for measure and a description of your . . . er . . . problems. I have prepared as best I could. Now we can try them and I will put on the fastenings so they won't cause you further hurt."

Imogen could have wept with gratitude. Amid all the chaos and work, FitzRoger had thought of this. No, she did not want to escape the marriage.

Master Cedric tried on various styles, marking, cutting and measuring. At last he held up one pair which were mere slender straps and sole. "These would be best for in the castle, lady, for they will protect the sole of your feet and come nowhere near your sores. I can affix the laces speedily."

Imogen nodded. "But I need something

would have completed the act no matter how she screamed. Men did take women by force, so why hadn't her husband?

She must remember, though, that Fitz-Roger acted always in his own ambitious interests. He'd achieved his main purpose; they were married. He doubtless knew she wouldn't announce her failure to the world. So, he probably thought it would benefit him more to treat her gently than to force her. After all, she'd be unlikely to loosen her purse strings for a rapist.

She sighed. She was very tired of brutal reality.

When the sandals were finished and on her feet, Imogen praised Master Cedric for his work and dismissed him, telling Martha to find him a place to work. She walked around her room, rejoicing in the simple security of a layer of leather between her skin and the floor.

Then she set out to explore. At last she had the freedom of her keep, and by walking along the walls she could survey most of the castle.

Imogen spent the day investigating and planning.

Considering the situation and the lack of servants, Carrisford was in surprisingly good condition. Even the pens of livestock were beginning to be replenished. New hens were laying, new milch cows had heavy udders, and in the dairy butter was being churned. She inspected and made a few changes in the arrangements, but had to acknowledge that matters were well in hand.

As the stables had burned, there was only a lean-to roof to shelter the horses, but that should be adequate in summer. Even with men out hunting, the stables were full, but peering down from the wall Imogen saw no familiar horses. She summoned a stable groom up onto the wall to speak with her, and he confirmed that her father's and her horses were gone.

"Don't rightly know if they be dead or not, lady," the man confessed. "I fled the castle, and by the time I came back, things were much as you see 'em."

"And what of the mews and kennels?" Imogen asked.

"The same, lady." But his eyes shifted in a way that told her there had been corpses. He was protecting her, as everyone did, but she let it pass, thinking sadly of her hounds, Gerda and Gelda, and her fine merlin.

Mere death was not enough for Warbrick. She'd like to roast him slowly over a fire.

She retraced her steps back to the hall. There was no need to replace her father's hounds and horses, for FitzRoger must have his own. It was a relief to see one thing that wouldn't need buying afresh. Carrisford contained ample treasure, but by the end of this it would be severely depleted.

She wondered if there was any possibility of gaining recompense from Warbrick, then laughed at the thought. Warbrick and Belleme needed money to fund their rebellion, which explained the attack on Carrisford in the first place. Moreover, if the king had his way, Belleme and his brothers would soon lose all their lands and property in England.

She stopped, thoughtful. Would the king give her some of the land in restitution? There were ramifications, but a chunk of Warbrick's land would round out the Cleeve-Carrisford holdings very nicely indeed.

The Cleeve-Carrisford holdings.

She relished that, for the first time appreciating how much power it represented, and what trust in FitzRoger the king showed in allowing it. In one stroke, FitzRoger had become one of the great magnates of the land. Perhaps the king planned it that way.

Imogen knew that in July, when Robert of Normandy had sailed to England to oust his younger brother, quite a number of the Anglo-Norman magnates had supported him. Robert, however, had not had the fortitude to carry through his plan, and had settled for a payment of three thousand marks. Since then Henry had been pursuing the traitors. Most he merely fined and settled with, but some, such as Robert Malet, Ivo of Grandmesnil, Robert of Pontfract, and Robert de Belleme, he intended to break.

Henry would certainly welcome a great lord he could trust. Imogen already knew FitzRoger enough to know that Henry could trust him. When FitzRoger gave his word, he kept it.

Imogen looked around her castle and saw it as the base for one of the great holdings of England. She nodded. Her father would have approved.

She wondered again exactly how the castle had been taken. FitzRoger had seemed to suspect the monks, but she'd heard nothing more about it. The last time she had raised the subject with FitzRoger, they had been distracted onto matters relating to their marriage. She must raise the subject again.

Carrisford must never again fall so easily to a conqueror.

Imogen returned to the keep, but when she entered the great hall she was struck again by how rough and bleak it looked compared to its glory days. It must be restored to reflect her husband's new power. Some of the hangings had come from Italy and beyond. How long would it take to replace them? The gold and silver vessels could be commissioned from craftsmen nearby, but not the glass.

She sighed. It was all going to take so long.

At this time of day the hall was deserted, everyone being about their work. The whores had disappeared, she noted, though she doubted they had left the castle entirely.

That recalled Renald's words about Beauclerk's lust, and the way his followers behaved as he did. She frowned slightly. Had FitzRoger used whores in his years at Henry Beauclerk's side?

Of course he had. What else did she expect?

But, ridiculously, it hurt.

Would he use whores if his wife would not satisfy his needs? Was he even now whoring in the woods?

That was sharp agony.

There was nothing she could do about that, but she swore that if he shamed her in her own castle, she'd use the knife he gave her.

She pushed the matter out of her head and strode off to investigate the path across the bailey to the weaving sheds. It was dry and packed, and so she followed it.

The linked rooms had always been humming with industry as women spun, wove, dyed, cut, and sewed, providing nearly everything needed for the hall and its people. Now the sheds were deserted, except for the laundry. This idleness was wickedly wrong. It was ridiculous, for example, that such a skillful woman as Martha should be spending her time taking care of Imogen when she should be here.

Imogen summoned Martha and set her to

gathering some women and getting these rooms working again.

"But the women are helping out elsewhere, lady," Martha pointed out.

"Then elsewhere can do without."

"But with the king here . . ."

"Even with the king here. He must surely make allowances for a place that has been sacked. Anyway, Henry is on his way to trounce Belleme, and I think he will leave soon. The first thing to do, Martha, is to see what cloth, wool, and flax we have still. If it is as I fear, I will order more."

It turned out just as she feared, with little remaining unspoiled. She sent off an order for wool for weaving, but they would have to wait a little for the flax crop to come in before they could weave linen.

She sent to Gloucester for ready-woven material to be brought for her inspection. By the time it arrived she should have the money in hand to pay for it.

She consulted with Martha and some other women and chose a girl called Elswith to be her personal servant. She was a quiet child of twelve, but well able to learn. Imogen took her to the tower room and explained some of the duties, then left the girl to some mending.

Imogen went to the kitchens to check and amend the food planned for the next days, hoping the king and his train would soon leave. She supposed she should be grateful that he had left most of his army to forage on Warbrick's land; the first stage of the man's punishment.

As soon as Henry received Warbrick's response to the call to justice — or when he ceased waiting for that response — he would seize the Warbrick lands, then move in force against Belleme. She hoped fiercely that he would crush both of them, but she wanted a more direct revenge. She wanted Warbrick brought low, and dead, and she wanted to be there to see it.

FitzRoger had promised to do his best to see him dead. She must remember to tell him that she wanted to witness it.

Imogen was in the pantry checking candles when she realized the implications of all this. When the king marched on Belleme, FitzRoger would go with him. He would fight, perhaps fight Warbrick. He would be in danger.

The man had been fighting all his life, she told herself. What point in her fretting about it now?

But she did.

She told herself that she simply did not want to be vulnerable again, but knew in her heart it was more than that. It was the feeling she'd had last night that he was now part of her life — like a father, brother, or son. One who could never be swept out, no matter what might happen.

"Ah, there you are, Lady Imogen." It was Siward. "A number of folk are in the bailey, returned to seek their places."

There was a twinkle in his eyes, and Imogen smiled. "Just realized Warbrick's gone, have they?"

"Just heard tell of the celebration, more like. We can send them away for a few days if you wish."

"No. We need them all." Imogen remembered FitzRoger greeting the returning workers, and smiled. "I'll receive them by the steps, Siward."

She needed money. She ran up to the solar and ransacked her husband's belongings. His treasure chests were all locked, of course, but at last she found a small pouch of silver farthings still attached to a belt.

Next she went to the office where Brother Cuthbert, the scribe, was working and took the list of castle servants. The she went to the bottom of the outer stairs and, like FitzRoger days before, checked each returnee against the list and gave each a silver farthing.

There, that should make it clear to whom they owed service.

The suitable women were sent straight to the weaving sheds to join the women already working there. Imogen thought she detected a trace of disappointment in some of them. She went with them, partly to help make the place ready, but also to make sure they settled to purposeful work.

The rooms were already clean and tidy, and the best needlewomen were repairing what linens were not beyond help. Others cut up the larger hopeless cases to make smaller items — hand towels and women's personal cloths.

Fine stuff was carefully preserved to serve as trimmings.

As they worked, the women gossiped. Though nothing was said directly it was clear that some of them had engaged in fornication last night, and expected to again tonight. It was also clear they looked forward to it.

Imogen worked alongside them, listening. She had never heard such talk before and guessed it was the fact that she was supposed to be a fully married woman that had broken their reticence. Or perhaps it was the fact that her powerful father was dead, for he had been the one determined to keep her innocent beyond reason.

". . . you wouldn't believe the size of it," one woman, Dora, murmured to another. "Didn't know what to do with it, though. Now, that barrel-chested one, *he* knows."

"I like a big man myself."

"Big where, though?" smirked Dora.

"Everywhere."

Laughter.

"You listen to me, Edie," said Dora. "It's

what's in their head that counts, not what's between their legs. The best futtering I ever had was from a wizened old man when I was just a girl. Showed me what's what, he did. I had to teach my Johnnie everything, or it would've been in and out every night of our lives."

Imogen wished someone would teach her what's what. On the other hand, she feared she knew. The women were talking of lust and sinful things, and just see what came of it. Dora was lewd and lost, ready to go with any man who offered. She probably *did* take a man's thing into her mouth. Imogen wondered if Father Wulfgan could show the woman the evil of her ways.

But then Dora sighed. "As it was, Johnnie were all I ever wanted. If he'd not taken that fever, I swear I'd never have let another man between my legs, no, not even the king."

"You didn't, Dora!"

Dora managed to look coy. "Didn't I then?"

"Oooh! What's he like?"

Dora looked around, pleased with her audience, but then seemed to notice Imogen for the first time. She went red. "I'm sure it's not proper to talk of it."

Now everyone was looking at Imogen. She forced a smile. "Don't worry about me. I'm a married woman, too, now."

"Yes, lady," they chorused, but the conversation was dead. After a while, Imogen put aside her work and left, hearing the voices spring up again soon after.

She was tempted to sneak back and try to listen, but she was Imogen of Carrisford, and above such things. And those women were low and doubtless sinful.

The idea popped into her head: FitzRoger surely knew what was what, and probably liked low sinful women.

Imogen was so deep in thought that her steps took her once more to her tower room. There she found Father Wulfgan awaiting her, frowning blackly. "We were to pray together today, daughter."

"Were we?" Imogen did not remember such a plan, but she knew she had not been in any state yesterday to remember much. She looked for Elswith, but the priest must have sent the girl away. Imogen wished she could send the priest away.

"Do we need to pray?" she asked.

"Indeed we do, daughter. For cleansing, for strength, or for forgiveness." He eyed her as if he could strip her down to the soul.

Imogen did her best to look completely blank, but Dora's spicy talk was still running sinfully through her brain.

Wulfgan fell to his knees.

Under his fiery gaze, Imogen had to do the same.

"Now, daughter," he whispered. "Speak through me to the Lord Jesus, who, though tempted day and night, never sullied thought or action with woman. What happened last night?"

Imogen couldn't think what to say, but even if everything had gone as expected she did not think it proper to discuss it, even with a priest.

"Is it possible?" Wulfgan asked in ecstasy. "Are you still innocent?"

"No!" Imogen instinctively lied, then waited for God to smite her.

Nothing happened, and Wulfgan did not appear daunted. "But did you avoid lust?" he demanded.

Imogen looked down at her joined hands. "Yes," she said, rather sadly.

"Blessed child! And did you help your husband to avoid lust?"

"Yes, I think perhaps I did."

His dirty twisted hands clasped hers. "Twice, thrice blessed! You have set your feet on the road to sanctity, and will take him with you to his heavenly reward. Now, pray with me for continued strength. *Christe, audi nos . . .*"

Imogen sighed and made the response to the litany. *"Christe, exaudi nos."* If they were to do a litany, they would be here for ages. Her knees would be as sore as her feet.

"Pater de caelis, Deus . . ."
"Misere nobis."
"Sancta Virgo Virginem . . ."
"Ora pro nobis . . ."

FitzRoger went fleet-footed to the solar, disconcertingly aware of something that might be eagerness. Inappropriate eagerness in view of the situation between him and his bride. His heart chilled when he found no trace there of Imogen. Not an item of clothing, not a comb, not even a long glittering hair on the pillows. The bed had been remade, as if it had never been touched.

Where was she? He could not allow this.

He left the empty room, walked briskly along the corridor and ran up the winding stairs to the pretty tower room that had housed the Treasure of Carrisford, the place where they had fought their battle of wits. Even without its hangings and glass window it had been an exquisite setting for a jewel, symbol of her life before disaster. She doubtless felt at ease there.

His jaw tightened. If she wanted a pretty casket, he would give her one, but it would be one they shared.

The drone of praying voices stopped him outside the door.

"*Ut nosmetipsos in tuo sancto servitio confortare et conseverare digneris . . .*"

Imogen replied, "*Te rogamus, audi nos.*"

To strengthen and preserve us in thy holy service . . .

We beg thee, hear us.

"*Ut mentes nostras ad celestia desideria erigas . . .*"

"Te rogamus, audi nos."

To raise our minds to desire the things of heaven . . .

We beg thee, hear us.

FitzRoger made a fist against the rough stone wall. After a moment he swung on his heel and returned to his room.

Toward Imogen he felt only impatience and pity, but he would like to throttle that guilt-mongering priest.

Chapter Twelve

When he reached the solar, FitzRoger looked down at himself and shook his head. Perhaps it was as well he had not confronted Imogen immediately. It had been a successful day's hunting and he stank of blood, sweat, and entrails. That would doubtless disgust his delicate bride even more.

There was a bathroom in the bailey at Carrisford, fitted out with tubs and a cistern of hot water. Lord Bernard had doubtless stopped off there to render himself pure before even entering his keep. Henry and the rest of the men were there now, scrubbing, and enjoying the whores. FitzRoger had been in no mind to join them and endure more of their lewd jests, and so he had come here, not even thinking that he might confront Imogen in this state.

That lack of thought bothered him.

He had always intended to command a tub in his room, and now he did so. He stripped off his soiled garments, then stood deep in thought as he awaited the bath.

Just what should he do about his bride? He was certain it would be better to rid Carrisford of the priest, but he had promised that Imogen would rule here, and he would keep his word if he could. An inconvenient chaplain was not a matter upon which he had the right to over-rule her, unless the priest interfered in military matters.

The more pressing issue was whether he should consummate the marriage tonight despite her pleas and protests. The way her body had tightened up against him dismayed him. He supposed force would work, but at what cost? The thought of painfully ripping into a terrified girl brought bile to his throat, but this situation was very dangerous. Henry could not afford to have anyone but Fitz-Roger hold power in this corner of England, and Henry would expect his friend and liegeman to achieve that purpose in any way possible.

FitzRoger turned his mind to a simpler matter: that of compelling her to move back into this room. That was essential if they were to conceal the situation.

He flinched even from that.

There was something very wrong with him.

The tub and water arrived, brought by ser-vants who glanced in nervous awe at his naked, scarred body. When Imogen had first seen it she had not been frightened, but that was before. Afterward, she had refused to look at him.

He waved the attendants away and eased

with a sigh into the hot water. As he scrubbed himself clean, he pondered his situation.

He supposed they could sleep apart. It would appear strange, but that was not the sort of factor that ruled him. One advantage of his life in Henry's libidinous train, and his reputation in combat, was that no one would think to question his virility.

Wouldn't they be amused, though, to hear that his bride remained an unsullied virgin? Well, not completely unsullied.

He leaned his head back and closed his eyes to contemplate sweet, painful memories of Imogen writhing beneath his touch, and to consider the mess that had developed out of a straightforward grab for power.

The door opened. He opened his eyes instantly.

Imogen went pink to see him in the tub. She had her arms full of clothes. "Oh, I'm sorry, my lord," she said, half retreating, then bumping into a girl who followed her with a small chest.

"Come in," he said. "We're married, remember?" He was experiencing an astonishing wave of relief. She was moving her belongings in here. She had never intended to desert him.

Eyes averted, she entered and put down her burden, directing the maid to place the chest against a wall. She was delightfully pink, and with her ravishing hair floating long and loose, she looked every inch the virgin she was. His body immediately wanted to rectify that, but he had never been ruled by his body before, and would not weaken now.

Even if he could practically feel her warm silky curves under his hands . . .

Her modesty amused him when she'd lain naked with him the night before. Was this a natural reversion — he'd never known such a gently raised lady before in his life — or a result of new exhortations by the priest?

She headed for the door again. "I'll come back in —"

"Stay." It came out as more of a command than he wished, but she halted.

"Girl," he said. "You may go."

The wide-eyed maid left and closed the door. Imogen appeared frozen.

What now? "Perhaps you could wash my back," he said.

She approached the tub nervously. With a bathhouse and bath attendants, he supposed there had never been any question of the Treasure of Carrisford bathing a guest.

"The king?" she asked in sudden anxiety.

She was right. Normally the presence of the king would demand the chatelaine's attention. "He will not expect your attentions, never fear. There are plenty of women in the bathhouse."

"Whores," she said with a look.

"Yes. Better the women who are happy to serve than the ones without a taste for it." He saw the expression that flitted over her face and almost regretted the words. Then he thought with irritation that a bit of guilt and jealousy might do her good.

She was standing there, undecided. He leaned forward to give her access to his back.

Imogen walked behind her husband and considered him.

His back was an impressive piece of sculpture: hard with bone and muscle, so hard, but scarcely marked at all except for what looked like a burn scar over one shoulder blade. The splash of shiny scar tissue almost looked like a badge of honor.

His skin was darkened by the sun to the color of rich, golden wood, but darkened more above the neck. She supposed it was paler lower down but couldn't remember. She'd only looked at him once, and her mind had not been on skin coloration.

Imogen took a cloth and dipped it in a dish of soap, then began tentatively to circle the cloth over him. He felt as hard as he looked. Why had fate linked her with such a hard man?

Because she needed one. And he wasn't always hard and cold. He'd shown her kindness and warmth, and her woman's instinct told her there was more, much more, if she could only find the way.

She remembered how good it had felt last night when he had stroked her back. That delicious stroking had not felt particularly lustful, just very sweet. Would he experience the same pleasure if she did it to him?

She rinsed the cloth and added more soap, then rubbed the soapy cloth on his back in circles. She watched for his reaction. He had rested his head on his knees, and he *looked* as if he was enjoying it. She began to use longer, sweeping strokes of the cloth, covering the whole of his back and wide shoulders. It was strangely pleasant to be doing it, almost as pleasant as when it had been done to her.

Had he enjoyed touching her last night? Had there been more than lust in him?

Imogen grasped her courage. She knelt and rolled up her sleeves. She let the cloth fall, and dipped her fingers directly in the soap. She used her slippery hands, both of them, to massage him, thumbs up the spine, hands splayed over the ribs. Up, around, down. Out across the ribs, following the fine lines of his muscles. Up and over the shoulders, hesitating momentarily at the roughness of scar tissue marring him there, then sweeping down again. She relaxed in delight at the silky feel of his resilient muscles flexing beneath the pressure of her hands.

Since it didn't seem to hurt him, she pressed harder and harder, exploring him down to the bones, and the feeling from it crept up through her hands and arms and into her soul, entrancing her. . . .

She became aware that her legs were cramping under her.

She eased away and up, her last touch being an irresistible gentle tangle with one of his damp curls. Back in reality and thought, she wondered nervously what he would say.

"Thank you." It was very soft, almost sleepy. "You're very good at that."

She smiled. It fact, she grinned. It was sweet in her heart that there might be something she could do for him that was pleasant for them both.

"Shall I rinse you now?" she asked.

"Yes."

She trickled a little of the clean water down his back, washing away the traces of soap.

He seemed to come to life. He stretched slowly, muscles rippling, then rose to his feet in a stream of soapy water. Imogen could not help but take a step backward, clutching the jug.

He glanced at her, and if there had been any relaxation, it was immediately disguised by the mask. "The cloth?" he said.

She quickly put down the jug and passed him the large cloth, trying to keep her eyes from his body. How silly she was. She noticed that he *was* paler, very pale, around the hips, that his male member was in its un-alarming state.

She breathed more easily.

"Perhaps you could find me some clean clothes. I don't mind what."

Imogen was pleased to turn away and bury her head in his chests. "Plain or splendid?" she asked.

He sounded slightly amused. "You choose."

Imogen investigated his three chests, and found it was not an easy choice. There was clothing here of all sorts from leather to tissue. He could outshine the king again, or appear almost peasant-plain. She knew it wouldn't matter; FitzRoger's presence did not depend on gaudery.

In the end she chose black braies, a white shirt, and a black tunic embroidered with green and gold. It was rich but not particularly showy. She added a pair of linen drawers and some green bands for his cross-gartering.

She turned to present them to him.

He was sitting on a bench with the drying cloth loosely wrapped around his hips. She should be getting used to his body, but she wasn't, and knew her face was coloring.

"When you've patched me up a few times, you'll doubtless find me unalarming."

"Patched you up?"

His eyes sharpened. "Don't you treat the sick? Why not?"

"Y-yes," she stammered. "But not . . . I haven't generally tended wounds. I know how . . . I think."

"You think," he echoed dryly. "Doubtless more of your father's pampering. Was he keeping you from the wounds, or from the men?"

"You are not to mis-say my father!"

"I will say what I please, Imogen. Perhaps your father could afford an ornamental woman. I cannot."

She tossed the clothes at him. "Then you shouldn't have forced me into marrying you, should you?"

He stood so the cloth dropped and pulled on the drawers. "I didn't force you, Imogen." He added pointedly, "In any sense of the word."

Imogen bit her lip at that.

He began to put on the braies. "And any man, even the noble Earl of Lancaster, would want a wife's tender care if injured. That presupposes, of course, that the earl would put himself in a situation to be wounded in the first place."

Imogen wished she had something else to throw at him. "Do you sneer at *everyone*? How wonderful to be so superior! Is it Lancaster's fault that he didn't have to claw his way up off a dung heap?"

He was cross-gartering his right leg and his hands did not falter, but she saw his jaw tighten. "Imogen. Take care."

Days of being attacked, bullied, coerced, and used boiled up in her. "Why? What will you do to me now? Hit me? For telling the truth?"

He knotted the laces and looked up. His eyes were wide and cold. "Come here."

A jolt of fear shot through her. What had possessed her to taunt the dragon like that?

"Come here," he repeated.

Imogen wanted to run, but her dignity would not permit that. She walked over to him, liquid with fear.

"Sit down," he said, indicating the bench.

Imogen almost collapsed with relief onto the bench. She kept her eyes on her own tight-clasped and none-too-steady hands.

"Imogen," he said levelly, as he resumed his gartering, "I intend to be gentle with you, but you can make that very hard. I am not . . ."

At the hesitation, she looked up, wondering. She'd never thought to witness FitzRoger less than certain of his every move. He was not looking at her, but seemed focused on the work of his hands.

"I am not well acquainted with gentleness," he continued, "whereas harshness and clawing my way off the dung heap are deep in my bones."

"I'm sorry," she said. "I didn't mean to hurt you. . . ."

His eyes flicked to hers, still icy. "You

didn't *hurt* me. You hit a nerve to which I have an instinctive response. That is a very dangerous thing to do. If you are wise, you will not raise my birth and background when you want to fight."

"I don't want to fight," she protested.

He finished the second bow. "How strange, then, that you do it so often."

"You provoke me!"

"You are easily provoked."

"Only by you!"

He twisted suddenly.

Imogen's wrists were snared by one hand, her hair by the other. His leg held hers captive. She was completely helpless in the trap of his rock-hard body. Her heart galloped and she let out a whimper of fear.

"See," he said softly. "Know with what you deal."

Her terror subsided as she realized he still intended her no hurt. "I never doubted you could best me physically, FitzRoger."

"And every other way, Ginger."

That annoyed her and she twisted, but only succeeded in hurting herself. His grip tightened to the point of pain as he gave no quarter. Held as she was, the only way to avoid his green eyes was to close hers. She didn't. "What am I then?" she asked bitterly. "A doll for your amusement?"

"What do you want to be?"

His body was still invincible on hers, but

his eyes were warming. That gave her courage. "I want to be your equal," she said, and thought he would laugh.

He didn't. "Then work toward that goal." He released her carelessly and picked up the shirt. Imogen shivered and rubbed the white pressure marks on her wrists. Looking at the power of him, she despaired.

"I am to practice with the sword?" she asked bitterly. "Try to grow muscles like yours?"

He pulled on the shirt and turned. "It's your dream. Achieve it how you wish. I was a puny eight-month child, after all, and called a bastard." He tied the laces at the neck of his shirt and pulled on the tunic. "But that is not necessary. I am stronger than the king, and could kill him in single combat. Does that make me his superior, or even his equal? No. I am his to command. I will fight on his behalf."

Imogen looked over his impressive body with new, thoughtful eyes. "You will fight for me, too?"

A brow rose. "I thought I had already done so."

"Yes, you have. . . ." Imogen was completely confused. "Why do you serve the king?"

"He has helped me to climb off the dung heap, so I owe him my allegiance. He can also reward me."

"Why will you serve me?"

He looked at her from under his lashes. "Perhaps for the same things."

Reward. That set the alarm bells ringing. "I can see that I have helped you climb, but what reward did you have in mind, FitzRoger?"

He turned away to take a gilded belt out of a chest. Dryly, he said, "I'm sure the Treasure of Carrisford has something to offer a dung-born bastard." When he turned back, she caught her breath. He looked magnificent and formidable in black and gold, and his words were laughable.

"Wherever you started, Lord FitzRoger, you have no need of pity now."

"The last thing I have ever wanted is pity, Ginger." He gestured ironically toward her clothing. "Are you not going to seek to equal me in display?"

"I have little." Imogen's thoughts were all on the man. Now and again she glimpsed something, something her heart yearned for, but that mask was between them and she didn't know if what she saw was foolish illusion or guarded treasure.

He started to sift through the pile of clothing she had brought — making a mess of it in typical male fashion. He chose a mauve gown and a gold silk tunic which she had only kept because of the magnificence of the material. "Wear these."

"The tunic's torn down the side and I

don't think it can be mended. Look at the way it frays."

He tossed it to her. "Wear it anyway. With enough jewels on top no one will mark the tear. I want people to see the Treasure of Carrisford tonight."

Imogen rose. "See what you have won?"

"Exactly." He slid two bracelets of gold on his wrists and then took a pouch out of his chest and gave it to her. "Your morning gift."

Color flooded her cheeks. "But . . ."

"I am not dissatisfied, Imogen."

She gazed into his eyes and saw only truth.

She opened the pouch and out spilled a girdle of amethyst and carved ivory. The work was exquisite and it equaled anything she had ever owned. She knew that this was a political move — he had to give her the gift or explain the lack — but tears pricked at her eyes anyway. "Thank you."

"Dress," he said. "The king will be in the hall soon."

He sat back on the bench and stretched out his legs.

He was going to watch? Imogen froze.

"Your naked body will not inflame me with lust, Imogen. Dress."

Imogen began to take off her tunic, then paused. She let it drop again, and faced him, dry mouthed. "No."

His face was completely still. "Why not?"

"It may be right before the law, it may be

right before God even, but it does not feel right to me."

He rose and walked toward her, menace radiating from him.

Imogen flinched. She had finally gone too far. With hopeless defiance she held her ground and met his eyes.

Then he relaxed and real warmth glinted in his eyes. "Well done," he said, and left the room.

Her legs gave way and she crumpled to kneel on the ground, trembling as if with an ague. How had she done that? She would never have denied her father in that way, never mind FitzRoger.

It was as if she were impelled to make these stands, to assert her rights, when she wasn't even sure she had rights. The only person who had advised her to stand firm on an issue was Father Wulfgan. Everyone else would surely advise her to be submissive to her lord in all things.

Especially in bed.

Except that her lord appeared to be encouraging her to rebel.

When Imogen descended to the hall, she wore the clothes FitzRoger had chosen and the beautiful girdle. She had summoned Elswith to plait her hair as a gesture toward her married status, but still could not wear a veil without a circlet.

The hall full of men fell silent. She saw in their eyes that they did indeed envy her husband, and she was pleased for it. He came forward to escort her to the high table, to sit beside the king.

"You are radiant," said Henry with a leer. "Perhaps Ty does know his business after all."

Imogen looked down, knowing her face was red.

"Ah, the charm of innocence. Pity it so quickly passes. I warrant you'll be more eager to leap into bed this night, eh? No need to push you." Imogen could have crept under the table for shame. "Sets up a fine appetite in us all, this kind of thing," the king went on. "Where's —" He broke off what he had been saying and Imogen could swear FitzRoger's hand had moved in some sort of sign.

The whores were not in evidence and Imogen realized the king was willing to bend in this matter. It was all an interesting reflection of powers. The king was FitzRoger's liege lord, but he would modify his behavior to humor him and her.

Why?

Everything was a question of who needed what most.

Henry needed FitzRoger on his side. A king needed powerful men to act for him in the land, and preferred ones he could trust. He

would humor and reward those who served him well.

And punish those who didn't.

Could the same be said of FitzRoger? What did he need of her? Eventually he would need sons, but for the moment he had everything he required unless she told the world that the marriage was incomplete.

For his part, he would humor and reward her if she were dutiful, and punish her if she were not.

He had implied the situations could be reversed. But that meant she should reward him for his service, which presumably meant the treasure. She didn't think that punishing FitzRoger entered into it. It was all very well for him to be drawing analogies between her and the king, but the fact was that she had no power to oppose him even if she wanted to.

She accepted it. It was the way of the world.

Thinking on these issues recalled what had started their disagreement. Her medical skills. He was justified in upbraiding her. In that respect, she needed to do better.

She had been well trained is such matters, but had never been allowed to practice on serious war wounds or the more noxious diseases. Perhaps her father had been at fault in that, though his aim had merely been to protect her.

She was certainly sure that if FitzRoger were carried home from battle wounded, she would want to be able to care for him properly.

Where were the men wounded in the taking of Carrisford? Doubtless they had been taken to Grimstead monastery nearby, and the number should include Bert, injured by her recklessness. Tomorrow, she would go there and begin learning.

"Why do I think you are plotting something?" FitzRoger murmured.

Imogen started. "I? I am not plotting. Just thinking." She didn't want to tell him of her plans just yet. She wanted to surprise him.

His eyes seemed to read her secrets. "Thinking of what?"

She turned to face him. "Are my thoughts not to be private, even?"

"How can they be otherwise, now you have learned to wear a mask?"

"Have I?"

"What?"

"Learned to mask myself from you?"

"Apparently." He washed his hands in the bowl between them, and dried them.

Imogen did the same, wondering at the implications of his words.

The food was served and talk veered safely to the successful hunt. Two roebuck had been found and killed, as well as a number of smaller venison. As the musicians played

in the background the moves of the chase were retold with vigor by the men, the virtues of hawks and hounds were debated.

It was all like, and yet unlike, the way it had been so few days ago. A melancholy swept over Imogen, and she had to fight tears. She kept looking up to speak to her father, but he was not there. There was a stranger in his place. She expected to hear Aunt Constance's voice, and yet the only female voices were the muted ones of servants.

FitzRoger rose abruptly, and Imogen looked up, startled. Her first alarmed thought was that he was going to take her to their room for marital matters, but he went to the musicians. He relieved one of them of his harp and carried a stool over to the middle of the room.

Conversation ceased as everyone paid attention to him.

He sat, and tested the instrument. He glanced around almost humorously. "You rogues doubtless expect my usual style, but tonight I sing for my bride."

He did not have an exceptional voice, but he sang competently, and amazingly it appeared that the song might have been composed for her.

Treasure incomparable, such is my lady,
Set among roses, played to by love-birds,
Nourished on honeydew, and finest wastel
*   bread*

Such is my lady, flower of the west.
Let her step softly, over the smoothest
ground,
Let her sing lightly, only of pleasant things,
Let her weep tears of joy, and touch me
gently.
Sweet is the treasure she brings to my
chest.

The men were pleased by this appropriately sentimental offering. Imogen was just amazed he was capable of it, and wondered if he had hired a jongleur to compose the piece for him. She had not missed that last line, however.

Treasure. Always the treasure.

He stood and bowed.

She smiled.

She rose in her turn and came to take the harp from him.

"You will sing?" he asked, almost warily.

"I will sing lightly, and only of pleasant things, my lord." He gave her the instrument, reluctantly, but kissed her hand as he passed it over, unsettling her.

Imogen sat and summoned her wits. She and her father, along with the professional musicians brought to train her, had played these improvisational games, making up long interwoven poems. She was very good at it.

She struck a note. "I sing for my husband," she said to the men.

The treasure of Carrisford, rescued by
  courage,
Safe in her true home ever shall be.
Tending her people, nourishing, guiding,
Sharing the wastel and honeydew, she.
I sing of the courage of Tyron FitzRoger
I sing of his honor in coming to aid me,
My tears are of joy, my touch will be gentle
A treasure preserved just where it should
  be.

She could swear she saw a flash of genuine humor in his eyes in response to the last line.

"Very pretty!" declared Henry, "and a lovely voice. Come, Lady Imogen, sing us some other piece now you have done your duty."

"Oh, it wasn't duty, sire, but pleasure, I assure you."

Imogen went obligingly into a song of Charlemagne's knights, a Provençal piece of more elegance than martial. It was only as she sang of the great king's twelve paladins and their adventures with the beautiful princess, Angelica, that she wondered why that particular song had come to mind. She glanced at her own darkly thoughtful paladin.

Why was he frowning? The company seemed well pleased with her offering, and she knew that in this one respect at least, her husband could not find her lacking.

She resumed her seat at his side.

"You sing beautifully," he said. "Doubtless a result of many years of expensive training."

Imogen raised her chin. "And many years of arduous practice, my lord. Doubtless you were engaged in other matters."

"Yes. Many years of arduous practice. Did I sneer? I beg your pardon. It is merely envy. I hope you will sing privately for me from time to time."

She glanced at him, and though he was cold as ice she judged him serious. She should have realized his strength and skills had not come easily, especially to a puny eight-month child. "Of course," she said, even though his words carried implications of unbearable intimacy.

One of the knights was singing now, in a fine bass voice, and they paid attention.

There was the sudden interruption of a bellow from the watchcorn's horn. The music broke off. FitzRoger glanced at Renald, and the darker man slipped out of the hall. At a signal, the singer continued.

Renald returned to murmur to FitzRoger, who then said, "Sire, it is the Earl of Lancaster. Is it acceptable to you that he be admitted?"

"The laggardly lover?" said the king with a malicious grin. "By all means!"

The order was given, but Imogen sensed a new tension in the air coming from the men on either side of her. It was not fear, but a kind of readiness, as men show before battle. Why? This doubtless would not be pleasant, for Lancaster would not be happy about the marriage, but what was done was done.

Except, she realized with a jolt, that it wasn't done.

She toyed with a piece of fruit as the king and FitzRoger spoke quietly across her of Lancaster. It became clear that the earl was not a man Henry could afford to ignore, and that it was even possible Lancaster would throw his support behind Henry's enemies if offended. He was known to have met with Belleme.

It was also clear that Henry's distrust of Lancaster had been behind the move to marry her to FitzRoger, and behind the haste.

Lancaster might have been told she had agreed to marry FitzRoger, but he had come anyway. And they had known he would come.

To confirm her interpretation, Henry said, "Good thing it's all settled. What happened to the sheet? We might have to wave it in front of him."

Imogen stiffened, but kept her eyes shielded and hoped no other part of her revealed her anxiety.

"There was no mark on it," FitzRoger said calmly.

"What?"

Imogen looked up at that, fearing she was about to be shamed in one way or another.

"That casts no doubt on Lady Imogen's honor," said FitzRoger. "Merely a matter of position and care."

The king turned red. "By heaven, Ty, that was stupid. A wedding night's no time for games like that!"

Lost, Imogen glanced between them. Games like what?

FitzRoger's fingers turned his table knife. "Do you think Lancaster will contest my lady's virtue? I hope he does."

"Stop snarling," said the king shortly as the Earl of Lancaster strode in. "I can't afford a fight between you."

The Earl of Lancaster was a big, fleshy man who generally looked magnificent in layers of finest clothing. Today he looked haggard and muddy. He clearly had, for once, rushed.

He scanned the situation and bowed. "Sire! I have made all haste to assist Lady Imogen, my affianced bride."

FitzRoger rose and arranged seating for the earl by the king's side. "I fear you are in error, my lord," he said politely. "The lady is my bride."

Lancaster froze, "But . . ."

"We were married yesterday."

The earl looked at Imogen in shock. "Lady Imogen," he said with an attempt at a smile.

"How can this be when you are promised to me?"

Imogen swallowed. "Nothing was settled, my lord."

"But your father's wishes were quite clear, and should be sacred to a dutiful daughter."

Imogen felt rather sick, but she kept her chin up. "Nothing was settled," she repeated.

"Come, Lancaster," said the king cheerfully before the red-faced earl could explode. "It is a suitable match and has my blessing. There is nothing to be done now. There are prizes aplenty in the land, and I promise you will have your pick of them. You have ridden hard. Take your rest. Eat. Drink. You are very welcome. We go shortly to bring Warbrick and Belleme to heel. You and your men can join us."

Imogen saw that distract Lancaster, for though he always provided his due in soldiers for his liege, he was not a man to engage in battle himself.

She turned to her husband, and found him looking at her in that catlike way she hated. She knew he was watching for any move she might make to announce her virginity, ready to forestall it. She wondered how he would manage that, and was almost tempted to find out. . . .

He took her hand and rose. "Will you excuse us, sire? My Lord of Lancaster." The latter was not a request.

"Of course, of course," said Henry jovially. "Off you go!"

Lancaster looked as if he would object, but after a glance at FitzRoger, he thought better of it.

Imogen thought of objecting also, but there was truly nothing to object to — it would not have caused comment if she and FitzRoger had kept to their room for a week. Still, she felt shamed by this blatant show of possession.

"We're married," she pointed out when they were in their room. "You've won. You don't have to rub his nose in it." She went to look angrily out of the window, trying to put space between them.

"What a suspicious nature you have. Lancaster can choke for all I care, but Henry's patience is not limitless."

Imogen turned. "What do you mean?"

"He's waiting anxiously for the whores to be let in again."

"*What?* But I said they were not to be permitted in the hall. In my father's day —"

"Your father had his arrangements, but you can hardly expect the king to wander off to the village, or sneak into the bathhouse in the dark."

Imogen was almost spluttering. "My father had no such arrangements. He loved my mother deeply!"

"Grow up, Imogen. Your mother has been dead for two years and was frail for many years before that. You have two half brothers and a half sister being raised in Gloucester. When you take up your duties and go over the accounts, you'll find your father provided for them handsomely."

"Bro—" Imogen snapped her mouth shut and tried to collect her scattered wits. It never occurred to her that FitzRoger might be lying, though. "How do you know this?"

"The business of Carrisford has been disrupted, but has not ceased entirely. Someone has had to authorize payments."

Imogen wanted to protest that he had exceeded his authority, but as he said, someone had to do it. It was her fault for allowing personal matters to block out her duty.

"Tomorrow," she stated, "I will take up the management here."

"Excellent. You can also calculate what you owe me." Before she could respond to that, he said, "I'm surprised Lord Bernard didn't wed again, especially when he was without an heir."

The matter of her father was still raw. She had brothers and sisters? "Some men, My Lord Bastard, take marriage more seriously than others."

His eyes narrowed. "I assure you, no one takes marriage more seriously than a bastard. If you die without giving me at least two sons, Imogen, I'll marry again at the first opportunity."

Imogen sat with a bump on the bed. "You really are a horrible man."

"Of course I am. It's my stock in trade." He came to lean on a post. Looming. "Are you saying you want me to mourn you in celibacy all the days of my life? Hardly realistic. I wouldn't expect it of you."

She met his mocking eyes. "After this experience, my lord, I am hardly likely to marry again, even if I should be lucky enough to be free of you."

"Unfortunately, I seem to live a charmed life."

"Unfortunate indeed." Imogen didn't really want to be saying such cruel things, but it was as if she were being carried along by a stream in flood, a stream of vitriol.

"There's always the knife," he said helpfully. He took it from where it lay on top of her chest and placed it beside her on the bed.

She just gave him a disgusted look, and remembered where all this had started. "Those whores —"

"Are now serving their king."

Imogen opened her mouth and then interpreted the look in his eyes. "Is this one of those matters in which I must be ruled by you, my lord husband?"

"Yes."

She smiled tightly. "Then I'm surprised you aren't down there availing yourself of their services."

"So am I, since there'll be little amatory release to be found here." He returned her humorless smile. "After our touching song play, however, it would be a shame to shatter the picture, wouldn't it?"

"Little . . ." Imogen was off balance again. She had assumed he was determined to consummate the marriage, particularly now Lancaster had turned up sniffing for an excuse to break it; a good part of her bitterness had been a desperate rear guard action. "What do you mean?"

He looked at her derisively. "Are you keen to assuage my husbandly needs then, Imogen?"

She could feel her color flaring. "I know my duty," she muttered.

"Do you? As laid down by Father Wulfgan, I suppose. I'm afraid I'm too degenerate to be satisfied with that." He moved away from her, opened a chest, and took out a chess board. He placed it upon a small table by the window and began to set up the pieces with swift, deft fingers. "I assume you play."

"Yes," said Imogen, bemused by his unpredictable moves.

"Well?"

"Yes."

"Good. I like a challenging game. You can be ivory."

Imogen moved to sit across the board from him. The board was inlaid in dark and pale woods; the pieces were silver and ivory. It was very lovely. She touched her elegant pale queen. "My father had a set similar to this," she said.

"It was smashed, but the silver is around somewhere. It can be reworked." His matter-of-fact voice was designed to give no quarter.

Imogen gritted her teeth and made the first move. She supposed it was a hopeless cause, but she would do her best to trounce him. She would dearly love to defeat him in something. Soon all her attention was fixed on the board as she fought for her life. FitzRoger played an unpredictably brilliant game, but she was holding her own.

Just.

While she contemplated a particularly complex series of moves, he rose and poured them both wine. She drank it absentmindedly, fighting excitement, checking for the third time that her plan wouldn't spell disaster.

She couldn't believe that she actually had a chance to win.

Struggling to look impassive, she moved her bishop three squares. Still standing, he moved a rook. She moved a pawn seemingly at random. He raised a brow and took it. She moved her queen. "Checkmate," she whispered.

He sat rather sharply and studied the board for a long time. "So it is," he said thoughtfully.

Their eyes met and a grin started on

318

Imogen's face that she couldn't stop. She was gloating, but couldn't help it.

He suddenly laughed, his face lighting in a most amazing way. "A true victory," he said, and toasted her. "Remind me never to underestimate your mind, especially when mine is distracted by lust."

It was like a dash of cold water. Imogen glanced nervously at the bed.

His smile faded. "I'll give you notice, Imogen. I do believe that in time you will come to be comfortable with me. I am willing to wait if I can."

"If you can?" she asked.

He shook his head. "I'll wait. But you have to try to overcome your anxiety. It would help if you didn't keep running off to that priest to have your fears reinforced."

"I didn't . . . I don't . . . Why should I believe you, not him?"

"For no reason at all. But there are other opinions. When we have opportunity, perhaps you would like to ride to Grimstead monastery and consult with the abbot there. I have met him and he seems to be both good and wise."

Imogen nodded, relieved by such a reasonable suggestion. "I would like to do that."

"Good. I assure you, the last thing I want is to force you to act against your conscience, but this situation cannot go on indefinitely."

"Particularly with Lancaster around."

His glance was quick and sharp. "Quite."

Imogen's fingers tightened on her goblet. "What did you mean about position and care?"

He lounged back and sipped his wine. "With most women, if a man takes care, there's little blood and pain, and if you weren't on your back on the bed, there quite likely wouldn't be blood on the sheet."

Imogen opened her mouth and then shut it again. She had questions, but they were not ones she felt able to ask. She liked the fact, though, that he had answered her question so directly. She was used to people telling her not to worry her pretty head about things.

She should tell him about Warbrick and Janine. Panic seized the back of her neck just at the thought.

She took another tack. "I am ready to do my duty, Lord FitzRoger. I'm sure if you would just *do* it, it would be all right."

She wasn't sure, but if he were quick, surely it would be over with before the worst of her fears had a chance to gather.

"It might come to that, Imogen, but it's not my way. And I hope for better." He turned his goblet thoughtfully, then looked up at her. "You may not realize this, but it would have been no easy matter to complete the marriage last night. Perhaps it was the way you fought me, or perhaps it is the way you are made, but I could not have entered you without using a great deal of force."

She hadn't realized. "I'm sorry."

"I'm not sure it is something you can control, but I'm sure it will help if you can ease your fears. Even if it does hurt you the first time, it is a natural thing, after all." He was looking at her in that considering way, seeking out strengths and weaknesses. "Come here."

Her nerves trembled, but warily she rose and obeyed.

When she was standing by his knee, he took her hand. He played with her fingers. "Tell me what you fear. The pain of losing your maidenhead, if there's pain at all, will be soon over."

"I don't fear the pain." Imogen wanted to tell him, but could not find the words. Could he explain why he feared closed spaces?

"You cannot persuade me that you do not like to be kissed and fondled."

Her cheeks were burning. "No, I like it well enough. From you, at least."

"A compliment!" he declared. "We progress! Who else has kissed and fondled you, though?"

The edge in his voice made her nervous, but she answered. "My betrothed kissed me on the lips now and then, and Lancaster once. His breath is foul."

Still, he played with her fingers in a mesmerizing way. "So, why are you afraid,

Imogen? I don't bite. Or only," he added, raising her hand and nipping her fingers, "in the nicest ways."

She snatched her hand away. "That! That's what I fear. Your urges are wicked!" It was a paltry, lying evasion, and she knew it.

He shook his head slightly and considered her. The silence stretched until she felt fit to scream. What was he planning?

"For this night," he said eventually, "I give you my word, I will do only what you wish. If you say stop, I will stop."

He held out a hand. Tentatively, Imogen placed hers in it. He pulled her down onto his lap.

"What are you going to do, then?"

"Kiss you," he said, and did.

His lips were soft and warm, and his hand played gently at her neck. Imogen easily put all the words of Father Wulfgan away and relaxed. She snaked her hands about her husband's neck and submitted happily.

Even when his hand wandered over her breasts she stifled any protest. If she just kept her attention on the kiss, perhaps she could keep dark thoughts at bay. . . .

The mere idea caused them to hover around her like a storm cloud. It was as if she were afraid of being afraid. No, she wouldn't give in to this insanity. There was nothing here to stir her fears. Warbrick had never touched Janine's breasts. There was no connection.

She kissed her husband fiercely, trying to drive the shadows away. This could not be too hard a thing to do, especially when she could tell that her body wanted what he offered. The wanting was like warmth trickling through her and coiling sweetly in her belly.

He said she'd tightened against him. She didn't think she was tight now.

He murmured something approving and unclasped her precious girdle to let it slither to the floor. It clattered carelessly in a way that made her wince. His hand invaded her tunic to be one layer closer to her skin.

Her body moved with desire. Her mind said this was right.

The terrors, though, the terrors screamed, *Stop!*

She blocked them and said, "Yes," even though her heart was pounding with fear.

He was studying her and she looked into his eyes for strength. He captured her hand and held it to his chest. "Yes?" he asked.

She nodded, fighting the demons with every fragment of strength she could find.

Who was in control of her body and her mind, she or them?

She *could* do this. She could.

"You look frightened," he said on an unsteady breath, "but we'll go very slowly, and I'll stop if you want."

"I'd rather it were fast," she protested. "I know it can be fast. I've heard —"

He put his fingers over her lips. "It will be easier for you if we take our time. Trust me, Imogen. . . ."

He was slow as he took her hand and slid it down his hard body until it touched where he was harder. She flinched, but he held her there gently. "Don't be afraid of it," he said. "It won't hurt you, or at least, only the first time. You are made for this, Imogen. Accept it."

Yes, she told herself. Women are made for this. She remembered the needlewomen and their anticipation.

No! shrieked her fears. Remember the pain. Violation. Blood. Screams.

Martha, she reminded herself fiercely. Dora. Those whores down in the hall taking ten men a night. Her mother and father.

Janine!

Women have endured this since time began. It is natural. I can be calm and let him do his duty.

I can. I can. I can.

Her heart was speeding so, she feared he must hear it.

In her effort to gain control she clutched at him. He jerked under her hand and swelled. She looked into his eyes and saw the power of his need.

Her control broke. She pushed away violently. His hold was lax so she fell bruisingly to the floor.

At the look on his face, she scuttled backward. "I'm sorry, I'm sorry," she said, tears streaming down her face. "I tried . . ."

He buried his head in his hands. "Then don't." He surged to his feet and turned toward the door.

"Please don't leave me!" Imogen cried, then she shook her head. "Oh, I'm sorry. Go, if you want. Go to a whore. I won't mind. It's all my fault."

He was like an ebony statue, except his face, which was ivory-pale. "I will never use a whore in your house, Imogen. I will only be gone for a short while. If you wish to be kind, get into bed, but keep your shift on."

Imogen watched the door click shut, heart-sick. How could something she wanted so much be so impossible?

She obeyed him, though. Trembling, she used the water left for washing, then climbed into the bed in her shift.

She was discovering that life wasn't a chess game. She couldn't plan the moves, and she needed more than her brain to win. Despite all her good intentions, she wasn't in control of her body and couldn't will herself to behave as she wished.

It was like rats. No willpower on earth could make her pick up a rat, even a dead one.

How could it be resolved?

But FitzRoger had gone into the secret passageways to save his friends.

How did that help her? She'd tried to be brave tonight, and it had been nothing but disaster.

He had vomited when he came out of the passageways. Would she vomit if they consummated the marriage? What would that do to him? Perhaps, after all, she should go to the nunnery.

She didn't want to. She wanted to stay with FitzRoger.

He returned, calm in a way that was not natural. It made the hairs raise on Imogen's skin, though not with a sense of danger.

Father, she begged, *what do I do now?*

There was no answer.

FitzRoger stripped down to his drawers, then climbed into the bed. He did not touch her, but lay on his side, looking at her. She met his eyes. She owed him that.

"Imogen," he said, "it would help, I think, if you could send Father Wulfgan away. The monks at Grimstead would take him in and doubtless some of them would appreciate his brand of piety."

Imogen knew Father Wulfgan wasn't the major problem, but just the mask she was using to hide from the dark. Sending the priest away, however, was a little enough thing to ask. "Very well," she said.

He nodded. "And I would like a promise from you."

"What?"

"That you will never endure anything from me in lovemaking. If you feel at all uncomfortable, let me know. It is . . . extremely hard on me to be misled in these matters."

Imogen swallowed. "But I'm not sure if . . ."

"We can at least try."

She searched his eyes and told herself that he knew what was what. "Very well. I promise."

"Good. Now, go to sleep." He turned, and cut off communication with absolute finality.

Imogen turned wearily in the other direction, wondering how this was to unravel.

Chapter Thirteen

The next day, Imogen again awoke to find herself alone, but she had no fear that he had abandoned her. No matter how tangled it all became, FitzRoger would never abandon such a source of wealth and power. The more likely hazard was that one day he would tie her down and rape her.

When she ventured down to the hall she learned that FitzRoger and the king were again out hunting. They were insatiable, and in the king's case, inexhaustible. The hall gave silent evidence of another wild night, but at least there were no whores in sight.

Imogen intended to continue her organization of Carrisford, but when she was told that the Earl of Lancaster had pleaded the exhaustion of the journey and declined to hunt, she grew wary. She retreated back to her room to avoid a meeting. Any meeting between them was bound to be unpleasant, but it could also be dangerous.

What would Lancaster do if he suspected the marriage was unconsummated? He would do something, and it was clear the king did not want to move directly against the earl.

Henry's position was still precarious, and he could not afford to offend such a powerful man.

Considering the possibilities, Imogen wanted, quite desperately, to be in a consummated marriage with FitzRoger. Everything then would be relatively simple, both for her and for the kingdom. Here, in the calm of the moment, she couldn't understand why it was impossible to achieve. If FitzRoger had been available, she would have dragged him to the bed to try again.

She laughed at the thought.

For the moment, however, she had plenty to occupy herself. If she couldn't be a full wife to him, at least she could manage their properties properly. Today she would tackle the accounts and pay all her debts.

That meant a trip to the treasure vault.

The shoemaker had sent the new shoes, and she found the man was good at his work. The shoes did not rub any sore place, and fitted snugly. The raised cork soles would protect her from any mud.

She wasn't looking forward to the trip, for the passages were dark, damp, and noisome in places, and she had never gone to the treasure vault alone. This, however, was just a fear, and one she could face, unlike the other. The main hazard was that she might encounter a rat, but she had never met a rat there. They tended to avoid the lantern light.

Keeping an eye open for Lancaster, Imogen made her way to the lower floor by a tower staircase that led to the buttery. After ensuring that the paneled corridor was deserted, she moved one carved panel and slipped into a stone alcove behind, easing the wood back in place. The alcove did not look unusual to the uneducated eye, but a push swiveled the wall, causing an opening.

Imogen slipped through and let the stone swing heavily back, enclosing her in the musty damp. Panic choked her for a moment, for there was only the glimmer of light through small openings in the wall designed for just that purpose. She had expected this, though. She fought her fear and waited for her eyes to grow accustomed to the dimness.

Her ears sought betraying scratching noises but heard only blessed silence broken by the drip of water in the distance. Her heart rate began to settle.

The floor here was smooth stone and she walked quickly to her left to where the lantern was kept. What would she do if it wasn't there? Go on, she told herself. Go on to the next one closer to the treasure room.

The lantern was there, along with flint and tinder. She lit the candle inside with hands unsteady with relief. The thin light seemed startlingly bright, but only showed stone walls striped by green dampness, and a lot of cobwebs. Now she had a light, however, Imogen's fears receded.

She went through the passageways purposefully, coming to forks and turns, but always knowing the way to go. She stopped at one unmarked place and loosened a stone. From behind she took the key to the treasure room.

She pressed on, feeling the way slope downward. The passage became damper, the floor slippery.

Now two clear passageways lay before her, and one that appeared hopeless. Thick cobwebs curtained the entrance, indicating that no one had passed that way for years. Beyond the ground sloped apparently into deep water. Imogen ducked as low as possible under the cobwebs and skirted the slimy little pool which, in fact, was only ankle-deep. Beyond was mud, but it was only a thin layer. It squished unpleasantly under her cork soles, though, and at least one garderobe discharged deliberately down the outside of the nearby wall, filling the place with a foul smell.

Looking ahead, one would swear the passage soon dead-ended in rough-hewn rock, but she went forward. At the rock face, a narrow turn was revealed which widened into a space blocked with an ironbound door.

With a relieved breath, Imogen slid in the key and turned the well-oiled lock. The door was open to the treasure of Carrisford.

There were chests, bags, boxes, and — on shelves — golden plates and goblets.

It was tempting to take some of the splendor up to the hall to restore the magnificence of her home, but with the king here it would be unwise to produce new treasures. She needed coin for her debts, and a few of her jewels, that was all. She went to a box and took out two bags of coin.

From a chest she selected a few favorite jewels, including two circlets. That reminded her that she had given FitzRoger no gift. She wanted to give him something.

She opened her father's jewel chest. Everything was here, for all his jewels had been brought down after his death, brought by herself, Siward, and Sir Gilbert, the only ones who knew the full secrets of Carrisford.

Tears pricked her eyes at the sight of these familiar ornaments, last seen on Lord Bernard's person. She lifted a magnificent egg-sized ruby on a chain, remembering how she had loved to catch the sun in it as a child. Aunt Constance had said she'd cut her teeth on it.

She let it fall. It was not suitable for FitzRoger.

She checked through soft leather bags, knowing what she sought. At last she had it: a magnificent chain of heavy gold set with smooth cabochon emeralds. It was perhaps the most precious item in the treasure and little worn, for it had not suited Lord Bernard's looks. It would be magnificent on FitzRoger, though.

She hesitated. When she gave it to him, he would know she had been here to her treasure.

So be it. He'd know anyway when she paid her debts.

She put her collection in a pouch made of her tunic skirt and locked up carefully behind herself. She made her way back along the muddy passage and left it, disturbing the cobwebs as little as possible.

Letting her breath out with relief, she hurried back along the passageways and returned the key to its place. Then she went on to where she had to leave the lantern. From there, however, she took a slightly different route, for she didn't dare exit in the buttery, where it was hard to tell if someone was close by.

She came out instead in a garderobe near the hall. She slipped out of there and headed up to her room. To the room she shared with FitzRoger.

As she turned into the tower stairs, she heard a voice call her name. Lancaster. God rot the man. She ignored the call and ran up to the solar. She dropped her treasure into her chest and locked it, then quickly brushed away the cobwebs.

She had just finished when Father Wulfgan stalked into the room without a knock.

"Daughter, where have you been?"

Imogen almost said, That's none of your business, which startled her considerably. She remembered then that she'd promised to get rid of the priest, and felt her knees knock.

Under FitzRoger's eyes it had seemed easy enough. Face-to-face with Father Wulfgan, it was almost impossible.

"I was inspecting some of the storerooms, Father," she said.

"You were looked for, and not found. My Lord of Lancaster seeks to speak with you. You owe him that."

"Do I?" Why on earth would Wulfgan be on Lancaster's side?

"He is a godly man," said Wulfgan. "He does not lust after war. He is generous in support of holy works. If he had become your lord, he would have founded a new monastery on this land, one truly dedicated to a life of mortification."

Imogen sighed. So even Wulfgan was not above bribery. Was he to be abbot of this foundation? It did offer a possible solution to her dilemma, though. "Perhaps Lord FitzRoger will found one such," she offered.

"He would corrupt everything he touches! Do you know your husband has brought foul women into this place?"

Oh dear. "They are for the king, Father."

"Impious king. He has a wife, so does not even have that excuse for his depravity!"

"At least FitzRoger is not so depraved."

"He has you upon whom to slake his foul lust." He fixed her with a penetrating gaze. "Did you stay pure in heart, daughter? I witnessed him dragging you from the company before the sun had decently set."

"We played chess!" she said in quick defense.

"Chess?" His eyes sharpened.

"Yes." Imogen couldn't endure another inquisition and prayer session. She'd rather face the earl. "I will speak with Lord Lancaster in the garden," she said. "Please tell him that."

Wulfgan narrowed his eyes at the command, but blessed her and obeyed.

Lord, how was she to dismiss Wulfgan when he reduced her to a child so easily? It was tempting to let FitzRoger do it, but she knew it was for her to do. But first she must face Lancaster.

It was interesting and dangerous that Lancaster had moved to bring Wulfgan on his side. The earl clearly had not accepted defeat. Could he suspect the truth? Had she said anything to Wulfgan to make him believe that the marriage was unconsummated?

She didn't think so.

So now she had to convince Lancaster.

Imogen wiped damp palms on her skirt and called for Elswith. The girl came running, and Imogen had her check that there were no smudges on her cheeks or marks on her skirts. First thing in the morning Elswith had woven Imogen's hair into two fat braids twined with silk ribbons, but now, to make a point, Imogen put on a veil and anchored it with a heavy gold circlet.

Then she made her way with stately grace down to the garden.

This garden had been started by Imogen's mother in a walled square next to the keep. Lord Bernard had cherished it carefully in his wife's memory, and Aunt Constance had tended it, too. Imogen loved it, but knew better than to tamper with it, for she had no skill with plants at all.

She needn't have bothered. This enclosure had escaped her scrutiny up till now, and she was appalled. Why had she thought the garden would have escaped Warbrick's spite?

The precious roses were stripped of blooms and most of the branches were bent or broken. She suspected that only the thorns had deterred the invaders from ripping them up as they had ripped up some other bushes. The smaller plants — flowers and herbs — had been trampled into the earth.

Two men were working there, trimming away destruction and easing plants free of mud.

"It will have to wait until next year to be remade," she said sadly to one of them. "And

even then it will be years until it regains its glory."

The man bowed and smiled. "Nay, lady. Give it weeks, even. It looks rough, but there's little loss. We can survive this and be as good as ever, if not better."

When Imogen looked closer she saw that the man was right. Plants appeared fragile, but had their own strengths. Many could bend rather than be broken. Warbrick's men had clearly been in too much of a hurry to do the job thoroughly and most of the plants would survive.

Here and there, roses bloomed valiantly, even if short of half their petals and drooping on a bent branch. Not all the leaves were gone, and she saw buds which would bloom later. The trampled plants were already straightening under their own power and putting up new growth, new blooms.

Imogen leaned and broke off a bent sprig of rosemary. She brought it to her nose and inhaled the rich aroma, stronger when it was crushed.

The garden was a symbol of the future. Carrisford could revive from brutality, and so could she. Was she not called the Flower of the West? Flowers were not weak. She would be stronger for having been crushed. . . .

"Ah, there you are!"

Imogen turned with a grimace to see Lancaster striding toward her, rested and groomed

into his usual sleek magnificence, his thinning fair hair curled around his face. She moved away from the gardeners, knowing this would not be a pleasant interview.

The earl surprised her. The arrogant anger she had heard in his voice disappeared as he said, "Imogen, my dear child. How you have suffered." He held out his fleshy, beringed hands, and she felt obliged to put hers into them.

He squeezed them. His hands were soft, warm, and sweaty, very unlike other hands. . . .

"I was stunned when I heard the news of Lord Bernard's death, my dear. I had thought it merely a sickness, and was sure that my physician would soon have him on his feet again. . . ." He touched his eyes, though she could see no tears. "As soon as Master Cornelius brought word of the terrible event, I hastened here."

"It came as a shock to all of us," she said, leading the way to a marble bench that her father had said dated from Roman times.

It had been his favorite seat.

She sat, and Lancaster sat beside her, his girth so wide that his leg pushed against hers. They had sat thus before and she had not been so aware of such things. Now she wished she could sidle away.

"A great shock," he agreed, patting her thigh. "And even more of a shock to hear

that you were invaded. How did they force you to marry such a man, child?"

"It was the Lord of Warbrick who invaded." Imogen gestured angrily at the ruined garden. "He wrecked Carrisford."

Lancaster's eyes narrowed, and she reminded herself that he was not a stupid man. "Carrisford is nigh impregnable, Imogen. How did Warbrick take it?"

"Do you think we let him in? That would have been madness. There was clearly treachery." She saw no reason not to tell him of their suspicions. "We think some monks who were resting here might have been false, and overwhelmed the guards at the postern gate."

He frowned. "But when Lord Bernard wrote to me, he said that during his illness he had ordered Carrisford sealed."

"So he did. But the monks were already here when my father was wounded. Had been here for some days. They were traveling to Westminster but one of their party fell sick. It seemed to cause the man great pain to be moved, so Father gave them permission to rest here instead of Grimstead. He was always . . . always kind in such matters."

"Indeed he was," said Lancaster, but absently. "But, my dear girl, this surely means the whole tragedy was planned."

Imogen looked up sharply. "Planned? How could it have been planned?"

Lancaster was frowning at a broken-stemmed lily. "It means your father's death was no accident."

"No accident? But it was just a minor arrow wound. Even if the wound was given with malice, how could anyone count on the infection?"

He turned to look at her. "Master Cornelius was puzzled by the course of the illness. He suggested that a wound from an arrowhead dipped in excrement would be more likely than not to fester. Whose arrow was it?"

Her father had been *murdered?* Imogen's thoughts were scrambled by this. "We never found out, and lacked time to search thoroughly. A poacher, we supposed, but a sweep through the forest turned up no one."

"Long gone. And paid for by whom?"

Thoughts steadied and focused. "Warbrick," Imogen spat. "He was the one ready to move. May his soul rot in hell for eternity!"

"Or FitzRoger," countered Lancaster oozingly. "He, after all, is the one who has benefited."

"No." It was an instinctive response. Imogen sought to shield it by giving reasoned arguments. "That makes no sense, my lord. If the Lord of Cleeve had murdered my father, he would have been quicker off the mark to seize the advantage. I assure you, my husband is very efficient in such matters."

"So I understand," said Lancaster sourly.

"But he might not have realized great speed was required. He possibly intended a less brutal wooing than Warbrick. Your father had refused his suit, you know."

"He had?" Imogen wanted to clap her hands over her ears and run, but she was stronger now. She would not flee.

"Yes. Would Lord Bernard have joined you to one of such suspect birth? I see Beauclerk's hand in this. With Duke Robert a constant threat, and Belleme gathering power here in the west, Henry needs a secure base hereabouts. He sent FitzRoger to dispose of that weakling brother and secure Cleeve. Their next move was to acquire Carrisford. I'm sure they would have preferred to accomplish their ends in more ordinary ways, but once your father rejected FitzRoger's suit, he had to die. Interesting, isn't it? Henry's brother, King William, died of an arrow wound while out hunting, and here we have the same method again. . . ." He looked at her sadly. "I fear your father would have been most disappointed with you, my dear."

Imogen felt sick. His words made a great deal of sense, struggle as she might not to believe them. Hugh of Cleeve's death had been looked at askance, and the whole country had its suspicions about the death of King William Rufus. She *couldn't* suspect her husband having a hand in the death of her father, though. She'd go mad.

341

She must have given away some hint of her feelings. Lancaster took her hand. "All is not lost, Imogen. I am sure this marriage can be broken. A claim of force, perhaps. Or abduction."

Imogen shook her head. "There are many to swear that I consented freely, as I did."

She saw the angry frown, quickly concealed, and reminded herself that no matter what FitzRoger was, the earl had his own self-centered motives for all this. She tried to sift through all he had said. . . .

He watched her carefully. "The women say there was no blood on the sheet."

Imogen's mouth dried. She should say what FitzRoger had said, that it was a matter of position and care. What if Lancaster asked for details, though?

"Well, Imogen? Are you a true wife, or has FitzRoger proved unable . . ."

Imogen met his eyes. "He is completely able." That was no lie.

He studied her and she hoped her mask was good. "Is that the truth?"

"Yes."

Perhaps her mask was not very good, for he said, "And do you vow that the marriage is complete?"

"What else would I mean?" Sweet Mary, help me. She had never given a false oath in her life.

"Imogen, you mustn't be afraid of such a

man. But for the king's favor, he is nothing, and I can protect you from the king. It is by no means certain anyway that Beauclerk will hold his throne."

"That's treason!" she declared, hoping to distract him.

"That is merely a wise man's opinion. Father Wulfgan seems to think you have not, as he puts it, been corrupted."

Imogen realized that Lancaster had disastrously misinterpreted the priest on that and felt an insane urge to giggle. If only FitzRoger would appear to handle this.

Scenting blood, Lancaster pulled out a jeweled cross from his pouch. "Make a solemn vow to me on this, Imogen of Carrisford, that you are a true and complete wife to Bastard FitzRoger."

She tried to pull away, but he took a vicelike grip on her wrist. Despite his sleek softness, he too was very strong.

"You have no right to demand such a thing, my lord. I have told you —"

"Say it," he hissed, "or I will put the matter before a Church court and have you placed in a nunnery until the matter is decided. An examination will soon determine the truth."

Imogen froze. She could scream for help and receive it, but the threat would remain. If she admitted the truth, she could end up wed to Lancaster; Henry could not thwart him forever. The very best that could happen was that she and FitzRoger would be given another chance, and her husband would force her ruthlessly.

She'd rather that than the other, but it would destroy them.

She begged God's forgiveness, then placed her hand upon the cross. "I avow on the cross that I am a true and complete wife to Tyron FitzRoger, Lord of Cleeve." She pulled away again and this time Lancaster let her go.

No thunderbolt shot down from the sky to shrivel her, but she felt soul-dead.

Imogen stood unsteadily and straightened her skirts with shaking hands. "That was not well done of you, my lord. You know I was gently raised and such matters embarrass me. I am sorry you are disappointed in your wish to marry me, but if you serve him honestly, I am sure the king will make good his word and find you a prize even greater."

Lancaster stared at her hotly. "There is no prize in England greater than you, Imogen of Carrisford. When I think of the care I have taken these last months . . . I treated you like the Blessed Lady. I should have thrown you down and raped you."

She stepped back from the hot malevolence in his eyes. "My father would have killed you."

He sneered. "Your dear father was a pragmatist and I was his equal in power. There would have been nothing he could have done other than get us married." He rose to tower over her. "One way or another, Imogen of Carrisford, you will be mine."

With that, he turned and stalked away.

Imogen felt sick. That last threat had been against FitzRoger as well as herself, and she knew now that healthy, powerful manhood was no proof against premature death.

Her father had been murdered.

And now she had made a false oath.

She wanted to race to the chapel to pray for guidance and for forgiveness, but she suspected Lancaster would be watching her, looking for just such evidence of deceit.

She wanted to confess to Father Wulfgan, but that would be even more disastrous.

But what if she should die with such a sin on her soul?

She paced the garden fretfully. What was she to make of her father's death? She couldn't, wouldn't, believe that FitzRoger had had a hand in it, but perhaps the king had brought it about.

It was more likely Warbrick.

She grasped that with relief. Yes, if anyone had murdered her father, it was Warbrick. After all, if it were the king, FitzRoger was tarnished by association.

But Henry had surely brought about the death of his brother. By an arrow, out hunting.

And now Lancaster was enemy to FitzRoger. Would her husband be the next to suffer an accident? He was out hunting now. . . .

She made herself stop such thoughts before she went mad. He'd hunted yesterday.

Lancaster hadn't been here then.

But now she was suspecting *Lancaster* of treacherous murder! He couldn't be guilty, or he'd not have sent his physician, or taken so long to come here. . . .

Imogen saw the gardeners glance at her curiously and knew she couldn't show her terror like this. Nor could she do as she wished and ride madly in search of FitzRoger.

She forced calm on her skittering mind and went to work on the accounts.

With effort she could put away thoughts of murder and treason, and of betrayal of the worst kind, but she could not wipe away the knowledge that she was in a state of terrible sin. She had sworn a false oath on the cross.

At first her jangled mind could make no sense of the records and tally sticks, but in time she settled. Together with Siward and Brother Cuthbert she went over the records, glad to have something to do.

She didn't do very well at it, though, for the oath swamped her mind. Nothing good could come of such perjury, but what else could she have done?

"Perhaps this is too much for you, Lady

346

Imogen," said Brother Cuthbert kindly.

Imogen forced herself to concentrate. She would seek forgiveness, but not of Wulfgan. Startlingly, she didn't trust him with the truth now that there was an alliance between him and Lancaster. That alliance, combined with his rabid hatred of FitzRoger, made the situation perilous.

Nor, she realized chillingly, could she confess her sin at all until the marriage was consummated. She would be expected to rectify it by telling the truth. That she couldn't do.

Sweet Mary, aid her.

"Lady Imogen," prompted Siward. "Do you approve the purchase of new hangings?"

"What?" Imogen forced herself to think. "Oh, yes. And send to London to see if we can find some like the ones we had from Italy."

"That will be very costly, lady."

"We can afford it. I want Carrisford to be restored."

"Perhaps we should consult with Lord FitzRoger. . . ."

"No," said Imogen, affronted. "I rule Carrisford, and I decide how my wealth will be used."

She saw the two men exchange a glance, and foresaw trouble. She almost surrendered, for this was petty compared to the real problem shadowing her life. But she didn't.

They returned to the records.

Fortunately, Siward had managed to hide Carrisford's record book and tally sticks, and the chest of deeds and documents. Imogen had been trained to understand such matters, so once she disciplined her mind, she could easily see what had been going on since her father's death.

Nothing untoward. There was no sign that FitzRoger had taken any money out of the estate, and many records of his paying for needed supplies. Imogen made a careful tally of the amounts. She checked Siward's records of things required for the domestic management of Carrisford and resolved to demand an accounting of the other senior officers. Beeswax and brooms, salt and cinnamon; they needed almost everything.

She calculated how much Siward required for immediate expenses and added in the debts for supplies provided by the local people — wool, dairy goods, poultry and such. After a moment's consideration, she added the money owed to FitzRoger. She would prefer that Siward pay it back.

The immediate debts took nearly all the coin she had brought up from the treasure chamber.

At last she felt that she had gone over everything, that she was beginning to take control. She had even seen the records of her half brothers and sisters, though Siward had tried to conceal them, and was pleased to see they were being well raised by a merchant's family. Whether she should do more for them was a matter for the future.

It unsettled her, though, that such a significant part of her father's life had been kept entirely from her. She would have thought, at the least, that there was honesty between herself and Lord Bernard.

What was illusion and what was real?

Having finished that task, she took the midday meal in the hall. With the hunting party out, and many men on guard, the company was thin. Lancaster was there, however, watching her like a hawk. Even Wulfgan was present, and he too seemed to be trying to strip her down to her soul. She couldn't stand another session with him, but nor could she gather the courage just yet to banish him to Grimstead.

With relief, she suddenly remembered her intention of visiting the Abbey at Grimstead to check on the wounded men and learn something of the treatment of wounds. Perhaps she could also speak to the abbot there — about lust, and about false oaths. Perhaps there was a way to receive absolution for the oath without telling the truth.

She needed an escort. Today, Renald was also out hunting, and big Sir William was in command of the castle defenses.

"An escort, Lady Imogen?" he said suspiciously. "But why would you be wanting to go to the monastery?"

Imogen could tell that the stupid man suspected her of trying to escape. Where on earth did he think she had to go? "To visit the wounded," she said. "It is my duty to ensure their welfare."

"They are being cared for, my lady, and I am not sure if such a journey is wise."

"Sir William, it is scarce more than a league! Hardly out of sight of the watchcorn. With an adequate escort, what harm can possibly befall me?"

"I do not like it."

Imogen's patience snapped. "Sir William," she hissed through her teeth, "if you do not provide an escort, I will ride out alone. Unless you are willing to restrain me forcibly, you will not be able to stop me."

He looked as if he'd be delighted to restrain her forcibly, and lock her up as well, but his nerve failed him. With great ill will he selected six men to ride with her.

It was a small victory, but it heartened her. Imogen found it refreshing to be out in the countryside and in charge of her own mount. The horse she was riding was not her own sweet Ysolde, but a rather large, rawboned dun. It was well behaved, though, and her spirits lifted.

Halfway through the short journey, she had a momentary qualm as to whether her riding would give away her virgin state. She assured herself that any soreness from her wedding night would surely have passed. She hoped that was true. She wanted to give Lancaster no reason to revive his doubts.

At the abbey the porter greeted their patron's daughter, now their patroness, with great warmth. Imogen was disappointed to hear that Abbot Francis was in Wells engaged in Church business and so not available for counsel, but she could pursue the other part of her plan.

Brother Miles, the infirmarian, was a little doubtful about the wisdom of Lady Imogen's visiting the wounded men. He clearly remembered her father's days, so recently passed, when she was not to be exposed to any unpleasantness. Imogen was gently insistent and he gave in, if skeptically.

He guided her around the ten beds which contained those wounded in taking Carrisford. One man had lost a leg which had been crushed by a barrel.

He was pale and haggard, but said cheerfully, "Don't you fret, lady. 'Twer my own fault, not yours. Just careless, I was."

"Still," said Imogen, "it happened in my service, and I will see you have a livelihood."

" 'Tis gracious of you, lady, but Lord FitzRoger will care for me. He's said so."

"He's been here?" she asked of both the monk and the soldier.

"Assuredly, lady," said Brother Miles. "Nigh every day."

"For sure," said the man, showing a broken

tooth. "Right scathing, too, about me being in such a fix, but he'll see to me."

She wondered when her husband had found the time, and felt like a useless good-for-nothing in comparison.

Imogen went on to a worse case where fever had taken hold. The man tossed and turned in delirium and a novice sat by gently sponging him.

"Will he live?" she asked quietly, remembering her father. They had kept her from him until the last. . . .

"It is in God's hands, but there is hope."

"And the best treatment is to wash him thus?"

"And herbs to balance the humors and keep away devils."

"Vervaine and betony?"

The man looked at her with more respect. "Aye, lady. And pimpernel."

They moved on past other men recovering well, though one would not see through his right eye again.

"I hoped there was a man here called Bert." Imogen saw no sign of Bert. Had he died of the stab wound — the wound caused by her insistence that they join the fighting in Carrisford?

She turned to the infirmarian.

"Ah, we have him in a small room apart, lady. Do you wish to see him? I fear it is not a pleasant case."

Poor Bert. "Yes," said Imogen. "I want to see him."

The room was a small, cool cell with white walls and a crucifix over the bed. An old monk made vigil by the bed, praying quietly. The once hearty Bert was shrunken down, and his skin was the color of old ivory. He made a strange, gurgling sound with every arduous breath.

"Chest wound," said Brother Miles quietly. "Poignard. It festers deep. Very little hope, but he lingers. Sometimes I think it would be kinder . . . But then sometimes they rally. Or a miracle can happen. And after all, his sufferings will reduce his time in purgatory. It is in the hands of God."

There was a sickly smell which sharply reminded Imogen of her father's death chamber. The smell of pus and decaying flesh. "He looks to be unconscious."

"Most times he is, and when he revives, I doubt he knows where he is. When men recover from such things they rarely remember them, which gives me hope that he does not truly suffer."

Just then Bert heaved in the bed and groaned incoherently. The old monk prayed louder as if to mask the sounds. Imogen instinctively went forward and laid a hand on the wounded man's shoulder. He was burning with fever. "Lie still, Bert," she said soothingly. "You won't get better if you move around so much. Would you like a drink?"

He said nothing, but looked at her, and delirious or not she knew that he recognized her and that he suffered. For her. If she'd not insisted on going into Carrisford while the fighting was in progress, Bert would be drinking and whoring up at the castle with the rest.

He hadn't answered her question, but Imogen poured water from a pitcher to a wooden beaker. She raised the man's head slightly and trickled some fluid into his mouth. Most of it spilled down his bristly chin, but she saw him swallow some.

Imogen looked up at Brother Miles. "I am going to stay here a little." She meant, until he dies.

"It could be well into the night, lady," the monk said dubiously.

"So be it. Send one of my escort back to the castle with word."

The monks conferred and then the elderly one bobbled away, leaving his stool for Imogen. Brother Miles drew her out of the room for a moment. "There is little to do other than to wipe his brow with the infusion there now and then. I will bring a soothing draft at compline." He was still eyeing her dubiously.

"I have little experience with wounds, Brother, but I have sat with the sick."

"Aye, lady, but as I said, it could be long.

And sometimes such cases turn violent near the end."

"Then I will call for help. It is my fault he is in such a state, and I must aid him as best I can."

The monk shrugged and left. Imogen took her seat by the dying man's bed. Herbs on the floor could not disguise the smell of putrefaction and death, but in a way she welcomed it. She would do vigil here as she had not at her father's deathbed.

They had kept her from Lord Bernard throughout that brief illness, assuring her everything would be well. Only at the end had she been allowed to see him. Her father had been bathed and shaved, and his room had been heavy with perfumes, but all that failed to conceal the agony and decay.

He had looked a lot like Bert — a strong man collapsed to lumpy, pasty, suffering flesh. After his gasping instructions she had been hurried away, and back then — in another life, as it seemed — she had not had the resolution to object.

Imogen took up the cloth and wiped it around the man's head and neck. "If I had it to do over again, Bert," she said, "I can't see much to change, but I would have stayed up in the woods until we got word all was safe." She put the cloth back in the bowl and took Bert's heavy-jointed, callused hand in hers. A sixth sense told her he might be hearing her words.

"Do you know all's gone well? Warbrick got away, of course, and left the castle in a terrible mess, but Lord FitzRoger has done a lot to straighten things up, and now I'm taking charge. I should have done so from the first, but I'm not used to this sort of thing, and that's the truth . . ."

She drifted off into her own troubled thoughts, but then the flaccid hand in hers moved in what could have been an attempt at a squeeze. She looked at Bert's face, which showed nothing but the weight of suffering and gathering death, and heard each agonized, wheezing breath.

She picked up the story. "Did you know we're married, and the king's come . . . ?"

Chapter Fourteen

Late that afternoon, FitzRoger strode across the monastery courtyard to the infirmary, running his leather hawking gauntlets through his hands. This hadn't been one of his better days.

He'd had to handle Henry's irritation about the lack of bloody sheets to wave in front of Lancaster, knowing all the while that his unpredictable bride could expose the situation with a word, knowing too that he shouldn't have left her alone all day with the earl. She'd shown distinct preference for the sleek, older man. Doubtless he reminded her of her beloved father.

FitzRoger had no great opinion of fathers.

He'd had to wonder at the way he was handling this situation. Why hadn't he simply taken the girl's virginity and put an end to this? Doubtless many gently bred brides wept and fought at the crucial moment, but soon recovered from the experience. Perhaps many of them tightened so that force was required.

He knew in the same situation, he would do the same thing.

It worried him.

Thank God Henry didn't suspect the truth or he'd mate them at swordpoint, or claim *droit de seigneur* and do it himself. Henry was capable of anything in pursuit of his goals.

The king had been justified, however, in his irritation that FitzRoger had not artificially stained the sheets. That omission worried FitzRoger deeply. Imogen of Carrisford seemed to have stolen his wits.

And what in the name of the chalice was she up to now?

He and Henry had returned from an unsatisfactory and acrimonious day's hunting to receive a message that Imogen was staying at the monastery. Henry had been brief and forceful on the subject. The marriage must stand, and he wanted Imogen back at Carrisford acting the proper wife to be sure of it.

Her actions made no sense. If she were seeking refuge, surely she wouldn't come to the monastery, nor would they allow her to stay, even though Carrisford was their patron. Their rule forbade the presence of women overnight.

The porter had said Imogen was in the infirmary, but had assured him she was not ill or injured. FitzRoger was going there to find her, and if necessary to drag her home by her long beautiful hair. He was very inclined to beat her.

Halfway across the garden courtyard, music stopped him in his tracks.

It was compline, and the soothing sound of the monks' voices swept over the herbs and flowers. The flowing chant blended sweetly with the hum of insects and the joyous singing of birds. In this world of order and tranquility, he became discordantly aware of the stink of blood on his clothes, memento of their one kill of the day.

Perhaps he should have taken time to bathe.

The brothers sang of their fear of the night, and their fear of a sinful death — the everlasting night. They begged God's loving protection against the shadows of darkness.

FitzRoger had spent a brief time in a monastery as a boy. His mother's family had sent him to a monastery in England, though, and Roger of Cleeve had heard. He had compelled the monastery to throw him out.

That was when he'd gone to Cleeve, and his present life — for better or worse — had begun.

Roger of Cleeve had ordered his unwanted son thrown in the oubliette with the appropriate intention of forgetting all about him. In that hellhole a terrified child had tried to use the prayers of compline to drive away the dark and the monsters it held.

To no avail.

That time of horror still lingered in the

one weakness he had never truly conquered: the fear of tight, dark spaces.

By tooth and claw he had made a place for himself in the light, but now he had this new darkness in his life, centered on a troubling girl whom he could break but could not compel to his mold, and who could beat him at chess.

Which reminded him of his purpose. He strode on.

Brother Miles was not in the chapel, but just coming into the infirmary from a corridor. "Good evening, my lord."

"Good evening, Brother. I believe my wife is here."

They both spoke softly in the presence of the dozing patients.

The monk's expression became wary, doubtless a response to FitzRoger's tone. "Indeed, Lord Cleeve. She sits with Bert of Twitcham."

"Why?"

"I believe she feels some responsibility."

"By the cross, if I sat by every man I sent to his death, I'd have blisters."

"Yet you have visited every day, my lord."

The men's eyes locked — one strong in body and war skills, the other in the spirit and in knowledge of human frailty.

FitzRoger spoke first. "You look as if you're guarding that corridor from me, Brother Miles."

"I doubt I could stop you did you care to overwhelm me, but if you intend to beat your wife, Lord Cleeve, I ask that you do so elsewhere."

"Why should I beat her?"

"Why indeed, and yet your expression speaks of it."

FitzRoger consciously relaxed. "I merely intend to escort her home. The king cannot be ignored in this way."

Brother Miles stood aside.

FitzRoger went forward and heard his wife's soft voice. Soft and a little hoarse. What on earth was she doing?

Imogen had long since exhausted recent events, but if she stopped talking Bert's hand would make that feeble movement that seemed to urge her to continue. He was noticeably worse, and fever was being replaced by a clammy sweat. Brother Miles had come and worked a little of a soothing draft into the man's mouth. He had indicated that Imogen's presence and talk might be easing the man's last hours.

Bert's breathing was now even more labored and sometimes she thought it had stopped, but then, with excruciating effort, it would take up again like an old creaking bellows. The noise, she had realized, came not from his throat but from the air whistling in and out of the hole in his chest. She found herself praying for him to die — for his sake, not hers. But she kept talking.

"I had a puppy when I was little. Such a roly-poly creature, and golden brown. I called him Honeycake, which was very silly when he grew, but he would answer to nothing else. He was a fine bird dog and a dear friend. I last had his daughters, and they were good dogs, but not like their father. Warbrick must have killed or stolen them. My father's hounds too . . ." Her voice faltered as unwelcome memories seeped back.

So much death, though she had seen little of it. But here it was in front of her.

Something alerted her and she looked up to see FitzRoger leaning in the doorway, watching her. The sun was setting and the high window was small so that she could hardly make out his still features. Perhaps it was just an emanation that sent a shiver of unease through her. Even so, she put a finger to her lips.

A movement of his head commanded that she step outside to speak with him, but as soon as she tried to move her tired hand, Bert's closed on it with surprising strength. She looked helplessly at FitzRoger and saw the tightness of his jaw.

"Bert," she said. "I must go away for a moment. I will be back very soon, I promise."

Reluctantly his hand released her and she stepped into the corridor, her heart hammering. She waited for her husband to speak.

"What are you doing here?" His voice was quiet, but she could not miss the anger in him. She could not remember ever having been the focus of such anger before.

She didn't know why he was so angry. "I'm visiting the wounded men."

"You've never done so before."

"My father would not permit it, and so I did not think . . ."

"Perhaps I should not permit it."

"Why not?"

She realized for the first time that he was in his hunting leathers, well stained with blood and mud. She could not help but wrinkle her nose.

"I offend you?" he asked dryly. The menace was distinctly less.

"You'd be the better for a bath."

"And had intended to take one had my wife been where she should be and ready to wash my back."

Imogen colored, as much at memory as anything. "I'm sorry. I would have been back for your return if it hadn't been for Bert."

His eyes snapped to hers. "You did not intend to stay here?"

"I doubt they'd let me, and why . . . ? You thought I had run away here?"

"The idea did cross my mind. Your message spoke of staying, and said nothing of returning."

"Oh, I'm sorry. I did not intend that." That he might think she would run away startled her.

Silence fell, woven through with the distant ebb and flow of the chant and the closer rasping breaths of the dying man.

"I must go back," she said.

But when she moved he caught her arm. "I cannot let you go to Lancaster, Imogen."

She had thought on this and wondered whether she should not allow Lancaster to weave his plans. This marriage, consummated or not, put FitzRoger in grave danger. "The king promised the earl another rich bride," she said. "He could do as much for you."

"But not one with lands so convenient to mine."

Imogen tried to find something other than blunt practicality in the words, and failed. Well, they'd laid out the terms of their bargain days ago. He was strong and she was rich.

She spoke in a whisper. "He could find you a bride who would not fight you in bed."

He released her arm and his fingers traced the turbulent vein in her neck. "I don't mind the fighting. It's the terror that unmans me."

Imogen closed her eyes in shame. "I'm sorry."

"So am I." His hand slid around to raise her chin. "Look at me."

Imogen obeyed, wondering at his troubled expression.

"I have to take back my word, Imogen. I will try to give you time, but if it comes to it, I'll tie you down and rape you before I allow Lancaster to have the marriage contested."

Though her innards knotted with fear, for she knew he would do it, she said, "I hope you do. I . . . I . . ." Now it came to the time, putting her sin into words choked her.

All uncertainty fled and he grasped her shoulders. "You what?"

Impaled by his green eyes, Imogen forced the words out. "I swore on the cross that we were . . . that it was done!"

"Hush." His hand covered her lips. His eyes gleamed in the dim light, and for the first time he smiled. "Did you indeed?"

She jerked free. "Don't gloat, FitzRoger. I decided I didn't trust Lancaster's loyalty, and I've no mind to link Carrisford with a traitor. You can tell Beauclerk if you want that the earl seems very inclined to favor Duke Robert."

"We know that." He captured her again in his arms, and though she stood stiff she knew better than to fight.

"The monks will throw us out for lewdness," she said.

He touched his lips to hers. "We're leaving anyway."

Then she did struggle, fruitlessly. "No we're not! Or at least, I'm not. I promised Bert."

"Imogen, have sense. He's unconscious. The king wants you in Carrisford, and he's impatiently awaiting his meal and entertainment."

"Then you go and entertain him. I gave Bert my word."

He slung her over his shoulder and carried her out of the building.

After the first moment Imogen didn't struggle, for she knew she couldn't win a physical fight. When they reached the stables he put her down, watching her.

"You realize I am right?" he asked warily.

She straightened her skirts angrily. "By your lights, I'm sure you are. I didn't fight you, my lord husband, because I know that I cannot match you in strength. But I intend to return to Bert's side at the first opportunity, starting now." She began to walk away. He seized her arm and turned her back.

They stood frozen there as the music stopped and the monks began to emerge from the chapel.

"And I suppose if I take you back to Carrisford you will return as soon as I turn my back."

"Yes." Her heart was pounding, but this was one battle she could not turn from.

"I could tie you to the bedposts," he said.

"Yes."

His jaw tightened with impatience. "He'll be dead within hours."

"All the more reason."

He suddenly released his grip. "Imogen. If

you don't bend, I may break you."

"I've been doing a lot of bending, my lord husband. Perhaps it's time you learned how." There was something in his eyes, and she honestly couldn't tell if it was anger or not, but she knew that for all she had been willing to bend to survive, to preserve her home, and to protect her people, she couldn't bend on this. In the infirmary a man was dying because of her, and he seemed to find solace in her presence and her voice.

"I am going back, now," she said. "If you want to stop me it will have to be with force, and if he dies while I'm gone I am not sure I will ever forgive you."

FitzRoger's hand flexed with abrupt impatience and Imogen flinched.

"You don't know him. He was no saint. He was too fond of drink, and lazy."

She made herself meet his eyes. "Do you think that matters?"

His hand moved to grasp her, then stilled. He lowered it. "Very well. Stay. I will return as soon as I can. Don't leave here until I return. I don't want you abroad in the dark with only a handful of men. I'll leave my escort as well as yours. This place could be easily taken."

It had never occurred to her that she might be in danger this close to Carrisford. "But who . . . ?"

"Warbrick," he said tersely, then spun on his heel and left her.

Imogen stood for a moment, staring after him, reaction dizzying her. A few short days ago she would not have believed herself capable of defying FitzRoger in such a matter, never mind prevailing.

And now, though she knew she was morally right to insist on staying with Bert, she was not sure this enterprise was entirely wise. She had never considered that she might still be in danger. FitzRoger had re-created her security to such good effect that she'd almost wiped away what had happened, but she was still a treasure to be seized. Moreover, she was still a virgin, and thus vulnerable if anyone found out.

So many reasons to rid herself of this silly burden. Once the marriage was consummated she would be irrevocably bound to FitzRoger so that no examination, no oaths no matter how terrible, could change it. She would be able to confess her false oath and receive forgiveness. Being tied up and raped almost had its appeal.

As she hurried back to Bert, she shuddered at the thought of being asked to swear an oath on a relic, or on the host. No, she didn't think she could swear a false oath on the host. In fact, she didn't think she could swear a false oath of any kind again. Some fears, once faced, disappeared, but there were some experiences that were worse once known. This state of sin was such a pain on her soul that she would remember it all her days.

Brother Miles was in Bert's room, and seemed surprised to see her. Bert was very restless. "I do believe he missed you, Lady Imogen, but he is very weak."

Imogen took her seat again and put her hand in Bert's, using the other to soothe his brow. "I'm back," she said. "That was Lord FitzRoger, but he's had to go back to Carrisford because of the king. Kings are a lot of bother to my mind. Did I tell you this one's brought loose women into the castle? I wasn't having any of that . . ."

Bert settled, and Imogen thought she saw Brother Miles's lips twitch as he went to see to his other patients.

Things rapidly grew worse. Bert's face seemed to swell and when Brother Miles came by he said it was fluid under the skin. There was nothing they could do. The man became more restless and didn't seem to hear Imogen anymore, though he clung to her hand. If he'd more strength he would have broken her fingers.

He broke out in a cold sweat, and his pulse became rapid and weak.

Imogen ceased her chatter and fell to her knees beside the bed to pray earnestly for his release. She only realized she was crying when she saw her tears bouncing off his swollen hand. She tried to stop them, but couldn't.

Brother Miles came in and stayed, also praying quietly, prayers for the dying. *"Si ambulem in medio umbrae mortis . . ."*

Though I walk in the shadow of death, I will have no fear, for you, Lord, are by my side.

It was full dark, and just one small lamp glowed.

The end came suddenly. Bert gave one final, gasping exhalation and went on to a more peaceful place.

"Sweet Jesus be praised," breathed Imogen, resting her head on the man's limp, puffy hand.

Someone raised her and led her away. She only slowly realized it was FitzRoger. "Where . . . ?" she asked dazedly.

"Hush, I've been here for a while, doing vigil in my own way. After all, it was my fault, too. I should have realized Bert would be soft wax in your hands."

Imogen burst into tears. She was swept up and carried away. She expected to be taken to the horses, and though she had no idea how she would ride, she had learned that a person was capable of extraordinary things.

Instead, she was laid on a bed.

She looked around at a small room lit by candles. "Where are we?"

"A guest room. Normally women are

obliged to sleep in the special house outside the walls. I convinced the good brothers that your safety required that you be inside. The fact that you pay for nearly everything here might explain why an exception to the rule has been made. There are two conditions, however. One is that I stay with you to control your Eve-like outbursts of ungovernable lust. The other is that we don't indulge in carnal union on holy ground. I don't think we should have trouble with either of those conditions, should we?"

His tone was brittle, but she suspected that for once it was being used as a shield, and rather transparently. She didn't know why she thought that. If there was warmth in him, only a sixth sense could detect it.

Imogen eased into a sitting position, feeling drained. "No, I don't suppose we will have trouble with those conditions."

He picked up a wooden platter and beaker from a table. "Just bread, cheese, and meat," he said, passing them to her.

"That sounds wonderful." She began to eat. "What about the king? Is he very angry?"

"On being assured that you have not run away, he chooses to see you as a noble vision of womanly tenderness. At the moment he's not likely to take serious offense at anything we do as long as it doesn't affect matters of loyalty or cast doubt on the validity of the marriage. His mind is largely absorbed by matters military. Warbrick's reply has come, and it is defiance."

"The king will march against him?"

"He has already sent word to move on Warbrick Castle. Once that is secured, we will move on Belleme."

"Will you go?"

"Of course. I would have thought it might be a relief to you."

Imogen ducked that one. "What of Lancaster? I don't want to be left with him."

"Don't worry. When I leave, I'll be sure the earl and his men leave with me."

"I suppose he's no danger anymore, now that I've lied to him."

"I'm not sure. He is down but not defeated. He seems to have spent time with Father Wulfgan and grown encouraged."

There was a question behind it, and Imogen answered it. "I haven't told Father Wulfgan that I am still a virgin."

"So I would hope. But might he have guessed?"

Imogen knew that once the answer would have been yes, but she thought her mask was better now. "I don't know."

"Need I remind you," he asked coldly, "that you were to dismiss the priest?"

She looked down. "I meant to. Then I came here." And in part, she knew, she had been running away from just that task. Sometimes she despaired of ever finding the depth of courage she needed.

FitzRoger dropped onto the one bench and lounged there, drinking from his own cup and eyeing her. Imogen's nerves shivered. "I meant what I said earlier," he said.

"I know. I meant it too. If it comes to that point, take me by force. I don't want to end up married to Lancaster. There probably is someone in England I'd rather be married to than you, but my chances of finding him seem slim."

He raised his brows and she supposed it did sound blunt and ill-mannered, but no more ill-mannered than things he had said to her. His only response, however, was, "Just so long as you don't find him later and try to act on it."

Imogen faced him. "I will be true to my vows, my lord. When I lied to Lancaster, that was the first false oath I have sworn in my life, and it will be the last."

His lips twisted. "Whereas I can only try to be true to my word. I do, however, try."

"I know," said Imogen softly. "That's why I trust you."

His look was direct and unreadable. "Do you? You should be in bed. There's a privy just outside the door, but few other amenities."

Imogen used the privy and returned to eye the narrow bed. "It won't be easy for two to sleep there."

"I'll sleep on the floor. I'm not unaccustomed to such hardship, and we wouldn't want to be tempted to carnal union, would we?" There was a bitterly sarcastic edge to the comment and Imogen knew that for some reason her husband was in a terrible mood.

Frustrated lust?

She eyed the hard, narrow bed, wanting quite desperately to have it over with. She thought perhaps here, away from Carrisford and its memories, it might go better. But she couldn't be sure.

She stripped off her tunic and jewels and slipped into the bed in her shift. She watched as he placed his sword carefully to hand. For the first time, she noticed his chain mail, helmet, and shield lying neatly in a corner. This second time, he had come fully armed.

"Do you really think we're in danger here?" she asked.

"There's danger everywhere these days. That's one of many reasons I serve Henry. England needs a firm hand so that people can sleep safe in their beds."

"And you think he can be that hand?"

"Oh yes. Henry is nothing if not firm."

"Sometimes you don't sound as if you like him very much."

He flashed her a look. "Sometimes I don't like myself very much. Henry, like me, has the ability to do what has to be done, and if given a choice, will do what's right. There is considerable virtue in efficiency."

"It would be pleasant to have peace in the land."

"We will."

"What of Warbrick and his ilk?"

"They will be crushed, and soon."

"And then you will hold this part of the country in orderly security."

"Yes."

"And I am just a means to this end."

There was a hesitation. "Yes."

Imogen knew this was an unproductive conversation, but she couldn't help but pursue it. "If I had been a foulmouthed hag, you'd have married me, wouldn't you?"

"Yes."

"And bedded me?"

"Yes."

Imogen had known the answers, and they were completely reasonable. She couldn't think why they depressed her so. She reverted to the earlier point. "So you don't think I'm in particular danger now?"

He sighed. "I'd rather you were behind castle walls, Imogen, but I have twenty men out there, so this place is well guarded. Warbrick would need an army to take us here, and if he has an army in this area, I'll have my scouts gutted."

She should have known he would have it all *efficiently* in hand. "Why would Warbrick want to take me now? He can't know . . ."

"Partly spite. None of that family can bear to be bested. But more than your luscious body, he and Belleme want the Carrisford Treasure to fund their rebellion, or if not that, to reestablish their power abroad. He'd bargain you for your wealth."

"What it is," said Imogen, "to be a walking treasure chest. And would you pay?"

The movement of his hand was sharp and revealing. "I'd not easily leave anyone in that family's hands."

Anyone. Not her in particular. She was just a means to an end to everyone. She cleared her throat. "I wouldn't mind now."

"Being captured by Warbrick?" he asked in surprise.

She knew she was red. "No. Carnal union."

"Yes you would," he said flatly.

"I'd like to try."

"I've promised we wouldn't do that, and I never break my word without great cause. Go to sleep."

Imogen felt like weeping. "I know you must be sick to death of me, but I wish . . ."

He cursed softly and came over to stand by the bed. From Imogen's perspective he looked tall and formidable, but she knew the stirring within her was desire, not fear. Surely it would be all right here, now.

"Why the sudden desperation?" he asked. "I assure you, I'm not going to disown you."

"Of course not," she said acidly. "I'm the Treasure of Carrisford."

"Precisely. So?"

She looked down at the sheet and found she'd knotted it in her fingers. No wonder he wasn't impressed by her willingness. "The oath," she muttered. "I can't confess because I would have to tell the truth. I can't . . . I'd hoped the abbot would have some advice, but he's not here. . . ."

He leaned down to rescue the sheet and smooth it out. Imogen looked at his shadowed face, wishing she could read his thoughts, wondering what he was going to do, ferreting about in herself, trying to sense what her unreliable body and mind would do if he did take her up on her invitation.

He captured her hands and wove his fingers through hers. After a moment he spread her hands so she was vulnerable before him. Nerves jumped all through her body, but it wasn't really fear, and she hoped he knew that.

Slowly he leaned down, pushing her hands back until they were on either side of her head and he was settling over her, the coarse sheet and blanket between them. His eyes were intensely watchful.

Imogen made herself relax and meet his eyes. Then his hands loosed hers and threaded sweetly into her hair. The warm weight of him pressed against her whole body in a most comforting manner. "Perhaps a little love-play without fear would help," he said.

"What do you mean?" Imogen's lips tingled from the nearness of his, only inches away.

"I've made a promise we won't indulge in carnal union here, and I won't break it. But there are many things other than carnal union."

"Are there?" A tremor of excitement ran through her. He was going to kiss her, and there was no fear of the darker side in that.

His lips settled onto hers gently, teasingly. He played but refused to deepen it until she grabbed his head and pulled him down to her, kissing him fiercely. The sweet taste of him seemed something she had known all her life, and his shape on her fitted perfectly. It felt so right, so good, and she couldn't believe that this time it would not work for them. At this moment, she couldn't imagine rejecting him. Perhaps he could be brought to break his word. . . .

He pulled back. "Remember," he said softly, "we are absolutely not going to consummate our marriage here."

"I . . . I think I could."

"Even so, we will not. Remember that."

Then he was between the blankets, side by side with her on the narrow bed. He gathered her into his arms and kissed her again. His hands played on her back, and so she did the same. One of his hands wandered up to find the delicious sensitivity of her nape, and so she copied it. His hair, she realized for the first time, was very silky, despite the curls which suggest a rougher texture. Just rubbing it between her fingers was delight.

He had bathed, for there was no longer a stink of blood, but instead a delicate aroma of the herbs in his rinsing water. Beneath that was a spicy scent that she already recognized as his, and which seemed able to fever her all on its own.

His mouth wandered from her lips to her neck and she instinctively stretched back to grant him access, staring at the beamed ceiling as she floated on warm sensuality. His lips ventured onto her chest, tracing the neckline of her shift. A tiny spark of anxiety flared, but she stamped it.

It wasn't going to happen anyway. He'd given his word.

As if he sensed that fragment of tension, his hand soothed her, and he said, "Don't forget, even if you plead and beg, I'm not taking your virginity here."

That brought a gurgle of laughter from her and he blew softly against her face, smiling.

The hand that had been stroking her side slid up to stroke her breast, sending a shudder through her. She tested it carefully in her mind and decided it wasn't fear. Growing bolder in her mind, she tentatively sought those terrible dark fears. They weren't there, not even as distant clouds.

Was it possible that just knowing he wouldn't do it could keep them away? Perhaps if he promised, and then . . . But it was because she believed in his promises that it was working. . . .

He eased back her shift and his lips tugged softly at her nipple.

"Oh, why is that so sweet?" she whispered.

"God's holy plan?"

"Don't say such things!" But she didn't want him to stop, not at all.

"Time to talk about Father Wulfgan's warnings, Imogen," he said against her tingling flesh. "Let's get them out in the open. What does he say is so evil?"

"I don't want to . . ."

"Tell me, Imogen." His tongue touched her softly.

"What you're doing," she gasped. "That is evil. And tongue-kissing." Once started, she let it all run out like a flood. "And hands almost anywhere. Anything but . . . you know. Putting it in me. And that's only permissible because it is necessary to make more souls for God."

He sighed. "The man is mad, you know."

Imogen thought about it. "I think he is too," she said at last, reluctantly, for it felt like heresy. "Yesterday, when he was talking to me, he seemed to be trying to force me to tell him all we had done. He seemed . . . It sounds silly, but I thought he was growing . . . excited. Do you know what I mean?"

He eased away from her breast to look at her. "Yes. I suspected he might be like that. So, wife of mine, are you willing to let me tongue-kiss you, and touch you everywhere with hands and mouth, and pleasure you?"

Years of exhortations are not easily erased, but Imogen nodded.

"Remember," he said, "we are not going to indulge in carnal union, but I can give you pleasure if you will let me. This is not a duty or a penance. If you don't like it, or if you become frightened again, tell me. Yes?"

"Yes," said Imogen, though she was determined not to stop him. "What are you going to do if you're not going to . . . ?"

"This," he said, and returned his attention to her right breast. He eased over a little so his fingers could play with her left.

Imogen shivered with pleasure. "What should I do?" she asked.

"Nothing. Just tell me if I hurt you, or if you don't like it." His teeth gently abraded the top of her nipple and her body startled her by arching like a bow.

"Good," he murmured, reassuring her. "I like you to stretch and move for me. But remember, I'm not going to enter you, not even with my fingers."

"Fingers?" she gasped.

"Don't you remember? Devil hunting."

Imogen had her eyes shut, but she sensed he was looking at her and opened them. He was deliberately bringing back memories of their wedding night. Watching her reaction.

"It's all right, I think," she said, wanting to beg him to carry on with what he had been doing.

He slid up to kiss her lips and she opened her mouth willingly to him. His shirt brushed against her tender nipples and she moved herself to intensify the sensation. A tremor passed through her.

He laughed softly into her mouth, then drew back. "Oh, my sweet wanton, you'll be the death of me."

She was guilt-stricken. "I'm sorry."

He silenced her briefly with his lips. "Don't be. I want to do this. I want to drive you wild with pleasure and watch you."

"But won't that be breaking our word?"

"I only promised we wouldn't have carnal union."

Imogen hadn't been aware that she had opened her legs until his thigh slid between them to press against an ache there. She gripped him with her own thighs, then gazed at him, confused.

He read her aright. "Nothing we do here is wrong, Imogen. Nothing you do could possibly be stupid or wrong. Just show me how you feel."

She gripped his thigh more tightly with hers and drew his head down for a kiss. She thought she heard him groan. His hands traveled her. She shivered when one traced the underside of her raised thigh and brushed along the edge of her buttocks. Then it traveled over to the front and in a move, replaced his thigh between her legs.

She tensed for a moment, gripping more in defense than desire, and he stayed perfectly still, waiting. Imogen could feel her flesh there pulse with the need to be touched, but it almost felt too sensitive for any kind of contact.

"I'm not sure," she said.

"I'm just going to stroke you, very gently. I'll stop if you want me to."

She surrendered warily. "It seems a strange place to be stroking someone."

His hand gently stroked, then circled, flirting with a place of exquisite sensitivity. "But perhaps not," said Imogen, and released her resistance.

She closed her eyes so as to sink deeper into the heated sensations he was summoning. When his mouth returned to her breasts, she sucked in a deep breath. "Angels of heaven, aid me," she whispered. "This is most peculiar." A moment later she added, "Don't stop."

"I won't."

She wasn't even holding him. She had spread her arms and was gripping the edges of the bed as if her life depended on it. "Should I hold you?" she gasped.

"It's all right."

The pressure of his hand became slowly stronger and she lifted to it, stretching to it. She dimly heard an encouraging murmur and that liberated her to move, to writhe.

Teeth. He'd said something once about biting . . . She felt his teeth press at her nipple. "You're biting me!"

He stopped.

"It . . . I didn't mind."

He laughed and she felt his teeth again.

"I never would have believed this," she muttered. Then: "I don't know what to do." Her heart was pounding so that she could hear nothing but that thunder, and yet she heard his voice softly in the distance.

"That's it, Ginger. Let it happen. This is how it's supposed to be."

"What? Tell me what to do!" Her protests turned into a cry, and he caught it in his mouth. She kissed him desperately, wondering if she could survive this, begging into his mouth for release.

It came.

It was as well he still covered her mouth with his, for she screamed as her body convulsed. He moved to press her down even as his hand continued its circling. Her body fought him and that battle seemed to cause an explosion of ecstasy.

He was still touching her, but swansdown soft. His weight was still on her, but unconfining now. His mouth slowly released hers, and Imogen sucked in an enormous breath through bruised lips.

"Sweet heaven," she said softly, and stared at him.

"Yes, isn't it?" His expression was enigmatic, but she thought, she hoped, that there was warmth in the depths of his shadowed eyes.

A part of him moved against her hip and she realized he was hard and ready for a woman. Guilt invaded her delight. "But shouldn't it have been like that for you, too?"

"Sometimes. Not every time. I'm not feeling deprived. Well," he said dryly, "not very much." He drew her lazily to lie on his chest.

"Can't I do the same for you?" she asked.

"No."

"It's not possible?"

"It's not appropriate."

He was relaxed and yet his tone was austere again. She tangled a finger in the open neck of his shirt. "That doesn't seem very fair."

"It's fair. I enjoyed doing that to you."

"Then wouldn't I enjoy doing it to you?"

He pulled her up so they were eye to eye. "No, Imogen."

"No, I wouldn't enjoy it?"

"Just no."

Since he was taking her weight, she rested her elbows on his chest and put her chin in her hands. "Not even if I pout?"

"Pout? I'm supposed to be moved by a pout?" There was a distinct glimmer of amusement in his eyes that looked like a victory banner to Imogen.

"Cry then," she said. "Not even if I cry?"

"If you ever use tears to sway me, I'll rosy your behind." Despite the words, his expression was no threat to her posterior.

Imogen was aware of a glowing happiness almost as wonderful as that passion he had summoned. She was glimpsing the warm, relaxed side again, the one few people ever saw.

What would it be like when he abandoned all barriers and joined her in rapture? She wanted that, more than rapture of her own. She knew what he had meant when he said he had enjoyed watching her pleasure. She would enjoy watching his if she knew how to achieve it.

She realized with frustration that Father Wulfgan's warnings had not included enough about wicked things a woman could do to a man.

There was that business of the mouth . . . No, surely not.

She became aware of his hardness beneath her hips and moved, but gently. Such hard, engorged flesh must be very tender and she was afraid of hurting him. He caught his breath and seized her hips.

"No, Imogen."

She studied his face and didn't think it was pain she saw there. Despite his hold she managed tiny little movements.

He swatted her behind quite stingingly, rolled her off, and escaped from the bed.

Imogen sat up grinning, perfectly aware that her shift was off her breasts. "Aren't you going to share the bed?"

"I said I'd sleep on the floor. I'm supposed to defend the monks against your outbursts of ungovernable lust, and it looks as if it could be a mighty battle."

There was no hint of a smile on his face when he blew out the candle, but Imogen laughed as she slid down under the blankets. She had tasted the power of her womanhood when it was unencumbered by guilt and fear, and it was delicious.

Silence fell, and she gently explored her body beneath the sheet. It felt the same, and she supposed it was. She was still a virgin after all. But it was not the same. It was awakened. It was hungry. She really didn't feel there would be a problem with consummation the next time they tried.

That sweet ecstasy had nothing to do with the rape she had witnessed.

"I wish you'd done that before," she said into the dark.

"I tried, as I remember."

"It would have helped if you hadn't gone on about devils."

"It seemed an amusing device at the time. I underestimated Wulfgan's effect on your mind."

"I had been raised to view him as a saint. Not a comfortable person. A thorny conscience, but right." Some doubts lingered, and she knew they were in her voice.

"And yet your father begat three bastard children. I'm sure Wulfgan didn't approve."

Imogen sighed and her hands touched her newly alive body wonderingly. "I'm sure he didn't."

"Imogen," said FitzRoger into the dark. "I think your father, like many loving fathers, was uneasy at the thought of his daughter in a man's bed. Father Wulfgan was part of his defense, along with the sort of men he put forward for you. Older men that he knew would wait."

"You have waited," she said softly.

"But not for much longer. You want me now, don't you?"

Her hand found the hot moistness he had touched, and she moved restlessly. "Yes."

"Then tomorrow night we will put an end to the beginning."

Imogen wanted to beg him to do it now, when it was right and her body still hummed with need, but he was a man of his word, and he had given his word.

Tomorrow she would truly be his.

Chapter Fifteen

For the first time in her life, Imogen was awoken with a kiss but FitzRoger was already in his armor and completely the commander, not the lover.

Imogen eyed him as she dressed. The night almost seemed a dream. But the memories of it would never leave her, for they changed everything. The horror of Janine and Warbrick was set apart in her mind — not forgotten, but apart along with death, disease, and war.

A man's body close to hers, FitzRoger's body close to hers, his touch, her needs, were something else entirely, and they lingered like the taste of honey on her lips and in her mind. Nor could she view these matters as evil. Spoken of crudely they could disgust, but shared with trust and care they were surely of the angels, not the devil.

The state she was in was not a state of sin.

FitzRoger had given her — generously, carefully — that explosion of the senses. Her body and mind were still sensitized, even to the cool water with which she washed, and the sliding touch of her own clothing.

And sensitized to him.

Even now, after sleep and the passage of hours, the lightest brush of his hand brought back quivering memories. The smell that was his alone lingered in the sheets and melted her. Now she knew why newly married people were so strange and were given time apart. They were adrift in this powerful new sensuality and unable to cope with everyday matters.

Was he?

As Imogen pulled on her stockings, she slid a look at him.

She sighed. Of course he wasn't.

He was completely unaffected, and his mind was doubtless entirely taken up with practical concerns. As if to prove it, he looked over at her impatiently. Then his gaze stopped and lingered for one revealing, heated moment on her leg.

Imogen's breathing caught and she lowered her head to hide a smile. She took rather longer than she needed to put on her stockings.

She remembered knowing, last night, that it was not easy for him to give her pleasure and take none for himself. Perhaps, behind the mask, he too was drowning in sensual torment. Her legs felt none too steady as she rose to join him by the door.

He stood aside so she could pass through.

Then he moved.

His mailed hand pinned her to the door jamb at the neck with precise control — not roughly, but not gently either.

He kissed her, and that too lacked control in its heat and its force.

A jolt of longing shot through Imogen and it came from him. He jerked his head back, eyes closed, as if shocked by his own actions. His very stillness spoke of need far deeper than she could understand.

For her? Or just for any woman. As far as she knew he'd had no woman for quite some time.

He raised heavy lids to expose darkened eyes. He moved his hand as if it were a stranger to him and looked at her neck with frowning concern. Imogen raised her hand to cover her neck, though she knew there was no mark.

Her lips felt bruised.

She waited for him to speak, but he touched her briefly and steered her out into the fresh day.

Would they even wait for tonight to resolve all this? There was nothing to stop them, as soon as they arrived back at Carrisford, from retreating to their room. There was no *need* to wait for night.

Imogen quivered with nervous longing. She was full of need, but the violence of that kiss frightened her. She had a dragon on a chain; he could warm her with his breath, and soar her high on his wings, but he might, almost absentmindedly, devour her.

When Imogen and FitzRoger emerged from the monastery, she found, as he had said, that twenty men had been on guard. She appreciated his care of her while thinking it excessive. The road from the monastery to Carrisford was well maintained and clear, and curved invitingly before her. The sun was burning away the last of the morning mist, slowly making invisible the lacy spiders' webs strung between the grasses; birds sang cheerfully in the greenwood all about.

There was clearly no danger out here, and they would be home in a trice.

She heard a groan and turned.

At first there was no evidence of a problem, but then she noticed that one of the men was pale, though busily saddling his mount. Then he swayed slightly, grasping the pommel to keep his balance. FitzRoger had seen it too.

He moved forward. "You are sick?"

"A gripe, my lord, nothing more . . ." The man moved to mount, then doubled over and vomited.

In moments, most of the men were moaning or vomiting. Five were not, and Imogen realized that these all wore FitzRoger's colors while the others wore Lancaster's.

Danger after all.

FitzRoger beckoned one of the healthy men. "Gareth. What did they eat that you didn't?"

The man looked uneasy. "Not eat. Drink, my lord. Lancaster's men had a wineskin."

"But you did not drink?"

"No, my lord."

FitzRoger turned to Imogen. "You see why I flog men for drinking on duty."

"But why do you have Lancaster's men?" Fear was turning to terror. This was a plan, and the only purpose could be her undoing. She looked again at the road. Now it was as inviting as a beast's lair.

"I couldn't take all my men out of Carrisford," he said almost absently, "but I wanted extra escort for you, so I brought some of the earl's. From hindsight, a mistake."

She began to retreat toward the monastery. "We'll have to stay here. . . ."

His hand on her arm halted her. His eyes traveled over the men, well and sick; over the ten-foot-high monastery walls; and over the road to Carrisford.

Imogen's nerves settled a little. No matter what was happening, FitzRoger would protect her. He was her champion and supremely skillful at the job.

His voice was calm when he said, "The monastery offers little security from an enemy indifferent to God's wrath, and there's some plan afoot. If we act quickly we may forestall them. Can you ride?"

"Of course."

"I mean, can you ride hard and fast?"

Her heart speeded, but more with readiness than fear. "Yes. I like to hunt, remember?"

It was a feeble attempt at humor, but he rewarded it with a smile. "Good." He grabbed one of the smaller of Lancaster's pitiful men and roughly divested him of his boiled leather jerkin and his conical helmet. "Put these on."

Imogen bit back a protest and obeyed. The jerkin hung loosely, but the hardened leather would stop an arrow. She hated the thought that it might be needed. Until her father's death no weapon had ever been turned against her. She was determined not to fail this test, though. She tossed away her circlet and jammed the helmet on over her veil.

FitzRoger picked up the gold band. "We can't afford to waste this, wife," he said, and the glint of amusement in his eyes steadied her nerves.

It was impossible that he not prevail.

She tucked the circlet up her tunic, held there by her girdle. Then she saw that one of the sick men had a bow and arrows. She took up the bow, strung it, and tested it. It was stronger than she was used to, but she thought she could manage it for a few shots. She slung the quiver over her shoulder.

FitzRoger turned from giving orders to his men. "Can you use that?"

"Yes."

He made no further comment, but helped her into her saddle.

In moments, they were ready, just seven of them against who knows how many. But FitzRoger had said he was sure there couldn't be an army nearby, and it was possible that their enemy, not knowing of FitzRoger's strict standards, would expect all the guards to be sick.

Her husband rode alongside her and passed her a shield. "Put the strap over your shoulder and your left arm through the bands." She did as she was told. It was a round one, smaller than his kite-shaped shield, but it was still heavy on her shoulder and her arm.

She felt rather ridiculous. Her arm would be aching just from the weight before they reached Carrisford, and she doubted she would be able to use the shield in any purposeful manner. It would certainly stop her from using the bow.

"They won't want to harm me," she protested.

"Who knows what they want?" His eyes searched ahead. "It is my task to protect you, Imogen, and I will do so. Ride by me and keep up. And obey any order instantly."

"Or what?" she asked, trying for a bit more humor.

"Or I'll beat you if we survive."

She knew that this time he wasn't teasing.

He drew his sword, surveyed his small troop, and gave a quiet command. They left at a gallop, two men ahead and three behind.

Imogen had told the truth when she said she could ride hard, but the too-large helmet kept slipping onto her face, and the heavy unwieldy shield bounced, bruising her leg and causing her horse to break pace and jib. She began to fall behind. FitzRoger slowed and leaned to grab her reins. Imogen didn't contest it, but took a grip on the mane and concentrated on managing the shield and staying on.

She wished, though, she could have kept up on her own.

They thundered between the trees and there was no sign of any enemy.

Then arrows whined through the air. One of the front men and his horse went down in a screaming tumble of legs, blocking the road.

FitzRoger hauled to a halt. He and the remaining men swung efficiently into a protective circle around her.

Imogen looked in shock at an arrow driven well into her shield. It could have been in her body!

She saw FitzRoger wrench an arrow out of his chest. After an appalled moment she understood that it couldn't have penetrated far. If it had cut into his mail at all, it must have been stopped by his padded haqueton. But it could have been in his heart.

More arrows hissed through the air, low and at the horses. It was luck that sent most through their legs. One horse screamed, but the rider controlled it. Imogen saw a scarlet gash on the beast's belly. Not deep.

Sweet Savior, were they going to die here?

The man who'd been brought down stayed down. It was Gareth, the man who'd told them about the wine.

But she was no use to Warbrick dead, she thought wildly.

She was no use to anyone dead.

Except the king. If she died, Henry would have Carrisford.

Surely not . . .

The arrows ceased. It was an eerie moment of calm that seemed to last much longer than it possibly could.

Then ten armed men crashed out of the woods, hurtling against her defenders in a screaming, shrieking tumult. Above all other sounds was the broken-bell clanging of metal brought against metal in an attempt to hack into flesh and bone.

Imogen's horse plunged and turned, spooked by the clamoring melee all around. She controlled it viciously, looking for any chance to be of use. Her bow fell from her arm, but she didn't bother with it. It was no use in this kind of fighting.

She was bemused by how slow everything seemed. It was only moments since Gareth came down and yet it seemed an age. Everyone, friend or foe, seemed to move at dreamlike speed around her.

She saw an enemy wide open to attack, and yet a man of FitzRoger's right there took no advantage. If she'd had any kind of blade, she could have spitted him. Her swinging horse showed her FitzRoger moving as slowly as a doddering ancient, but more efficiently.

His sword swung mightily against an exposed torso and Imogen could almost hear the ribs break before the man screamed and toppled off his horse. That was more like it! She let out an exultant cry of victory, as if the blow had been her own.

One of their men screamed and went down. The protective circle fractured.

Her joy soured. There were too many against them.

Imogen concentrated on preventing any attempt to seize her. She wished FitzRoger had given her a sword even as she knew she could never have managed it. Then she remembered her arrows. She whipped a handful out of the quiver, ready to stab with them if anyone tried to seize her.

The attackers were too busy to try for her yet, though. They seemed to concentrate on FitzRoger, as if they knew that downing him was the key to her. He was fighting three, calmly, efficiently, always able to block the blows.

Her heart leaped to her mouth as she saw a mace swing viciously at him from his blind side while he fought another man. She screamed a warning, but he was already moving to avoid, to react, as if he could see all sides at once.

In a split-second gap between blows he grinned at her as if this were an amusement.

She was amazed to realize she was grinning back. This was not amusing, and yet she had never felt so vibrantly alive. If she died here, it was better than many deaths.

But she would not be taken prisoner.

A sword whistled through the air at FitzRoger's head. He blocked it with a fiery crash, turning his horse with his legs to face the attack again.

Another of FitzRoger's men went down, but the enemy was losing more. FitzRoger had accounted for at least three. Imogen longed for someone to come in range so she could stab him. She screamed defiance, and exulted at each death.

Another of their men down.

An enemy rode straight at Imogen. She reared her horse to thwart him, and screamed a warning. FitzRoger was fighting two men, but he swung his horse back on itself to cover the new threat.

He was fighting for his life and guarding

her at the same time. It was impossible.

Then the rump of his nearest opponent's horse swung into Imogen's leg, bruising her. With relish, she stabbed it deeply with her arrows.

The horse bucked wildly. The rider was not thrown, but for a moment he was beyond defense.

Still it was so eerily slow.

The opening at his neck between the flaps of his mailed coif was as clear to Imogen as the bull's-eye on a target. FitzRoger's sword found it with deadly precision. Before the man realized he was dead, FitzRoger swung brutally at his other opponent and broke his arm. The man howled and fell.

FitzRoger flashed her a grin. "Well done!"

Her heart sang.

Three other men were coming at him now, but they reined in for a moment. Why?

Not surprising if they feared to face FitzRoger.

Arrows hissed.

One glanced off Imogen's helmet, jarring back her head, making her yell with fright. Most hit FitzRoger on his right, shieldless side.

At least seven of them. He looked like a hedgehog.

He cursed fluently even as Imogen realized again that they hadn't done much damage. But they were stuck there, sharp points

surely cutting through into his skin, crippling his right arm. He switched his sword to his left.

The last of their guard went down and the two attackers turned to join the three waiting. She saw one grin expectantly.

Everything stopped.

She saw the three men ahead blocking the way to Carrisford.

She saw the two men behind, beginning, so slowly, to move toward them.

She saw the blood oozing from FitzRoger's many cuts.

When he turned toward the trees and said quite calmly, "Into the woods," she had already thrown away her burdensome shield and quiver of arrows and was beginning the only possible movement.

They raced their horses recklessly into the woods, leaping them over fallen trees, gathering them from almost disastrous stumbles. To slow was death for him, and worse for her.

He was with her, but she knew that in this race he could not help her or they would lose.

She could hear the crash of pursuit behind them, but fading.

Her helmet went, caught by a branch that would have knocked her out. After that she rode low.

Her skirts were snagged and ripped, but she thanked God they were frail so the entangling branches didn't drag her off.

He swerved down a deer track and she followed, the way easier now.

Twisting, climbing, then down a mad slope she'd never have attempted sane, almost falling.

A stream.

He hauled up his foam-mouthed horse. "Can you jump it?"

"Yes. How are you?" Most of the arrows had been broken or pulled out entirely, but there seemed so much blood!

"Go!" was all he said.

She set her horse at the stream and leaped it cleanly, pulling in to wait for him. He leaped his horse after her.

The pause gave Imogen a moment to think.

"Up ahead!" she gasped. "There are caves. We can hide." Then she wondered if that was cowardly. "Or I know the way to Carrisford from here."

"The caves," he said.

She led the way up a gradual slope toward the hummocky hills where the stone often broke through the greenery. She began to fear that she couldn't find the caves, for it was years since she'd visited them. Then she saw some rocks and remembered. She urged the tired horse on, up to the cliff.

She slid off her horse to lead the beast through the narrow opening into the chill gloom. FitzRoger did the same behind her.

"Is this wise?" she asked as she shivered in the sudden dampness. "It seemed like a good idea, but it's like a child hiding under the bed, isn't it? We're trapped here if they find us." Her voice echoed slightly, though the cave was not very large. For better or worse she'd chosen a cave that did not link into the warren that riddled these hills.

"We've lost them," he said, "and I can defend this place for quite some time."

The peculiar slowness was still there. It was fading, but still there. And an unnatural calm held her in its grip. Surely she should be shaking with terror. "Let me look to your wounds," she said.

"Leave them," he said, assessing their refuge and pulling out arrowheads like someone pulling off teasels.

One he didn't touch.

She saw that arrow was much deeper. It had managed to go through the mail and into the flesh of his arm. Most of it had broken off, or he had broken it off, but it moved as he moved and must be extremely painful.

It was also causing bleeding with each movement. "We can't leave that one," she said.

"We have no choice. The mail won't come off with it there and I can't grasp it well enough to pull it out."

"Then I'll have to do it." Imogen prayed that she could.

He looked at her, one quick, doubting

glance, then presented his arm.

Only a little-finger-length protruded from the mail and it was both sticky and slippery with blood. Imogen took hold of it as best she could and tugged. Nothing happened except a hiss of pain from him and a new welling of blood.

"I'm sorry," she said miserably.

"It's barbed, and will snag on the mail." His voice was steady. "You'll have to pull with all your strength."

Imogen took a deep breath. It had to be done and she *could* do it. Still, she first explored as gently as she could to see if she could somehow work the mail over the shaft. "Perhaps I could cut the shaft," she offered.

"I suspect that would hurt more and take a lot longer."

Imogen looked at the shaft again, one part of her mind clearly telling her that she could not do this, that if she left it everything would turn out all right, that someone else would take care of it. Another part of her knew that this had to be done if he were to have any chance of fighting with that arm without losing more blood than he could afford.

"Lie down," she said at last, startled by the commanding tone of her voice.

He looked at her. "Why?"

It seemed ridiculous to be giving FitzRoger orders, but she said, "The only way I'll be able to do it is with you on the floor. Just lie on your front."

He eased down without protest. Now the arrow shaft poked straight up. Imogen put the ball of her left foot on his forearm and the whole of her right foot on his shoulder. "Does that hurt?"

"Not particularly," he said, and added with a trace of humor, "In some places it is considered amusing to have a woman walk over a man's back. . . ."

"What sort of places? Or should I not ask?"

"Probably not."

Imogen bent and wiped off as much of the blood as she could, as gently as she could, willing her hands to be steady and her strength to be adequate.

His voice was warm with humor when he said, "I'm willing, as you must have noticed, to let you walk all over me. . . ."

She ignored his nonsense and wrapped a tattered piece of her skirt around the stub for better grip.

"It is said to loosen tightened muscle — *God!*"

The arrow was out. She had felt it sickeningly tear through muscle and skin, and grate against metal. The force she had used toppled her backward and she sat there fighting the urge to be sick.

He rolled up and grasped his arm,

breathing roughly. "I don't feel particularly loose at this moment."

"I'll have to practice . . ." She choked on a sob and crawled over to his side. "I'm sorry."

His eyes spoke of pain but were warm as well. "I've had worse treatment. We can work on the other at some more convenient time."

She took refuge in a minatory look. "Let's have the mail off you."

That was painful too, but they managed it, and the leather haqueton as well.

He was covered with blood.

Most of it oozed from the small gashes made by the arrows. The wounds were not dangerous, and some had already stopped bleeding, but they must be painful.

The deeper wound was a mess of torn, bleeding and swollen flesh, and she knew most of the damage had been done in ripping that arrow out. "Dear Lord," muttered Imogen. "It has to weaken your arm."

He flexed, causing a new gush of blood.

She grabbed him. "Stop it!"

"It's not too bad, and I can use a sword left-handed."

"I hope you won't have to fight anymore. After all, the castle will send out a party to look for us." Imogen ripped her skirts to make a pad and bandage, cursing the fact that they didn't have so much as a drop of water to tend to the wound, never mind herbs. She thought briefly of going to look for something, but knew it wasn't wise.

"What am I going to do if you die?" she muttered as she pulled the bandage tight.

"I won't die from this, Imogen."

"My father didn't expect to die from his wound," she pointed out forcibly, then added, "Lancaster said that the wound must have been poisoned."

He turned to look at her. "So it occurred to him too, did it?"

She stared. "You thought of it? Then why didn't you say anything?"

"To what purpose? You needed no extra reasons to hate Warbrick."

She gave the knot an extra, angry tug. "Just because I had a right to know! How many other things have you kept from me?"

He moved warily away from her ministrations to lean against a wall. "We all have things we hoard."

Imogen sucked in a breath. "Oh, the treasure again. Are we going to fight about the treasure again, FitzRoger?"

"I don't think it would be wise to fight about anything at the moment," he said calmly. "I made enquiries about your father's wound, Imogen, and there was no reason for it to putrefy as it did. There must have been poison involved. The obvious culprit is Warbrick, since he was ready to attack."

Imogen controlled her irritation. He was

right. This was no time to squabble. "Lancaster accuses you, or the king."

"Does he? And what do you think?"

She glanced at him, then said, "That it couldn't have been you."

"Why not?"

Because my heart says so. But she wouldn't say that. "You'd have moved faster. You're nothing if not efficient."

"I'm glad you appreciate something about me." He leaned his head back against the wall and gripped his arm in a way that admitted the pain.

Her anger faded. "Does it hurt very badly?"

"As much as one would expect. The bleeding should stop in a while. Then the only real problem will be stiffness. We'll have to hope I don't have to fight."

Reaction was setting in, or perhaps it was just the chill of the cave. It was a warm summer's day outside, and Imogen was dressed only in the remains of light linen and silk. She shivered. "Why didn't we head straight for Carrisford? It isn't that far. You could get better help there."

"Instinct." She saw him studying her. "If that attack was Warbrick's work, how did he know we were at the monastery?"

"If he had us watched . . ."

"That's possible, though I've had patrols through the woods here daily to at least disrupt any serious activity. But how then would he arrange for the tainted wine?"

"If someone gave it . . . But Gareth said Lancaster's men had it with them!"

"A detail that escaped me at that moment. I apologize."

"I don't expect you to be infallible."

"That's good, since you seem to turn my brain to a dumpling."

It was said so flatly, she didn't take it in at first. Then she giggled at the absurdity. "I do?"

"Yes, particularly now." He was looking at her, though she couldn't read his shaded face.

"Now?"

"Now that I've seen the fire in you."

"You mean last night?"

"Then a little. I mean today. Come sit by me."

Wondering, she inched over until she was by him. He used his good arm to lift her onto his lap. "Do you realize you were screaming the most foul insults back there, and cheering every death?"

She closed her eyes in shame. "Yes."

His strong left arm held her close. "You are a virago, my wife, a warrior woman. And if it wasn't for my arm, and the danger, I'd ravish you here as a virago deserves to be ravished when all bloody from battle."

Imogen realized she was blood-splattered, and he was worse. It hadn't bothered her before.

"I feel terrible," she whispered. "How could I have —"

He kissed her hard and fast. "Don't bemoan it. It excites me as nothing else has ever done." He put her hand against his neck and she could feel the speed and power of his blood, hot beneath the skin.

"It's the wound," she said.

"No."

The beat of his blood beneath her hand seemed to be pounding into her. "I feel strange too. All shaky and excited, and wanting more. But not more danger. . . ." Then she remembered the night before, and knew what she wanted. She turned his head to hers.

"We can't, Imogen. It would be recklessness." But he let her draw his head down to hers and his mouth was hotter than his blood, and the kiss sent them reeling closer to disaster.

He pushed her gently but firmly away. "No. Sit over there, Ginger. We need to talk, and with as clear heads as possible."

She didn't want to, but she knew he was right. She scuttled back, a piercing ache inside telling her exactly what her body wanted. If it hadn't been for his wound, she might have demanded it.

Up against the opposite wall, six full feet of space between them, she clasped her hands and said, "So, talk."

"I suspect Lancaster of being behind this

attack, and the main purpose must have been to kill me, not to capture you. You were vulnerable to seizure a number of times, but no one took advantage of it. The attack focused on me as much as possible. That last flight of arrows was aimed to kill me, or maim me enough for them to finish me off. I saw it coming too late."

"You saw it? Was it slow for you too, then?"

His eyes came alert. "It was slow for you?"

"Yes. Strangely slow. I couldn't understand it. It made every move so obvious, and people looked so stupid."

"Me too?"

"No," she said, remembering. "You were slow, but you always did the sensible thing."

He leaned his head back and laughed briefly. "Not just a virago, but one with the gift. I wondered how you managed that ride. Let's pray our sons inherit it."

"It's a gift?"

"The most precious one a fighting man can have. The more urgent the fighting, the more it slows, so every move can be considered, every hazard avoided."

"Not everyone has this?"

"Not one in a thousand. Not one in a hundred thousand."

"It hardly seems fair," she said severely.

"Nor is ambush, or poisoned arrows."

That brought the discussion back to the

chilling point very bluntly. "So you think Lancaster tried to kill you, and we are in danger if we return to Carrisford?"

"It's possible, and I thought we had better have time to think. I have not been my usual efficient self these last few days. Henry and his men will have left at first light to take Warbrick Castle. Lancaster, however, was to stay behind to await the return of his men before joining the king. If he has other men in the area, it would have been easy enough to set up this attack. Then he would have been on hand to comfort and seize you."

"Could he really think I would go from your arms to his in a day?"

"I hardly think your wishes would have entered into it," he gently pointed out.

"But the king, the king would not have stood for it!"

"He would have had little choice unless he had proof of Lancaster's hand in this. He cannot afford to break openly with the earl just yet. Henry would have grieved my passing. He likes me, and more than that, he finds me useful, but once I was gone he would take the next practical step. He would probably hope that the bribe of you would keep Lancaster loyal."

Imogen hugged herself. "Do you know how much I hate this? Being a prize to be passed around."

"I can imagine. If anything happens to me,

Imogen, try if you can to make it to Rolleston in East Anglia, or to Normandy, to Castle Gaillard."

"Why? Oh, but they are . . ."

"Ruled by the brothers of Roger of Cleeve, yes. My uncles."

Somewhat hesitantly she asked, "Do they accept you?"

She saw the slight smile turn his lips. "Yes. The old man, Count Guy, accepted me long since, but didn't contest the Church's ruling. I suppose he knew there was no point in it, but in my youthful arrogance I would not admit that. I spurned the connection, but the family will aid you, for blood's sake, and for justice. They are powerful enough to stand against Lancaster if they have cause."

"There will be no need of this," Imogen said, unable to tolerate any notion of Fitz-Roger's death. "Let's talk instead about what we should do. Surely if we get to Carrisford we will be safe. You have other men there, including Sir William and Renald."

"Will has gone with Henry, but I hope Renald is stirring himself to look into things and mop up any trouble. I thought it better to give them time, though. It is possible that Lancaster has men watching, and if we had headed straight for Carrisford it would have been too easy to kill me. I am only one man and not impervious to all attack."

Imogen was looking at the bandage on his

413

arm. "What if that arrow was poisoned, too?"

"Then I suppose I will die."

She leaped to her feet. "No you will not! We have to get you to Carrisford. I know of herbs and fomentations that are supposed to draw out poisons."

He was looking at her strangely. "Is all this heat for me? I wonder why. Lancaster will be a tolerable husband if you don't balk at him."

"Is it strange that I don't want you to die?"

"Yes."

"No, it isn't."

He shrugged and said no more. He rose to his knees and moved his arm cautiously. "I don't think it will do great damage for me to rearm. Perhaps you could help me. Then we can head cautiously back to Carrisford."

Imogen picked up the bloody haqueton, feeling as if something were left unfinished. But surely the main aim must be to return to the castle; other matters could be resolved later. She helped him into the padded leather garment, trying to move his arm as little as possible. She knew once on it must gall the wound.

Then she hauled the heavy mail over his head, feeling sympathy at the weight of it settling onto his many wounds.

He rose to his feet and flexed thoughtfully.

"How is it?"

"Adequate. Don't worry. I can still serve you."

"This isn't a matter of serving me," she snapped. "It's a matter of survival. Mine and yours."

"You are not in much danger, other than from a stray arrow."

"I am in danger of losing you!" There, now it was out.

She clasped her hands and looked at him, hoping.

His mask was in place. "Don't care too much, Imogen. One man is much like another in most respects. If I die, you'll find another man will suit you just as well when you grow accustomed to him."

"Oh, shut up," she said, and thrust his sword belt at him.

He finished arming in silence. Imogen swallowed tears. After all they had been through it seemed ridiculous to be overset by this cool practicality, but she was. For a moment a while ago, she'd thought he was going to confess to warm feelings for her. It must have been the wound talking after all.

She focused her unhappiness on the state of her clothing. Her skirt was in shreds, and even her shift was missing at one side where she'd cut away stuff for his bandage.

"I don't feel as if I've been in a decent state of dress for weeks," she muttered.

"With God's favor, you will soon have your life back."

In truth, she didn't much care whether she

ever had her pampered life back — in fact, didn't want it back.

She wanted FitzRoger. She wanted the fighting and the challenging, the kissing and the passion. She even wanted the danger, the excitement that made her blood sing. She didn't care at all about clothes, and hangings, and gardens.

But she said, "Good. What are we going to do about Lancaster?"

"Hopefully send him on his way to join Henry, and guard ourselves well in the future." He slid her a look. "Once you are clearly with child, his fangs will be drawn."

That was doubtless the only reason he wanted to bed her at all, to mark her as his and get her with child. "Why can't you tell Henry what the earl's been up to?"

"I will, but he can't act without proof, and I think proof will be hard to find. Warbrick will be the obvious suspect, despite the questions, and it will suit Henry to have further reason to move against Warbrick and Belleme. You know the way to Carrisford from here?"

"Yes."

"How far is it?"

"Not far. Perhaps two leagues, though it will take some time if we stay in the woods. The riding would be easier if we joined the road, but . . ."

"But, no. Through the woods, and carefully."

It was mid-morning when they emerged from the cave, and the bright warmth was almost shocking. Everything appeared peaceful and normal, but they both scanned the area with care.

"What will they have done once they lost us?" Imogen asked.

"That's the interesting question. I suppose at least some men are spread out between here and Carrisford, hoping for a chance to pick us off."

"Pick *you* off," she said tightly.

"Yes." He faced her thoughtfully. "Imogen, I have no wish to die, particularly now, but I learned years ago that worrying about it serves little purpose."

"It would be nice," she said tartly, "to see you worry about *something!*"

He smiled slightly. "It worries me that I might die without making you my wife in all senses."

"We could go back into the cave . . ."

He laughed; he actually laughed. "Have pity, woman. It would mean taking my armor off again." He began to lead his horse down the slope. Imogen followed, wishing she knew just how to take him. She'd never seen him laugh like that before.

The man was likely to drive her mad, but he was fascinating enough to last a lifetime.

A long lifetime, she hastily amended, and started to pray.

She decided that they needed all the help heaven had to offer and was halfway through a litany of her favorite saints when he stopped.

"What?" she whispered, breaking off her prayer to Saint Adelaide.

"Just that we are about to move into the open a little. I want to watch."

Imogen was reminded of the time they watched Carrisford and she told him so. "I thought you were like a castle," she said. "Cold and hard."

"Just as long as I am a good one."

"Is that all that matters to you?"

His intent gaze did not halt in its search of the area.

"What purpose is there in life other than to be proficient?"

"You could be proficient at something other than death."

"I hope I'm proficient at survival. Come on."

He moved forward toward the trees. Imogen followed, wishing she hadn't given in to that irritation. But she wanted him to be more than her defender and champion.

They mounted in the woods, and she didn't allow him to help her into the saddle, but used a fallen tree. He had his sword in his right hand, and his shield hanging from its shoulder strap, but she worried about his wound and his strength.

"If you can't fight, tell me," she said.

"Why?"

"Because I need to know."

"Imogen, just lead us to Carrisford and let me do my job. I won't fail you."

Imogen turned her mount's head sharply and headed through the trees.

This area had always been secure under her father's rule, and she had played here as a child. Her companions had been her father's wards and numerous castle children. Lord Bernard had seen no harm in her playing with those of lower orders.

In time, however, Imogen had stopped coming here. Her playmates grew and had more work to do. The wards left to marry. Imogen spent her time with books and music, and her forays into the woods were for hunting, not games.

But she knew them.

She remembered the oak she and the farrier's son liked to climb, and the thicket of bushes with a space inside which had been the girls' house. And there was the fairy circle magically free of trees where they'd danced and tried to cast spells.

She glanced back. FitzRoger looked both relaxed and alert, every sense attuned not to her but to the woods around them. She pressed on.

She had to constantly choose between following foot and deer paths that wound away from their destination, or going straight through undergrowth and across uneven land.

Once they had to backtrack when they were confronted by a bog she did not remember from before.

She looked anxiously at him then, but he said nothing. She began to worry that his impassivity might be a sign of distress — that he was in pain, or weak from loss of blood, or suffering the first effects of poison. If she asked, he'd doubtless deny it.

"Men," she muttered to herself.

Carrisford could not be far now. She glimpsed its towers. Fretting about his welfare, she took a risk and headed straight for it.

The rift in the earth was new and deep. Her horse stepped into it and she heard its leg snap even as she was tossed. The world spun, then hit her with numbing force.

Her horse screamed.

Then was silent.

She looked up to see that FitzRoger was off his horse and had slit the beast's throat, but the scream echoed through the woods, and birds still whirled, repeating the cry.

"Oh Jesu, I'm sorry," she whispered.

He held out a hand. "It can't be helped. Come, we must be close."

But before they could mount his horse, they were surrounded. Perhaps thirty hardened men. And Warbrick.

Chapter Sixteen

"Beauclerk's green-eyed hound," said Warbrick, and spat. "And the Treasure of Carrisford."

Imogen felt blind terror grab at her, and fought it. "What are you doing on my land, Lord Warbrick?"

"Looking for a little reparation. For me, and for others. You are so eagerly sought, Lady Imogen. Does it please you? Don't be bashful, my lord. Come forward."

Imogen couldn't think what he meant, until the Earl of Lancaster was urgently hustled forward. He was in mail, with a rich silk surcoat, every inch the mighty warrior except that he looked flustered and even frightened.

What on earth was going on?

She glanced in confusion up at FitzRoger. He was giving away nothing.

She realized it was strange that Warbrick was not in mail, but had greasy stained leathers stretched over his bulk. He hardly looked as if he were on campaign.

She turned to the Earl of Lancaster. "My lord, what are you doing here?"

Lancaster's eyes shifted and he made no reply.

"He was waiting for you," said Warbrick with a shallow smile. "After he took care of your escort with poisoned wine, you were supposed to be easy pickings."

"You were supposed to take care of FitzRoger," spat the earl. "Ten men you had, and here he is, hale and hearty."

"You said none of his escort would be fit to ride."

Imogen glared at Lancaster. "You toad! You were responsible? You tried to kill FitzRoger! Do you think I would marry you even if I were free?"

Warbrick laughed and hooked his thumbs into his massive, studded belt. "You, Lady Imogen, will do as you're told. Listen to your fate. You will marry the earl, and I will have your treasure. With your wealth behind us, Beauclerk will soon be a landless wanderer again." His eyes moved over her, finding every gap in her torn clothing. "But before I make off with the treasure of Carrisford, I intend to enjoy the Treasure of Carrisford."

Imogen stepped back, closer to the graven statue that was FitzRoger. But what could even he do against so many?

"By the thorns, you will not!" blustered the earl. "Our bargain was clear, Warbrick. She's mine. Bad enough she's been polluted by one man."

Imogen wondered if she could sow discord between these uneasy allies. "My Lord Lancaster," Imogen said clearly, "you should know that when Warbrick took Carrisford, he intended to wed me."

"What?" Lancaster turned on the bigger man.

Warbrick laughed again, belly shaking. "*Marry* you? Are you still so naive after days of the Bastard? What point in marrying you with Beauclerk at my throat? But I certainly intended to enjoy you. There's particular pleasure in hearing a frightened virgin scream as you broach her. Such a delicate, sheltered morsel would have been sweetly terrified . . ."

He dropped the false bonhomie, and his piggy eyes narrowed. "But you escaped me, you little bitch. You'll pay for that. Escaped and took the secret of your treasure straight to Cleeve. You won't do that again." He took a couple of menacing steps closer to Imogen. "Beauclerk moved on Warbrick Castle today and I hardly had time to escape. I need all the gold I can get."

Imogen stepped back, pressing against FitzRoger. His hands came strong about her arms, bracing her. "You can have it," she said. "All of it. Just let us go."

"Us?" Warbrick asked in mock astonishment.

"FitzRoger and me."

"You prefer the Bastard to Lancaster?" He dug an ungentle elbow in the angry earl's ribs. "There's one in the eye for you, my lord earl."

"She's besotted," snarled the earl.

"So it would seem."

"I'll teach her better. She needs a few lessons."

At last FitzRoger spoke. "If we are contesting possession of Lady Imogen, perhaps we should fight over it."

"No!" It was both Imogen and Lancaster together.

Warbrick laughed. "Bastard, you amuse me! By all means. But win or lose, I take my share of the Treasure."

Imogen closed her eyes in terror. She knew he did not refer to the gold.

Could she survive it? She knew in logic that if the act did not physically kill her, she should be able to survive and put it behind her, but she didn't think she could. And she knew FitzRoger would not live and let it happen. She could feel the tension in him from staying calm during this exchange.

For him to interfere just now would achieve nothing, but it could not be easy. *The particular pleasure in hearing a frightened virgin scream as you broach her.*

And she certainly was a frightened virgin.

She didn't realize she was clinging to FitzRoger until he gently put her aside. She opened her eyes to see him take a shield on his arm.

The earl was in armor, doubtless prepared

to ride after the king, but he did not look warlike. Imogen felt a hint of pity for him, but only a hint. She didn't understand the whole of it, but he had betrayed her castle and tried to kill FitzRoger.

It was quite possible that he had killed her father.

Had her father refused Lancaster's suit?

If so, she thought suddenly, it could have been because her father was already considering an alliance with FitzRoger. She had thought that if they met, they would like one another.

Who was to say they had not met?

For the first time she wondered about the death of Gerald of Huntwich. So many convenient deaths. Had Lancaster had a hand in all of them? And apparently to gain her, not the treasure, judging from the bargain he'd struck with Warbrick.

But then she knew with bitter certainty that Lancaster had intended to cheat Warbrick, just as much as Warbrick had intended to cheat the earl.

Lancaster was still protesting. She saw that there were some men of his among the soldiers, but they were outnumbered and too terrified to interfere.

Lancaster was about to die, and they all knew it, but how would it help her and FitzRoger?

Warbrick drew his sword and poked Lancaster in the back. "Fight, my lord earl, or I'll spit you here and now."

"You can't do this," the earl raged. "Kill the man and have done with it. What benefit to you to let him fight?"

"What benefit to me in killing him outright? You were of use to me, Lancaster, because your doctor could drug the garrison and open Carrisford to my men once Lord Bernard was dead. That was all you ever had to offer. Your man failed to secure the heiress, though. She was supposed to be drugged in her bed, waiting for me."

Imogen gasped at the net that had almost entrapped her.

"I never guaranteed that," blustered the earl. "You let her slip through your hands! And again today I did my part. It wasn't my fault his men didn't drink the wine. . . ."

"Whatever happened, I have her now, and she's going to lead me to her treasure." Warbrick smiled at Imogen. "I think she'll do it more eagerly to save FitzRoger than she will to save you. Won't you, my little chicken?"

Anything to save FitzRoger. "Yes."

"And you'll lie with me willingly to save him, won't you?"

Imogen heard the sob that escaped her, but she said, "Yes."

FitzRoger turned his head and looked at her. There was no expression on his face, and yet something flashed between them.

He turned back to look past Lancaster to Warbrick. "Take the treasure, Warbrick, and leave England, and I will not pursue you. Do more than that and you will die in agony."

Warbrick sneered. "Crow, cockerel. You have no spurs." He poked Lancaster viciously in the back. "Fight!"

The earl yelped and drew his sword. Eyes wide with fright, he staggered forward.

It took longer than it should have, and Imogen was afraid FitzRoger was weakened, but then she realized he was spinning it out to make the earl suffer. He was a great deal angrier than she had thought, but no angrier than she should expect.

He despised treason, and he would let no one tyrannize those under his protection.

But still, what could he do about Warbrick, one man against so many?

Would help come?

They were so close to Carrisford, and surely FitzRoger's men must be out searching.

She prayed, not about the fight in front of her, but about the fight to come. She would give up her treasure willingly — that treasure she'd bargained and tussled over — just to have FitzRoger safe.

But could she give up her body to Warbrick and live?

The earl was gasping and desperate, his

arms and legs both weakening. He had not given up hope, though. His glazed eyes sought desperately for the careless moment that would allow him to snatch victory from death.

Imogen knew such a moment would not come.

To her, FitzRoger seemed to have all the time in the world when he finally executed his opponent. His sword swung in a mighty blow against Lancaster's neck, breaking and half severing it, so the man crumpled like a well-stuffed doll to the ground.

FitzRoger seemed hardly stirred by it all, but Imogen could tell by a subtle awkwardness in his arm that he was in pain, and possibly weakened. Doubtless the wound was bleeding again.

"Dull, that," said Warbrick. "I'd heard you were good, and for once rumor does not lie. I wish I could try you."

"I'd welcome it," said FitzRoger with a distinct edge.

Imogen saw the temptation flash in Warbrick's eyes. He was a fearsome warrior, and he doubtless thought he could defeat FitzRoger by might alone. She prayed that he would take up the challenge, for with him dead they had a chance.

But he said, "The treasure first. I need you alive to make sure the little heiress does my bidding. Give up your sword now, Bastard."

FitzRoger made no move to obey.

Warbrick said, "You won't tempt me to fight you now. My men will disarm you. You may kill some, but they'll do it, and relish damaging you. Then there'll be less chance for you if I do decide to let you fight me later. Perhaps fight for your wife's virtue."

It was a callous piece of bargaining, and hollow, but there was little choice. FitzRoger tossed down his sword.

"Good," said Warbrick. "Now, we have a man of yours captured by Lancaster's soldiers, one who knew something of the passageways. We need him no longer, I assume. How else would you have sneaked into Carrisford if Lady Imogen hadn't told you the ways?" Warbrick looked around. "Then we have the earl's men."

Imogen saw six men turn pasty white. With reason.

"Kill them," said Warbrick.

Imogen cried a useless protest. As the killing started she covered her face and was pulled into FitzRoger's arms. She could hear, though. She heard the screams, and the babbling cries for mercy, and the callous laughter. It was as if she were back in the damp passage at Carrisford listening to the sack of her home. It was as bad or even worse now, for the death was all around her, and the smell of it was heavy in the air.

She wanted to hide. She was willing to die if it were only quick.

She heard Warbrick say, unmoved, "Now, we must wait for dark. Fulk. You said there were caves nearby?"

"Aye, my lord. An hour or so."

"Then we will go there."

Despite her resistance, FitzRoger firmly moved Imogen around and she knew it was time to face Warbrick again. Her head was filled with mist, and her limbs were water. She stared at him hopelessly.

Warbrick looked her over. "Still not accustomed to death, Lady Imogen? You should be when you are the cause of it. A beautiful woman is nothing but trouble. Your husband here has doubtless learned that. You should smile at me, girl! I have saved you from one unwelcome suitor." All the time, his eyes assaulted her, as if she were already spread for his invasion.

She stepped back into the strength of FitzRoger and he put his hands strong on her shoulders.

Warbrick grinned. "I love to see a woman in fear, and we've hardly started yet." A beefy hand moved toward her, but halted. "No, it is not time for that. You see," he said, and touched her cheek in a macabre caress, "I have control when I need it."

His eyes flicked over her head to Fitz-Roger's. "And what of you, My Lord

Bastard? Without Beauclerk, last and landless son, you are nothing, and Beauclerk will soon fail. Robert of Normandy will be king here, and he has promised my brother lordship in the west. England will be our hunting ground, with none to say us nay. But war is costly and we need the treasure."

He laughed, rocking back on his heels. "I'm going to plunder both your treasures, Bastard, and watch you squirm. Will you kill her first? You should, shouldn't you? *When* will you kill her? Will you kill her too soon, unnecessarily? Perhaps you'll be rescued. What a pity to only have a corpse to kiss. Or will you wait too long and hear her scream to you for death?"

Imogen felt FitzRoger's hands tighten to the point of pain before he regained control.

Would he kill her?

If he didn't, would she wish he had?

Warbrick reached out and seized Imogen's tunic, dragging her to him. She felt FitzRoger's grip resist for a moment, then release her. She cried out as Warbrick pulled her against him, the smell of old blood and dirt all around him. But then he spun her off to another man. "Lig. Ride with her in front and with your knife at her face. If he gives any trouble, any trouble at all, slash her. But don't kill her or I'll roast you."

Imogen fell stunned into the thin man's arms, knowing neither threat was empty. Her gaze locked with FitzRoger's for strength. There had to be something they could do!

There wasn't.

He held her eyes calmly. His look didn't promise anything, and yet it steadied her. He was only human, as was she. They would do what they could, and if he could, at the last possible moment, he would give her the gift of a swift death.

They rode back along the ways to the caves. The route was different, but not by much, and Imogen marked it as if that were a purposeful thing to do.

Her guard, Lig, kept an arm tight about her, and his sharp blade glinted in the corner of her eye, but other than that he ignored her. She knew, however, that he would slash her without hesitation even at a false alarm.

The hills and the caves came as a welcome destiny, though Imogen had no reason to think things would improve here. At least she didn't think Warbrick would rape her here; he must know that one way or another she would be useless to him then. Hope, slender hope, would keep them dancing to his tune.

There were other torments, however. He could torture FitzRoger and still keep him alive enough to bargain with.

They watered the horses at the stream before climbing up to the caves. They had fodder with them, and the horses were settled with guards in one of the larger caves, one of the ones that honeycombed together.

If they were put in one of those caves, Imogen could find a way through the linked spaces to freedom. She knew the caves well.

Warbrick inspected and chose the cave they had used before. "In here," he said. "It does not link with any of the others. Mark my kindness." He leered at them. "I put you together for a few brief hours. Will you enjoy one another one last time, or has terror sapped your manhood, Bastard? I don't mind. It's nothing to me who's gone before once a woman's broken to a man."

They were thrust into the gloom. "There are four guards at the entrance," said Warbrick, "each knowing hell is mild compared to my vengeance if they let you slip. I will come for you at dark. Meanwhile," he sneered, "I wish you joy."

Then they were alone. Imogen fell into FitzRoger's arms and he encompassed her. "I'm sorry," he said. "I'm failing you."

She pulled back a little. "One man against thirty? What are you supposed to do?"

His lips curved slightly. "Perform a miracle?"

"Well," she said, trying to match his tone, "if you can . . ."

He touched her face gently, thoughtfully. "I had one not quite miraculous transformation in mind," he said softly.

"What?" But she knew.

"Virgin into wife."

"Here?" Her eyes were growing used to the gloom, and she looked around at the stone walls and earth floor. She could see the silhouette of one guard blocking the door.

"Not ideal, I grant you, but . . ." He cradled her head in his calloused hands and she felt the slight unsteadiness of them. "I'm not sure I can kill you, Imogen. I'll hope you can survive. But I'll die to protect you —"

"I don't want you to!"

"Can I live?"

"Can I?"

He held her close.

"If you can, Imogen, I want you to live. Warbrick is right — in this I am a coward. If I were going to kill you, it should be now, but I cannot do it. By the time all hope is gone, it will be too late."

She put her fingers over his lips. "Don't. Don't speak of it. And you're right. If we're to die, I want it to be as your wife." She didn't add the other — that if she was to be raped by Warbrick, she would rather it not be as a virgin. She still had hope that Warbrick would bargain her willingness for FitzRoger's life, and she'd pay, though what would come of it afterward, she couldn't imagine.

His face lightened as if they were not in peril of their lives. "Then I intend to remove my mail, foolish though it may be."

"How long do you think we have?" she asked nervously. She might want it, but it seemed a mad thing to be doing.

"Long enough. There's a few hours before dusk." He glanced at her and grinned. "Let's hope they don't intend to feed us."

Amazingly, that summoned a laugh from her, and she felt lighter. "Should I undress?" Imogen asked, hands already at her girdle.

"No. If we are interrupted, the last thing we want is for you to be naked." Then he added, "Perhaps the tunic."

She slipped it off, still well covered by her kirtle and shift. "But . . ."

"We'll manage, Ginger. This isn't what I wanted for you, but it is all we can be sure of. For now," he added. "Perhaps one day I can love you as I want."

She knew he didn't believe it.

She pondered the word *love,* but it was just a word to him, she decided, describing an act, not an emotion. Perhaps, in this situation, it was as well.

Love would weaken him.

She helped him off with his mail, and saw the wound had bled a little, but not too much. The other gashes looked healthy. He was so healthy it seemed impossible that he might die within the day. . . .

She put her hand on his chest, drinking in the living strength of him, feeling the beat of his heart. For this moment, they were alive and together, and they would celebrate it. "What should I do?"

He drew her to the back of the cave, some twenty feet from the entrance. "It's as well I always planned this with you on top," he said, as he subsided to the floor and pulled her on top of him.

Imogen sprawled there. "What? Why?"

"Why not?" he murmured lazily, and kissed her.

Everything disappeared: the damp, the gloom, the guards, the danger. There was just FitzRoger's hard body beneath her, his arms around, and his mouth soft and welcoming beneath hers. She plundered him for sensation, tasting him, stretching him. When his mouth escaped to roam around her neck, she arched up and felt him hard beneath her hips.

"Now?" she gasped.

"Not yet, my hungry virago."

He ripped the front of her kirtle.

Imogen gasped.

Then, under her astonished gaze, he slid down her loose shift so her breasts were exposed, held up by the bands of cloth. Her nipples were rosy and already standing proud.

"More precious than any treasure," he said softly, and drew her body down. His mouth was hot, and for a moment, gentle. Then he sucked hard. Imogen cried out and clutched at him.

"Hush," he said, half laughing. "You're a noisy bed partner, but if you make too much noise they'll want to come and watch."

She didn't think that was a joke either.

"What's going on in there?" called one of the guards, his black shadow blocking out the trace of sunshine.

"We're talking," said FitzRoger a bit unsteadily. "Is that a crime?"

"You, woman," the guard growled. "Are you all right?"

"Yes," said Imogen, stifling a giggle.

"Then keep talking. I don't want him slitting your throat when *I'm* on guard."

"*What?*" Imogen exclaimed as the guard retreated.

"You heard the man," said FitzRoger, and she could swear he was amused. "Keep talking or he'll be back to check that you're alive."

"Lord save me," she muttered. Her mind was blank to all but his body, and his mouth tormenting her. "I can't do this!"

"I have great faith in you. You can do anything." His tongue teased the tip of her breast in a way that sent shivers through her.

"I've been thinking," she said desperately, "that we could have colors on the walls in the hall."

FitzRoger laughed softly and his mouth settled on her breast again.

"Pink, perhaps, or yellow. Something bright . . . *Oh, Sweet Heaven*. . . . Flowers! At Cleeve too."

"Over my dead body," he muttered, and

turned his attention to the other breast.

"Hangings!" Imogen said desperately. "We had. . . . *Oh, my.* . . . We had silk ones from Florence, you know."

His skillful teasing of her breasts fractured thought. "They were . . . *FitzRoger!* They were . . . They were . . ." A wave of intense pleasure finally rendered her speechless.

"Silken treasures," he prompted, easing her away a little. "Very beautiful, like you."

"Very beautiful," she repeated weakly, and sought him in the shadows. "Like you."

Humor crinkled his eyes. "If your Florentine hangings were only as beautiful as I, Imogen, you were cheated." He moved her gently to straddle his thighs, pushing up her skirts in a stroke of his strong, callused hands.

"You *are* beautiful —"

But his fingers had found her most sensitive flesh and she melted into dizzy silence.

"Keep talking, Ginger."

She gulped. "You're enjoying this!" she hissed.

"Yes. Aren't you?"

A shuddering spasm passed through her. "You're mad. . . . Wine!" she said loudly. "We need wine! Lots of wine!"

"Lots and lots of wine. And honey. Up on your hands and knees for me, sweet honey."

She rose up so his mouth could reach her breasts while his hand stroked between her thighs.

"What else do we need?" he asked between licks. "Herbs, spices? You're very spicy. Fruits? Melons come to mind. And oranges. Oranges from Spain. You taste sweeter than the sweetest orange. . . ."

"I love oranges," she gasped. "So juicy. FitzRoger, I need to kiss you."

"Not yet," he replied, and teethed her.

Imogen just managed to swallow the cry of pleasure. "I can't *not* cry out when you do things like that!" she protested. "It's not fair." Her hips were moving against him. She was aching deep inside.

"Oranges," he prompted as his fingers slid toward the ache.

"They're . . . *Oh!*" She sucked in an enormous breath. "Don't! Don't stop! They're orange!"

"They're orange," he agreed as breathlessly as she. "And you're juicy. Now it's time, Ginger."

"Thank the Lord."

"And you're going to do it."

"*What?*"

"In case you still have any problems about this." He unfastened his linen drawers to expose his erection. "Take me into you."

Imogen looked at it wide-eyed. It seemed rather larger than she remembered, and rather larger than she could comfortably contain.

But an ache inside said otherwise.

She put her hands around him and the heat startled her.

The movement she caused startled her too, as did his sucked in breath.

She hesitated. There was a big problem here.

She hated to admit it, but she whispered, "I don't even know where it goes."

He closed his eyes briefly. "You don't know your own body?" He took her right hand and placed it between her thighs. "Slide your fingers back. You'll find the place."

She slid her fingers back through what felt like cream, and paused. "Oh, it feels almost as sweet as when you touch me there!"

"Remember that if I'm away."

One of Father Wulfgan's more mysterious warnings finally made sense. "But that's a terrible sin!"

"But one you're least likely to be caught at. Come on, Ginger."

She heard the urgency in his voice and could feel the tension in his body between her legs. It was echoed in the need that thrummed in her. She moved her fingers farther and her body told her she had found the need he could fulfill.

"Found it?" he asked unsteadily.

"Yes."

"Now take me, and put me there."

Imogen put her hand around him to guide him. Her hand was slick now from her own juices and slid against his rigid heat, so she moved it around him. She felt the quiver her touch caused, and looked at him in wonder. Even in the gloom she could see his hot need.

She could do this to him, and she delighted in it. She explored him with her hand, gently, and then, remembering Wulfgan again, impulsively ducked and licked up the length of him.

His whole body heaved beneath her, almost throwing her off.

"Imogen!" he gasped. "Another time, yes?"

"But you like that?" she asked, grinning.

"Yes, I like that." It sounded as if his teeth were gritted. "But take me into you. Make me your husband, Ginger."

She laughed shakily at that and rose up to guide him into the place that hummed in readiness. As soon as he began to fill her she gasped at the tightness.

"You'd better say something," he whispered.

"I want this," she said quite clearly, wanting to tell the world. "You can't know how much I want this."

"Oh yes I can," he muttered, causing her to laugh again.

"You are rather big, though," she said as she eased carefully down. "Are all men . . . ? Oh." She froze.

"It's for you to do, Imogen."

There was pain. Real pain. She could feel

the barrier and it was going to hurt to go any farther.

She pushed down gently and the pain grew, so she stopped.

"I don't know . . ." she said anxiously. "I'd hoped it wouldn't be like this, this time. . . ."

He reached up and pulled her down for a kiss. "Would you rather I do it?"

It became a test. "No. I can do it, but cover my mouth. I'm afraid I'm going to cry out."

"Bite me," he said, and put his hand edgewise between her teeth.

Imogen set her teeth against his flesh and reared up a bit to push down. The pain blossomed, but she kept pushing. The pain just got worse, but she wouldn't stop even though there were tears running down her face. She pushed and pushed even though she thought she could not bear any more pain. Then with a small explosion of agony, the pressure broke and left only a burning soreness.

She tasted blood and realized she had bit him. She hastily released his hand. He sucked it. "That certainly hurt me as much as it hurt you," he said almost soberly. "You must have had one of the toughest hymens in Christendom. No wonder you made such a fuss before."

Imogen was just sitting, full to bursting with him, rather sore, and miserable. She felt a kind of triumph, though, that she'd gone through with it, and knew that if she'd been under him, it would have been worse. She'd have screamed and blamed him. "It's not like that for everyone?"

"I don't think so. Is it very bad?" His voice was controlled, but Imogen could tell it was hard for him to just be lying there. She could imagine from last night, from the pleasure without the pain, how he felt.

"I'm all right," she lied bravely, moving, trying to adjust to the pressure inside and the soreness that remained. "What now?"

He pushed up so he was sitting against the wall and brought her legs behind him. The pressure eased a bit.

He began to touch her again, and kiss her, to suck at her and pleasure her, even as his hips rocked gently. She could sense the awesome control in him, the tension, and she almost wanted to beg him to do it, to release that pressure before he exploded.

And yet she feared it. Feared more pain.

Tears ran again.

"What's the matter?" he asked, touching her cheek. "We'd better talk again anyway."

"I'm not doing this right, am I?"

"You're doing wonderfully, but we're going to have to finish it. Try to come with me, dear heart."

She didn't know what he meant, but he began to move her hips around him. At first she tensed from the soreness, but then it eased a little and she saw what she was doing to him.

She moved on her own despite the discomfort, watching him, loving him, wanting to give him this in case there was no tomorrow.

He closed his eyes and stretched back, but his hand found her, and touched her again so she shuddered around him.

"Christ's wounds," he muttered, and pressed harder.

They were supposed to be talking, but she couldn't. She could scream, though. She wanted to scream. She couldn't. That would bring the guard in for sure. She thrust her own knuckles in her mouth and moved faster, watching his every reaction.

He was gasping, his head moving restlessly.

Was it wrong for her to rejoice that here, at this moment, he was not in control at all?

He clutched at her and thrust up into her.

His eyes opened and she was sucked into them, lost in them. She felt his seed burst deep inside her and choked onto her knuckles.

Then he relaxed to stillness, and she settled against him. She knew what he had meant the night before. She was left unsatisfied, but she had loved giving him that pleasure.

Then he pulled out of her, and rolled her onto her back in the dirt. His mouth caught her cries as his hand carried her forward and into a madness of her own. She shattered, more violently than last night, shattered to the point of agony and destruction, beyond the point intent would take a sane person. She was left weak, trembling, and dazed in his arms.

"Oy, you in there! I told you to keep talking."

"Oh, shut up!" shouted Imogen. "I'll scream if he tries to kill me, all right?"

"You need a fist in your mouth," grumbled the guard back, but he left them alone.

FitzRoger was helpless with silent laughter beside her. Imogen thumped his chest. "What's so funny?"

"At this moment, everything." He gathered her into an embrace more tender than she could ever have imagined. "I can at last die happy."

That brought her back to reality. "Well I'd rather not," she said, pulling out of his embrace severely. "It seems to me you are falling apart, FitzRoger."

"Am I?" he said, sitting up and hugging his knees. He was tousled and still happy. She hardly recognized him.

"Will it always be like this?" she asked.

"I hope not. I want to make love to you slowly and gently, in peace and security. If we sacrifice a little of the wild pleasure for it, I'll be content."

Imogen looked down at her tattered skirt. For the first time she wondered what she looked like, but it didn't seem important. "Do you mean that?"

"You think I want to love you always in a damp cave in peril of our lives?"

She looked up. "Do you mean love?"

He sobered. "Ah," he sighed. "Imogen, I don't know. If such a thing exists, it is not familiar to me. You are very precious to me. I will guard you with my life."

"You'd have married me if I'd been a hag," she accused again.

"Yes."

"You'd have guarded me with your life." "Yes."

"You'd have consummated the marriage."

"Yes. But probably rather sooner."

Imogen gazed into his eyes and crawled into his arms. "I'm getting scared again."

He held her. "Try not to. It doesn't do any good."

She shook her head against his chest. "We have to make plans."

"Do you have any plans?"

"Yes." She moved back purposefully. "We're going to go through the passageways . . ." Then she remembered what this meant to him. "Oh."

"Oh," he echoed. "I'm trying hard not to think about that."

"It doesn't do any good to be scared," she repeated back at him mischievously.

"I could probably take my mind off it

quite well by beating you." But there was warmth in his eyes and he wasn't denying his frailty.

"The guard would think you were murdering me."

"But when he found I was just blistering your skin, he'd cheer me on. You heard him. He doesn't approve of saucy women."

Another gurgle of laughter escaped her. "Oh, stop it. I don't want to laugh just now."

"I want to make you laugh." But then he sighed. "Go on, then. What plan have you come up with, my virago?"

"Warbrick doesn't know it yet, but he'll never fit into the passageways."

"True," he said with interest. "Will he trust any of his men in without him? Yes, because there'll only be the one way out for them."

"So, we'll have a better chance."

He shook his head. "He'll keep me with him as warranty of your good behavior. On the whole, I'm grateful."

"You can't be!"

He met her eyes. "The fear, Imogen, is overwhelming. Death seems light by comparison."

"But you went in after Renald. . . ."

"Yes, and it's probably the bravest thing I ever did. As it was I made a short distance on my feet, then crawled, shouting until they came back for me."

Imogen just stared at him. She would never

have believed he would open himself to her like this. She couldn't think what to say, so just placed her hand over his.

"I wanted, desperately, to crawl out again," he said, "but I think they thought I'd fall down the cliff. Which was probably true. Renald did the kindest thing, and knocked me out. They didn't dare leave me in case I came around, so they carried me and I still have some bruises to show for it. I came around before the end but managed not to go mad by keeping my eyes shut and telling myself I was in a large bright hall. As soon as I was out, I was vilely sick."

"I know," she said gently. "Some of the servants saw you."

Amazingly, he flushed. "I'm surprised I have any credit left."

"They just thought you'd eaten something bad."

"And you?" he asked. "What do you think?"

"Am I supposed to think less of you?"

He pulled her closer and kissed her. "I am very fortunate in my wife. Now, listen to my plan."

"Yes?"

"Warbrick will have to divide his forces. You will presumably lead the way for the men who go into the passages to get the treasure, and he'll send his more experienced and trusted minions. If you can persuade them to do without a light, or if you can kill the light, you should be able to slip away from them in those passageways. I presume you can find your way in the dark?"

"But . . ." Then Imogen decided not to mention rats. If he could go into the passage-ways — certain terror — she could risk rats. "Yes I can. But you'll still be in Warbrick's clutches."

"At least one of us will be safe, and you can alert Renald."

"Then what?"

"Then you and Renald think of a way to rescue me," he said lightly. "I have great faith in my virago. I have a few suggestions, though . . ."

Chapter Seventeen

As the light outside faded, Imogen lay in FitzRoger's arms. They could not be silent, and so he spoke restfully and openly of his life, and she responded with her own simple experiences. They did not compare in any way with his, but she offered them all the same because she knew that he was, in a way, saying farewell.

She prayed that it not come to that, but he had laid out the facts with steely precision. Warbrick would keep him alive and largely uninjured as long as he was a weapon to force her compliance. He would, however, make sure he was powerless, and such things were easy to achieve.

If anything was to be done, she would have to do it, and though they had worked through a number of possibilities, there were too many unknowns to make firm plans.

She would have to act, and react, alone, and he would simply have to wait.

The faith he was showing in her was terrifying. She wanted to protest that a sennight ago her most taxing decision had been whether to wear blue silk or red; her closest brush with violence had been the loosing of her merlin.

But she didn't, because she was their only hope, their only chance of defeating Warbrick and surviving.

"As a boy, I enjoyed the challenge of rough active games but had no taste for brutality. Are you surprised?"

"No. I don't think you have a taste for brutality now." Imogen let a finger trace a raised vein on his strong arm. She couldn't seem to help touching him.

"True," he said. "If I kill, I kill quickly."

It was a somewhat bleak definition of kindness, but she understood. "How did you come to be a warrior, then?"

"I met my father. That convinced me that I never wanted to be in such a man's power again, or leave those in my charge in such a man's power. That is why I say I am failing you."

"Some things cannot be avoided. Perhaps it is God's will."

"There is nothing of God's will in this," he said flatly. "Would it surprise you to know I was destined to be a monk?"

She twisted to look up at him in the gloom. "A monk? You must have hated it." Imogen couldn't imagine FitzRoger under monastic rule. Poverty, chastity, and obedience?

"I loved it," he said softly. "I was happy

there as I have never been since. Everything was order and discipline, and there was the opportunity for learning."

Happy as he had never been since. That hurt, though why she should think he might have found happiness in the few chaotic days since they had met, she couldn't imagine. "Why didn't you stay, then?" she asked.

"The monastery was in England. My mother's family, quite understandably, had sent me as far away from home as possible. Unfortunately this put me in my father's sphere. He didn't want me nearby, and ordered the abbot to send me back to France. The abbot had little choice but to obey."

"How old were you then?"

"Thirteen. A difficult age. I was furious at the injustice of it. Instead of going back to France, I set off for Cleeve to confront my nemesis, full of righteous indignation."

Imogen winced. "Oh dear. What happened?"

He smiled slightly. "Exactly what anyone with sense would expect. Roger was not as bad a man as Warbrick, but rock-hard to the core and without a drop of compassion. When I confronted him he had me whipped. When I wouldn't shut up, he had me thrown in the oubliette."

It was said quite calmly, but Imogen felt the tension that spread through him. "What did he hope to gain?"

"I think he quite literally intended me to

rot there, forgotten. I wonder now whether he was trying to forget what I represented. He had only one acknowledged son — weak, vicious Hugh. Roger could be vicious, but he was never weak. His second wife was barren and cold, but not likely to die soon. He was not a happy man.

"Are you feeling sorry for him?"

"No." It was said flatly and followed by an eloquent silence.

Imogen wondered if he would stop speaking, now he had come to the dark heart of his story. She hoped not. She was gathering these scraps of his life into her heart.

He shifted her in his arms a little and carried on. "My childhood had not been easy, but at home and in the monastery I had been fed and cared for. The oubliette . . . the oubliette was a sudden descent into hell.

"They threw me in — ten feet down — so I was bruised. It was like a well, not even wide enough for me to stretch my arms out. The floor was damp earth and foul. My own excrement soon made it fouler. I was sure I would suffocate in the smell, but I didn't. It was pitch-dark, and though I knew the hatch was far above my head, I was terrified that it was pressing down on me to crush me. . . ."

He shuddered. Imogen touched him gently, not sure what to say.

"I wept. I screamed. I begged for mercy. I was not at all brave."

"You were thirteen years old," she said. "At that age I still made a fuss over a cut finger."

"And yet at fourteen, when you broke your arm, you endured the setting without a whimper."

She stared up at him. "How did you know that?"

His finger traced the line of her jaw. "I have made it my business to learn about you."

She didn't know how she felt about that. What had been his purpose? "The arm hurt too much to make a fuss," she said. "Does that make sense?"

"Yes, and the fact that you knew people were trying to heal you. I knew Roger wanted me dead."

"How is it that you didn't die?"

He shrugged slightly. "The people there decided to feed me. They all hated Roger and Hugh, and one man I've met since then said they recognized a look of the family and knew I was his true son. Whatever their reasons, they weren't about to risk setting me free, but they fed me."

"Dear Jesus. How long were you there?"

"An eternity. I had no sense of time. I gather it was just less than a month. Eventually Roger left the castle to travel to London. They freed me then, putting in the carcass of a pig, hoping that would fool Roger if he ever cared to look. Apparently, he never did." She felt him stir as he said, "The bones were still there when I checked the hole a few months ago."

The callousness of it stunned her. "He never thought of the son he had condemned to a lingering death? Never even checked his fate? He must have known in his heart that you were his son."

"Who knows what he thought? I would dream sometimes in later years of forcing him to tell me. . . ." He took a deep steadying breath.

"What did you do when you were free? Go home?"

"No. There was nothing for me there. I set out to become a warrior."

Imogen twisted to peer at him in the dark. "That can't have been easy."

"No, but I had a purpose. I wasn't quite clear on my purpose," he said ruefully, "but I knew it necessitated being strong and powerful so I could have vengeance on Roger of Cleeve. And, of course, never be in such hands again."

Their present situation came to hover like a dark miasma.

He sighed. "Most people thought I was mad, and laughed at my dreams, of course."

"You didn't laugh at mine," she said softly.

His fingers played gently with her plaits. "I know the power of dreams."

"How did you achieve it without wealth or sponsors?"

"Luck. I fell in with a mercenary troop in need of servants. I watched and studied as they trained, and then began to copy them. I realized I needed strength, and my natural build was scrawny. I set out coldbloodedly to create muscle. Arno, the mercenary captain, saw what I was doing and encouraged me when he was in the mood. He even let me train with the troop, until I beat one of his best and biggest men."

Imogen smiled. "Then he realized he had one of the greatest warriors of the age."

His lips twitched. "Then he realized I'd injured one of his best men. He flogged me."

"*What?* That's not fair."

"Amazingly, Ginger, life frequently isn't fair."

"Like now," she said.

"We can't blame life for this one," he said dryly. "This is wickedness combined with stupidity — mostly mine."

Imogen protested this, and he retaliated by kissing her, which led to kisses that passed a lot of time. Eventually, however, he made her stop her hungry assault, and took up his story.

"Arno was interested in me, though, because he realized I had the gift. He trained me, but he made it clear he'd take it out of my skin again if I did serious injury to any of his men. I learned to fight with a great deal of control."

That brought a gurgle of laughter from her.

"I'm sure you did. How did you become a knight, though?"

"Arno took us into Flanders to fight, and I showed up well. He persuaded the count to knight me. Arno paid for my horse, armor, and weapons, and then set me to fight in the tourneys. That had been his plan all along."

"Tourneys? As in mock battles?"

"Not so mock. Men die. That is why it is not permitted in England. But a man can become very wealthy on the tourney circuit."

"And you were good at it."

"And I was good at it. Arno just sat back and managed my prisoners, splitting the ransoms."

"That wasn't fair either," she grumbled.

"Yes it was. I was paying him back for his training and the start he'd given me. In time I decided I'd paid the debt. There wasn't much Arno could do about our parting."

"What happened then?"

"I met Henry."

"The king?"

"Not king then. Just the Conqueror's youngest, landless son. Henry wanted England. He has always felt, very strongly, that as the only son born in England it is his by right."

Felt strongly enough to kill for it? Imogen wondered. But she kept the question to herself.

"Henry likes tourneys," said FitzRoger,

"and is rarely beaten. I took him prisoner before I knew who he was. He didn't like it at all and demanded single combat to settle it. His freedom if he won. A hundred marks extra if I won."

"I let him win, but did it skillfully enough that I don't think he has ever realized. If he has, he will not acknowledge it. He boasts of being the only man to down Tyron Fitz-Roger."

"I cannot like him," said Imogen. "He is ruthless."

"A weak king is no benefit to anyone. I must serve someone, and Henry has qualities I admire, not least intelligence and efficiency. But I wish he had more scruples."

"When I first met you," said Imogen, "I didn't think you had scruples either."

"Good. That's what I want people to think."

There was something strained in his voice. Imogen glanced at the entrance and saw that the light was beginning to go, and she guessed his deepest fears were gathering. Probably this talk was distracting him. "So you joined Henry's court?" she prompted.

"Yes. And thus came to England. And to Cleeve." He touched the tip of her nose. "And to you."

"Via the death of William Rufus." Then Imogen bit her lip. This was no time to be raising disputes.

"Via the death of William Rufus," he agreed calmly. "Are you determined to rake all the coals?"

"If Henry killed his brother, it can't have been right," she insisted.

"Who can determine right? Rufus was bringing the country to the brink of ruin. Henry in his own way loves England, and he is efficient. Order will be established and ruthlessly enforced."

She remembered FitzRoger speaking lovingly of the order and discipline of the monastery. "And you want to be part of that."

"And I want to be part of that."

She saw it come to him that he probably wouldn't be. That instead, his personal dream would die today. And that if Warbrick took the treasure, it might be the turning point in the struggle for the control of England.

"What sort of king would Duke Robert be?" she asked. She had not heard much good of King Henry's brother.

"Disastrous." He rose to his feet, pulling her up with him. "Time for me to gird for battle again, I think. I hope," he added. "It's getting dark in here."

Imogen assisted him, but her whole body trembled. It was like arming him to ride out to a hopeless cause. And though it was he who armed, it was she who would have to act if they were to survive.

A short while later, the guard called for them to come out, and FitzRoger murmured, "Praise be." At the entrance to the cave, however, he paused. "I have a request to make."

"What?" Imogen asked, hearing *last request*.

"I'd like to hear you call me by my given name."

She flushed with guilt. "I find it hard to think of you as anything other than FitzRoger." She reached up and kissed him. "God be with you, Tyron."

He swept her in for a hard, hungry kiss. "May God be with us both."

They walked out into the gloom of dusk to find Warbrick and his company already mounted. Imogen was pulled away and passed up to Lig. FitzRoger — Imogen tried to think of him as Ty, and failed — was led to his own horse. It was a well-trained animal and there would be little to stop him from breaking away and riding free, other than the fact that she would suffer for it.

They were each hostage for the other.

Imogen knew now she was bound by love. What bound her husband?

A certain fondness, she thought, and strong desire. But mostly it was duty. As he'd admitted twice, he would have done almost as much for any woman he married, and he had married for wealth and power.

Imogen had been raised to be practical in

these matters, but she was aware of a painful emptiness in her heart where FitzRoger's love would fit like a precious jewel.

Imogen composed herself and began another earnest litany. Surely, if God cared about man's purposes at all, He must be on their side in this dispute. Warbrick was clearly a tool of the devil.

An hour later, they stopped in the dark woods within sight of Carrisford. All looked normal. Imogen wondered what everyone there thought of the disappearance of the lord and lady, and the slaughter of their escort. Had Lancaster and his men been found? The watch at the castle would be strict, and surely, as FitzRoger had supposed, Renald would keep some watch on the entrance to the passageways.

FitzRoger had based his plan on the assumption that Renald would not try to block the entrance, but would watch it. When the invaders were within, he would strike, probably from the first joining passage. Imogen would have to be ready to escape then, and avoid inadvertent danger.

If that did not happen, she was to escape anyway at the first opportunity. If she got an opportunity.

FitzRoger had pointed out that most luck was made, and that she should create an opportunity.

She still had her small eating knife, and in

case anyone thought of it, she had concealed it beneath her garter against her thigh. She was in danger of cutting herself, because she had not dared to move the sheath from her belt and FitzRoger had sharpened the blade on a stone. She had bound the blade with more strips torn off her garments, and hoped.

What use such a small blade would be, she did not know, but it felt better to have some weapon than nothing.

The horses were tethered well back among the trees. Imogen now told Warbrick what she had once told FitzRoger. "The entrance is narrow. Only the lighter built men will be able to pass through, and only without armor."

"What?" Warbrick almost bellowed. "You mean I will not be able to enter?" He slapped her so her head rang. "You lie!"

She heard a commotion and knew FitzRoger must have reacted and was being overwhelmed. The briefness of the struggle told her he had regained control. She prayed that he keep it. She could not imagine what it must be like for him to have to stand passively by, but he must. They could not risk his being more seriously hurt before he was needed.

"No lie," she said to Warbrick, swallowing blood from her cut cheek. "Come up if you want and see."

"I will," snarled Warbrick, "and if you have lied, you'll pay."

He began to arrange which men would climb the cliff, which would stay behind.

Imogen risked a glance at FitzRoger. He was backed against a tree caged by six swords wielded by terrified but purposeful men. He had a swelling at his temple and his left hand bled, but she didn't think it was serious.

His look was the calm one of his greatest efficiency, but she could tell the effort behind it. Their eyes met briefly, and she smiled for him, but he could doubtless tell the effort and pain it cost her.

Warbrick grasped her arm bruisingly. "I'm pleased you're fond of him, Lady Imogen. You'll not risk damaging him, will you?" He turned to the men imprisoning FitzRoger. "Let him free."

The swords moved, but FitzRoger didn't.

"Frozen?" sneered Warbrick.

It was as if FitzRoger was a statue. Imogen knew he was at his most dangerous like this, but there was nothing he could do. Nothing. Any resistance would be paid for by her.

Warbrick smiled. "Tie him to the tree," he said to his men, "and make it tight."

FitzRoger's arms were dragged back to be bound behind the tree, and Imogen saw him catch his breath as his wound was tortured. She felt tears gather. Even if he were unwounded that position would be agony.

Warbrick checked the bonds and nodded. "Make some cudgels," he said to his men. "Any trouble, any trouble at all, splinter his ribs. Mail can't guard against that, and with luck, he'll take a nice long time to die."

FitzRoger didn't so much as blink, but Imogen felt sick panic. How could she risk that?

How could she not?

Warbrick saw her feelings. "Don't distress yourself, Lady Imogen. As long as you behave, I see no benefit to myself in killing either of you. When we are back here with the treasure, I will allow you to buy your husband's life by pleasuring me in front of him. You have only been married a few days, but I'm sure he has taught you something."

And, sick though it made her, Imogen knew she would pay the price. But she tried another tack. "I am very religious," she said primly. "Pleasure in the body is a mighty sin."

Warbrick guffawed and destroyed any hope of the ploy working. "I don't give a piss if you get pleasure or not, so your soul won't be jeopardized by me. If you don't know what to do, I'll teach you, and relish it all the more if you hate it." He smirked at FitzRoger. "Perhaps you'll thank me for what I teach her, Bastard, if you can bear to touch her afterward."

Still FitzRoger didn't react. Warbrick walked forward and slapped him so his head snapped to the side and his lip split, gushing blood. "Are you alive?" Warbrick taunted. "Or are you paralyzed by fear?"

The green eyes blazed, but otherwise FitzRoger did nothing. Warbrick laughed, but there was a touch of uneasiness in it now. "You'll react, Bastard. I'll use your woman until you do. I want you *begging*."

Then he seized Imogen and dragged her toward the edge of the woods. He halted suddenly and glared at her. "I hope you know what's wise."

"Yes," whispered Imogen. "I know what's wise." She knew they had no chance other than to try their plan.

He nodded, satisfied, and towed her onward.

Imogen thought she knew what FitzRoger felt like. The hate, the desire to destroy, were overpowering, but they were deep and cold. They would last forever, or until satisfied.

She had thought she hated Warbrick before, but she had not known true hate until today.

Chapter Eighteen

The moon was waning and there were clouds, so it wasn't hard for the twelve men with Imogen and Warbrick to slip over the open ground around the castle and up the slope of the craggy rise on the east side of Carrisford.

They moved in short bursts, darkly. Warbrick was a massive black shape, but Imogen knew that from the castle he would be just a shadow. The tightest watch was not kept on this side because apart from the passageways it was impossible to assault this sheer, blank wall. She wondered if Renald was keeping special watch tonight, though.

FitzRoger had tried to guess how his friend would think, but they couldn't be sure of anything, which was why it was all up to her. She kept an eye on the walls. She saw nothing except the shadowy shape of a patrolling guard who seemed oblivious. She prayed that continue. No good could come of an alarm at this point.

Once at the cliff face, they all stopped to relax for a moment.

"Where?" grunted Warbrick.

Imogen looked up. "It can't be seen from here, but we climb." She looked down at her ruined skirts. Some torn tendrils had tangled her feet as they'd crossed to here. "I need a knife to cut my skirts."

He gave her a hunting knife with insulting lack of concern. She wondered what would happen if she stabbed him. To begin with, it seemed impossible that the blade reach any vital spot in his great bulk.

She trimmed her skirt neatly at the knees and passed the knife back. "Shall I lead?"

"You know where we're going." But he produced a length of rope and tied it around her waist. He gave the end to the ever-obliging Lig. "Keep hold of her leash. We wouldn't want to lose the Treasure of Carrisford, would we?"

Imogen began the climb, giving thanks for the knife pushing at her thigh. Nothing was certain, but at least, if the occasion arose, she could cut the tether.

Despite the appearance of the cliff, it wasn't a hard climb. There were ledges which made it almost like climbing steep stairs. Imogen had done it only once, at her father's insistence, and remembered from then how new muscles had complained, but it still was not particularly difficult.

She could feel the pull now, and the scrapes on her hands from gripping the rough rock. She doubted she had any unbroken nails. She was aware all the time of a soreness between her legs, but that pleased her. That was a reminder of the fact that she was Tyron FitzRoger's wife in every way.

She even smiled against the rock as she remembered. She had made him her husband.

After a while she began to worry that she had missed the way, that she would never find the entrance, but then she spotted the arrowhead rock and breathed a sigh of relief. In moments she was in front of the narrow black shadow that was the secret entrance to Carrisford.

More than three men couldn't gather by the entrance, and Warbrick had brought twelve. Most had to find their own resting places on the nearby rocks like birds of prey. Warbrick pushed forward to join Imogen and Lig.

He scowled at the narrow space. "This is the only entrance?"

"Yes."

She could see he'd love to hit her, throw her down the cliff even, but as he'd said, he had control when he needed it.

"Then I will wait here, Lady Imogen. If you are not out with the treasure by the first hint of dawn, I will go down to amuse myself with your husband. Do you understand?"

She shuddered but said steadily, "I am not stupid, Lord Warbrick."

"All women are stupid and good for one

thing only." He seized her throat and kissed her. The foul taste made her want to gag, his tongue choked her, but worse than that was the sense of smothering in his bulk and sweaty miasma. When he released her she crumpled to her knees.

He dragged her up by her plaits. "Get on with it." He pushed her toward the entrance and Imogen scurried into it with relief. Anything to be away from him. She felt the rope tighten then slacken as Lig followed. She went a little way and waited.

She heard someone striking flint. "It's better to do without a light," she said, her voice echoing in the passageway.

Lig reeled in the rope until she was close to him. "You'd like that, wouldn't you? No, I want to see what you're up to."

The man with the lantern was three back, so Lig wouldn't be able to see very much. Imogen couldn't help but be grateful for the light, which would keep away rats.

She began to lead the way, which required no thought, as the narrow passage offered no alternatives. The next opportunity would be at the trap.

She could undoubtedly cross over without warning Lig, and send him hurtling down into the oubliette, but even if she cut the rope and so wasn't dragged down with him, the other men would not be caught. They would go back to Warbrick, and even with the alarm sounding, Warbrick would have time to return to the woods and kill Fitz-Roger slowly before anyone could interfere.

When they came to the trap, she carefully explained it. It had one good effect. Lig relaxed, convinced that she was too frightened to try any tricks.

She led the way on, keyed up and ready to act. She didn't know if her state of mind was healthy or not. Her heart was racing, and her limbs felt almost weak, but she could sense that her body was prepared for action. She wished the slowing would come on her again, but she didn't sense it.

They were still passing through solid rock, but soon they would enter the castle and the walls would be stone. She wouldn't point it out to them. Shortly after, there was the first adjoining passage, a narrow one designed for the ambushing of intruders.

It had been on the drawing she had so reluctantly done for FitzRoger a lifetime ago, but she hadn't emphasized it. The chance of it being used then had been remote.

If Renald had found the map, would he recognize the passage for what it was? And would he use it?

She eased the knife out from her garter, praying that the shadows concealed her. She felt the sting as she cut herself, but it didn't matter. She had the knife in her hand now.

She gripped the rope and began to cut at it against her waist, trying not to let the motion travel back to Lig so close behind her.

She was only half through when they reached the passage.

It was empty.

Imogen swallowed a mixture of disappointment and relief. She wasn't really ready yet, but she was afraid of time and hovering disaster. How much time had passed? How soon till daybreak?

She forced herself to consider her real dilemmas. Ahead, the passage would soon branch. One arm led toward the treasure but also through out-of-the-way passages. The other led up, closer to the hall, where Renald might have watchers.

If she went up, though, it would take much longer to get to the treasure and carry it out. She'd give Warbrick her wealth, every last coin, to buy FitzRoger's life.

She paused for a moment, then headed up. FitzRoger had wanted her to get help, so she'd try. Another advantage was that the higher passages had more intersections. She passed two more junctions without any sign of help and knew she was going to have to act on her own.

"How much farther?" whispered Lig, and she heard his fear. Strange, she'd been so absorbed in her plans, any fear of these dark ways had left her.

"Not far," she said back, and worked at the rope a bit more.

"What're you doing?"

"The rope galls me," she complained.

"It'll do more than gall you in a moment. Move on."

"I need a key," she said, thinking he'd have to hear her thundering heart. "It's here somewhere. Bring up the light."

Surely her breathy, tremulous voice would give her away. But then she understood that he expected her to be terrified, and would hear only fear.

There was a sidling and a shifting as the lantern was passed forward. Imogen took the opportunity to slash the last threads of the rope, keeping hold to maintain the tension.

She realized with joy that the slowness had come. The men were moving as if in water, against pressure. Her mind was clear and fast, and able to choose between a score of options. When Lig slowly reached forward with the lantern, she had all the time in the world to smash it into the wall, plunging them into darkness, and to leap away and run.

But her guard flailed and caught one of her long plaits, yanking her back. Again she had time to think.

She gripped the imprisoned plait near her head and slashed it off.

She ran, hand lightly on the wall for guidance, hearing the clamor behind speak of panic.

She even laughed for the joy of the first victory.

But she needed more.

She twisted left, the map in her mind, then up some narrow stairs. She pushed the wall and it swung, flinging her out into the space beneath the hall stairs.

Voices.

Sudden caution.

Instead of rushing around the wall to burst into the hall, she crept, all senses alert, to check if further disaster awaited.

Renald was there with a bunch of men, arguing, worried.

She ran in. "Renald! There are men in the passageways, and we have to block their return. Now. I know how. Come."

They gaped then obeyed. She led them fleet-footed down the hall stairs and across the bailey to the guardhouse by the gate. There she commanded four bemused armed men to follow, too.

She opened a way there into the passage. "Go down," she said crisply. "Go forward. There are no turnings. Your passage will meet another. Wait there. Men will come back. Stop them. Kill them if you have to. Try to be as quiet as possible."

The dazed men looked to Renald for confirmation. "Do it," he said. "Stephen. Go with them."

One of the younger knights immediately obeyed.

As soon as they were gone, Imogen collapsed against a wall, shaking, all the power drained from her. She became aware of a sting on her face and her hand found a cut there. Her mind ran back over the last little while and she recalled a shard of the lantern horn hitting her as Lig grabbed for her. . . .

Renald picked her up and carried her to the wooden table and sat her on a bench there. He poured some of the mead the men had been drinking and held it to her lips.

"What's going on?" he asked. "Hell's fires. Who cut your hair?"

"I did." Imogen wanted time to mourn that, but didn't have it. She drank the mead and let the strength of it seep into her. Then she looked at them. "Warbrick has FitzRoger."

"Warbrick!"

"He has him tied to a tree not far into the woods, and Warbrick is waiting at the entrance to the passageways. That's why I had to stop the men getting back to him. He would have gone straight back to kill FitzRoger. Now he'll wait until first light unless he suspects trouble."

Renald glanced at a window slit. "About three hours, perhaps."

Imogen sucked in a deep, calming

breath. "We have to rescue FitzRoger before that. Heaven knows what they're doing even now. . . ." She caught herself up. That way lay madness.

"If we come on them unawares . . ." said Renald.

"It still might not be enough. Warbrick's men have cudgels, and orders to break his ribs at any sign of trouble. They're more afraid of Warbrick than of death itself, and with reason. There's about fifteen of them in the camp, four with orders to do nothing but guard FitzRoger. Warbrick intends to kill him anyway, I'm sure of it, but he's keeping him as a sword to hold over my head." She suddenly covered her face with her hands. "Oh, Mary, I'm so frightened!"

Renald gathered her into a firm embrace. "With me by your side? Come, little flower, you have done well. We will find a way."

Imogen steadied herself. "FitzRoger had a plan."

"Then how can we not succeed?" asked Renald with a cheery grin that summoned a watery smile from Imogen. "Tell us what we are to do."

"We are to take some of the treasure and slip out of the postern. Then take it back to the camp, saying it's the first of the load and they are to begin to share it out. We're hoping that the sight of such wealth will distract even Warbrick's men for the moment it takes for you to free him."

"Is that it?" asked Renald, dismayed.

"It's all we could come up with at the time," she snapped. "However, Warbrick is waiting at the passage entrance with only four men. Perhaps we can take him to bargain with."

"On a cliff face? I doubt it. We could probably kill him, but who's to say what his men will do then?"

"We could wait for Warbrick to go down at first light."

"And risk the attack being seen by the men holding Ty. No. We'll have to try your plan, though I've heard better. Are you sure Ty came up with this one?"

"It's not easy," Imogen pointed out, "making plans for unknown situations when in fear of one's life. We did think," she added bitingly, "that you might already be in the corridors, expecting something like this."

"By the cross," said Renald admiringly, "you're even beginning to sound like Ty. I'm sure he will have words to say. But we didn't even know there was a problem till noon, and certainly never expected an attempt to enter the castle. It . . ." He rubbed his nose. "It didn't exactly surprise us that you and Ty were dallying on your way home."

Imogen colored. "Are the men in the corridor taken care of?"

He stood with a wink. "I'll check."

Within moments, Sir Stephen was back, a little rumpled but uninjured. "Those men fight like wild animals. We're bringing up three prisoners, but the rest are dead or close to it. We lost one. Kevin."

Renald just nodded, but Imogen felt her hard purpose waver. So thoughtlessly she'd ordered a man to his death, a man who'd been sitting here drinking his ale and scratching his fleas . . . But then she thought of FitzRoger, waiting bound for her to act.

Lig was one of the survivors. He snarled at her. "I'll get you! And your man'll die screaming once Warbrick hears of this." Behind it all was sheer terror.

"Don't worry," said Imogen sweetly. "Warbrick won't live to make you pay. Strip and secure them," she told her man. "We need their armor, and men of ours who can impersonate them. Three should be enough."

The men cursed as they were forced to strip, so she ordered them gagged. She had no time at the moment for any trace of compassion. Their white naked bodies reminded her of maggots and she waved them away to a dungeon.

Three men-at-arms of the right build put on the leather armor and conical helmets, and she assessed them. "It will do in the dark for the few moments we need. The nasal helms obscure your faces. But remember, as soon as we get into the camp you are to flaunt the treasure. We want everyone's attention on it."

She turned to Renald. "The rest of you will be ready to take advantage of whatever happens."

"Of course." But she saw the bemused look in his eyes. In all their eyes.

She heard herself giving crisp orders and almost felt she should apologize. But she stopped herself. Survival was all that mattered.

She led the way at a run to the best entrance to the passageways, not caring anymore who knew of them. She plunged into the darkness without a thought for rats, lit the lantern with steady hands, and went quickly to the key.

Then, followed by the clanks and bumps of the clumsy men, she led the way to the treasure. She realized the gift was still with her. She could weave through a nest of blades without hurt.

But then she remembered FitzRoger caged in just such a nest of blades and faltered for a moment, offering a prayer. She collected herself and hurried on.

She struck straight through the curtain of spiders' webs, waded the shallow pool, turned into the corridor, and clicked open the lock.

Once in the chamber she stood back. "Take what you think most tempting."

The men, even Renald, gaped at the glittering hoard.

"Move!" she snapped, infuriated by their slowness. "Take what you would most want. If FitzRoger comes out of this whole, you can have it."

"Imogen . . ." said Renald hesitantly.

"Do I care?" she overrode him, and swung on the bemused men-at-arms. "Well?" She flung open a chest full of silver pennies, and another containing gold. She opened her father's jewel chest and pulled out pouches, spilling chains, rubies, and pearls.

She remembered the chain she had selected for FitzRoger. Dear heaven, she had never given it to him.

The men suddenly scrambled into action. One grabbed an armful of golden platters, another the whole chest of jewels. The third took the chest of gold coins.

"Imogen . . ." Renald said again, but she just said, "Are we ready?"

The men nodded.

She led the way back into the castle. The idea of giving FitzRoger the emerald chain, of putting it on his live, healthy body, had become an obsession.

They had not been secretive about all these activities, and rumors of events were beginning to spread through the castle. Renald hastily assembled his force of men, dressed for quiet dark work in the woods. Another party was to watch for Warbrick coming down the cliff. There were not that many men in the castle, though. About the same number as Warbrick had had to begin with.

To Imogen it took so long, but the rescuers must be ready when she created her diversion.

She suddenly thought of something. "Renald, I want a good knife. A useful one."

Without a question he brought her a long blade in a sheath and she fixed it on her girdle. It would not be noticed in the time they had, and she needed something.

Knives made her think of her hair, and in the midst of all this turmoil, that almost caused her to weep. She felt the stubby end of it . . . She stopped being maudlin when she realized it could be noticed by someone. The short end came just past her shoulders. She tucked it into the neckline of her tunic.

At last, at long last, they were ready. They all moved quietly out of the postern gate. They would have to work their way around to the east through the woods, which would take time. Imogen looked anxiously at the sky, but there was not even a hint of morning grayness.

The woods were full of night life, and they slipped quietly through, trying not to cause a disturbance that might alert their quarry.

Imogen was sure it was growing lighter and whispered so to Renald.

"We have at least an hour, Imogen. It's just that your eyes are growing accustomed to the dark."

Her eyes might be growing accustomed, but her body wasn't. There seemed to be a limit to how long she could hold the power, and it was leaching away, leaving only fear. Sweet Lord, what would they find when they got to the camp?

She was assailed with visions of FitzRoger bleeding, bruised, perhaps already dying of splintered bones.

Then came the time when Imogen and her three men would have to part from the larger force, so as to appear to be coming from the castle. Renald grasped her and kissed her. "For luck, little flower. Don't worry. We'll do it."

She clung to him a moment before heading out of the woods, down the open slope. This was the time when they were most likely to be seen, but the approach of morning was bringing a hint of concealing mist.

Then they began to climb again, heading toward where she thought the camp must be. Now the mist was a hazard. They could miss entirely.

A sharp whistle from the left.

They headed toward it and found one of Warbrick's men peering at them in the gloom. "What's going on?"

This was the tricky part. It would be more logical for one of the men to speak, but their voices would give them away.

"You have your treasure," said Imogen angrily. "That's what. So much treasure that

Lord Warbrick wants more men to carry it down the cliff."

"That right?" asked the man of her "guards."

Her men grunted in agreement.

"Don't expect much of them," she sneered. "They're too busy clutching the choice items."

The man moved nearer, eyes glittering. "Let's see then . . ."

"I want to see that my husband is safe," snapped Imogen. "Out of my way!"

The man swung a fist at her, but halted it. "You'll get yours from Warbrick, you shrew. I'm going to enjoy that, I am."

With a start, Imogen recognized the voice of the man who had guarded them at the cave, and almost broke into nervous giggles. Instead she plunged ahead to the camp, her men following. A quick glance showed her the guard following too. He was trying to keep an eye out behind as well, but clearly the lure of the glinting gold was too much for even a man of Warbrick's.

She silently praised the man who had picked up the platters. Those shining disks of gold were lures of the most potent kind.

They stepped into the camp. There was a small, carefully shielded fire and it gave just enough light for her to see Warbrick's men sitting around, and FitzRoger by the tree still guarded by the four club-wielding men.

He was slumped. Mary, Mother of all, don't let him be unconscious.

The man carrying the plate let one drop with a clang. It spun, flashing gold, near the fire. The second man tripped, and his chest of gold spilled. The third clutched his part of the treasure like a true miser.

For a moment, no one moved, then one of Warbrick's men reached to pick up a gold piece. Another man moved. Then another. In moments a madness took them.

But the four guards by FitzRoger didn't move. They twitched. They yearned. She could almost see their need to scramble for some of that gold, but they stayed by FitzRoger.

Imogen spun on the last of her men. "Give me that chest, you oaf. That's my father's jewel chest. You shan't have it!" She pulled it out of his suddenly lax grasp and it spilled, by her careful design, toward the guards.

She had taken the time while they waited in the castle to empty all the pouches, knowing those men wouldn't know how unlikely it was that such ornaments be all jumbled together. Precious gems sparkled through the air toward them.

She scrambled after them, wailing.

They lunged to get there ahead of her.

Renald and his men stormed in

One man was cutting FitzRoger's bonds before Imogen got there, but her husband was hardly free before a guard realized what was happening and swung viciously with his club. FitzRoger twisted and caught it awkwardly on the back of his shoulder, falling to his knees. After hours of bondage he lacked his natural, fluid grace and Imogen feared that blow must have done even more damage.

She ran forward to defend him, pulling out her poignard.

The guard swung again, this time going for the ribs. FitzRoger's men were all around, but seemed so slow, and Imogen had all the time in the world to choose her spot. She remembered FitzRoger saying once, "Go for the neck." She plunged her long knife to the unguarded side of the man's neck. He screamed and arched as blood fountained out onto her.

FitzRoger staggered to his feet and pulled her into his arms before the man hit the ground.

"Truly a baptism of blood, my virago," he said with a shaky laugh.

Imogen used her tattered tunic to wipe blood and tears from her face, telling herself it was not so different from pig-killing time, but she was shaking head to toe. She stayed in her husband's arms as the fighting swirled around them. She needed his comfort and protection, but she was also protecting.

Like a vixen with one cub, she would let nothing happen to him.

Renald ran by, laughing, and tossed

FitzRoger a sword. He caught it left-handed, but awkwardly. Just how badly injured was his shoulder? He made no move to join the fight, but stood guarding Imogen and flexing his body carefully to overcome the stiffness.

As the fighting dwindled, he released her to stretch more thoroughly, working his damaged body as best he could. He said just one word. "Warbrick?"

"Is on the cliff or coming down." The sky was definitely beginning to lighten. "We set some men to guard the way."

Those of Warbrick's men not defeated were realizing that they had no chance, and were surrendering. FitzRoger's men were efficiently disarming and binding them. They had brought torches and now lit them from the fire to light the scene of carnage.

FitzRoger walked forward, arm around her as if he could not let her go.

Renald came over. "Your crazy plan worked after all, Ty." His joy at his friend's safety rang through the prosaic words.

"Greed works every time." There was something flat in FitzRoger's voice that made them both look at him.

"Warbrick?" asked Renald, almost with a sigh.

"Where is he?"

"I hope our other party has stopped him. He must have heard this."

"I hope so too."

"Ty, we can take him for justice," said Renald. "Henry will see to him."

"Henry will probably only dispossess and exile him."

"That'll get rid of him."

FitzRoger made no reply to that. He let Imogen go and walked forward toward the edge of the woods.

Imogen looked at her husband with clear sight for the first time and saw what Renald saw. FitzRoger's face was a mess; he had clearly received a few more blows after she'd left him. That wasn't the important thing, though; his movements were awkward. The arrow wound must be hurting his right arm, and it would be a miracle if that cudgel blow to the left shoulder hadn't cracked something. He was also favoring his right leg.

He was in no condition to fight anybody, least of all Warbrick.

She knew it would be pointless to say that. She prayed that someone had had the sense to kill Warbrick as they took him prisoner. If she'd anticipated this, she would have ordered it.

She peered into the dense wispy grayness at the base of the cliff, but it was impossible to tell what was happening there. Nor could she hear. The activity in the camp blocked out more distant noises.

They began to descend the slope. Imogen stayed anxiously at FitzRoger's side, Renald just one step behind. Some of the men brought torches, creating pearly pools of light.

"That was a nasty blow on the shoulder," Renald said.

FitzRoger ignored him.

"Is something wrong with your leg?"

"Mere stiffness."

"You seem to have some stiffness in your sword arm, too."

FitzRoger ignored that, as well.

"He has an arrow wound in it," Imogen said.

"Ty . . ." Renald protested.

"No."

It was all FitzRoger. The sort of command no one ever disobeyed. Imogen prayed that Renald would knock his friend out before he went on with his madness. He'd done that in the passages, after all. Unfortunately, it didn't seem to occur to him now.

They found Warbrick pinned at the base of the cliff like a maddened bear surrounded by mastiffs. And like a baited bear, he had drawn blood. A body lay nearby and Warbrick's great sword glinted red in the torchlight.

FitzRoger pushed forward and Imogen went with him. When Warbrick saw FitzRoger, he cursed viciously. "I'll have my men's guts around their necks."

"They tried," said FitzRoger almost sweetly.

Warbrick straightened. "Well, Bastard. What now?"

"Now I kill you. You deserve to die for your many sins, but you will die for touching my wife."

Warbrick laughed. "I did more than touch her! Has she told you what happened up there? Of course not. She'd lie about it."

Imogen would have protested, but Fitz-Roger's hand gripped her arm, telling her to be silent.

"She wouldn't lie. But no matter what happened, only you will suffer. Shield."

The one-word order immediately brought him a kite shield.

"And for him."

More reluctantly, one was passed to Warbrick. Imogen took some comfort from the fact that it could not possibly cover his bulk.

Imogen pulled FitzRoger back a little, and he allowed it.

"This is madness," she hissed. "Hang him. He deserves it."

"I promised to kill him for you," he said quietly, flexing his shoulder.

"Then use a rope."

"No."

"I take back my request. Let the king deal with it."

"No. He must die by my hand."

She wanted to hit him. "You're in no state!" she protested. "You've that wound, and it's a miracle that blow didn't break your shoulder!"

His hand covered her mouth, and not gently. His eyes were almost cold with the killing fury that possessed him. "You will be silent," he said. "You will stand here where it is safe, and watch in silence as a good wife should."

When he released her, she snapped, "And what am I supposed to do if you lose?"

He shook his head. "I'll have to take to beating you, won't I? If I lose, at least don't give yourself to the victor."

She watched him limp away, filled with exasperation. Merely a stiff leg? She doubted it. If she thought she had any chance of accomplishing it, she would order his men to tie him back up to a tree while she hanged Warbrick herself.

They'd never obey.

The idea came to her.

It terrified her.

But these past days she'd done so many things that terrified her that one more hardly seemed to matter. Before she lost her nerve, she picked up a fist-sized rock and swung it hard at her husband's unprotected head.

She'd not wanted to kill him and she thought for an awful moment that she'd not hit hard enough. He staggered and turned, rage blazing in his eyes.

Then he crumpled at her feet.

Chapter Nineteen

"Christ's wounds!" Renald expressed the horror on the faces of all the men.

All the men except Warbrick. He guffawed. "Know he can't beat me, eh?"

Imogen turned to look at Warbrick. "Kill him," she said coldly to the men. "I don't care how. Kill him."

There was an eerie stillness, then a man with a bow coldly nocked an arrow and let loose. Cursing, Warbrick caught it on his shield, but another man had a bow and stuck him in the arm. Imogen watched as her enemy became bristled with arrows as FitzRoger had once been, but this time without the protection of mail.

Warbrick was not a coward. He charged his attackers, but cold-eyed men drove him back to be victim to more arrows.

He was roaring and staggering about, threatening his assailants like a maddened animal. Then at last an arrow took him deep in the chest and he crumpled with a last cry of agony and defeat.

Silence fell.

Sickened back to her wits, Imogen turned

away from the man's final twitching moments, wondering just what her husband was
going to do to her. Bone-rattling shudders
began to rack her. She had actually knocked
FitzRoger out to prevent him from taking
part in what he probably regarded as a duel
of honor.

She half expected to find him facing her,
rage still sheeting from those green eyes, but
he was on the ground and trussed up. He
appeared to still be unconscious.

"I had to give him another little tap," said
Renald, shaking his head. "By the thorns,
Imogen, I don't know . . ."

"N-nor d-do I," she stammered, hugging
herself. "You haven't t-tied him too tight,
have you? H-his wounds . . ."

"He's tied tight enough to hold him,"
Renald said. Grimly he added, "I hope. I'm
working on the belief that he'll regret it afterward if he throttles you with his bare hands."

Imogen covered her mouth with her
shaking hand. "H-he'll be that angry?"

"I have no idea how angry he'll be.
Nothing like this has ever happened before.
My plan, however, is to escort you to Cleeve
while the men put him in a bed with a
strong sleeping draft. Then we just hope that
he's too wounded to set out after you until
he's cooled down a bit."

Imogen desperately wanted to tend her
husband with her own hands, but she had

some sense left. "Yes please," she said meekly. "But please untie him as soon as possible."

Renald gave his orders, and those for disposing of Warbrick, then escorted Imogen around to the gate to get horses. Her knees were weak, and her head as misty as the gray morning. She shivered constantly and not just with cold.

What was going to happen to her? If she was lucky, he'd just beat her half to death.

Her terror was that he'd cast her off.

Renald took time to find her some wine and a thick cloak, but then he and six men carried her off to Cleeve at an urgent gallop.

Imogen managed to stay on her horse, but when she dismounted she collapsed, and the next thing she knew she was in a bed at Cleeve, sore from head to foot, and miserable as the devil.

Given the situation, she rather wanted to keep her eyes closed forever, but she opened them a crack, then wider to search the room. She had expected FitzRoger to be there, waiting to visit his rage upon her. When she realized he wasn't, her heart sank and her mind immediately conjured up the worst.

He was too wounded to move.

He was dead.

He never wanted to see her again.

Imogen turned and wept heartbreaking tears. She could clearly hear him once saying,

"I hope at least that you never cry because of me, though I suspect you probably will." She didn't think either of them had expected her to cry at his loss.

Imogen slept again, the sleep of exhaustion, and woke in the evening no better in mind or body. This time, however, she did not weep, but started wearily to put together some sort of existence.

When she sat up, aching in every part of her body, she found ale and bread by the bed. The bread had begun to harden, and the ale had caught a few flies, but she ate and drank anyway.

Then she assessed her physical hurts. Her feet were sore again in places, and when she inspected them, some of the worst wounds had been revived. No matter. She had nowhere to go.

She had an alarming number of bruises and scrapes with no recollection of how she had acquired them, but the sorest spot was her face. She gingerly felt her jaw, which Warbrick's blow had made very painful; she had no doubt she was black and blue there. Her fingers found another hurt, and traced the jagged gash in her cheek made by the flying piece of the lantern.

A thin wail escaped her when she realized she would be scarred. She shut her mouth on that weakness, but she could not stop the tears that rolled down to drip off her cheeks.

A woman peeped around the door, then came in. "Why, my lady, what's the matter? Never fret. All's well now."

That struck Imogen as hilariously funny, but she managed not to giggle. "My face!" she gasped.

The middle-aged woman grimaced. "Aye. It'll never be quite as it was. But it'll look better when it's healed, you'll see. I'll get some of old Margery's salve for it. That'll help." She came over and picked up the cup and platter. "Now, lady, do you feel ready for a bath?"

Imogen realized that she was stripped to her shift, but even that was stained with dirt and blood. Her hair was sticky with gore. She stank of blood. "Yes," she said.

When the woman had bustled off, Imogen climbed wincing out of bed and looked down at herself. In disgust, she tore off the ragged shift and wrapped herself in a sheet. The shift was good for nothing but rags now, she thought, then she saw one particular set of bloodstains.

Among all the other stains no one would note them, but Imogen knew they were the marks of the consummation of her marriage. She slid down sadly against the bed, clutching the garment. For a brief while then, at their darkest hour, she had been happy and so had he. FitzRoger had opened himself to her as perhaps he had never done to another. He had trusted her.

And she had betrayed him.

It had been a betrayal.

Honor said she should have let him go to his death.

She could not have done that, though. She contemplated the matter sadly and decided that she would do the same thing again. If she had the courage. That was what was lacking now — the insane recklessness of living with death for twenty-four hours.

Servants brought the tub — the same tub she had used when she had first come to Cleeve. She'd been in a disgusting state then, too, she thought wryly. They lined it with cloths and filled it with warm herb-scented water. Imogen was assisted into it among horrified exclamations at her scrapes and bruises.

Then one woman exclaimed, "Oh, lady! Your hair. Your beautiful hair!"

Imogen's hand flew to the severed plait, finding the ragged end brushing her collarbone. She clutched at the other, still thick down to her thighs.

The women began to unravel the long plait in deathly silence. It only took fingers to untangle the stubby one. No one said a thing, but their shock echoed in the room. Hair was any lady's glory, and length was one of the most prized attributes. Some ladies had to content themselves with plaits down to the waist, or even to the breasts. Many extended their deficient hair with false braids.

No lady had hair that was almost too short to braid at all.

"Cut the other side," said Imogen flatly.

"Oh lady . . ."

"I can hardly have one side long, one side short. Cut it."

A woman fetched a sharp knife and with unsteady hands trimmed Imogen's hair until it was all the same length.

"Oh, lady," said one, incautiously. "You look just like a boy!"

"At least it will be easier to wash," said Imogen staunchly. "Does this place boast a mirror?"

"Oh, I don't think . . ."

Imogen fixed the ditherer with an icy stare. "Get it." The woman rolled her eyes and scurried off.

Imogen forced herself to relax and let the women wash her. What can't be changed must be endured, and at least her hair would grow. How long, though, would it take to achieve its former glory? She had no idea. Her hair had not been cut since she was a child.

Years, she suspected.

Among all her other troubles, this should be nothing, and yet it clogged her mind and heart like a dismal cloud.

At least, as she had said, it was easy to wash out the grime and blood, though the women were stumped as to what to do with it afterward. "I could make it into plaits, lady," one said dubiously.

Stubby little plaits? "No, leave it. Where's that mirror?"

Eventually it arrived, a plain one of polished silver, but adequate. Imogen was dressed by then in a borrowed shift. She held the mirror at arm's length. Braced though she was, she could not suppress a gasp.

One side of her face was black, blue and yellow, and swollen to boot. The other was marred by an angry weeping gash. Her eyes were red and puffy. Her hair, which had always been merely wavy when long, was now drying into a frizz of unruly curls.

And in a beam of sunlight, it *did* look ginger!

Imogen thrust the looking glass into a woman's hands and retreated, lips quivering, to the bed. "Go away!" she commanded, and the women went.

A little later there was a knock on the door. Imogen ignored it. One thing was certain, FitzRoger would not knock. The door opened. Imogen looked up, hoping despite sense. It was Renald.

She saw him wince at the sight of her, and turned away. "What are you doing here?"

"You think I'd rather be at Carrisford?" he asked dryly. "Mind you, the state you're in I think I should perhaps have left you there.

Ty would have to be a monster to take vengeance on you now."

Imogen gritted her teeth. "Renald, if you think that is any comfort, you're wrong. I'm a freak."

He came over to stand in her line of sight. "Wounds heal, Imogen. I've seen enough, and yours won't leave serious marks."

"My hair!" she wailed.

He shook his head. "Amid everything, you're worried about your *hair?*"

She looked at him miserably. "How is he?"

"I don't know. There's been no word."

"Oh." After a moment, she said, "Perhaps we should send a messenger."

"That would tell him where you are."

She sat up abruptly. "He doesn't know? Then send one!"

Renald wrinkled his brow. "That may not be wise, Imogen. Give him time."

Imogen couldn't believe this. "If he's conscious, he'll be concerned. It's not right to worry him so."

"*Worry* him!" exclaimed Renald, wide-eyed. Then he shrugged. "I haven't understood you two from the beginning, so if you want me to send a messenger, I will."

"I want you to."

"Are you sure?"

"Yes!" shrieked Imogen, then winced as her jaw complained. Her already shaken nerves were jittering even more at Renald's uneasiness. Did he really think FitzRoger would charge in here and take her apart, piece by piece?

Perhaps he did.

Renald went toward the door, then turned, very serious. "One thing, Imogen. Don't even think about trying to hold Cleeve against Ty. I'll truss you and toss you over the walls first."

"I wouldn't!" she gasped.

He shrugged. "Just wanted to make it clear. I don't know what you'd be likely to do anymore."

Imogen collapsed back against her pillows. She knew she should be terrified of her husband's knowing where she was, but all she wanted was news that he was safe.

No news came that night and Imogen settled to sleep, suddenly aware that she was sleeping in FitzRoger's bed. Of course they would bring her to the castle solar. Where else?

There was nothing to mark the place as his, for most of his personal possessions were at Carrisford, and the others were locked in chests. But she thought she could sense his presence lingering here.

She hugged a pillow that presumably had cradled his head, and drifted off to sleep.

When daylight woke her from tormented dreams, matters looked no better.

She had to accept that for a woman to

strike her husband, strike him unconscious, was a very grave matter. She wasn't even sure it wouldn't cost her her life.

She couldn't believe that FitzRoger would demand that penalty, but he could hardly allow her to go unpunished. Confinement on bread and water? A public beating? Her greatest fear was that he would cast her off entirely.

What was she going to do if he sent her to a convent? She wondered if what she had done was grounds for divorce.

She laid her hand over her flat belly. There was a small chance that she was with child. She earnestly prayed that she was. She knew, with his history, that FitzRoger would never put aside a wife who was bearing his child.

But even if he took her back, would he ever relax with her again? Ever trust her again?

Still she knew that in the same situation she would do the same thing if she could. She'd burn at the stake to save his life. Her thoughts trudged around and around in weary circles.

A tap on the door brought servants, servants bearing familiar chests and even Imogen's harp. One of the maids was Elswith, nervous but smiling.

Imogen sat up, heart in throat. Her chests? Her maid? What did this signify? Renald followed. "Ty is apparently in his bed with a fever, but alert enough to have your clothes and woman sent here."

Imogen swallowed. "He's not dangerously ill?"

"Not as far as anyone knows."

"Er . . . what did he say about me?"

"He ordered your things to be sent here."

Imogen didn't know if that was good or bad. "Is that all?"

"He sent a message to me. You are not to leave Castle Cleeve for any reason." He suddenly relaxed and smiled a little. "At least this means he's not going to kill you in his first rage."

"Thank you," said Imogen faintly.

"And I doubt that he'll beat you severely, Imogen. Ty would only do that in cold blood if he thought it would serve a purpose."

"It might," she said bleakly, "just make him feel better." She hadn't missed the fact that Renald took it for granted that Fitz-Roger would beat her.

Renald laughed. "Give him time, Imogen. He'll forgive you."

Imogen took that prediction to heart, for surely Renald knew FitzRoger better than she, and a mild beating would be welcome as the price of forgiveness.

That recalled to her that she still had not confessed her false oath. At least now there was no point in reparation. The oath was now true, and Lancaster was dead. All she needed was a priest.

Heartened, Imogen rose from her bed and sent for a priest.

Within the hour, one came up from the village. He was a simple man and she did not burden him with details, but confessed that she had made a false oath upon the cross. He was suitably horrified, but once assured of her full repentance and that there was no way to make reparation, he granted her absolution. The only penance he imposed was that she pray on her knees each night for a sennight, begging Christ's Blessed Mother for strength to avoid sin in the future.

Imogen welcomed it. She had a great deal to pray about.

Imogen sent the man away with the promise that in time she would make a special gift to his church. She wondered if it would be within her power, but she knew that no matter how else other matters might work out, FitzRoger would make good her word.

She even sang in the bright morning light, for the only act that had truly burdened her soul was now washed away.

Elswith dressed Imogen in the clothes her husband had sent over. The young maid was distressed at Imogen's appearance but otherwise seemed happy and unfearful. She had little news to add to Renald's report.

Lord FitzRoger was in his bed recovering from wounds, Elswith told Imogen. He was eating normal foods and supposed to be doing well. Rumors were flying around the castle about Warbrick, and that Imogen had struck her husband down, though few believed that possible. None of the men who had been at the scene seemed to have a clear memory.

Imogen realized that Renald had brought all the men who had witnessed that scene here to Cleeve as her escort. The mist doubtless had made things unclear for the rest. This gave her hope. If it was just a matter between her and FitzRoger, it would go better than if it were a public scandal.

According to Elswith no one was quite sure why Imogen was at Cleeve, but most thought that during her husband's sickness she was setting the place in order in case the king should wish to visit.

A clever rumor. Put about by FitzRoger? Imogen hoped so.

The waiting was going to be the hardest part, the waiting to hear her fate. When the news of it arrived, she wanted to look the best she could, however. She was still Imogen of Carrisford, and lady to FitzRoger of Cleeve.

She pondered dismally the question of her hair, and decided she might as well wear a veil to hide the worst of it. She draped a length of fine linen over her head. "Give me a circlet, Elswith. The gold rope one."

At the silence, Imogen turned. The maid had colored. "I wasn't allowed to bring your jewels, lady. The master's orders."

"None at all?" Imogen asked, chilling.

The girl shook her head.

"Not even my morning gift?"

"No, lady."

Imogen turned away, heart sinking at this news. The absence of the special gift almost dissolved her into tears again, for it made a clear statement. Was FitzRoger even now in the process of casting her off?

This also meant he was in complete control of her wealth, both her personal jewels and all the treasure of Carrisford. Surprisingly, Imogen found she couldn't fret about that. In part she simply didn't have the energy to care, but also she knew now that he wouldn't squander their wealth.

One way or another he would use it to increase their standing and power.

If he still regarded them as a couple.

Imogen gritted her teeth against tears and said, "Then I'd better see if I can make a headrail out of a long scarf, Elswith. Find me a longer piece of linen."

Imogen had no desire to go about looking as she did, and so she and Elswith spent the morning hemming the white lawn and devising ways of winding it around Imogen's head so that it was secure and concealed most of her hair.

Eventually they achieved the best they could, though Imogen was sure she still looked a freak. She spent the rest of the day in the solar lackadaisically practicing on her harp. FitzRoger had enjoyed her singing. Perhaps she could win back his regard with her voice.

It took only the first day, however, to convince Imogen that sitting in her room gave her far too much time to think, and would drive her mad. On the second morning she found she could wear her sandals again, and so she set about the management of Cleeve Castle. At first she wondered if there would be some objection — after all, she was as good as a prisoner here — but, if anything, the servants were happy to have a chatelaine.

Imogen found that under FitzRoger's hand the castle had been well run, but that a number of womanly arts had been neglected. The needlework and preserve areas were not as efficient as they could be, and when Brother Patrick was away, medical care was chancy at best.

Thoughts of Brother Patrick had Imogen standing in a doorway, worrying about FitzRoger's health.

After a moment she took up writing equipment and wrote,

To Brother Patrick.
  Of your kindness, Brother, please send news to Cleeve if My Lord Husband should be close to death, so that I might come to him.
    Imogen of Carrisford and Cleeve

The note was sent and brought no response. Imogen chose to take that as reassurance.

Each day Renald sent a messenger to Carrisford. Each day the messenger returned with information, but with no word directly from FitzRoger to either of them.

They heard that he was recovering from his fever.

Fever, thought Imogen in panic. *He had a fever?*

Next they heard that Lord FitzRoger was out of his bed, but using a staff to walk. His knee had apparently only been badly bruised.

A few days later came the news that Lord FitzRoger was training again in armor.

Imogen began to let go of her terror for his safety. Now, however, she had only her own future to worry about. She had to believe that someday her husband would decide what to do with her and end this limbo. At the very least, some day FitzRoger would want to visit his castle.

At least he would find it in good order.

She threw herself into the work at Cleeve with a vengeance, trying desperately to make days pass faster than nature allowed, and hoping that her husband might be mellowed by her effort and competence.

She put more looms to work, and organized the still rooms and larders more efficiently. She ensured that all was ready for the winter stores, and set some men to whitewashing the hall to make it brighter.

Every time she walked through the plain hall she thought of ordering flowers painted on the walls, and smiled sadly.

Then, two weeks after her arrival at Cleeve, a spark of rebellious mischief stirred in Imogen's mind, and she did just that.

She had the Cleeve scribe, who knew something of illustrating, make a simple design, then worked with some of the men to use dyes to tint the whitewash. Soon after, the men were copying the design all over the walls.

Renald came in as she was directing the workmen. His mouth fell open. "Imogen . . ."

He shook his head. "Flowers. Pink flowers."

"It will brighten the place considerably," she said. "I think the messenger to Carrisford should see our work here before he leaves."

Renald gaped again, but then a trace of admiration lit his eyes. "Ah, little flower, you are either mad or splendid. Quite possibly both."

Imogen spent the day in a nervous frenzy, anticipating her husband's response.

The messenger returned that evening with Father Wulfgan.

Response, retaliation, or mere coincidence?

The priest stalked into the hall and scanned it with a withering glance. "Daughter in Christ!" he declared. "You have done a terrible thing!"

Imogen heard herself say, "I don't think the flowers are that bad," and suppressed a nervous giggle.

"On your knees!" thundered the outraged priest. "You are a rebellious, undutiful imp of the devil!"

Imogen almost obeyed, but she stopped herself. "Perhaps we should talk in the solar, Father," she said, and led the way without a backward glance.

Somewhat to her surprise, Wulfgan was behind her when she arrived there, but as soon as the door was closed he began again. "You have sinned most grievously, daughter."

Imogen clasped her hands demurely. "In what way, Father?" She honestly wasn't sure which of her many crimes would be most heinous in Wulfgan's eyes.

"To strike down your husband, your lord in God's sight!"

"You never approved of him," she pointed out.

"He is still your lord! God's representative for you on Earth. Your holy duty is to obey and cherish him."

"But I *was* cherishing him," Imogen protested. "If I hadn't struck him down he would have been killed."

It occurred to her that if her exile here was designed to turn her into a proper submissive woman again, it was failing miserably. Was Wulfgan going to report back to FitzRoger?

"Death is not to be feared, my child," he retorted. "Only dishonor."

Imogen lowered her eyes to think on this statement. Was it possible that FitzRoger was using Wulfgan as a messenger?

"I am willing to do penance for my sin," she said at last, "though I fear I cannot repent."

"You wicked child," he whispered. "How can you be so lost to all sense of your duty to your lord and to God? I have told him," he declared. "I have told him again and again that he must beat you publicly and severely, both to reclaim his honor and to save your sinful soul."

Imogen swallowed but managed to say, "My husband's honor is not in doubt."

"He is a laughingstock if he does not punish you!"

"It is widely known, then?"

"Could it be otherwise?"

Imogen supposed not. But still, she raised her chin proudly. "No matter what he does, FitzRoger could never be a laughingstock."

Wulfgan stared at her. "You are deep in sin."

"Am I?" asked Imogen. "And what of you, siding with Lancaster?"

"Lancaster?" queried Wulfgan. "I favored the earl over the upstart. What has that to say to anything?" But for the first time ever he looked unsure of himself.

Imogen realized that FitzRoger must have

managed to keep the earl's wickedness secret. There were still men of Warbrick's who could reveal it, but FitzRoger had doubtless taken care of them, too.

How?

Were they dead?

There was no point in worrying about that now.

She covered her error. "You were supporting the earl over my God-given husband."

Wulfgan's fiery gaze wavered. "He was a more Godly man."

Imogen pressed her advantage. "But my duty was to my husband."

Unwise tack. Wulfgan was on firm ground again. "Aye, and yet you wickedly assaulted him! What will the world come to if women can strike their lords? Why should not anyone raise his hand against his better?"

"I have said I am willing to do penance." She certainly wasn't looking forward to being beaten or flogged, but she could see a certain justice in it, and if it would wipe away her sin, she would almost welcome it. "Are you come to accompany me back to Carrisford, Father?" she asked hopefully.

Wulfgan was taken aback. "I? No. I was presenting my views to Lord FitzRoger yet again, and he told me I would have more purpose preaching to the sinner, and ordered me here."

Imogen's lips twitched. She could almost imagine the scene. Not a messenger then, she thought sadly, so much as a penance. But she detected a touch of humor in the gesture, which gave her hope.

"What does FitzRoger do with his days?" she asked the priest.

"What any man of his type does. There is work to do in administering the castle, and he trains with his men. I suppose," he acknowledged sourly, "that it is such a man's duty to hone his body as I hone my spirit."

"A paladin," Imogen said softly, then shrugged. "Father, you are welcome here, but I suspect you would find it easier to hone your spirit at Grimstead monastery."

To her astonishment, Wulfgan nodded. "You may be right. I fear you are beyond me now, daughter. I fear for you, but cannot allow my soul to be imperiled by yours. I admit, too, that in listening to the Earl of Lancaster I may have been tempted by things of the world. I will build an anchorite's cell by the walls of the monastery and live there in penance all my days."

"Good," said Imogen, hiding her astonished relief. "Perhaps you would like to go there now?" she added hopefully.

He nodded and sketched a sign of the cross in the air. "God guide you, daughter, though I fear you are lost."

Imogen saw him away down the road to Grimstead, wondering if such an easy victory would count with FitzRoger.

She went in search of Renald. "When the next messenger goes, Renald, be sure he tells people at Carrisford that Father Wulfgan has gone to be an anchorite at Grimstead." She couldn't help a mischievous smile at the end.

Renald shook his head. "And for your next miracle?"

Imogen's smile faded and she sighed. "I would like to turn myself into a true wife, but I don't know the secret of it."

She climbed to the battlements and looked wistfully in the direction of Carrisford, though she couldn't see it from where she stood. Her instinct told her that FitzRoger was no longer in a rage, but she could not be sure that he would ever send for her. Her courses had been and gone, so there would be no child to bind them.

She was tempted to set out for Carrisford on her own initiative, sure that face-to-face they could achieve more than at a distance. She was not closely guarded. On the other hand, she wanted to convince FitzRoger that in most respects she would be dutiful and obedient.

The next day's messenger brought the news that the king was at Carrisford. Warbrick's castle had been seized and razed, and all his men dispersed, those who had not been hanged for crimes. The messenger brought wild rumors of evil and torture found in that place, and Imogen suspected that most of them were true.

"And what of Lord Warbrick's death?" she asked the messenger. "What do they say of that?"

The man's eyes grew concerned. "They say the king is not pleased, lady. I am told he said he wanted no rough justice in his land."

Imogen retreated to her room with a whole new level of concern. She knew she had been floating on a trust that FitzRoger would never be really harsh with her. But the king? As FitzRoger had said, Henry's first concern was his kingdom, and he would take whatever steps necessary — no matter how brutal — to impose the kind of order he wanted.

A penitential life in a convent seemed very likely, and a few tears escaped. How could she live without seeing FitzRoger again?

The next day, the messenger had little to report except that the king and FitzRoger had spent much time together in discussion, and that FitzRoger had practiced the sword with Sir William — a bout so fierce that all had gathered to watch, fearing it would come to death.

Imogen didn't need Renald's sober face to tell her that boded no good.

Early the next day, a troop of the king's men bearing his banner came to escort Imogen of Carrisford back to her castle. They were led by a stone-faced older knight, Sir Thomas of Gillerton. He would say nothing of their purpose, and would not be drawn, but Imogen had to believe that she was being taken to face the king's justice.

And FitzRoger had nearly killed Sir William.

Imogen turned in panic to Renald, and he took a steadying grip on her hands. "Ty will not let anything too terrible happen to you, Imogen."

"But that's what I'm afraid of!" she gasped. "Will he oppose the king for my sake? I'll cause his ruin!"

A flicker of concern passed over Renald's face before it was shielded. "I can't believe even Henry would destroy Ty to avenge Warbrick."

"I could flee . . ."

His grip became firm. "No, Imogen." It was as absolute as any statement of FitzRoger's.

Imogen accepted it. It was time to face the consequences of her actions. But that "even Henry" tolled in her mind as she prepared for the journey.

She would have to find some way to prevent this new disaster, to prevent FitzRoger from destroying himself in her cause.

But at last, at long last, she would see him again.

Chapter Twenty

Despite everything, Imogen couldn't help but smile when she set eyes upon Carrisford Castle in all its beauty, pennants flapping in the brisk breeze.

Surrounded by her escort she rode through to the inner bailey, eyes roving in search of her husband. Surely, for better or worse, he would be here to meet her. Despite her eagerness, she couldn't help wondering what he would think when he saw her. Her bruise was almost gone, and the cut was not too horrible now the scabs had come off, but her hair was still an unruly mop which her scarf could not disguise.

But then the atmosphere brought more serious concerns to the front of her mind. Everyone — Carrisford servants and men-at-arms — looked up in solemn silence to stare at her as she rode by. She couldn't decide if they were angry, horrified, or concerned about her, but no one smiled.

Then one of the men spat into the dust. She swallowed fear; it was clear what *he* felt.

Her heart began to pound and she looked around again for FitzRoger. She'd give anything for him to be here to meet her and lead her to her fate, even if he was about to flog her. He was not here, nor were any of his or the king's knights other than Sir Thomas.

He it was who came to help her dismount, and directed her gruffly up the stairs to the hall. Imogen looked up then, knowing that something terrible awaited, but she had no choice. She raised her chin and walked steadily up to meet her fate.

At the top of the stairs there was a short passageway leading to the great hall doors. The doors were closed and guarded, but the men there swung them open at her approach to reveal a room full of sober, frowning men.

Imogen swallowed as best her dry mouth would allow, and walked in.

The king was sitting in the central place behind the great table, but Imogen sought FitzRoger. He was seated to one side of the table.

She drank in every detail. He was in black — *mourning?* she wondered wildly — with no jewels other than his ring. He looked un-marked by their adventure. He returned her gaze unreadably, though she thought perhaps he frowned slightly.

"Lady Imogen!" The king's sharp voice brought her attention to him. "Approach us!"

Imogen took a steadying breath and walked forward to stand before the table. She curt-sied deeply to Henry.

"Ha! So you know some proper behavior,"

he said. "Imogen of Carrisford, you have only been granted a hearing before this assembly because of your unusual status as overlord of Carrisford, a status which may well be rescinded."

There wouldn't be much point in being overlord of Carrisford if she were in a convent; Imogen could see that.

"You are here," said Henry, "to face two charges of assault upon my vassals. One being your lord and husband, whom you also took prisoner; the other being Lord Warbrick, whom you killed out of hand. What say you?"

Imogen almost panicked. She'd never thought that her actions might be seen as attacks on the king's vassals, therefore attacks on the king himself.

Her knees weakened, but she gathered her strength. "I admit both acts, my liege, but neither was designed against Your Majesty."

A hiss rumbled through the room at her flat admission. Belatedly Imogen realized that she would have been wiser to give in to collapse, preferably in tears and begging for mercy. She could have claimed madness brought on by her sufferings. . . .

She flicked a glance at FitzRoger, but he was completely masked. He was turning his ring, though.

"Do you have any justification for your acts, woman?" the king demanded in exasperation.

She wondered if he, too, would have preferred weeping repentance. Well, if that was the case they should have forewarned her.

Imogen considered carefully, for she feared she was fighting for FitzRoger's life as well as her own. Despite his impassivity, she knew in her heart, in her soul, that her husband would never stand by for her brutal punishment.

"My Lord King," she said at last. "As overlord of Carrisford, I had the right and duty of exacting vengeance against Lord Warbrick. He had assaulted my castle, killed my relatives and people, despoiled my property and land, and attempted to rape and kill me. Being a weak woman, I could not prevail against him single-handed, and so I used my troops as proxy, as is allowed."

"Not *your* troops, Lady Imogen. Your husband's!"

Imogen was framing a response when FitzRoger spoke. "By your leave, sire, that is not exactly so. By the marriage contract witnessed in this hall, my wife retains the suzerainty of Carrisford, and those men were Carrisford men."

There was an uneasy rustling, but no outrage. Was it possible, Imogen wondered, that FitzRoger was on her side? She didn't dare look at him.

"So," said Henry, rapping his bejeweled fingers on the table, "the question is whether Imogen of Carrisford, as lord of this castle, had the right to visit summary justice upon Lord Warbrick, or whether she should have arrested him and brought him to trial."

Imogen hoped the two men were going to debate the subject for her, but it appeared not. Henry snapped, "Well, woman?"

"My Lord FitzRoger thought summary justice was his right, Your Majesty, and so did I."

Now there was an outraged stirring and muttering in the room. Imogen was coming to believe that Father Wulfgan had been right: FitzRoger would have to beat her publicly to recover from this. In view of the situation she thought that might be to get off lightly.

"But your husband would have offered Lord Warbrick fair combat," Henry pointed out. "You gave your enemy no chance."

Imogen answered proudly, "If my husband had not been wounded, sire, his skill would have given Lord Warbrick no chance." Too late, she realized such a spirited answer was unwise.

Henry glared at her. "Are you not aware, woman, that the hand of God settles trial by combat? The weakest in the land could prevail against the mightiest if God were on his side."

It was like a door opening into sunlight, though Imogen almost hesitated to walk through it, it was so tempting. She took a deep breath. "Then surely, sire, God was on my side."

Another stir in the room, but not quite so

malicious. Imogen thought she heard a chuckle, but she could have been mistaken. It occurred to her that none of the barons could contest her right to punish her enemies without weakening his own rights in such cases. In this matter, the men might incline more to her side than to the king's.

Imogen saw something flash in Henry's eyes — anger or admiration? She was almost dizzy with the pressure of this situation. Perhaps she would collapse before them after all, and completely involuntarily.

Henry's fingers continued their irritated rap. "You have too clever a tongue, Imogen of Carrisford, and must be schooled. Now tell me, can you talk yourself out of your attack on your husband, too?"

Does that mean I've talked myself out of the first charge? Imogen thought dazedly.

"Well?" the king demanded.

Imogen tried, but she found no clever words. "I thought he would die," she said simply.

Silence rounded the room as loud as cries.

Henry leaned back. "You thought Lord FitzRoger unable to defeat Lord Warbrick? You just said otherwise."

A flickering glance at FitzRoger still told Imogen nothing. The mask was complete. She lowered her head. "I thought he misjudged the extent of his wounds, sire." She knew there was no defense in any of this, and awaited judgment.

The king surprised her. He addressed her husband. "My Lord FitzRoger, is your wife correct? Do you think Warbrick would have killed you in that duel?"

"As always, sire, I put my trust in God," said FitzRoger.

Imogen risked a glance at him. Still as hard as black iron.

"With hindsight," persisted the king irritably, "do you think your wounds would have made victory by ability alone unlikely?"

"Very unlikely," said FitzRoger flatly. "I was without effective use of both arms and one leg."

Imogen wished she could risk a look around to see how the men in the hall were taking this. They were the ones that mattered here. But she knew they would never accept the idea of a woman taking matters into her own hands so forcibly, even to save a man's life.

The king addressed the hall. "So. On the first charge, Lady Imogen contends that as overlord of Carrisford she had the right to seek vengeance against Lord Warbrick for the crimes committed against herself and her people. Does anyone speak against that?"

Imogen allowed herself to hope. By phrasing it that way, Henry made it unlikely that any would object. In fact, the knights and barons would support a lord's right to act in such cases, even if the lord were a woman.

Henry took in the silence, and said, "So be it. But be it known that it is our intent that justice be fair and equal throughout this land. If Lord Warbrick had been other than he proved to be, if there had been any doubt as to his guilt, *I* would have spoken out today."

Imogen felt relief seep into her, and it was dangerous, for it weakened her. But the major charge, surely, was removed.

"Now," said Henry, "we must address the other charge. Lady Imogen does not deny that she attacked her husband, my vassal, and caused him to be made prisoner. Her excuse is that she was acting for his greater good. The implication is that she thought her husband unable to manage his affairs without her assistance. Despite this, Lord FitzRoger is inclined to be merciful and make her punishment light. Out of respect for his great services to us, we are willing to overlook any offense we might have been caused."

Imogen was hardly breathing.

"But," said the king, "does this matter go beyond his personal indulgence, and ours? Does anyone wish to speak to this?"

There was a positive roar of voices, and Imogen winced.

Henry brought order on proceedings and the men stepped forward in turn. The words differed, but the message was the same: women could not be allowed to overrule men, nor to take charge of their lives, even for the man's protection. Were men as infants, to be kept from sharp blades and the fire?

And are women infants? Imogen thought. *Yet you protect us from making our own mistakes.* But she had the wisdom to clamp her lips on such words.

When all the men had had their say, Henry asked, "And do any speak for Imogen of Carrisford in this?"

Imogen couldn't help it: she looked at FitzRoger. But though he met her eyes, and he had not spoken against her, he did not now speak for her. She lowered her head.

"Imogen of Carrisford," said the king, "you are young, and have undergone many trials in recent days. First you lost your beloved father, then your castle was sacked. Witnesses have told us how you acted with courage and resolution to preserve your home. Just before your crime you had been in great personal danger, and had been forced to act against your woman's nature to escape. In view of your husband's faith in you, we accept that the strain of being forced to these unwomanly acts disturbed your mind in a temporary way. We put this penalty upon you, and this only: that you kneel here before us all and admit on the cross that what you did was wrong, and beg your husband's pardon."

A sober-faced monk came forward and presented Imogen with a jeweled reliquary cross.

Imogen took it, looking around wildly. Her

eyes fixed on FitzRoger's and she saw a strange look flit across his impassive features. Did he know she couldn't take such an oath?

She sank to her knees, clutching the cross to her chest. "On the cross," she said, "I am truly sorry for having caused all this distress, and I sincerely beg the pardon of my husband, my king, and all here present."

It was not to be so easy.

"Lady Imogen," said the king, "I am sure you are sorry for causing yourself to be here today. You will have to be more specific."

Imogen tried again, without much hope. "On the cross, I am most heartily sorry that I had to take such steps against my husband, and I beg his pardon."

The muttering started up again, swelling to a roar. The king shook his head. "You are not going to swear, are you, Lady Imogen?"

She faced him, tears blurring her vision. "I have made one false oath on the cross in my life, sire, and that was so painful to my soul that I cannot bear to do it again. I love my husband, Your Majesty, and I cannot believe it was wrong to preserve his life, even though I suffer grievously for it. I do, however, most sincerely beg his pardon, and yours, and that of all here present, that my actions have caused such distress, and that my refusal now will doubtless make matters worse."

Henry looked nothing so much as exasperated. His fingers rapped angrily.

In the silence, FitzRoger stood. He held out a hand. "The whip."

Imogen started as she realized one had been there waiting all along. She stared at her husband as he walked toward her. She noticed that he still limped slightly.

"Remove your cloak," he said to her.

Dry-mouthed, Imogen undid the clasp and let it fall to puddle around her.

She gazed up at him, so tall and dark. The first time she'd seen him, he'd been flogging a miscreant.

"Do you accept that it is my right to punish you?" he asked.

She nodded, then found her voice, "Yes, my lord."

"I suppose when you were about to strike me down with a rock you fully expected to be punished for it."

"Yes, my lord."

"I would hate to disappoint you." The whip hissed and Imogen gasped under the fire across her back. She stared forward, still clutching the cross, praying for courage.

FitzRoger walked away and tossed the whip on the table. Imogen stared as he turned to face the hall and her. "Any further discussion of this matter between my wife and myself will be in private. But if events here should get home to your wives, you men may at least tell them that Lady Imogen was publicly whipped for her sins."

The muttering grew, and then one man rose angrily. "I say it's not good enough. It's to condone her actions! If Lord FitzRoger is too squeamish to whip his wife here and now, I'll do it for him!"

"Any man who injures my wife in any way, ever, will answer to me."

Silence fell, and the standing man sank back into his seat.

FitzRoger looked around the hall. "Does any man here speak against my decision in this? I will be happy to put the matter to the test of the sword."

No one spoke. It was not surprising. Imogen could hear the killing anger in his voice. She was close to fainting under the weight of it, for she feared it was mostly directed at her.

FitzRoger raised Imogen to her feet with an ungentle hand on her arm. "Then my wife is restored to her honor in the world's eyes, and will be treated thusly." He bowed to the king. "By your will, my liege."

Henry frowned, but said. "So be it, but as a husband myself, I think it best if no word of events here escapes to infect the women of England."

Imogen couldn't help but think that a little of that infection might do everyone good, but she hastily lowered her eyes and resolved to keep her mouth shut.

Perhaps not hastily enough. "Take your

wife away, Ty," said Henry testily, "and teach her proper behavior. And take the whip. I think you'll need it."

FitzRoger led the way, and Imogen followed in submissive silence, nervously watching the whip tap against his leg as he walked, but also noting his limp with concern. Was it permanent?

When they entered the solar, Imogen looked around the scene of old pain and battles and wondered how life and herself could have changed so much since she had last been in it.

Then she looked at her husband, black from head to toe and angry, and her knees knocked.

He walked away from her and turned, whip still in hand, eyes blazing with contained anger. "You are in the wrong. Say it."

She swallowed, "In the eyes of the world, I am wrong. I know that."

"I warn you, Imogen. I'd *enjoy* beating you." Then he seemed to see the whip in his hand, and he hurled it away to clatter on the floor. Imogen almost crumbled in relief.

"Do you know how much trouble you've caused? You irritated one of Henry's sore spots — justice — and I've had to apply all my skills, and some risky pressure, to have the matter handled so lightly. *Do you understand?*"

Imogen nodded and tried very hard to stop her lips from quivering under this verbal lashing. "I'm sorry," she said.

"Sorry for what? That's the question."

She glanced at him. "Sorry that you're angry with me," she admitted.

He laughed shortly. "Always honest. Your besetting sin."

"You'd rather I were dishonest?"

"It would make life easier for all."

Two tears escaped, and Imogen brushed them away and sniffed.

"By the Grail, Imogen" — and the rage was lessening — "I'm not angry at you for being truthful. Though if you'd taken that oath, it would all have gone a great deal easier."

She raised her chin. "I won't take another false oath, FitzRoger," she said bleakly. "It hurts too much."

"My all-too-honorable virago." He sighed. "Don't you know yet, Imogen, that life is an affair of tooth and claw, not a pretty tale of paladins and princesses?"

She shook her head.

He took to pacing the room. "You terrify me! You're like me at thirteen, facing down Roger of Cleeve and listing off his sins. Virtuously right, but headed for bloody martyrdom."

She met his eyes. "But right."

He jabbed a finger at her. "Don't forget the bloody martyrdom."

"I don't. You rescued me, my paladin."

He shook his head. "Imogen, I'm no paladin."

"You are to me. You've been trying to rescue me from my own foolishness since I hit you, haven't you?"

He collapsed down on the bench. "So I'm transparent now, am I?"

She just looked at him.

"Yes," he said with irritation, "as soon as I regained my wits I knew we had a problem. With hindsight it would have been better if Renald hadn't carried you off to Cleeve. Better politically, but not for your skin." He looked for a telling — almost longing — moment at the whip, then back at her.

"Once there, however," he carried on, "I thought it better to keep you at Cleeve until I could see my way clear. I was hoping that the evil found when they seized Warbrick Castle would sway Henry, but it was by no means certain. He is determined to have good justice in this land."

"I confess I didn't think much of my execution of Warbrick. I was far more worried that you would cast me off for assaulting you."

His eyes turned serious. "I would never do that, Imogen."

There was no warmth in it, but it warmed her all the same. She worried, though, at the sense of something yet to come. Surely he had forgiven her. . . .

Imogen became bold enough to sit on the edge of the bed and to put aside the cross she had been clutching like a ward against evil. "Thank you for trying to clear up the problem I caused."

"What else could I do? You are my wife." There was still no tenderness to read in him.

Imogen could have wept. Was this all there was to be, this detached concern? Would they never regain those hours in the cave — bleak hours of fear, and yet the sweetest of her life? She too looked at the whip. If it would get them past his anger, she would present it to him on her knees.

"Anyway," he said, "you rescued yourself from the more serious charge with your quick wits." He groaned. "Jesu, but my heart was in my mouth when you threw Henry's words back at him."

"Was that dangerous? I wasn't sure. But I couldn't think what else to do. I was so afraid."

"Imogen, didn't you know I'd never let you really suffer?" She could almost think he was hurt.

"Of course I did," she assured him. "That was what I was afraid of."

He exploded to his feet. "By the Host, Ginger! Haven't you learned yet? You're not *supposed* to protect me. *I'm* supposed to protect *you*."

The use of his special name brought a

glow to her heart. "I can't help it, FitzRoger, I love you."

He stopped as if she'd hit him on the head with a rock again.

"Tell me something," she said softly, and he looked up, eyes shadowed and unreadable. "Would you rather I had let you fight Warbrick?"

"Make no mistake, Imogen. If you'd been within reach during my first anger, you would have suffered dearly for your action."

"You did warn me to keep out of range of your first rage."

He shook his head in exasperation. "Are you even aware that most of those men hope I'm beating you black and blue?"

"Yes. I'm also aware that you're evading my question."

He shook his head again, but he answered. "No. At this moment, I would not rather you had let me fight Warbrick."

Before she could comment, he added, "But don't ever do anything like that again."

"That doesn't make much sense."

"Perhaps not. But from now on, you will behave correctly according to your sex and station."

Imogen sighed for what might have been. "You had better send me to a convent, then. I've come to the conclusion that I can't be a meek, dutiful woman anymore. It's as if something has broken, something that can never be mended."

He laughed sharply. When she stared, he said, "I'm trying to remember when you ever *were* a meek, dutiful woman, Imogen."

"I was before all this started," she assured him earnestly. "Before I knew you." It seemed amazing to her that there had ever been a time when she had not known him.

"Were you? Your father was better at managing you than I am, then." He prowled the room again, kicking the whip out of his way. "Do you think," he demanded at last, "you can at least *act* the part — excepting life-threatening situations in which you feel you have to save my life?"

She flinched at the edge in his voice, but nodded. "Yes. I promise."

"In public," he added.

"Of course," she said, confused.

He smiled, and at last it was a true smile. "Because I rather like my all-too-honest virago in private."

Imogen felt tears of happiness swell and didn't hide them. Tentatively, hopefully, she held out a hand. He came to her and carried it to his lips. But once by her side he pushed back her scarf and Imogen remembered her appearance. "I'm sorry," she said, looking away.

He turned her back. "God's blood, Imogen! Why would I care about your hair?" He pulled her into his arms, and his lips lowered to hers. She expected a fiery kiss, but it was one of tender gentleness. "I only care that I haven't been able to protect you from all this." His lips trailed up to touch first one eyelid and then the other. "If I'm your paladin, Ginger, then I'm an arrant failure."

"No, you're not." Imogen melted under his sensual assault. "But, oh, I love you too much. . . ."

He carried her back onto the bed. "I fear that's true."

She looked up at him and the mask was down. He was open to her again and she smiled in blissful welcome.

He played with a tendril of her hair. "I can imagine no greater gesture of love, Ginger, than that rock to the back of the head. Because you knew the consequences, didn't you?"

"Yes."

He began to unknot her cord girdle. She stilled his hands, not sure if he was really understanding her. "FitzRoger, I knew the consequences. And I will do it again if need be."

He laughed. "No you won't, Ginger, because I, at least, learn by my mistakes. If we're ever in a similar situation, I'll tie you up before you get the chance."

Imogen at last allowed herself to surrender to happiness.

He pulled off all three layers of her

clothing in one, leaving her in only her stockings. He touched faint bruises and marks gently. "It was quite an adventure we had, wasn't it?"

"Yes." Imogen watched his expression. "What about my face?"

He kissed her scar. "Imogen, wounds of war don't bother me. You saved us both. I don't forget that. I didn't raise the matter in the hall because it would have made matters worse rather than better, but if you hadn't acted so bravely and wisely in the passages and after, all could have been lost."

She began to cry with relief and happiness, and stretched up her arms. He came to her, kissing her, a kiss that turned from conscious care and comfort to unconscious need, so that they rolled together, absorbing one another.

She tore at his clothes, and he helped. One way or the other, they were off and he was naked. She pushed away to look at him, to anxiously study his wounds like a new mother with a babe. All looked well, though there was rough scarring on his arm, and his shoulder and knee were still shadowed with bruising.

"You still limp," she said. "Will it get better?"

"Yes." His fingers trailed hungrily over her body. "You won't believe this, but it was completely better until I tripped on a hummock while training yesterday."

She clucked like a worried mother. "They say you were in a killing match with Sir William."

"Hardly that, though I took my rage out on him. I'd failed to persuade Henry to drop the matter. As it was, I was too distracted to notice a patch of rough ground."

"Distracted by what?"

"By concern for you."

Imogen gave him her thanks as a kiss. For the first time she noticed a scar on his lip that hadn't been there before. Caused by Warbrick's blow.

She kissed it.

She kissed each hurt, and then she couldn't stop kissing all of him, every bit of his hard body. "I can't believe how you frightened me at first," she mumbled. "You seemed so hard."

"I wasn't as hard then as I am now," he teased, pushing the hardest part of his body at her.

Imogen blushed and laughed again, light and free. He brushed the hair gently from her eyes. "I hope the devils haven't come back now we're in this room again."

"Oh no," she said, but flustered. Such things were still unfamiliar, and it was broad daylight.

"You're bright pink and delicious. Do you want to be on top again?"

She shook her head. "Can you . . . Can it

be like it was in the monastery?" She was sure she'd gone from pink to red. "But . . . but everything?"

He pushed her gently down and smiled at her. "I'd like that very much. My gift to you, my dear virago."

His clever hands explored her, finding every point of delight. His mouth accompanied his hands perfectly, summoning rich new sensations and building them, moment by moment, to her ecstasy.

This time there was no need for restraint, and nothing to fear. This time there was no pain, though when he entered her — slowly, oh so slowly — there was an amazing fullness and she tensed.

Imogen had closed her eyes, the better to drown in the dark pleasures he had summoned, but now she opened them to find him watching her in careful concern. "Just give it a moment, dearling. It's only your second time, after all."

Imogen considered the sensation and shifted her hips around him. "It is in a way, quite pleasant," she said. "Just strange." She shifted again and saw him catch his breath. The feelings she was stirring in herself were thrilling, but the look on his face was more so. She began to rotate her hips.

"By the Tomb," he muttered, but he made no objection, and moved in counterpoint to her.

"Oh, my," said Imogen. "I think I'm going to . . . with you in me."

"Good."

Imogen could no longer control her movements. "FitzRoger . . ." she muttered. "I . . ."

"It's all right, Ginger," he soothed. "It's all right." His hands and mouth continued to pleasure her, but it was their joining that was driving her wild.

Imogen was aware of thrashing upon the bed almost as if she were fighting him, and of his mighty body skillfully restraining her so that the madness built. "FitzRoger," she gasped. "Remember that I scream!"

"Scream, my sweet virago. Scream the castle down."

And Imogen did scream when she exploded. She screamed, *"Ty!"*

When she came to herself she was limp and drenched with sweat. Her heart still pounded. "I'm like a goblet shattered into pieces," she whispered.

His hands soothed her, though they themselves trembled. "You're quite whole, dearest one, and remarkably, so am I."

She closed her eyes to absorb the trembling memories of her body's ecstasy, and relive them. "I think I screamed rather loudly. Why didn't you stop me?"

"I wanted everyone to hear you scream. If they think I'm torturing you, so much the better."

She opened her eyes to frown at him, but then just sighed and burrowed closer to his wonderful body. "I missed you so. Don't they know that was a far worse punishment than even a beating?"

He tugged her hair so she had to look at him. "You thought that was a punishment? Then I punished myself. Even when I wanted to throttle you, I wanted you here to be throttled."

"Then why did you keep us apart?"

His hand explored the pleasure points of her back, touched gently on the sting where he had had to strike her. "Once you were here, I knew I'd have to deal with it, and there was always the chance it could come to combat. I couldn't risk fighting for you until I was fit again."

"I thought of running away to save you from that," she said. "And from offending the king."

He shook his head. "You are not *supposed* to try to save me, remember?" But he was smiling. "I guessed. That's why I made sure you had no money, and nothing you could turn into money."

"Oh, I thought . . ."

"You thought what?"

"My morning gift," she said shyly.

He slid from under her and went to his chest to take out the girdle. "You thought there was some symbolism? No." He clasped the girdle around her waist. "You are mine for all time, Imogen, never doubt that."

The words and the action were perfect, and yet there was something . . . something suggested by the way his eyes did not meet with hers.

Anxious to make all right, Imogen scrambled out of bed and ran naked to her own chest, the ivory and amethyst girdle clacking merrily. She opened the box and took out the leather pouch. "This is my gift to you," she said, almost shyly. "I never had the chance to give it to you."

He spilled out the emerald chain. "By the Rood . . . !" He was clearly pleased, and yet the shadows gathered more darkly, frightening her. What was wrong?

He dropped the chain over his head so the smooth stones glittered against his brown, muscular chest.

At last he looked at her, but his eyes were serious.

Imogen sat cross-legged on the bed before him. "Ty, what is it?"

He smiled, eyes sparkling like the jewels with pleasure. "You are using my name."

"Yes." Imogen wasn't deflected. "What is worrying you?"

He touched the large central emerald, then met her eyes. "I took back your promise to the men who carried the treasure. They were well rewarded, but not given all they carried.

That would have been madness, and they were as happy as not to be relieved of such responsibility."

"Very well," said Imogen. "But I would have given it all for your safety. I hope you know that."

"I know it, and am still amazed."

"So," she said. "What else bothers you?"

He smiled ruefully. "You can read me like a book, can't you? I have given Henry one half of the Carrisford Treasure."

"Oh." Imogen wasn't pleased, but she was surprised by how light the displeasure was. "Well, I suppose after the trick we played, the whole world knew about it."

"The king and I knew about it months ago. I came to this part of the country with instructions to win your hand one way or the other. The understanding was that half the treasure would eventually go into the king's coffers. That was the price I was to pay for you and your lands."

"You were to buy me with my own money?"

"Yes."

"And when I came to you at Cleeve, you were preparing to seize me, weren't you?"

"Yes. But for your protection. In the end, though, Henry would have given you to me."

Imogen looked down and fiddled with the ivory girdle. "I suppose I shouldn't ask," she said, looking up. "But will you please give me your word that you had no hand in the death of Gerald of Huntwich?"

He was surprised. "Your first betrothed? I assure you, Imogen, I had no part in it, or your father's death, but it was Huntwich's death that started Henry and I planning. It was too good an opportunity to miss. It's possible that Lancaster poisoned him, or even Warbrick and Belleme, but it could have been a natural death."

"Are there any more secrets?" she asked warily.

"Not of mine," he said, and the shadows fled.

Imogen smiled radiantly and took his strong, callused hands, his warrior's hands. "Nor of mine. So, what does the future hold for us, my mighty champion?"

He shook his head at the name, but said, "Under God's will, peace in England. A long reign and strong sons for Henry, so that we and our children may live our lives as sweetly as this moment."

He leaned forward and kissed her. "Lives guided always by love."

She hardly dared to hope. "Are you saying you love me?"

"God's breath, Imogen! Why else didn't I whip you soundly down there?"

Imogen whooped with delight and set to tickling her mighty champion to death.

Author's Note

A historical novel such as this is a blend of fact and fancy. The historical events are true, but the only real person on stage in this book is King Henry, and I have tried to be as true to his complex character as I can.

Robert of Belleme really lived and terrorized his part of England. He had at least two brothers, one of whom was called Arnulf, but little is known about the man. Arnulf of Warbrick, therefore, is mostly my own invention, though I doubt he is much worse than the real man.

Lancaster became a noble and important holding in future centuries, but at this time it was not a title. There is no link between my Earl of Lancaster and the future ones.

Imogen made frequent mention of "paladins," likening FitzRoger to one — somewhat to his irritation.

The word paladin is ancient, and means one who lives in the palace: in other words, one close to the king.

It was applied particularly, however, to the twelve closest followers of the great King Charlemagne, who reigned in France from

768 to 814 — heroes somewhat like the Knights of the Round Table. Unlike Arthur of England, there is no doubt Charlemagne existed and reigned, and did so magnificently, but the stories which grew up about his paladins are mostly myth.

Despite that, the word came to mean a truly noble knight, one who fought for right, not for his own interests. You can see why it made FitzRoger uncomfortable to be described that way.

And what does the future hold?

FitzRoger and Imogen were destined for more than thirty years of stable rule in England. Henry I was in many ways a cruel king but he was firm, and established the rule of law throughout his land.

He had many illegitimate children, but unfortunately only one legitimate son, Henry, who died when his vessel — the White Ship — sank en route from England to France. Henry tried to make his vassals accept the rule of his daughter, Matilda, but his nephew, Stephen, was more favored by the barons.

Thus began a civil war which was to trouble England for nearly twenty years.

Let us not think of that, however, but of the thirty-four years of peace ahead for Cleeve and Carrisford.

I have written other novels connected to this one, the most direct being *Lord of Midnight*, about Renald de Lisle, which was published by NAL in 1998. It is still available. If your bookstore doesn't have it, they can order it for you at no extra charge.

Lord of My Heart, reissued by NAL in October 2002, is about FitzRoger's uncle, Aimery de Gaillard. That should be easily available. FitzRoger makes an appearance in *The Shattered Rose*, which is currently out of print.

I also write romances set in the Georgian and Regency periods, and I hope the sample from my next new book, *St. Raven*, will make you want to read more. That book will be available soon. It follows *Hazard*, which was published in May 2002 and should be easy to find. You could read that while waiting for Tris and Cressida's adventures.

You will find a list of all my books available from NAL in the front of this book, and more details on all my work on my Web page at www.jobev.com. I enjoy hearing from readers. You can e-mail me at jo@jobev.com, or write to me c/o Meg Ruley, The Rotrosen Agency, 318 East 51st Street, New York, NY 10022. I appreciate a SASE to make a reply easier.

All best wishes,
Jo